INVADED!

Paige sat down happily to read, conscious now and again of June's picture looking down upon him. He liked to feel that she was there reading with him. He did not know that the door had opened. But he suddenly became conscious of someone standing there in the doorway and he looked up, startled.

There stood Reva, her eyes, with actual hatred in them, upon the picture. Before he could move, her eyes came to look him over and then to concentrate with a still darker look of hate mingled with a queer kind of fear when she saw what he was reading.

Suddenly she reached out with a quick motion and snatched the Bible from his hand, flinging it angrily across the room. . . .

Grace LIVINGSTON HILL

AMERICA'S BEST-LOVED STORYTELLER

WHERE TWO WAYS MET

LIVING BOOKS®
Tyndale House Publishers, Inc.
Wheaton, Illinois

This Tyndale House book
by Grace Livingston Hill
contains the complete text
of the original hardcover edition.
NOT ONE WORD
HAS BEEN OMITTED.

Copyright © 1946 by Grace Livingston Hill
All rights reserved
Cover illustration copyright © 1988 by Steven Stroud

Living Books is a registered trademark of Tyndale House
Publishers, Inc.

Reprinted by permission of Harper & Row, Publisher, Inc.

Library of Congress Catalog Card Number 88-50905
ISBN 0-8423-8203-8

Printed in the United States of America

01 00 99 98 97 96
15 14 13 12 11 10

THE sky was dark and the wind was cold. There was slush on the pavements from a late snow. The young man shivered as he turned his collar up and buttoned his coat more closely about him.

It was late February and supposed to be near spring, but the grim clouds hurrying across the leaden sky gave no suggestion of spring. Rather they had the air of going out to battle, as if they were hasting to obey a sharp imperative emergency command in a case of unanticipated dire necessity! There was nothing encouraging in the night scene to lift the heart of one who was already troubled from within.

Paige Madison had gone out earlier that evening with high hopes, to get a job and establish himself in a new and successful life, now that the war was over. Nothing was really changed from the promises of the day before that had sent him questing to a great and influential man who had seemed so favorable, and willing. But there was an uneasiness within him since the evening's interview he could not quite analyze, an uneasiness strong enough to haunt him as he went on his way and prevent his rejoicing, as he really had every right to do, he told himself. What was the matter?

Could it be just a little shifty look in one director's eyes? A crafty set of jaw on the great man who had promised so much and been so complacent? Or the very streamlined look of most of that bunch of men gathered about that directors' table? Could that be what had disturbed him? There was one there who looked like nothing in the world but a slick crook. Oh, he was well groomed of course or he couldn't have been numbered with that respectable group. He was cleanshaven, his thin hair cut just right below the bald crown. His pale shifty pop-eyes above his sly mouth did not miss a thing. He wore a nifty outfit, not quite in the same class with the others, but his half deprecating smile was veiled by an amused swagger.

Paige had never thought of himself as a discerning reader of character, yet in spite of himself as he trod the midnight slush, the faces of those men with whom he had spent the evening, came out and were pictured vividly against the blackness of the night. He found himself studying each one as he had not dared study them while he was sitting face to face with them. And now he saw qualities in those faces that plainly denied the fine high descriptions of them that had been given to him before he met them. Then he blamed himself for allowing his mind, or his imagination, to play such tricks on good benevolent men who were kindly offering to open their ranks and take him into a group where his future success would be practically assured. There was Harris Chalmers, the president, well dressed, smug in an all-but-elderly dignity, beaming with affable content, well-pleased with himself and all he had done, glad to extend a helping hand to a young man just returning from distant, dangerous warfare in which his own part had been merely financial.

There was Mr. Chalmers' personal lawyer, Dawson Sharp, keen and cold and missing no point that he was so well paid to keep before the minds of these other crooks, for crooks they all seemed to him now, down the line to the tawdry unmistakable crook at the foot of the table, to whom they had each and all referred now and then as "Jimson". "Jimson'll take care of that when the time comes," they had said, with a casual wink and smile and a slight shrug.

As he plodded along toward home he drew a deep sigh. How tired he was! Perhaps that was the matter. The long journey, the excitement of getting home, the hope of a good job by means of which he would be able to look after his mother and his father, who was failing greatly and was no longer really able to be working.

And now this let down. It wasn't thinkable! It couldn't be that such respectable men, men with such fine reputations, could be dishonest! He was crazy! It was just a part of the weary reaction after the danger and turmoil and chances of war.

He would go to bed and get a good sleep. In the morning of course things would look different. He was hired, anyway, and he did not have to worry about that any more. If after he had thought it over there still seemed some questionable matters that he would like made clear there would be time enough to worry about them. Meanwhile he was too tired to be really sane.

As he neared the house he could see a bright light in the window of the living room. Somebody was waiting up for him. His heart sank. Probably his mother. Why did mothers insist on doing unnecessary things for their grown sons? Now she would expect to hear all about the evening. And if she was anything like she used to be before he went away, and of course she would be, she would see right through him and insist there was something the matter. She always could see through him. Never even as a child had he been able to deceive her. She always knew when he was in trouble, or even just disappointed. But now he must meet her and keep her from finding out about things. If she got an idea there was anything wrong about this job, she would be utterly against his taking it, and would make him miserable until he gave it up. Even if he found it was all right in the end, it would be almost impossible to disabuse her mind of prejudice against it. So he must be very cautious about what he said, if indeed she was still up.

He opened the door silently and stole through the hall as quietly as possible, but his caution was useless. There she stood in the living room doorway smiling, eager, almost as if she had been a young girl waiting for her lover. Though of course that likeness did not occur to him. But he was deeply touched. After all, he had been away and his mother was glad he was back. She was his *mother* and she was the one he had wanted so long to see.

"Mom!" he said with a sudden gentleness that the first sight of her after an absence always brought to him. And especially now when he was so fresh from the long years at war, and the deep longing for a sight of her blessed face.

"Yes?" she responded quickly, with that instant sympathy in his affairs as always, and that quick eager question as to the outcome of his mission. And then suddenly his heart fell. The job! She would want to know at once how it came out. She had been so confident he would get it, and he had been confident too, when he went out, and so eager, as eager as she. Well, he just mustn't let her see how he felt. That was all there was about it. He must cheer up and not show his depression. At least not tonight. And after tonight of course all was going to be right.

"Yes," he answered her firmly, trying to put the glad ring into his voice he had told himself he ought to feel.

His mother hesitated, turned on the hall light over his head and studied his face, the way she always used to study it when he came home from school, or college, to see if surely all was well with him.

"You—?" she hesitated an instant, her keen eyes still searching his face. And he let her search it and tried to look happy.

"You—*got* the job?"

"Why sure, I told you I was going to get it, didn't I? Of course I got it. There wasn't any question about it. I thought I made that plain before I left." He tried to grin and swagger as he used to do when he was a little boy and came to tell her of some trifling achievement in school, or athletics, but still she stood there looking doubtful.

"Then—what *is* the matter, son?"

"Matter?" he said gaily. "What could be the matter? I went after the job and got it. What more is there to say?"

But still she was silent, studying him.

"Then what *is* it, son? Something has disappointed you."

"Now mother, you aren't going to put on that old line of questions, are you? I never saw the like. You aren't God, you know, to put me through a grilling."

"*Son!*" There was piteous sharpness in her rebuke.

"Oh, forgive me moms, I didn't mean that. I guess I'm a bit tired. It was a long meeting, and I'm not used to sitting up late yet, since I was in the hospital."

His mother's voice softened at once.

"Yes, dear boy. Of course! I forgot. Come, let's go into the dining room. I have some hot coffee for you."

"Coffee!" he exclaimed brightening. "That'll be great. Some of *your* coffee again."

After she had him seated at the table with the steaming cup of coffee before him, sugared and creamed just as he liked it, she sat down beside him and took his hand gently, softly, with that tender little mother-pressure that he had dreamed about when he was far away. Gradually the deep lines around his mouth faded and he grew relaxed, almost happy-looking again.

"Oh, moms! There's nobody in the world like you!" he said as he drank the last swallow of coffee and handed her back the cup.

She smiled and filled his cup again, almost like a sacrament. Then she sat down beside him, still holding one of his hands lightly.

"Now, son, suppose you tell me what is the matter."

He was still a long time, though his fingers pressed hers tenderly and a light of warm love grew in his eyes.

"Well, mother," he said at last, "I don't know as it's anything. I guess I'm just a bit goofy. But somehow they all seemed so slick and satisfied. I guess it's just because I've come home out of terrible things. Back here they don't even seem to know there's been a war, except as they couldn't get meat and butter and things. But I guess maybe I'm prejudiced. Somehow they all looked too slick and happy. I just couldn't quite seem to trust 'em the way I trust my own folks. The way you taught me to trust God when I went into danger."

"Well," said the mother thoughtfully, "they are businessmen and they were in a business session. And you wouldn't expect them to talk religion of course. Though Mr. Chalmers is supposed to be a very godly man. At least he's very active in church affairs, and gives greatly to missions."

"I know, moms! I told myself that, but somehow watching him tonight, I wondered."

"I know what you mean, son. Last Sunday he helped pass the communion. He's one of the elders, you know, and it was his turn I suppose. Afterwards when he sat up front before they passed the wine, I studied his face. Maybe I shouldn't've, but I had it in mind that you were coming home and were going to try for a job with him, so I looked him over while the minister was reciting Bible verses, and somehow I couldn't feel quite happy about his face. But then you know we are told not to judge one another, and some people have very unfortunate expressions. It just isn't fair to judge a man by his expression in church perhaps. But surely they wouldn't put him in as an elder if there were any question about him. I've always supposed our church was very particular about whom they made elders."

Paige grinned.

"He's a rich man, moms. It would mean a whole lot to the finances of the church to have a man like that in a high office."

"I know," sighed his mother. "But I'm not sure we should dare judge him."

"Of course not, moms. Oh, forget it. And I suppose of course he's all right. I guess the trouble was in me."

"But son, what was it you saw, or heard, that gave you this uneasiness?"

"Nothing, moms. It was just that the whole setup seemed so slick and well-satisfied with themselves, as if they owned the universe. I guess I was just tired. I'll get a good sleep and then things will probably look all right to me. But they were really swell to me, offered me more than I expected. I'm to go down tomorrow for a conference and get my bearings on things. My job begins next week, so I'll have time to get the right clothes. Now go to bed moms dear, and don't you worry about this. It all comes of this old habit of yours that you have to look right through me as if I were made of glass or cellophane, and analyze my innermost thoughts. You'll have to get over that now I'm a grown man, and have been to war. You'll get us all mixed up if you don't. I'm not a little kid any more."

"I know, son, I'll just have to take it out in praying for you."

"That's right, moms, you take it out in praying, but don't sit up any later tonight to do it. Look what time it is! Let it rest till tomorrow."

The mother smiled gently.

"Oh, son, it doesn't take but a minute to put you and your affairs into the hands of the Lord, and there I can always trust any matter that troubles me."

She stooped and gently kissed him, and then they parted for the night.

The young man went to his room, made short work of disrobing, and with a sigh of relief he dropped comfortably into his clean sweet bed. His own home bed, with smooth sheets that smelled of sweet clover and lavender, as his mother's sheets always did. He drew a breath of thanksgiving for that cleanness and comfort, pushing far from him the memory of other nights not yet so far away, when there were no sheets—or at least not clean ones—and no comfort, relegating with them a hovering memory of disturbing thoughts that had depressed him when he came home. He sank into a deep dreamless sleep, somehow made possible by that brief talk with his mother.

And the mother was even then softly on her knees beside her bed before her Lord.

"Oh, my Lord," she was saying, "here is something that I do not know how to deal with. Won't You take over, and manage this? If there is any advice I should give, show me what it should be. If I should keep out of this entirely, then put a guard over my lips. Guide and keep my boy."

Then she too lay down upon her bed, and sweetly trusting, slept.

Paige Madison slept late the next morning, after all the excitement of the evening before. He enjoyed the restfulness of being at home again and not having to hurry unduly.

He took great care with his dressing. His best uniform with every button bright and every ribbon in place. In a very few days now he would be done with uniforms and into civilian clothes, but he realized that the uniform counted for something just now, his first day in his new job. It would mean something to his fellow workmen, to his employers, to the officials about the place. It gave him a bit of prestige, timely interest, a certain standing to start out with.

His mother too looked proudly at him as he came downstairs, and motioned him to the late breakfast she had prepared for him. How proud she was of him, how glad he was safely at home! She put aside the twinge of fear that crossed her mind as she thought of all the temptations and discouragements that awaited him in this new-old world to which he had returned. She must not fear. She had trusted him to her Lord, and He would guide.

"What's new, moms?" he asked as he drained the orange juice with relish and put down the glass. "You know I've hardly had time to ask you any questions since I got home, what with all this to-do about hunting a job. Is everything hereabouts the same as ever? No marriages or births or deaths?"

"Yes," the mother looked thoughtful. "Nettie Hollister got married to a lieutenant stationed in India and went out with him. It was kind of sad, because her mother had just died, and Nettie was sort of alone. And Randa Goss married that wealthy Bert Hickens and got a divorce from him two months later. That was sad too, because her mother did everything she could to keep her from marrying him. And now she's come home with the saddest look I ever saw on a girl's face."

"Well, she might have known what she was getting into. That Hickens guy was always a low-down bum. And by the way, your old minister passed away, didn't he? I suppose you'll miss him a lot."

"Oh yes," said the mother with a tender little smile, "but he was ready to go. He really wanted to go after his wife died. And he had suffered a lot. He was sick for the last ten months. But we've got a new minister now, and I think his coming made it easier for old Dr. Bowen. This man is the son of an old seminary classmate of Dr. Bowen's and when he came it seemed to cheer him up wonderfully, the last few days of his life. It seemed as if his last worry were gone, when he could leave his precious church in such good hands."

"Well, that's good. Is he a young man, this new minister?"

"No, not so young," said the mother, "I should say he was about forty-five or eight. He has a son in the service, not yet returned, and a daughter, a very sweet girl. I think they are going to be a great addition to the community, though of course I haven't seen much of the daughter. She has just got home from somewhere. But I like the mother very much. I think she is going to be a delightful neighbor and friend. You know they are living just across on the next corner in that little new stone bungalow. The old manse has been sold and the church bought this. I think it is going to be so much pleasanter for the minister so much nearer the church, and it's a very pretty cosy house."

"Well, so that hideous old manse has passed out of the picture, has it? That's good. Who bought it?"

"Why I think someone wanted the ground for a filling station, or something. Anyway they tore it down. I only wish the Bowens could have enjoyed the new manse before they left. But I guess they've likely found their Heavenly mansion better."

"Let us hope!" said the young man with a grin. "I'd hate to think they had anything as run down looking as that in Heaven. Well, now, moms, I'm off. Do I look okay? If there's any turning down to be done on this job *I* want to do it. I don't want anyone to turn me down because I didn't look nifty enough."

The mother smiled admiringly.

"You're all right, Paige, my lad. And I'm praying that all will go well with you."

Paige smiled half ruefully.

"Thanks, mother, I'm sure it will then."

With a gay flinging on of his service cap he hurried away, and his mother watched him down to the street, with a prayer in her heart.

As he passed the next corner he caught sight of a young girl sweeping the porch of the new stone cottage, and he wondered if she could be the minister's daughter, or was that a new maid they had hired? She was pretty, anyway, he thought from the brief glimpse he caught of her before she turned and went into the house. She had golden hair, and a blue dress with a white apron. Or was that purely his imagination? But she was probably a young girl they had hired, someone who had grown up since he left town. Silly speculation! What difference did it make anyway? He had seen her so briefly that he probably wouldn't know her again if he met her face to face. Although that hasty glance had told him one thing. She was wearing no make-up, and her face looked young and fresh. Well probably a hired maid, and not even pretty if he saw her close by.

But he wasn't interested in girls now. He was interested in jobs, and if this job that he had secured last night didn't turn out to be the right one, he must hunt for another that was definitely the right one, without any question, even if the salary weren't half so large.

Then he signalled a bus, swung into a seat, and thought no more about it. Except that he hoped he wasn't going to be too close to that minister's daughter. It would be awkward if she was tiresome or stupid. His mother had always been so closely associated with the church and all its doings, and it would be entirely natural that he would often be called upon to escort a girl like that to church doings. But he would be careful about that and not get involved even the first time, if he could help it. But of course with an important job such as he had he could always have the excuse of being too busy.

At the next stop a paper boy stood offering his wares. Paige bought a paper and absorbed himself in the news, and in just no time at all it seemed, he was downtown at his destination.

As he turned into the big office building he noticed a handsome car draw up before the entrance. A gaily dressed girl got out. She spoke a word of direction to her chauffeur, and turned toward the office building. He gave only a casual glance and strode toward the elevator. He was not interested in girls just now, he told himself again, especially not in a girl who rode in limousines like the one at the curb.

Of the girl he had a closer glimpse as she stepped out of the elevator, just ahead of the one in which he was riding, and he was distinctly aware of the heavy breath of expensive perfume which floated about her and preceded her as she stepped out into the hall. The only clear impression he had of her now was of excessively red lips and a velvety artificial complexion.

Then the great marble clock that faced the elevator caught his attention, and the girl passed out of his mind. He did not even notice which way she went. It was the hour that Mr.

Chalmers had set for his arrival at the office, and with long strides he went down the corridor to the door that bore the magic name "Harris Chalmers."

He tapped on the door, and in answer to the response from within stepped inside and closed the door behind him, entirely unaware of the clicking heels that followed him down to the door.

The lady barged into the office just after him, noisily, as one who had a right, and addressed the secretary at the desk in the tones some use to address a menial.

"Hi, Jane, is Dad here yet?"

"Yes, Miss Chalmers," answered the girl coldly. "He just came in, but he gave direction that he is not to be disturbed. He is expecting someone for conference."

"Oh, *really?* Well that doesn't mean me. If I want to disturb him I certainly will, no matter how many conferences he has. No, you needn't announce me. I'm going in without announcement."

The dignified secretary controlled the angry flush that started to her cheeks and turned her attention to the young man in uniform.

Paige Madison handed her the card of identification that Mr. Chalmers had given him the night before, and a look of instant recognition passed over her face.

"Yes, Lieutenant," she said quickly. "Will you step right into the next room. You are expected."

She turned and opened a door just behind her desk, though not the door that bore the name "The President." But the quick-witted, petted child of fortune knew that this door meant the visitor was very special, and had been granted a speedier entrance than other callers might have gained. Quickly she stepped up beside the young man as he reached the door and smilingly accosted him.

"Hi, soldier! You don't mind if I go in along with you, do you?"

Paige Madison looked down at her with courteous haughtiness, took one step back, looked from her to the secretary who was escorting him, and said calmly:

"That would be something that is scarcely within my province to grant." Then he stepped ahead of her into the next room and the secretary closed the door.

And that was the beginning of Paige Madison's acquaintance with the daughter of Harris Chalmers, his new employer. It was probably not a diplomatic way to further his own interests, but somehow the young man for the moment did not care. If his job depended at all on getting in right with this girl, perhaps it would be just as well not to have it.

As he stood for a moment alone in the room to which he had been sent, he thought he heard the echo of angry voices. Or was it only one angry voice, and another quiet and controlled? That last would probably be the secretary's voice. Then the door opposite to the one by which he had entered opened, and Harris Chalmers, quiet, self-assured, heartily welcoming, greeted him, with friendly hand outstretched.

"I see you're on time, Lieutenant," he said cordially. "Come into my inner office and we can get right down to work on the details of which we spoke briefly last night."

Paige followed his new boss into the luxuriously appointed office beyond, where quiet conservative elegance reigned, with an air of righteousness. He had scarcely sat down when another door on the other side of the room opened sharply and the girl he had left in the outer room breezed in gaily and triumphantly, with a grin toward the poor soldier boy, that would have thoroughly snubbed any young service man who cared.

"Hi, dad!" called the girl gaily, with a note in her voice that utterly belied the quiet dignity of the room. It flung a challenge to the atmosphere her father had intended to create.

The father turned with an annoyed look and frowned at her:

"Reva!" he said in his harshest voice, "how did you get in here? I thought I gave special instructions to Miss Dalworth that *no one* was to be admitted here until my morning conferences were over."

"Oh, you did, dad! Your Dalworth pussycat did her best to keep me out, but you can't think I would stop for that, can you? Besides, dad, it's important, what I need to talk to you about, and it won't take long. And I can't wait, *really* dad! It's *quite* important! You see I went to the bank this morning to cash a check I needed at once, and Mr. Reyburn at the bank was very stuffy about it. He said I had already overdrawn my allowance for this month and he had no authority, without a word from you, to let me have any more. You see, dad, this is a debt of honor, and I simply *must* pay it at once. I certainly will be glad when I'm eighteen and this time of servitude will be over for me. It's ridiculous that I'm hampered so financially."

There was a weep in the end of each word as she pleaded, and the father frowned heavily again.

"I haven't the time to look into this now, Reva. Come back at twelve o'clock and I'll try and give you five minutes."

"I can't do it, dad. I'm going out to Rosemont to lunch, and I expect to meet the girl I owe this money to. I told her I'd bring it today. She's leaving at midnight for a trip to California, and she's making all kinds of a clamor for her money. I simply have *got* to pay her, dad. It's a debt of *honor,* you know. And it won't take you a second, either. I've made the check all out for you, and all you've got to do is to sign your name. Please, dad—"

Impatiently the great man reached out and took the check she handed him, sat down at his desk, signed his name and handed it to her.

"We'll settle this tonight before dinner," he said in a low voice as he handed her the check, "and now clear out and don't bother me again this morning."

"But aren't you going to introduce me to your soldier boy?" pouted the girl, as she turned unexpectedly toward Paige Madison.

"Oh, yes, why yes," said the father impatiently, "of course.

This is my daughter, Reva, Lieutenant Madison. And Reva, Mr. Madison is going to be our new assistant."

At which the girl turned and gave Paige a prolonged stare, and treated him to a half contemptuous smile of derision, with a promise in her eyes of future annoyances, until she had him just where she wanted him.

"Oh, *yes*?" she drawled. "I didn't realize you were somebody important. Well, so long, dad. See you tonight, and thanks for the check."

She walked noisily across the room and slammed out the door, and her father, apparently embarrassed, turned to rummage in a drawer of his desk.

"Young people are unpredictable these days, I find," he sighed with an apologetic tone.

Paige lifted an amused glance.

"What do you think, young man? What would set the world right today?"

Paige Madison lifted an amused impish grin to his unobserving boss's back.

"Oh, I don't know," he said idly, "perhaps a year or two of real war experience might set most of them right. War takes a lot of ideas out of most fellows. It might do that for the girls, too, if they really tried it."

Mr. Chalmers turned a startled glance of enquiry toward the young man, and answered slowly:

"Well, I don't know but what you've got something there, Madison. Of course I wouldn't want *my* girl to go out to battle, but at that it might set some of her crazy notions straight. And now, shall we get to work? Here is a list of some matters I want to bring to your attention at once and that will give you a general survey of what I am expecting of you."

Paige Madison settled down to study it and to listen to the instructions of his mentor, trying meanwhile to rid himself of the feeling he had of distrust of this man. What was it that gave him that impression?

And in between, his thoughts reverted to the daughter.

Was that girl a sample of what the home girls had become while their brothers were off fighting? If so, he wanted none of them.

Then his mind jerked back to the phraseology of some of the papers given him to consider and sign. There were tricky sentences here and there that he wanted to consider further before signing, and he noted down their phrasing and location.

Cautiously he went through them slowly, not hurrying, and becoming more and more aware that he was being keenly watched as he progressed. Well, what of it? If there were anything phony in all this, now was the time to discover it and to bring it out into the open before he was committed to anything.

"Well?" said the older man at last, with a shade of impatience in his voice, as Paige came to the final paper and laid it thoughtfully down upon the rest before him on the table, "do you find it all perfectly understandable? Are you ready to sign them?"

The younger man lifted clear troubled eyes.

"I'm not quite sure," he answered gravely. "Perhaps I am not used enough to such phraseology to quite understand its import. For instance, the third paragraph of this first paper," and his eyes quickly searched out the sharp little check his pencil had made as he read the papers over. "Do I understand that there is no leeway given a man who fails in a payment at the required date, except the regular three months? I have in mind a man who has always been honorable in all his business dealings, and does not take ventures that he cannot reasonably expect to fulfill. Just suppose such a man were taken suddenly very ill, with a long tedious recovery which might take all his available funds. Do I understand that there would be no provision for him to catch up and recover his property when his health was restored? Would he lose at a blow all he had already paid?"

"Oh, of course—in such a case—if there were hope of his

getting back his earning ability, an exception *might* be made in his case," answered the calm assured voice of the rich man. "But you understand one has to be very clear in these statements, and not leave any loopholes for an easygoing man to slip out of paying. However, if you object to that phrase a few words more or less could be added, qualifying the statement. Just make a note of that and I'll see that it is changed."

"And here again," went on the young man, "in the fourth paper there is a questionable sentence. I would not like to attempt to try to sell something to a man in the face of that third sentence."

Mr. Chalmers bent frowning over the paper, and read the sentence carefully.

"Yes," he said thoughtfully, "I can see what you mean. But that too can be changed. In fact, I'll have my lawyer go over the whole thing and get this matter made entirely clear. I can see you are a conscientious young man, and perhaps not thoroughly conversant with the language necessary to be used to make a contract like this binding in court, but of course that does not mean we will not be careful to give every man his rights, even if it means in some cases being a little hard on ourselves. But suppose I take these papers to the lawyer, and you come back this afternoon. You and I can go over them again and see if you find any possible objection then, before you sign. And were there other places that troubled you?"

"Yes, here, and here, and here," Paige fluttered over the papers and left no doubt in the mind of his new employer that he was a keen young man who could not be easily hoodwinked, and must therefore be treated accordingly.

And at last Paige Madison went on his way thoughtfully, wondering just what was coming of all this, and whether he had been an utter fool to make this stand. Yet he knew in his heart that he was still troubled over the situation, without in the least being sure what it was that made him feel so doubtful.

2

"WELL," said Priscilla Brisco, the suburban dressmaker, placing the last three pins of her mouthful carefully between her thin lips, and talking skillfully between pins, "I see Mary Madison has got her son back from the Philippines at last, poor thing! I hope to goodness she'll be happy for a while. I just hated to see that sweet patient look in her saintly loving eyes. I always felt condemned for any frets I have whenever I saw her. Me, with no children, not even a distant nephew left to go!"

"Yes," said Mrs. Harmon, the Madisons' next door neighbor, who was having a dress refitted, "she is a good woman, and she did feel her boy's going a lot. He was such a good boy. But I don't know but I'd feel more worried about him now he's home. He's bound to be somewhat changed now he's been out in the world, away from that sheltered home his mother and father made for him. They simply can't expect him to stay the way they brought him up of course. They'll probably find out a number of things about their mistakes now he's home. I suppose he'll have an awful time now finding a job, like so many of the returned service men."

"Oh, no, I don't believe he will," said Miss Brisco, shifting a pin to the other corner of her mouth, "hadn't you heard? He has one already! Yes, isn't it wonderful? An important job with Harris Chalmers. Yes, that's definite. I had to stop at Chalmers' house last night to get a frock I promised to alter for Mrs. Chalmers, and I had to wait in the hall for the maid to go upstairs and get it, and I heard Mr. Chalmers telling about it. And he said they were going to have young Madison over for dinner Saturday night."

"You don't say so! Over for dinner! Are you *sure*? Then that must mean that Mr. Chalmers has really taken up the young man. Well, that's something to be proud of. Mr. Chalmers is an outstanding man. He's very prominent in our church, and very benevolent. Well, now it will be up to Paige, whether he can make good. And of course Mr. Chalmers has a daughter, very pretty and smart, and quite worldly. If he can just make up to her, his fortune will be made."

"It sure will," said the dressmaker, extracting the last pin from her mouth and fixing it firmly in the seam she was taking up.

"But then," she went on with speculative lips free to converse thoughtfully, "there again will be something for that mother to worry about. That Chalmers girl wouldn't be at all the style of Paige's saintly mother. But then I suppose she must expect that in these days of modern young people, there are girls everywhere, and he's probably been thrown with a lot worse across seas where he's been. Oh, I guess she's an all-right girl, only of course, she's not at all religious, and his mother is. But then after all they may not take a notion to each other. That Chalmers girl can have *anybody* she wants. She's good looking and wealthy."

"Well," said Mrs. Harmon, "Paige Madison is very handsome, of course, and that goes a great way with a girl. With almost *any* girl. I guess if *she* wants him she can have him. He certainly seems to have landed on his feet."

"Well, it's all as you look at it," said the dressmaker dubiously. "I'm just afraid his mother won't look at it that way."

"She'd be an awful fool if she didn't," said the neighbor. "Now, about this dress. When do you think you can have it done? I'm thinking of going away next week and I'd like to take it with me."

And so the talk drifted to other matters, and presently the dressmaker took herself away with the big bundle she was supposed to finish in two days. But Mrs. Harmon stood by the window and looked out across the two lawns that separated her from her neighbor's windows.

"Yes," she mused to herself, "if this is really so, they will presently be important people. I'll keep a sharp lookout and see whether the young man really gets—and keeps that job. I've always supposed they were very commonplace people. They never seem to go anywhere except to church, and not a very important church either. They're awfully quiet of course, and respectable, but if the Chalmers are taking them up it might be worth while to begin to cultivate them, now before it would be obvious. I might go over and call, make a pretense of borrowing something—or—no—that would be almost humiliating after all these years of ignoring her. I must think up something better than that. I wonder how she would react if I were to suggest asking her to go with me to our bridge club? Of course she doesn't likely play bridge, but I might say I'd teach her. It would likely be an awful bore, for quiet women like that who haven't been used to playing— Well, at least it might be a gesture. It would show I was friendly. And of course if the Chalmers take her up why it wouldn't be hard to get the ladies to vote for her. There's one thing, she's an awfully good cook, and makes lovely salads and things like that. It would be good to have someone who could take over the refreshment part, now Mrs. Powers has moved away. Of course she might wonder why I never asked her before, but I could tell her I knew she wouldn't feel like getting into social affairs while her son was away, but now he was home I thought it was a shame she couldn't be in our group, especially when she lives so near me and it would be so handy for us to go to the meetings together. Anyway let her think what she wants to. She likely has been envious of me all these years for belonging to everything, when she never goes out except to church. Well, I'll think it over, and keep a watch out for the young man. If the story seems to be true I better get in some good work before things get going, and somebody else gets hold of her. Of course if it doesn't prove to be true I won't need to bother about it. But Priscilla Brisco generally knows what she's talking about. I've never found her making mistakes in anything she reports, and there's never anything malicious in her gossip, it's always kindly and sweet. Maybe there is more to that Mrs. Madison than I ever thought. Priscilla certainly spoke beautifully of her."

Brisk steps on the pavement of the street made her turn and look out her front window. Yes, that was the young Madison fellow, and he certainly was good-looking. Of course a uniform is becoming to almost everyone, but this one had such fine proportions, such well-set-up shoulders, such a fine bearing. She could easily see how he would adorn an office. Yes, and fit into social life if it came to that. Well, perhaps it would be worth her while to cultivate the family, at least tentatively. And there was this about it, if she did it right away before this business connection of the son's became generally known, she would have the name of being intimate with friends of the Chalmers. Of course the Chalmers were a notch higher socially than she herself had ever attained.

She thought about it all that evening at intervals, and kept a sharp lookout on the doings of her next-door neighbors. She noted the lights that appeared in the windows, wished that the living room of the Madison place were not on the other side of their house. She certainly would like to be able to look over and get a little better acquainted with the family before she ventured to take any of them into her own charmed circle. When it came to things of a social nature one had to be very careful of course. It wouldn't do to be impulsive.

But on the other hand the Madison dining room was on her side of the house, and she could see them sitting at their tables in the evening when the lights were on, and that was an advantage. She would be able to tell later whether any of the Chalmers were invited to dine next door; that of course would be a conclusive proof that they were going to be socially accepted by the Chalmers.

When it came to Saturday afternoon Mrs. Harmon took her needle point, and the latest of her "book-of-the-month" novels, a pitcher of iced lemonade and a box of chocolates, and established herself where she had a good view from both front and side windows, and planned to stay there until the momentous question of whether Paige Madison was really going out to dinner that night or not was settled. Of course her husband was away in Washington for the weekend or she could not so easily have arranged this matter of spying on her neighbor. Then she let her maid have the afternoon and evening off and resolved that if anybody came she would simply not answer the doorbell. This matter was important, and there wouldn't be likely to be any interesting callers, so she would have no interruptions unless it was from the telephone.

It occurred to her that she was taking a great deal of trouble for a simple matter, but really it was better to go cautiously in a matter of social prestige, and anyway it was better to be sure before she took any step in this matter. It was easy enough to go on just living her own life and ignoring her neighbors as she had been doing for years, in case this was all a fantastic dream of Priscilla Brisco's imaginative brain.

Paige Madison came home hurriedly just at the edge of dark and went into the house. Presently the light flashed on his window, but was soon turned off. It didn't look as if he were spending much time on his toilet for a great occasion.

Surely he must have gotten a new suit and wouldn't still be wearing his uniform. Well, she didn't have much to go on. It was quite dark now and there seemed to be nothing unusual going on next door. Probably this was all wrong. Miss Brisco likely hadn't heard very distinctly. That was it, and her fine imagination filled in the way she thought it ought to be.

So Mrs. Harmon hurried to the kitchen and put on the coffee pot. She just must have some more coffee after all this strenuous watching. And it was just at that moment that Paige drove his father's old car out of the garage and down the driveway that passed her window. She heard the rattle of the old engine and hurried back to the window. But she was too late. She caught but one glimpse of the back of the old car, just its well-worn back as it swung into the road. Somebody at the wheel, of course, for it obviously could not drive itself, but surely the young man would never go to such an important place in the old car. At least he could have sent for a taxi. And most perplexing of all, she was sure, as the car turned the corner by the street light she had caught the flash of bright buttons on a uniform. Surely he wouldn't go to the Chalmers' to dinners now when he was supposed to be out of the service wearing his old shabby uniform. Or, perhaps he had a dress uniform. But he hadn't had a light up in his room but a minute or two. He couldn't have changed in that short time. It must all be a mistake and she was glad she hadn't yielded to the impulse she had had to run over and talk to Mrs. Madison in the afternoon when she first thought of it.

So she settled down with a book and the rest of her box of chocolates and put the whole thing out of her mind. At least she could tell later when he returned if there had been time for him to eat a dinner in a really fashionable place. But then there was no telling what a Madison might not do. They were unpredictable. They had ways of their own, and cared not whether they were popular and considered "smart" or not. It was as well. She better keep out of their affairs. Even if the young man should get a good job with the Chalmers firm, he probably wouldn't be keen enough to hold it.

But Paige Madison was not altogether unaware of what was required of a guest in a Chalmers' home when one was going to dine with his new employer. He drove the old car to a garage not too far from the pretentious mansion for which he was bound, and strode out boldly into the darkness. He had well calculated his time. Dinner was at seven-thirty. He would be there on the dot and the shabby old car wouldn't be at all in evidence.

Paige Madison stepped into the Chalmers' door a full minute before the costly clock chime in the hall pealed out the hour.

The young man went through the introductions to the family with dignity and a quiet poise that astonished the girl Reva. She didn't understand it. He didn't look old enough to be so grave and thoughtful.

He had not been much attracted by Reva, and beyond the mere courtesies of the occasion paid little attention to her, which of course did not add to his popularity with the girl. She was not accustomed to being ignored, and before the meal was concluded had determined that this sort of thing should not go on. She *would not* be ignored. She began by firing questions at him about the war, where he had been located, what his rank and duties. Of course she was fairly up on these things, as she had been going around with a lot of soldiers and sailors, playing at work in canteens, just naturally having a good time playing at war, for she had never been known to do any real work in her life, and well knew how to slip out of anything useful, while making it appear that she was very active and quite necessary to any outfit with which she chose to associate herself.

At first Madison's answers were exceedingly brief, but the girl refused to let him evade anything she really wanted to know, until at last her father caught a phrase from the young man's words and chimed in with his questions, and at last they got him started telling of some of his experiences.

Mr. Chalmers was a sharp man and knew how to ask questions, knew the names of the big men in army and navy, knew the location of the strategic points where notable fighting had been going on, and drew out his new man to tell his experiences. Not that Madison wanted to bring himself forward in any way, but the questions were so worded that if he replied at all he must make it apparent that these things had happened to him. And at last they got him to talking, with a fire of memory in his eyes. And Paige Madison could talk when he wanted to. He could mingle facts with pathos and tragedy and tenderness, until he had the whole table listening while he quietly told of happenings that were most dramatic, and if it had not been for Chalmers' questions interpolated "And were you there, Madison? Did you see that yourself?" nobody would have known that the young man had ever been near.

For once Reva was silenced. She sat watching the young man with astonishment in her face. He was good looking, of course, and that was what had appealed to her in him at first, but he didn't respond in the least to her, and she couldn't quite make it out. She set her vivid red lips determinedly. He wasn't going to get away with this lofty ignoring business. She would fix him somehow so that he would have to come crawling at her feet, demanding her attention. She would teach him that she was not one to be ignored. She, an heiress, daughter of one of the most influential men in town. She might have to change her tactics perhaps, but she would get him. She would teach him what he had done and punish him well.

Her jealous eyes watched him sharply as he talked. It was incredible, when he looked so young, and yet when he was talking he seemed so mature.

But suddenly Paige became aware of the interest his story

was creating at the table. Even the haughty Mrs. Chalmers had fixed her cold eyes on the young man's face as if she had seen him for the first time and were taking account of him most carefully. The young man relapsed into a shy silence, and his innermost heart told him that he was out of his natural sphere. Then, try as they would, they could not get him started again on any thrilling adventures.

But the deed was done. The family were intrigued, and determined each within herself to cultivate this brilliant young man.

Quite willingly Paige withdrew into the library with his new boss and entered into matters of business, matters which had been carefully planned beforehand, with the intent to impress the young man with the benevolent character and spiritual-mindedness of his new employer. It was quite necessary if they were to go on together in the business relations which the Chalmers outfit had planned that the young man should be deeply impressed with the Christian character of the head of the firm. And this was especially the case since the morning interview in which Madison had objected to certain phraseology in the contracts given him to sign. If there were any questions in the mind of young Madison on such a score, he would not be the asset to the firm that they had expected him to be. Of course the young man had been away overseas and might have changed, but before he went he was known in the vicinity to be most exemplary, and his people were careful, conscientious Christians. It was most important to Mr. Chalmers that his firm should be known as most honorable in every way, so it behooved him to find out thoroughly all about the young man. And the evening's conversation had pleased him well. He must remember to warn Reva that she was not to interfere with this young man, for the father well knew his daughter was not calculated to help any young man to maintain a quiet manner and keep in the background.

It was not desirable that his new assistant should take a place in the worldly circles, not at least until he had thoroughly established himself as one to be depended upon in every way.

So the keen businessman sat and conversed pleasantly with his new employee, guiding the conversation in the lines he had planned, that he might get a line on him from every angle. And Paige felt more at his ease now that the family were eliminated from the picture, for he had not liked the role of being on display, which the hostess, even more than her forward daughter, created. Of course he did not realize that the mother, recognizing certain interest in her daughter's eyes, was studying him to see just what attitude she should take regarding him in case Reva decided to take him over. Would this be an alliance—the mother called it in her mind a "friendship"—that she could approve and do nothing about, or something that would have to be fought out, even to the length of sending the girl away somewhere on an expensive trip till the danger was over?

Back in the living room they were talking it over, the mother and the sulky daughter.

"I think dad's perfectly horrid," said Reva, pouting in the corner of the big comfortable couch and lighting a cigarette, "making me stay home to entertain his new henchman, and then carrying him off for a private talk just when he was getting interesting."

"I didn't know you had any particular interest in him, Reva," said her mother, watching the girl sharply.

"Oh, I don't, of course," laughed the girl with a sneer. "He probably belongs to some common family, but all the same he's good-looking. Don't you think so, mother?"

"Oh, fairly so," said the mother indifferently. "Of course, being in the service, the uniform can make almost any ordinary fellow look really more or less distinguished. Go carefully, Reva, even at your father's request. He really has very little sense about looking after you."

"I don't need any looking after," said the girl with a scornful toss of her pretty head. "I've been around a lot and I think

I'm a better judge than you are of young men. I think he's rather swell myself. Of course he's a bit stuffy in his attitude, doesn't fall for a girl very easily. Seems terribly on his guard. But I can easily break that down if I decide I want to. But dad invited him here for us to look him over and now he carries him off to the library and keeps him there, and I don't like it! But he needn't think he can do that to me. I'll give him just five minutes more and then I'm going in there and start something."

"Now Reva," protested her mother, "you know your dad won't like that."

"I should worry," said the girl with another toss of her head. "I know how to manage dad, and if he wants my help with his hired assistants he'll have to do as I say."

"My child, that is no way to speak about your father. You know he insists upon your being respectful to him."

"Oh, yeah? Well, if he wants me respectful he'll have to be respectful to me, see? This is a day of young people and their parents can't lay down the law the way they used to do when you folks were young!"

"Reva! How perfectly terrible you are! I insist that you shall not talk in that ridiculous modern way! And you mustn't think of going into the library until your father calls you. Stop! Reva! Where are you going? I tell you, you mustn't think of it."

"Oh, I'm not thinking!" laughed the girl derisively. "It doesn't take thinking to defy dad. You just do what you want to, and then act all innocence! He wouldn't lift his finger to get it back on you."

Then the willful girl turned and flaunted herself toward the library door.

"Reva! Stop child! You simply mustn't interrupt your father when he's talking business."

"Ta! Ta!" said Reva as she vanished into the library and shut the door.

Mr. Chalmers had just been explaining some of his methods to his new assistant.

"You know you have all classes to deal with in a business like this and you have to learn to be all things to all men. That's where you come in. I hear that you have been well brought up and know how to be courteous, even to the people you would naturally despise. We naturally get all classes of people in our business, and almost any of them will work things to their own advantage if they possibly can, regardless of honesty. It will be your job to be both firm and courteous. Kid 'em along, you know, till you make them see they can't play their game with us. We mean business, and if they don't come to time according to agreement we'll take their property away from them.

"Now there are those people we were discussing last night. They are good-living people but a bit shiftless perhaps, and if they don't feel inclined to pay on the dot they will perhaps expect us to let things run along. For that reason I have made their contract a bit ironclad. And if they try to slide out of things, we have other men in our number who can deal with them, if we have to get rough. But they'll soon learn—"

It was just at this moment that Reva barged in, and her father looked up, annoyed. The steady, searching eyes of Paige Madison were on his face and he had an inkling that it was going to take some explaining before he had this young man educated in the ways of the wary world. Steady eyes that saw through evasions and clever devices, and objected to anything that was not in the open clearly, and he was just beginning to feel that he was getting somewhere in this explanation, he was just getting hold of the right words to express what he wanted to say, when this interruption occurred. He naturally frowned at his daughter.

"Now dad, you needn't send me out, for I won't go. You asked me to be here tonight and made me give up two most important engagements to stay at home and meet your new assistant, and now you get stuffy and take him off into another room with the door shut, and that's not fair. I demand that you come out and be interesting. We've got a bridge game ready, and we need you both."

Paige Madison gave a furtive glance at his wrist watch.

"I'm sorry," he said, "I don't play bridge, so I wouldn't be an addition to your company. I beg you will excuse me."

"Oh, but that's ridiculous," said the girl. "If you really don't know how, I'll teach you. I've taught a lot of people, and you're smart enough to learn quickly. I know, for dad said you were a good accountant."

"Thank you," said Paige coolly, "but I wouldn't care to learn. You'll have to excuse me!"

"Oh, for Pete's sake, why not?"

The young man smiled impersonally.

"I just wouldn't be interested," he said. "I haven't time to play."

"Oh, but you must," said the girl firmly. "Everybody has to have some recreation. Isn't that right, dad?"

But her father was sitting with an annoyed frown.

"Reva, you'll simply have to stop annoying us," he said. "We are talking business, and it's quite important. Run out now and shut the door."

"Indeed, no!" said the girl sharply. "You asked me to be here to dinner to entertain your guest, and you've got to keep your part of the contract and make me have a good time. If you can't make your guest come and play bridge, then what will you do? We might have some music. Perhaps he sings?" She gave a sharp look at the young man. "I'm sure you could give us some samples of the kind of song you used to sing in the army."

"No," said Paige, "I'm not a singer."

"Well, then, why don't you ask me to play? I can play myself. At least I've had enough expensive lessons to be able to amuse you a little."

Suddenly Mr. Chalmers rose and spoke sharply.

"That will do, Reva. You go in the other room for half an hour, and then we'll come out. Now go!"

"Indeed, no!" said the girl. "I'm not letting you off for any half hour. You can do your talking down at the office tomorrow. I claim tonight as mine!" she pestered, and twined her wheedling arm in her father's until she actually forced him to go with her, and the young man, of course, had to follow. Whereupon the girl took charge of the arrangements. She seated Paige quite near the piano and took possession of him as if he were her personal guest, and proceeded to exercise her arts on him, smiling insinuatingly, lifting her wide big eyes and throwing herself into musical lingo, asking what he wanted her to play.

Paige responded politely, asking her to choose what it should be, and she proceeded to play, not so well, but not so badly, and as she played the young man studied her.

She was pretty and graceful, yes, and he wondered at himself that he was not attracted by her, not flattered at her efforts to interest him.

But Reva was smart, and she realized the instant that she was losing the interest of the young man. She was using her usual arts and they hadn't worked. What was he, anyway? The uniformed men she had been familiar with had been most amenable to flirtation, and she knew she was attractive. Her mirror told her so.

Suddenly she tried another line:

"Let's go over to a night club and have a little time of it?" she said, gay as a child asking a favor. "I'm bored to death and so are you. You might as well own it. We can take my car and have the time of our life."

He gave her a swift, comprehensive look, and then with a glance at the great clock which was ticking away across the room he said:

"Sorry to have to be saying no all the time, but you see I'm not your type. Those things wouldn't interest me. And besides, I must be getting home. I'm a working man, remember, and I have to be at my desk in the morning. It's too bad I have to be so unsatisfactory, but that's how it is. Thank you very much for exerting yourself to be entertaining."

Then he rose from his seat and began to excuse himself and say goodnight.

But even then she didn't give up. She followed him to the hall, and with her loveliest smile offered:

"I'll drive you home if you like. That will be easier than going in the bus."

"Thank you," he answered coolly, "I have my own car down the street."

"Oh!" she said with a crestfallen pout. "You don't like me, do you?"

He gave her a boyish grin with a lifting of his eyebrows.

"I didn't say that, did I? I scarcely know you, you know."

And then he was gone.

3

"WELL, upon my word! Isn't he the most crude number you ever saw!" said Reva, staring at the door out which he had vanished. "You'll have to get rid of him, dad! I can't get anywhere at all with him."

"I don't know that you were asked to get anywhere with him," said her father coldly. "His province is the office, and yours is *not*. It's time you understood that. I don't want you coming down to the office any time you chose and barging in making a scene about your 'debts of honor' right in public."

"Now dad, that isn't fair of you! Didn't I stay at home from an important date to amuse your guest, and he turned out just to be a boor. That's all he is. A *boor* who doesn't know how to treat a lady. You certainly ought to get rid of him and find somebody more adaptable to our family if you are going to force your office people on the family."

"Stop!" said the father. "It is not your place to run my business for me, and when I tell you that I am having a guest and want your help to entertain, I want you to do so without a question. You are still my daughter, and I have always been reasonable with you. You have no call to behave in this way. Why you should presume to criticize that young man when

you can talk as you have to your own father, I don't understand."

Then the mother rose up to the defense of her child:

"And I don't understand why you are speaking this way to
your daughter, Harris. It is unforgivable of you to find fault
with her in that tone of voice when you know she gave up
something she planned for several days just to please you.
And why you should want her to waste her time on a young
man who didn't pay the slightest attention to her I can't understand. She gave up an important engagement to please
you. Why did that special young man have to be treated like a
young prince, may I ask? Is he a special pet of yours? I thought
he was rather rude to you."

"Because, Adella, he represents an important experiment I
am making in the office. I have searched a long time to find
just the right young fellow, who would combine keenness,
caution and conservatism to serve my purpose, and I particularly wanted to see how he would react in a home situation. If
Reva had cooperated with me it would have been a great help,
but since she didn't seem to understand the situation I suppose
it can't be helped. It was not a situation that called for a definitely hostile attitude on the part of anybody, and that was the
way that Reva acted during the early part of the dinner. I did
not ask him here to see how well he could flirt, and Reva's
idea seems to be that if a young man doesn't immediately fall
for her and start a violent flirtation that he is a boor. I am
ashamed of her. She is trying to make out that the young man
has no ability, and he has, definitely."

"Why, yes, Harris, I suppose he has. He really talked quite
well when he got to describing war scenes abroad. And he
seems to have a good education—" said Mrs. Chalmers, trying to smooth her husband's ruffled feathers, and at the same
time placate her child. "Reva, why can't you call up your devoted friend next door and get him to come and make up a
game with us. It isn't really so late, you know."

With a frown the head of the house growled, "All right."

He told himself he ought to have known better than to drag his family into his business affairs. His daughter was a selfish little fool and he ought not to have expected anything of her that would really count, and as for his wife, she always did take Reva's part. But it was strange they didn't take to the boy, he was so good-looking, and he had thought they all looked so interested when the young man was talking. Perhaps it was only chagrin on Reva's part that the young man didn't fall for her right away. Well, what difference did it make? It would all work out, and perhaps the young man's diffidence was due to his long stay in the atmosphere of war. It had made him shy. But that would soon wear off, of course, given the right atmosphere. Of course there were two or three nice girls, secretaries, down at the office. When he got to know them all that diffidence would wear off. But he definitely wanted him to be able to work among cultured people, quiet elderly people with money to invest, and perhaps granddaughters to win over, and he had thought a course with Reva would well prepare him to go among people of that sort.

It is a pity that Harris Chalmers couldn't have had a closer acquaintance with the older Madisons, and he would have seen that the young man he was seeking to train for his own purposes had been all his life under finer cultural advantages than he himself had ever had. He had seen them in church, of course, but the Madisons were not people to push themselves into notice and they had never been prominent socially, neither did their plain, quiet garb call attention to themselves or stamp them as being "smart."

But Mr. Chalmers had never taken in the fact that there was a higher culture than the kind that mere money and social standing could buy, and so he felt it incumbent upon him to train this young man for the position in which he was choosing to place him for his own ends.

Meantime Paige Madison, on his homeward way, had an uncomfortable feeling that he had not measured up to what

Mr. Chalmers had expected. Yet it was that girl that had made the whole situation, and her father must have known it. He showed plainly that he did not want her barging in when they were talking business. And they had scarcely got started. He tried to think back over the few sentences that had been said, and he couldn't for the life of him be sure just what they portended or how they had been going to end, and again, as after his first meeting with the board, he had that uncomfortable feeling that he wished he were out of this thing entirely. At least he was thankful that this evening's experience was over. But also he had a conviction that his boss was not altogether pleased with the outcome either. Well, perhaps that was as well. He might get the idea that his home was not the best place for a business consultation.

With a sigh of relief he turned his car into the home driveway and straight into the garage, reaching to turn on the light switch as he passed through the door.

And it was just then that Mrs. Harmon, keeping vigil at her side window, determined to find out if she could whether the young man had really been invited to dinner with the Chalmers. Of course it was no proof, for he might have gone to dinner somewhere else, but at least she meant to pursue this matter as far as she could.

And so she sat in her dark window and kept vigil, and when the light flared out from the next-door garage she arose and peered out, not to miss a thing. She saw the car halt, watched the young man get out, made sure it was he and not his father, saw him turn out the car lights, close the door and lock it, and then march up to the back door still in the full glare of brightness, for the garage lights turned out from the house as well as the garage. She had found that out long ago. Well, he was still in his uniform she noted as Paige passed her line of vision and she scanned his fleeting figure as he mounted the back steps and slammed the kitchen door, and an instant later snapped out the garage light. Then Mrs. Harmon arose wearily and went upstairs to bed. It had not been restful to watch so long and, after all, the outcome was still uncertain. Of course she did get a flash of gold or silver on his uniform, but that wasn't very definite. She couldn't be sure whether it was his dress-uniform or not. Well she would think it over, and if he went downtown at the usual hour in the morning for office men, she would perhaps go over and have a talk with his mother. She could take over a bunch of hyacinths and just be friendly a few minutes, and could likely find out something that way.

Paige walked through the house to the living room, where he was sure his father and mother would be sitting. He could hear voices in there, and wondered who was calling. Well, perhaps it was as well. There would be no opportunity for his mother to search him through and through to see just how well he had been pleased with his evening. Not that he minded his mother knowing anything about him, but he did not want her to sense that he was still somewhat troubled. His mother was gifted with a keener sense about a lot more than he was himself.

But this was likely some of the neighbors, and he would go in and greet them and then excuse himself and say he was tired and wanted to turn in.

He paused an instant and tried to identify the voices. A man with a firm, good voice and a pleasant-voiced woman. He did not seem to recognize them. Were they new people, or had he been away so long that he didn't remember them? Well, he must go on now. Dad and mother wouldn't like it if he didn't come in at all.

He stepped over to the hall rack and hung up his hat and topcoat, but just as he did so the people in the living room rose. They were evidently leaving. If he had only paused in the kitchen a couple of minutes he might have avoided them. But no, that was no way to do. He was at home now and he did not want to antagonize anybody. He was likely to live in this town for some time, perhaps, and he mustn't skulk away out of sight.

And then he heard his father say:

"There comes Paige now. I'm glad he arrived before you left. Come in, Paige. I want you to meet our new minister and his wife."

The young man turned and came into the room smiling, ready to greet the strangers, and was at once pleasantly impressed by them. A strong, fine-looking man of middle age with nice dependable lines about his mouth and eyes, and hair graying at the temple, and a sweet, quiet little woman with blue eyes and smiling lips—Dr. and Mrs. Culbertson. He was at once glad that his father and mother had such congenial neighbors, and a pastor who looked as if he might be a sensible man and a close friend. Paige, after he had shaken hands, did not carry out his purpose of excusing himself and getting away to his room, but stayed and stood talking with the rest in the genial home atmosphere, feeling that it was good indeed to be at home and enter into the old-time life of family and church and town. For the time his annoyances of the evening were forgotten, his uncertainties faded, his fears allayed. He was, within a few days, to be out of uniform and, like anyone else, a young man starting life with a respectable job and good prospects.

But he was glad that his father said nothing about his present employment, and he need not even think about it tonight. Things would clear up brightly by morning, of course, and he would soon be established in good and regular standing, associated with a firm that, at least in the eyes of the public, had a good name. If he found out later that the facts did not bear out this supposition he could leave, couldn't he? Why worry?

It developed that the minister was well acquainted with the chaplain who had been with young Madison's company, and had a nephew who had for a time been one of Paige's comrades. The minister stayed a little longer and they all sat down to talk again, so the hectic happenings of the earlier part of the evening were more or less wiped out of the young man's thoughts. When the callers were gone and they all retired for the night, Paige Madison went whistling up the stairs to his room with the old-time lilt in his voice, and his father said to his mother in the privacy of their room, "Well, Randa, the boy seems to be in good spirits again, sounds like his old self. I guess things must have gone well for him tonight."

"Yes?" said the mother with a questioning sigh. "Perhaps."

It was the next morning, about ten-thirty, that Mrs. Harmon arrived at the side door of the Madison house, with a handsome bowl of strawberries in her hands, and knocked. Just as if it had been a custom all these years for her to call on Mrs. Madison. Just as if she hadn't conscientiously treated the Madisons as if they didn't exist.

Mrs. Madison happened to be near the side door and opened it herself, looking at her caller curiously. Oh, she recognized her, for she had often seen her going by, and once she had narrowly escaped being on her list for a war drive campaign, but for an instant she wondered if her neighbor had made a mistake and thought she was going to the house on the other side of theirs. Then Mrs. Harmon's condescending tones voiced her little speech about the strawberries, and she quickly adjusted her own sweet smile to the front.

"Oh, that was very nice of you," she said. "Of course we like strawberries, and ours haven't come into bearing yet. It's early for them, isn't it? Won't you come in?"

To her surprise the invitation was accepted.

"Why, yes," said Mrs. Harmon, "I will for just a minute or two. I've really been so busy. These war demands are so strenuous, aren't they? I suppose you have been just as busy with all these drives and activities. And now your son is home from the war, isn't he? At least somebody told me he was. Is that right? Has he come to stay, or will he be returning overseas, or to camp, or something?"

"No," said the mother with a sigh of joy. "He is home now."

"Oh, then I know you are very happy and feel like celebrating. Will he be staying here, or has he a job in mind off some-where? That always seems to be the next question."

"No, I think he will be at home for the present," said the gentle mother voice, but giving no inkling of what he was going to do. And then smilingly commending the display in her neighbor's garden, "I've been admiring your daffodils. They are gorgeous this year. It makes quite a picture for our benefit."

"Daffodils? Oh, yes, well they are rather luxuriant this year, aren't they? But I never care so much for them. They always seemed to me rather common, just daffodils, but Mr. Harmon was always fond of them. He planted them, and we've just let them grow. They don't demand much and they are soon gone. Me, I rather like hyacinths better, but then one hasn't had much time during these war years to make changes in the garden. I think next year I'll try for some more sophisticated flowers. Azaleas are lovely and make such a dar-ling splash of color, especially some of the new shades. Don't you think so?"

"Yes, azaleas are lovely, too," said Mrs. Madison, "but while they are here I enjoy your daffodils."

"Well, I'm glad somebody gets some good out of them, I'm sure, for frankly I don't care for them. But then, dear me, everybody can't think alike. But I'm forgetting entirely the main thing that I came over for. You see our Woman's Club is making a drive for new members, just quietly you know. Each one of us is trying to bring somebody we think would be an addition to our number, just the right kind of congenial people you know, and I wanted to ask you if you wouldn't be my new member. You never have been a member here, have you?"

"Oh, yes," said Mrs. Madison serenely. "I believe I was one of the original members long ago. But I had to give it up and resign. I really couldn't spare the time."

"You mean you were a charter member, and you gave it up?" said the astonished caller, looking at the woman to whom she had been pleased to condescend with new respect. "But I don't understand. What was wrong with the club? I suppose that must have been in its early days when things were rather crude. I can't imagine any member being willing to resign now."

"Oh, there was nothing wrong with the club," said Mrs. Madison with a smile. "I just didn't have the time to give to it. I was a young housekeeper with three little children and my strength and my time were of course limited."

"Oh," pitied Mrs. Harmon, "what a pity! But you're not hampered in that way now. Your daughters are both married, and you have a marvelous maid I've heard."

"No, I wouldn't have the same reasons, but you see other things have come in and taken my time, and my church work really takes all my extra time."

"Oh, but you don't know what wonderful times we have," said the neighbor, waxing eloquent. "We are such a charming group, of the very best people in town, such *delightful* social affairs and marvelous lectures by the greatest men on all the subjects of the day. One gets such a clear idea of all the great themes of the day, political, psychological, literary, stated in such simple terms that the most dense can really understand. It's wonderful what that club has done for me. They even take up religion now and then, though not too seriously, because there are members from all denominations, and of course we wouldn't allow anything that would antagonize anyone. But it's just too delightful. You haven't attended in some time, I take it."

"Why no, I haven't," admitted the woman gently, "but of course I know a great deal about it, and I often see the notices of your program."

"Well, since you haven't been in some time, I don't think you ought to decide without going again, do you? Why can't you go over with me tonight and just sample it? You wouldn't have any trouble getting in, of course, if you find you want to join again, since you were a charter member.

They would just jump at the chance of getting you. Can't you go tonight? Of course we usually have our club meetings in the afternoon, but this evening, on account of its being an anniversary, we voted to have it in the evening, and they were hoping to get charter members. Will you go with me tonight?"

"Oh, I couldn't, not tonight," said Mrs. Madison. "I have another engagement."

"Oh, break it then and come with me. Please do!"

Mrs. Harmon was almost surprised at herself coaxing this hitherto despised neighbor to go to her precious club, but since she had been in the room she had been noting a number of tasteful, expensive things about the house that astonished her. The handsome antique rugs, the tasteful antique furniture, lovely bits of decoration, the china closet through whose glass doors she caught glimpses of priceless dishes and quaint silver such as she had longed in vain to possess. And also since this woman had been a charter member, why, of course, she must be far more worthwhile than she had ever dreamed.

But Mrs. Madison just smiled and answered quietly:

"I'm sure it is very sweet of you to ask me, but it would be quite impossible for me to go anywhere tonight. We have our Bible study class at the church tonight, and I never miss that."

"Oh, only a Bible class? Why of course you can miss a Bible class. You mean you teach a class of children the Bible? How self-sacrificing of you. But surely you could get a substitute to teach them just for once."

"Oh, I don't teach," laughed Mrs. Madison. "We have one of the best-known Bible teachers in the country. He is much sought after and has eighteen Bible classes a week, besides his church which he serves as pastor on the other side of the city. And it isn't children. It is grown people. Perhaps you'll come with me some time and visit? I assure you he is interesting!"

"Oh, thank you, but I don't really think I'd be interested. I always thought the Bible was frightfully dull. I don't see how you get people out in the evening just for Bible study."

"Well, we do. Our room is more than full, and it is so inter-esting we have to turn the lights out to make the people go home."

"Why, the perfect idea! Perhaps I might come sometime just out of curiosity if it were in the daytime. But my evenings are always so full. We always go to a play or go dancing, or to some dinner when my husband is at home, and he just doesn't see having me go off without him. If we don't have any more exciting engagement we go to the movies, so I real-ly haven't any vacant evenings. And besides, this wouldn't be at all in my line. But I do wish I could persuade you to come with me tonight, just for once. We really have a marvelous program. A star actress from Hollywood, a real star from Hollywood, is going to be present and will say a few words, and that's something you really can't afford to miss."

Again that gentle, quiet smile.

"I'm afraid I'm a good deal like you in my excuse," she said. "I think your program would be a little out of my line, and I wouldn't be interested. I am sorry to seem unapprecia-tive of your thoughtfulness, but I really can't accept your invi-tation, for I mustn't miss the class tonight. It's important. Some questions were asked last week that are to be answered tonight, and I'm anxious to take down the answers. But of course I thank you for your kind thought of me. And if you ever change your mind and would like to try out our Bible study class just let me know and I'll be glad to take you with me."

"Oh, that's awfully kind I'm sure," said Mrs. Harmon with a contemptuous toss of her well-groomed head, "but I'm afraid I wouldn't ever have time for a thing like that. Well, I really must hurry back! I have a very important committee meeting this morning, and I must give my orders for the day before I go."

She arose with another rather jealous look around the pleas-ant dining room, and a sudden remembrance that she hadn't made the slightest advance in the matter for which she really made this visit. She hadn't found out a thing about Paige Madison's job and whether he was really linked with the Chalmers Company. Suddenly she swung around:

"Oh, I forgot!" she said pleasantly. "I meant to say that if your son is hunting a good job somewhere, I'm sure my husband will be glad to put in a good word for him."

"Oh, that's very kind of you, Mrs. Harmon," said Mrs. Madison, "but I don't think my son will need to bother anyone. He has his own ideas of what he's going to do, you know. Now that the boys are home from service they seem even more independent than before they went. But I'm sure we thank you for your kindness, and we shall enjoy these strawberries a lot. And when my peas come into bearing I'll be sending you over some. I believe you said you didn't have any and ours have always been very nice and sweet."

"Why, how perfectly gorgeous. No, we haven't any peas in our garden, and I just adore them. Thank you so much, and I shall be just waiting eagerly for them to come."

And so Mrs. Harmon went soberly home reflecting that she hadn't gained the least bit of news about the Madison family, and hadn't even a guess coming as to whether young Madison was working for the Chalmers Company or not.

Was that plain, quiet-looking woman so very clever that she could see through what she had been trying to do, to get knowledge from her? And how neatly and coolly she had evaded all the questions! Even when she asked directly and offered to help her son, although heaven knew her husband had never offered to do anything for that next-door neighbor's son, and he never would. If she suggested it, he would only rage. He didn't like quiet church people who took their pleasure in studying the Bible. Imagine it! It would seem rank to him even if she ever dared to suggest it to him, and she was really relieved that her offer had not been accepted. Although, of course, she never would have asked him, she would have got around it in some way. There were always pleasant white lies whereby one could get out of careless promises, and she had no conscience against such.

So now she went home puzzling to know whether Paige Madison really had a distinguished job with aristocratic people, or whether he hadn't!

Well, anyway, she needn't worry, for though she had gone as far as possible in offering to sponsor Mrs. Madison in the Woman's Club, her offer had been firmly, almost amusedly, declined. What was the woman made of? Wasn't she human? To choose a Bible Class in place of the likelihood of being prominent in a flourishing woman's club! Imagine it! Well, that was that, and she was really glad she was out of it all. It might have been an awful chance she had taken if the woman had decided to go with her and she had been obliged to introduce her to Mrs. Chalmers! For Mrs. Chalmers had a way of making anyone very uncomfortable if they presumed to bring some undesirable to their sacred club, and instead of finding a royal road to Chalmers' favor she might have brought down retribution upon her aspiring head.

So she entered her own home, rather well satisfied with herself. At least she didn't have to watch any longer to find out if the boy next door went out to a regular job every morning and evening. Well, that was a relief at least. But there were those luscious strawberries, utterly wasted on a neighbor she didn't care a fig for. Well, next time she would wait till she was sure of something before she acted.

So Mrs. Harmon went into the house thanking her lucky stars that she was safely through this experience without getting into any serious trouble. It wouldn't be difficult to drop Mrs. Madison like a hot cake if it became necessary.

Nevertheless, in the back of her mind there lingered the haunting possibility that after all she might be missing a chance. If it just should be that young Madison had a job with the Chalmers Company, she could easily pick up the dropped threads and get in with the Madisons after all. Through those strawberries, and the green peas that had been promised, she could get a hold when something became sure.

So, with relief she went into her house and set herself to find a new maid and get her life into normal lines again.

4

THREE days later Paige came home from the office rather early. He had not seen Miss Chalmers since the evening he had taken dinner with her family, and he was not particularly anxious to see her. He had enough problems of his own without taking on a girl, any girl, even a girl who was expecting to be a great heiress. It just wasn't a question he cared to take up at this time. Girls were an awful nuisance anyway, always a complication when one had serious matters to consider. And the more Paige saw of the methods of the company he was working for, the more he was worried. He tried to convince himself that the whole feeling he had about business was because he had been so long where all considerations were matters of life and death, and not of how much money could be made in any given deal. Probably he would get over this extreme squeamishness about matters that really did not concern him. This was for Mr. Chalmers to worry over, not a mere assistant. And anyway, he had nothing definite to go on yet, just hunches.

So he was glad to get home a little earlier than usual and enjoy the sensation of doing just what he pleased, at least for an hour or so. But as he stepped into the house after parking the old car in the garage, he heard the telephone ringing. He heard the faithful old cook coming down hurriedly from the third story to answer it, but she would certainly not be down to answer before the people had hung up, not with her lame feet that had to clump down a half step at a time. Quickly he stepped across the hall and took the receiver himself. "Yes?"

Then a queer, excited voice began to speak.

"Is this somebody who lives across from the preacher?"

He had to ask over twice before he really gathered what was being asked.

"You mean do we live across the road from the minister?" he asked.

"That's right. Will you please go cross an' ask my girl's teacher to come right away. My girl is dying an' she wants her teacher. She wants a prayer before she dies. Please go quick! She's cryin' awful bad."

"Who are you?" asked Paige calmly.

"That don't make no matter," said the excited voice which had now added tears and occasional frantic sobs to the conversation. "Just tell her Nannie wants her. She'll know."

"But who is your child's teacher? Is it the minister's wife?"

"Na, na!" came the sobbing voice. "No wife. She is his girl!"

"You mean the minister's daughter?"

"Yah, yah, you get her *queek?*"

"You mean you want the minister?"

"No, no, I want my girl's *teacher!* You get my girl's teacher queek! My girl's dyin'!" and the voice broke in a hopeless sobbing.

"All right! But you'll have to tell me your name, and where you live."

"Tell her Nannie wants her," sobbed the woman. "She'll know."

"Wait a minute," said Paige, as he signaled the cook. "Come here Phoebe, see if you can find out who this is and just who it is she wants. She says her child is dying and she wants her teacher. If you can find out who she is and where she lives, perhaps you would know who her teacher is."

Grimly Phoebe took the receiver. She was used to answering calls for help from the minister.

"Yes? Who are you? Oh, Nannie Shamley's mother? What do you say? Nannie is dying? Who said so? Have you had the doctor?"

The words of the distressed woman came clearly from the instrument, and Paige heard them.

"No, no doctor. We can't have the doctor. We haven't paid his bill yet."

"That's nonsense!" said Phoebe crossly. "Any doctor would come to a dying person whether his bill was paid or not."

"No, no!" came the wailing protest. "My husband says no! He can't pay."

"All right," said Pheobe grimly, "I'll see what I can do." Phoebe turned around grimly to explain.

"It's Mrs. Shambley. They're awful poor people way out in the country and her little girl is in June Culbertson's Sunday school class, but Mrs. Shambley didn't know how to get Miss June. She says they told her the Culbertson phone was out of order. I guess I'll have to run across and tell Miss June. But I better stop and put the potatoes in the oven first. Your ma and pa'll be pretty hungry after that long cold ride."

"Where did they go, Phoebe?"

"Oh, they went up to that old Mr. Marshall's funeral. You know he useta be an elder in the church over here, and then he moved up to live with his son, the other side of Bryson Centre, and he had a stroke a few weeks ago, and has just died. I wouldn't wonder if Dr. Culbertson went too. If he did I don't see how Miss June's gonta get to that little Nannie, if she really is dyin'. If her father took the car she won't have any way to get there. But I'll run over and give her the message anyway after I get the potatoes in the oven."

"Oh," said Paige pleasantly, "don't hurry, Pheobe, I can

run over and give the message. I should think we ought to do something about a doctor, too, if it's really a matter of life and death."

"Well, yes, mebbe," said Phoebe. "I 'xpect your mother would say so ef she was here."

"I'll see," said Paige as he hurried out and over to the pretty little stone house his mother had pointed out as being the abode of the new minister.

It was June herself who opened the door, looking like a little girl in a simple blue gingham dress and a white apron, with the sunshine on her bright hair.

"I am Paige Madison," he said courteously, "and I'm bringing a message for Miss June Culbertson."

The girl's face lighted.

"Come in," she said in a friendly voice, "I'm June Culbertson."

"Oh," said the young man, "I wondered if you might not be. You see I'm just home and I haven't learned the changes that have come yet. But I guess perhaps there won't be time for me to come in. The message seemed to be imperative. It came on our telephone. The woman said they reported your phone out of order, and she asked us to let you know. It was from a Mrs. Shambley, and she said Nannie was dying, and calling for you. She wanted you to hurry!"

"Oh!" said the girl with a flutter of her hand to her throat. "Poor little Nannie! But—I'm not sure I can get there! Dad has the car. He and mother went to that funeral. And I guess your father and mother have gone to the same place. I wonder if I can get hold of a taxi in a hurry?"

"What's the matter with my taxiing you?" offered Paige pleasantly. "Of course our old car isn't much to look at, but it still runs on four wheels and does make fairly good time at that, if you don't mind."

"Oh, would you take me? Thank you so much. It's rather a long walk if there is need of hurry."

"I'll be delighted," said Paige. "And by the way, the woman said they had no doctor. She said the bill wasn't paid and her husband wouldn't let her get the doctor again. Do you happen to know who their doctor is?"

"Oh, why yes," said June, "it's Dr. Sherburn. I'll call him. He may not be at home, but they'll know where to contact him. And I'll be ready in three minutes."

"All right, I'll get the car," and Paige hurried home. He was back just as June came out the door and hurried down the walk.

As if they were old friends going on an errand of mutual interest they settled into conversation.

"I left a note for mother," she said, as he helped her into the car, "so they won't worry."

"That's good!" said Paige, "and what about a doctor?"

"Oh, yes. They said he was up at a clinic in the hospital and I got him and told him. He said he'd get some other doctor to take over and he would be out there almost as soon as he could get out of his uniform."

"So, he's that kind of a doctor is he? Ready to go to a poor family, even though they haven't paid their bill. He must be a pretty good man to tie up to."

"He is," said June. "I haven't been here so long myself, but from what I've seen of him he seems to be grand. Dad says he's always ready to go, day or night, if anyone is in distress."

"That sounds wonderful. And is he also skillful?"

"He certainly is. They tell me he has been practising around here since before the war, and he worked wonders in the hospital overseas. But he certainly was wonderful with little Nannie. We suspected she was undernourished and that proved to be the case. The doctor gave strict orders what she should eat, but I just don't believe they have been kept. You see the family are in reduced circumstances. I think they have been trying to buy their house, and they have let everything else go to that end. I tried to tell Nannie's mother how important it was that she should have the right food, and sometimes I've taken things over for her. They are always very grateful of course, but really quite embarrassed to take it. They are not the ordinary poor people. They are ashamed to accept assistance. That is why they have not sent for the doctor again. The father is very proud and terribly discouraged."

"Well, that's a sad tale, and their attitude makes it harder to help them in any way."

"Yes, that's true. Daddy has tried his best to get near to the father, especially now since he has been so ill himself, but dad can't seem to get anywhere. There! There is the house, down that little road. See the light at the end of the road."

"Yes," said Madison. "It seems a neat little house. Could stand some painting, but on the whole looks very well."

"Yes," said the girl wistfully, "but with mortgages and sickness, I don't suppose there is much money left for paint."

"No, of course not. Well, now, what's the order of the day? I don't imagine my presence will add to the picture. What shall I do? Just stay here till you come out? And will you let me know if I can be of any assistance?"

"Yes, I suppose that will be best. The doctor's car has not come yet. Perhaps you'll stay here and explain to him just what happened, and tell him to come right in. I'll take this soup and milk in. It may be needed at once. I have an idea that poor kid hasn't had a thing to eat all day."

"Why, here, I'll take those things in. Do you want this basket too?"

"Yes. I brought some oranges, and bread and a thermos bottle of coffee."

"That sounds good. Which door do we use?"

"This back door. The kitchen table is at the right. Put the things there. And hark, I think I hear the doctor's car."

"That's right. I'll go right back and meet him."

The girl vanished inside the house and Madison returned just in time to meet the doctor.

The doctor seemed to understand thoroughly the situation without explanation.

"I should have been sent for before, of course," he said, "but the father has that inhibition about bills. Poor soul! He is desperately sick himself. See if you can find him, and I'll be around to look him over when I get through with the child."

The doctor vanished into the house, going with the sure tread of one who thoroughly knows the situation, and Paige began a cautious survey of the premises. It was very still out there in the soft growing darkness, and there were no lights in the house to guide him, no sounds of moving feet or voices except those quiet ones in the room where the girl had gone.

Cautiously he approached window after window, and glanced into the dark rooms, but only darkness met his searching gaze.

At last as he went around the shed behind the kitchen he thought he heard a groan, but in trying to trace it to its source he came on the small figure of a young boy, flat on his face in the grass doing his best to stifle the sobs that were shaking his frail young shoulders.

Paige stepped quietly to his side, and softly kneeling, laid a gentle hand on the bowed head.

"What's the matter, kid? Is there anything I can do for you?" he asked in the tone of one young fellow to another.

The sobs stopped instantly. The shoulders were suddenly quiet. It was as if the boy had been frozen into suspended animation for an instant. But Paige remained kneeling there, his hand in kindliness on the stormy young head. Suddenly the boy raised his head, turned and sat up.

"Who are you?" he growled, glaring through the half-darkness into the young man's face. Then without waiting for an answer he demanded, "Is my sister dead? And are you the undertaker?"

"Oh, no!" said Paige half amusedly. "I'm just a fellow that brought your sister's Sunday School teacher up to see her. They said your sister wanted her to come. You see she didn't have a car she could use so I brought her in mine."

The boy relaxed limply.

"Oh!" he said wearily. "But she's dying, isn't she? I heard

my mother tell my father. And we can't have the doctor because our bill isn't paid."

"Don't worry about that, kid. The doctor has just come. It's going to be all right."

The boy looked at him with unbelieving eyes.

"Where is your father?" asked Paige. "Is he over there in your sister's room?"

The boy shook his head.

"No! He wouldn't go over there. He said he couldn't stand it there. He's sick himself. He says he's been an awful failure, and he's likely going to die himself before my sister does, and anyhow he's gonta lose the house and we won't have any place to go but the poorhouse after he's gone!" and the boy's shoulders began to shake again in great deep sobs.

"Now look here, kid, that's no way to react in a situation like this. Straighten up and let's see what we can do about it."

The boy sat up half angrily and his voice shook hoarsely.

"But there isn't anything we *can* do! My father said so. Tomorrow is the last day to make his next payment on the house, and we haven't got the money, and the man at the bank said if he didn't bring it before noon tomorrow we'd lose the house. All my father has worked so hard to pay! And it's all paid now but two last payments, too, and he's goin' to lose it *all*, and he just can't bear it! It's too much!"

"Well, now mop up and let's see about this," said Paige comfortingly, "the end of the world hasn't come yet, and there are always things that can be done. You take my handkerchief and dry those tears. We've got important things to do. If that money's got to be paid by tomorrow noon we've got to get a hustle on and find the money. How much is it, do you know?"

"Uh huh! It's seventy-five dollars interest, and a hundred on the principal. And dad's been everywhere all day tryin' ta borra some. He's only got forty-five himself, an some o' that he had ta use ta go places to try an' borra, but nobody had enny ta spare, an' dad came home so sick he couldn't stand up. He went off without even a bite ta eat."

"Well, now that's too bad," said Paige, "but look here, we've got more important things to do right now than bother about that money. I know places where we can get money. But what we need first is to see that your father is looked after. Has he had anything to eat yet since he came back?"

"Nope," said the boy, "he said he never could eat again. Hadn't any right to eat 'cause he was a failure."

"There now, kid, don't begin that bawling again. Where is your father? We'll see what we can do about it."

The boy at first wouldn't answer. Then he said: "Dad won't like it ef I tell ya."

"That's all right, kid. I'll make it right with your father. Where is he? He doesn't need to know you told me. Show me where he is."

"He's over on the old couch in the back shed," said the boy with a shudder.

"O.K. kid! Show me where that is. We mustn't waste any time. Your father needs something to eat, and we brought some soup and hot coffee. That'll brace him up and then we can talk about the other troubles. Hurry! We haven't any time to lose."

At last the boy was induced to lead the way to the forlorn little bare shed behind the kitchen where the man was stretched despairingly on a broken-down sofa, partially covered with worn Brussels carpet.

Paige turned on his flashlight, and the motionless figure stirred and looked up.

"Hello, brother. There you are! I'm hunting you to see if you wouldn't like a good hot cup of coffee. Then you'll be in better shape to help us get things straightened out."

"Is my—little—Nannie, *gone?*" asked the man's weak, anxious voice.

"Why no, man. What gave you that idea? The doctor's just

gone in to see her. He'll bring her round, and you've got to brace up and get ready to help us."

"There's—nothing—I can—do!"

"O yes, there is," said Paige. "Wait till you've had a cup of that nice coffee. Does this door open into the kitchen? I thought so. Kid, suppose you get me a cup and saucer, and we'll have your father fixed up in no time."

Paige threw open the old wooden door to a bare kitchen where a single candle burned on a mantelshelf. The baskets he had brought in were still on the table where he had put them. He could hear the doctor's cheerful voice across the next room, in the bedroom beyond, then a feeble child's voice, and a mother's sobs. Just then June Culbertson came quickly out and went efficiently to work preparing a cup of broth from the other thermos bottle. This was some girl taking hold of a situation like this and carrying on efficiently!

He went back to the father with the hot coffee, and an old cushion he had picked up from a chair.

"Now, brother," he said cheerfully, "suppose you let me raise your head a little higher so you can drink this."

In spite of his protests he was able to lift the man into a comfortable position, and coax him to swallow a few spoonfuls of the hot liquid, after which he seemed to revive a little, and finally sat up and drank the rest of the coffee.

"Oh, that's good," he said. "That's heartening. But I ought not to have taken it. My wife needs it more than I do. She's been up day and night nursing our little girl."

"There's enough for your wife to have some too," assured Paige cheerfully.

"But my little girl's going to die!"

"Oh, no she isn't, not just now," said the heartening voice of the doctor who had just come out of the sickroom. "All she needed was a little cheering up and some of that good hot soup Miss June brought along. Do you know what's the matter with this household? You've all been sitting around weeping and wailing. No wonder little Nannie thought she was going to die. No wonder your wife is almost dead on her feet, and everything is all wrong. Do you know where we found your kid son? Out in the grass crying because he thought you were going to die too. Now, brother, let's see what's wrong with you," and the doctor stepped determinedly over to the father and laid a professional hand on his wrist and then on his forehead.

"I thought so," he said, getting out his thermometer, "you're way below normal. What are you trying to do, arrange for a family funeral on the town? That's no way to do."

"But I can't pay you, doctor. I've been out all day hunting a job and trying to borrow money, and it's no go! I can't get a thing!"

"Yes? Well, if my bill is all you're worrying about, forget it. Things aren't always going on this way for you. You'll get a job. We'll all help you."

"But that isn't all, doctor. I'm going to lose this house, and there won't be any place for us to even die in."

"Oh, fiddlesticks. Here! Take this pill, and I'll give you another before I go. You talk your troubles over with young Madison, here. He's a bright young man interested in finance, and ten to one he'll find some solution for your difficulties. Now I'm going back to see how Nannie is. And Madison, I leave this man with you to find some solution for his trouble. He can't go on carrying all this burden, and then get up and do a man's work besides. It isn't possible. There's some way out of this, and we've got to find it, or I'm not a doctor."

"Of course!" said Paige cheerily. "Now come, we'll get you a bite more soup, and some bread and butter, and then you can give me the details."

The doctor's eyes twinkled as he looked back on the two and noted the expression on the discouraged father's face.

Paige lost no time in producing the soup, and saw that every drop of it was swallowed before he said a word about any troubles. Then he put the dish over on the table and came back, drawing up a chair to the old couch.

"Now," he said, getting out a pencil and paper, "just what is it that's worrying you most? This house? What makes you think you're going to lose it?"

"Because they told me that if I missed another payment, that was the end. I'd got to pay up interest and all or they'd have to close me out. And tomorrow's the last day. Twelve o'clock they close, tomorrow."

"Have you got any papers to show for all this?"

"Yes. Over in the drawer of that old desk in the corner of the dining room."

"Mind if I see them?" asked Paige.

"Oh, sure, but it's no use to try anything with those folks. They haven't any hearts. They don't care if we all die. And I'm dead sure there isn't anybody would lend a red cent to a poor old failure like me." The man drew a heavy, discouraged sigh and bowed his head on his hands.

Paige went to the desk and brought back a bundle of papers. To his surprise he saw that they were drawn in the name of Harrison Chalmers and Company, and his heart sank with indignant fury. So this was the kind of thing that his delightful bosses were carrying on under the guise of benevolence and righteousness! *Now,* what was he to do?

"Well, now look here," he said to the discouraged man, "you mustn't give up this way. I know where I can get this money for you."

"Oh, yes, you think you do, but just wait till they find out who wants to borrow it. Wait till they see my old rusty coat and the down-and-out-ness in my face. And wait till you find out the awful rate of interest they'll want to charge for it. Interest I could *never* pay, even if I did get well and get a job."

"No," said Paige firmly, with a strange feeling that he was somehow being directed from above, and must say these things. "No, there won't be anything like that, because I'll get the money for you myself. It'll be loaned *to me,* and I won't charge you a cent of interest. Not till you get on your feet and have plenty to spare. Then if you want to pay me back you can do it. But just at present you won't have *anything* to pay, and you won't have to sign any contracts. Your business is to get well, see? Now, let me look over these papers. I am sure I can arrange this for you. You'd better brace up and see if you can get the strength to take your payment in. Do you think you're up to that? Wait, we'll ask the doctor whether you can. Of course it could be mailed in if it would reach them in time."

"Oh, yes, I can take it," protested the sick man. "I'd rather. They'll think I've failed again if I don't come myself. But I can't let you do this for me."

"Oh yes, you can. We're brothers, you know. And if you don't like to let me do it for yourself, then I'll do it for your family's sake. Now if you'll show me about these different papers I'll try and get things in shape for you. I'll have to give you the money in the morning as of course I don't have that much with me, but if you can be ready to go back with me I can make the trip that much easier for you. I'll have to get back to the office where I work by nine o'clock. Will that be too early a start for you? And then about your getting back. I could pick you up at the noon hour and bring you home. But we'll have to see what the doctor says about your going at all, first."

The doctor had been standing just outside the door of the sickroom and now he came over to them smiling.

"Sure! Go and get your troubles off your mind! That'll be better for you than all the medicine in my chest. And if you've got any more of those financial troubles let's get them out into the open and get rid of them. Are there any more debts bothering you, brother?"

"There's your bill," sighed the man. "I guess that comes next."

"Well, we'll just forget that for the present. Let's get the other things out of the way first. How about the grocer's bills? Are they all paid?"

The man shivered as if a cold blast had struck him and he groaned.

"Yes, I thought so!" said the doctor. "Nothing like a lot of unpaid bills to put a person down sick in bed and ready for the undertaker. Let's get them off your chest."

"Are these all your bills, Mrs. Shambley?" asked Paige, holding up a bunch of papers he had brought from the drawer in the dining room where he got the mortgage papers.

The sick man looked up with a start, and then sank back.

"Yes," he groaned. "Those are all of them. But if I could get a job I'd soon have those out of the way."

"Well, it'll be time enough to talk about that when you get well and have a good job so you can take care of your family. Let's get these out of the way now. Madison, you add those up and I'd like to chip in and help with them. I want to see this man get well. Here's a milk bill. Twenty dollars, and it's dated two months ago! Is that why Nannie hasn't been drinking milk any more? Well, we'll see about that. I want her to have plenty of milk, and you too. The whole family needs milk. I'll just take this bill along and settle it up and see that they send some milk over right away tonight. And you get the other bills together."

"There aren't so many of them. Two groceries, and the shoe store; Johnny had to have his shoes fixed or he couldn't go to school. A small bill at the hardware. The ax broke and we *had* to have another to cut down a tree for a fire. There's a gas bill too, an 'lectric light, but they've been cut off for three weeks."

"There, now, don't worry anything more about it," said Paige. "These don't add up to so much. We'll be able to get enough to cover these, so don't worry. Now, let's go over them again, and see if we've missed anything."

Paige's matter-of-fact tone seemed to give a new kind of strength to the discouraged man.

"Now, are you sure there isn't anything else?"

"The bread man," murmured the poor man.

"Yes. But that's not so much. I can get you money enough to cover all these, and a little more to keep you going until you get your job. It won't pay you to starve yourself or your family. It only makes more bills. So now, let's get this thing straight. You are to eat some more soup and bread and coffee, and then you're to go to sleep, and put all your troubles out of your mind. That's the first step to righting things. The doctor says your little girl is not going to die at present, and will get well soon if you brace up and get well yourself. The doctor is getting a nurse tonight, too, so your wife can get some rest. And now I'll go and see if there is anything else I can do. Where is that son of yours? It's time he had something to eat too."

So Paige went in search of the boy and to find out from June what plans she had.

"I'm staying here till the nurse comes," she said, "but I think you should go home and tell my folks what has happened. Dad will come after me. And tell him to bring some more coffee and a loaf of bread. Now please go. I've taken enough of your time already, and I surely am obliged to you. I didn't know I was getting you into such an extended performance, but it certainly has been wonderful to have you along. You've done wonders with that poor discouraged man. Now go, do. Your mother will be worried about you."

Paige looked at her amusedly.

"So that's the kind of softy you think I am, is it? Leave you here to face all this music and go home to save myself? Not on your life, I don't do that. But I'll tell you what I will do. I'll go to the store and get some groceries. There's one store over near our house that stays open late, and even if they've retired I know them well enough to wake them up. So you wait here till I come back. I won't be long," and with that Paige vanished out into the darkness.

5

ALL the way back to the village Paige had a vision in his mind of the lovely girl he had left behind him, serving the poor and forlorn, and doing it so fully and so joyously. She must be an extraordinary girl. A girl worth knowing and having for a friend. He was glad he had been called aside from his own pursuits to have this brief experience with her in rescue work.

Knowing there was little time before the store closed, he hurried there first.

The grocer was surprised to see him.

"Why, Paige, your mother got her usual supply this morning," he said. "Are you sure she wants more butter? And eggs? Or has she got unexpected company?"

"No, Mr. Brand," smiled Paige, "these are for some friends who couldn't do their ordering today and as I was coming this way I offered to bring some things for them. They have sickness in the family and got pretty well cleaned out of supplies. Give me two loaves of bread please, and some crackers. Some of that cheese. About two pounds of butter if you can spare that much. Is butter still scarce?"

"Well, she ain't so plenty," responded the grocer, "but I guess I can spare you a little. I can let you have a half pound.

Will that do? Our butter man comes in the morning. And did you say you wanted some meat? Lucky I got a good-sized pot roast left. And how about potatoes and carrots and onions and cabbage and a bag of flour?"

"That will be fine," said Paige. He found himself fascinated by the number of things he might purchase to replenish that poor empty cupboard. Why, this was almost as good as Christmas, getting all these things where they were so sorely needed.

At last, with a big flour sack deeply loaded, and several smaller packages, and a box of oranges, apples and bananas he hurried to his own home and June's to explain what they had been doing, and to pick up a few things from each household to take back with him, and then he started.

As he turned into the highway he sighted the unmistakable Chalmers car in all its shining glory. As they passed at the crossroads the big spotlight above the street brought out the faces of the people in the car sharply. A large party of young people with Reva and an attentive young man in the front seat, into whose eyes she was adoringly gazing, while her laugh rippled out on the night. A moment more and they had passed by, but the startling image of the beautiful girl lingered with him. Complexion of roses and cream, vivid lips stretched wide in laughter, great eyes accentuated with artistic care. Dressed in something airy and soft and glittering, with lovely flesh appearing. The spotlight full on her face made a picture that could not easily be forgotten. *There* was a girl with whom he might easily have spent the evening if he had chosen, a girl so marked as a beauty, especially in evening array, that anyone who companioned with her would always be envied. And yet there was not a twinge of regret in his heart. He was glad he had escaped this affair wherever it was that the young people were bound. Far rather would he have been helping June.

He stepped on the gas and turned off to the side road, out of the path of the so-called fortunate of the world, and as he sped toward the little back road and the quiet little house with the small candlelights in the three windows he began to think over what he must do when he got there.

Of course, if the nurse had not come, or the doctor had not been able to get one, he supposed June would feel that she must stay, perhaps all night. In which case he felt that he should stay too, to help her out in any trying situation.

And in any case he must help the sick man into a comfortable bed. He was thankful that his thoughtful mother had put in a few clean sheets and pillowcases, and a couple of blankets. They could be used of course, and who but his mother would have thought of that?

The nurse had come, and taken over with Nannie, and June was engaged in getting some supper on the table. She received the addition to their stores with great delight.

Paige hunted up the boy and together they got some beds made up, and the father stowed comfortably in one, with an admonition to waste no time getting to sleep so he would be able to go in town with him in the morning. The doctor returned while they were talking and added his word, and a sleeping powder.

The little Nannie by this time was sleeping comfortably, and the mother under June's care was eating the first comfortable meal she had had for several days.

Yet in spite of all this it was almost two hours before June was ready to leave, and everything in shape for the early morning.

The nurse was capable and willing, and at last they started home.

"You must be almost dead," said Paige sympathetically. "You haven't had a bite to eat either, of course. Being the unselfish person you are, you wouldn't stop for even a mouthful."

June laughed.

"And how about you? I suppose you sat down and ate a

turkey dinner during that five minutes you spent in your home getting those supplies."

He laughed.

"Not a chance. I didn't even let mother pour down a drop of her nice hot coffee that she tried to choke me with. So, how about our stopping at the Sterling on our way home? It isn't but half a block out of our way, and I confess I could easily eat a whole cow if one was cut up into steaks."

"All right," said June, "I'm hungry too. But why do you have to choose such a swell place as the Sterling? Don't you think perhaps the sharp contrast might affect us badly? It certainly would be going from poverty to riches."

"I know," grinned Paige, "but I'm not sure that any other decent place would be open at this hour, and I really think we rate a good meal, don't you?"

"Well, it would be nice, but of course we could go home and get something decent there—either home, or both."

"Yes, we could, but I'm thinking it would be quicker and a lot more fun at the Sterling."

"Well, that's all right with me, only isn't the Sterling a pretty swell place? And I've only a plain little gingham dress on. All the high and mighties will be in evening dress."

"What difference does that make?" grinned Paige. "And besides, that's a pretty dress and very becoming. It just matches your eyes."

June rippled a laugh.

"I don't see where you've had time to see what color my eyes are, or my dress either, but if you don't mind taking a rather crumpled nurse to the swellest place in town, it's all right with me."

"Okay with me. I rather enjoy shocking some people. But we'll have fun."

"Well, I think you are a pretty good sport after all we've been through, that you can talk about having fun."

"Well, we had to do that in war, you know. Take a bit of

fun in between the desperate situations. And besides, things are coming out for our protégés pretty well. I think I can enjoy a bit of fun. By the way, how is Nannie, really? Did the doctor give you any more light?"

"Yes, he thinks she'll come out of this in a few days. She's undernourished, of course, but we can remedy that in time. But you, how did you make out with that poor discouraged father? It's his pride that has made all this trouble."

"Yes, he is proud, but I'm inclined to think the troublemaker goes farther than that. The mortgage people are cruel and have scared him out of his senses. Do you know he's spent the last two days tramping everywhere trying to borrow money enough to pay the interest and a pitiful little sum on the principal. Of course he is shabbily dressed, and he probably went to strangers and they wouldn't let him have it. But I told him I would arrange it for him, and he finally succumbed, ate some soup and coffee and dropped off to sleep like a babe."

"Do you mean you really can get a loan for him?"

"Yes, of course."

"But won't it cost him a horrible amount of interest these days?"

"No, I'll fix that all up for him."

"I think you are wonderful, Mr. Madison."

"Call me Paige, please. I'll feel more natural that way, and after all the things we've been through together this afternoon I don't see that we should be formal, should we—June?"

"Of course not," said June with satisfaction, "but I can't get over it that you went along with me and did all that," she said softly. "It was God who sent you, of course."

Paige grew a bit sober.

"Well, perhaps, though I wasn't conscious of heavenly direction. There was a telephone message that obviously was important, a little girl dying, and you had no car to go. Why shouldn't I take you? It wasn't a great thing to do."

"No, of course not. And it wasn't anything to lend that man the money to hold his house, and all the rest that you did.

Only a true servant of the Lord would have done all that, I am sure."

She gave him a bright look that had in it a question, and was almost embarrassing to him.

"Well, I don't know that I can exactly claim that title," he said with some hesitancy. "Of course I'm a church member, have been since I was a child, but that doesn't necessarily mean all that. You know in the army you learn to look facts in the face, and you don't rate yourself in the face of death the way you did at home where everything was calm and serene, and it was the respectable thing to serve the Lord. But out among the men who were many of them cursing and swearing and taking death as a part of the game, one got lax. I admit I did. I'm not just altogether sure what the Lord thinks of me now."

"Oh!" said June. Then after a pause, "But you'll be finding out pretty soon, I'm sure. After all, the world is alike everywhere, and there are too many risks in every day for a thinking person to let the really important things go."

Paige was silent for a full minute and then he said in a serious voice:

"I guess you're right about that."

They were coming into town now and presently came to the crossroads. Paige turned and looked down at the girl beside him, while the spotlight touched her lovely, earnest face, and thought how charming she was. Somehow the words she had just spoken went deep into his heart. He would be thinking about them again.

And now on the highway the traffic took his attention, so that they did very little talking until they swept into the curved drive before the imposing hotel.

June gave a little gasp as she watched a grand car disgorge a gay throng of passengers.

"Are you sure you want to take me into a place like that, looking this way?"

"I am sure!" said the young man firmly.

"But I haven't even a hat on!"

Paige gave attention to the people who were going in.

"Neither have a lot of them. But if it's a hat you want, we'll soon remedy that."

He drew up at the sidewalk and motioned to a man who was standing there conspicuously offering flowers for sale.

"Got any gardenias?" he asked nonchalantly.

"Sure thing," said the man, and produced a white box with three enormous lovely blooms.

"That's the thing," said Paige. "Got any pins to fasten them on with?" The vender handed over a little bunch of invisible hairpins.

"I see you are ready for all emergencies," said Paige. "There, June. Put them on and you'll be as well fixed as any of the other patrons. Those who pretended to have hats had nothing but a couple of big sunflowers or roses or something of the sort. Put them on."

"But Paige! With a gingham dress? Such lovely things! It wouldn't be suitable."

"But I say it would, and you're my girl tonight. I want to see them on. And who is to know your dress is gingham? And what if it is?"

"All right," laughed June, and presently the skillful fingers that had recently been soothingly bathing little Nannie's hot forehead, fastened the beautiful gardenias with a grace that could vie with any of the modern outlandish hats. She gave one glance into the little mirror over the windshield, patted one flower a little more to the right, and then looked up.

"Is that all right?" she asked amusedly.

"Perfect," said the young man. "I can recommend you as a milliner any time you want a new job."

"All right," she smiled. "Then let's go. But I warn you someone will laugh at me."

"Let them laugh!" said Paige, helping her out of the car and watching her admiringly. To his man's eyes there was nothing incongruous in her costume. And perhaps even a woman looking at her casually would notice nothing out of the way.

So they entered the building and followed the crowd to the great dining room.

Paige with quiet sense selected a small table unobtrusively placed where they could see without being too much in the public eye, and when they were seated he turned his admiration on the girl he had brought with him. How lovely she looked with those fresh gorgeous flowers nestled in her pretty hair! She might be conscious that her costume would not bear close inspection by the critical, but certainly she was beautiful and was in no way conspicuous.

An obsequious waiter provided them with menus and they soon selected their orders, for they were both hungry, now that they were in the neighborhood of food.

June was not a girl to sit and brood over her unsuitable garb. She promptly forgot it and entered into the festive time with pleasure.

"It seems like another world, doesn't it? So different from that forlorn little house where we've been this afternoon."

"Yes, it does. That's the way I felt when I got home from war zones. It was incredible that the same universe could contain both gaiety and misery. It didn't seem right somehow to be in a place of quiet restfulness and plenty, when some of my buddies were just starting off to go into death and pain and frightfulness."

"Yes, I understand," said June with sweet thoughtfulness, "and yet it must have been necessary that you should change your viewpoint from time to time or human flesh could not endure and keep on doing the work of a fighter."

"Yes, of course, there was that side, too. Although we didn't get to see much gaiety when we were in the actual fighting zone. People over there had seen fright and suffering enough so that they never got entirely away from the thought of it, the fear of it. But what got me was when I came home and found so-called decent, respectable men with pleasant incomes and palatial homes, gypping some of the poor returned men who hadn't a-where to lay their heads."

"Yes," said June with a blaze of indignation in her eyes, "like the man who is grinding down those poor protégés of ours. They tell me he is a very religious man and gives large sums to worthy causes. But look what he's done to these poor Shambleys. Do you suppose he knows them personally? Does he understand how desperate they are?"

"Probably not."

"Well, do you suppose it would do any good if somebody were to go and tell him? Could we possibly get him to go and see for himself?"

"Probably not. He would say he was too busy and that they were likely good-for-nothings or they never would have got to that state."

"Yes, I suppose so," sighed June. "But those poor souls! They don't seem like good-for-nothings."

"No, they don't. They have self-respect and a certain kind of pride. It may not be the wisest kind, that shrinking out of sight that doesn't venture to push one's self into notice, but after all, some of those so-called decent respectables don't even have that much dignity and self-respect. If they see a chance to make a penny by squeezing an unfortunate it wouldn't take much of their kind of philosophy to make them yield to the temptation. I'm beginning to conclude that that is how a good many of them got wealthy and influential."

"Yes, I suppose it is," sighed June.

And then the waiter appeared with their delicious looking dinner and they settled themselves to enjoy it.

Suddenly there entered a noisy group of girls and men, gay and noticeable in smart evening clothes, barging into the place as if they owned it, laughing and talking as if they might have been drinking already. Paige looked up from his dinner, and glanced annoyedly toward the newcomers. Something familiar in the loud, unrestrained laughter of one of the girls, reminiscent of unpleasant memories, made him look at her sharply, and there she was, Reva Chalmers! And coming right toward him purposefully, as if she had searched around and found him, and was coming to get even with him somehow.

His face grew stern as he watched her come, with that hateful challenging grin on her wide red lips, and his chin lifted haughtily, his eyes grew grave.

Reva marched at the head of her gay clan as if with entire intention, and brought up standing in front of the quiet little table where June sat in her blue gingham and gardenias, with surprise on her face.

But Reva was looking straight at Paige, chin up, a challenging sneer on her lips:

"So, *this* is where you were, Paige Madison, is it?" she accosted him, quite as if she had a right.

With an annoyed and somewhat puzzled frown Paige arose politely:

"I beg your pardon?" he said, looking at her with surprise, "I don't think I quite understand."

"No, *you* wouldn't," sneered the girl, " but I've been calling all over the place for you, and couldn't find you anywhere."

"Oh?" said Paige, "was it something important you wanted? Some message from your father?"

She burst into a laugh in which her huddled party joined boisterously.

"No, it wasn't any message from dad," she said when she could speak for laughter. "It was just to invite you to join our dinner party tonight. I had a girl for you but she backed out when we couldn't find you. But I see you have a dame of your own, so come on. What do we call your girl-friend?"

"Excuse me. This is Miss Culbertson, Miss Chalmers. Sorry, but I don't know the names of your friends."

"Oh, that doesn't matter. We'll soon get acquainted at dinner. Do come on. We're half an hour late now."

"You'll have to excuse us," said Paige haughtily, "we have other plans for the evening."

"Oh, you *have?* Indeed!" And Reva turned and gave June the benefit of the most prolonged appraising stare one could imagine, taking in the rumpled gingham frock, the gorgeous gardenias, puzzled to know just how to interpret them. Then she turned to her own crowd.

"Just like that they've turned us down flat! Can you imagine it? Tra la la! But they don't know what they're missing, do they, Bunny Faro? Well, come on!" and the giddy young cavalcade marched down the room to the great closed doors that shut off the private dining rooms from the main one, and left the two young people at the sheltered table to go back relieved to their interrupted dinner.

"Now will you be good?" giggled June. "I hope you understand fully what a terrible thing you did, bringing a soiled nursemaid in a gingham dress to such a place as this, to meet your boss's daughter in an imported frock with real jewels around her neck. If it hadn't been for your gardenias I should have sunk right through the floor, and died of shame. I hope you'll take a little advice another time and look out what kind of a girl you take to these swell places with your noble friends. I shouldn't be at all surprised if you lose your job for this performance."

Paige grinned back at her, and gave her a look of real admiration.

"If my job depends upon what that giggly-goo can do I should worry. You needn't say another word like that!" he said. "I was proud of my girl, and I shall certainly take her again if she will go. For I thought she was better looking than any girl in that dazzling crowd. Now, shall we have some hot coffee and begin again?"

"My coffee is plenty hot enough," said June pleasantly, "but I do feel troubled that I should have been along and hindered you from going to that other gathering. If I hadn't been here and made a fuss about not being dressed up you would have gone."

"I certainly would *not* have gone. I know what their parties would be like, and they are not my style, but I didn't even ask you if you would like to go. Perhaps I should have done so."

June laughed.

"I certainly was thankful you didn't put it up to me."

"Well, that's all right then. We're both happy," said Paige, "and now suppose you tell me about the little sick girl. Was she really dying, or did the mother only think so?"

"Yes, her mother thought so, but the child was frightened too. She had heard so much about dying, and in Sunday school we talked about getting ready to die. She had been too shy to ask questions."

"I'd like to have been there to hear how you quieted a fear like that," said Paige gravely. "I'm afraid I wouldn't know how. I've faced death myself a good many times, and it took a lot of courage."

"It isn't courage one needs," said the girl earnestly, "it's belief in the saving power of the Lord Jesus Christ. It's sin that makes people afraid of death, but Jesus took the sin, and paid the death penalty with His blood, and if we believe that and accept it for ourselves, we have nothing to fear. You believe that, don't you?"

"Yes, in a way I do," he answered, "but I've never really thought much about it."

The waiter appeared just then and they drifted into lighter talk, but somehow the subject lingered in Paige's mind. He decided, however, that this was no background for a serious talk. He would think it over and try to find out just where he stood before he brought the subject up again, but sometime he meant to find out just what she meant by this joyous faith that seemed to be a part of her very life.

They finished their dinner planning for the morrow.

"I'm going up there after Mr. Shambley at half past eight. Is there any message you want me to take?"

"Why, no," said June, "because I'm going up there myself. I told the nurse I'd be there early, so she could get some sleep."

"Very well, then I will take you, if you must go. And I'm

going to bring him back at noon, so I can take you home again if you are staying so long."

"Well that's very kind, and I'll be glad to go with you if you'll promise not to delay on my account. You know I can easily walk home in the daytime if for any reason I have to be delayed. And now, don't you think we should go home? Unless your 'other plans' that you spoke of to Miss Chalmers will still hinder us."

They went out laughing and got into the car, thankful that no stragglers from the Chalmers party had come out to challenge them again.

6

WHEN Paige reached home his mother looked a bit anxious as he came in from parking the car.

"Where in the world have you been all this time, son? Did you go with that Chalmers girl after all? She made a terrible fuss about not being able to find you here. She said her father had sent a very important message."

Paige grinned.

"Don't believe everything that girl tells you," he said. "Her father didn't send any message. She just wanted me to help out in some noisy dinner party she was having at the hotel."

The mother watched him with startled eyes.

"Did she find you? Did you go with her?"

"Yes, she found me. That is, she happened to walk into the hotel where June Culbertson and I were getting a bite of dinner on the way home."

The mother's face relaxed.

"Oh, I'm so glad. She certainly made a great fuss at not getting you."

"Well, don't let her worry you. She's a spoiled beauty who has been used to having her own way every minute of the day. She'll get tired of chasing me after a while."

"But—won't it—maybe get to her father's ears, and make trouble with your job?"

Paige's answer was a laughing shrug.

"There are other jobs," he said.

"Well, I'm glad you feel that way."

A little later when the family had all gone upstairs Paige went to the telephone and called up a friend from his bank.

"Tom, are you going to be in the bank by eight o'clock?" he asked.

"Yes, sure. That's my time for arriving. In fact, I usually get there at least ten minutes ahead of that."

"Okay," said Paige. "I want to run in and get a check cashed before I go to the office. I wanted to make sure you were open and I wanted to say hello to you. I saw your cousin Harold overseas and he sent you all kinds of messages. All right, I'll be there."

Then he went upstairs to a well-earned rest, but his head was so full of so many different things that had happened that evening that he did not find it easy to get to sleep.

Maybe his mother was right about Reva. Maybe it might affect his fine job if he didn't try to be friendly with her. Of course he wouldn't like to lose his wonderful job. Just when he was getting to a place where he would be needing money. And besides, how could he help Mr. Shambley without money? There was that side of the question he ought to consider, wasn't there?

Something out of his early training tried to whisper a little line to his conscience about the consequences of doing evil that good might come. But he hadn't reached that point of discernment where he fully realized that there might be evil in the very job he had been so pleased to get.

But a qualm passed through his consciousness about that business. He couldn't think of himself going to Mr. Chalmers and arguing with him about the way he was treating Mr. Shambley. And of course there might be other cases like his. He couldn't go to his boss and tell him how to run his business. This was the only case of this sort about which he knew definitely. The remedy in this case was for him to use some of his own money and help out this man.

After that there might be more light on this matter. That girl June seemed to be a mighty clear thinker. He might get to a place where he could talk it over with her sometime, if he got to know her better. He wasn't altogether sure yet about himself. She had asked some pretty stiff questions. At least they were not exactly in question form, but they were put in such a way that they pierced his soul like questions. That last one he must take out and think about when he got time. Just how was it put? "It is sin that makes people afraid of death. Jesus took our sin and paid the death penalty with His blood, and if we believe that, and accept it for ourselves we have nothing to fear." That was the way she had put it. Somehow her words seemed to be written deep in his heart, and he found almost an impatience at them. He had just come home from the war, from things serious, and he did not want to be made to consider a foreground of death constantly. Of course he didn't mean exactly that, but his business now was to be successful in some kind of business, and to stick at it until he was sure of himself. He was a Christian, of course. What more did he need? He had no desire to go into the world, a world such as Reva represented, but if being good friends with her meant getting on in life, why shouldn't he be a little friendly when he could? Well, he would look that matter over too, and see what he could do about them all.

As he looked back over war with all its horror and death he didn't know but life at home was going to be even more complicated than it was over there. Only in war one had to go where one was sent and do what one was told, and over here one had the right to choose. But one was not always sure whether one was choosing rightly. And of course it did depend a lot on what one *wished* as a goal. If your object was just wordly success, one might ride roughshod over many of the forbidden ways, and gain what you were after. Of course, being the son of such circumspect parents, he might not do that, but was he sure that he wanted to almost err on the other side of the subject? It wasn't his business, was it, if Mr. Chalmers conducted his business in an almost shady manner? Perhaps he didn't. He wasn't sure, of course. But suppose he did. That was no concern of his, was it? He was only working for him, doing his part of the work conscientiously. Well, anyway, there could probably be some fault found with any job anywhere, if you just happened to come across it.

But anyway, whatever came, there was tomorrow morning, and he must hurry to the bank and get that money, stopping at June's house to pick her up, and then away to the Shambley house.

From there his mind went carefully through the regime he had planned for giving Mr. Shambley the money, and advising him about the papers to be signed, and the way to conduct himself.

He found that all through this there was June in a little blue dress—he hoped she would wear it again, or one a good deal like it. He could remember how blue her eyes were and how they matched the dress, and June would be there, and perhaps go back with him at noon. If not, he would certainly be driving out that way that evening to see how his invalid had made out after the strenuous day.

But he must not let himself venture on any more serious topics until he had thought his way all out and knew just what to expect of himself. June was too keen-minded a person to be deceived by his own uncertainties. And yet he did not want to pass in her eyes as an indifferent Christian.

So he dropped to sleep and passed again before a tribunal of angels looking down upon his thoughts, and awoke some time in the night to find himself dissatisfied with his own conclusions. He had to spend time when he ought to have been sleeping, working back again through his own sophistries to his own comfortable conclusions.

shrill sound of the man's shrieks. He fired, and one of the Manglers squealed angrily, but it wasn't enough. After an instant, though, the man's cries ceased.

At least the damn things were quick.

Crying aloud himself now, Rafe started blasting the beasts at random.

"Come on, you misbegotten monsters! You want me? *Catch me!*"

He turned and ran as fast as he could. Behind him, he heard the gleeful growls and clacking as the creatures gave chase. They were faster than he thought. Desperately, Rafe hoped he hadn't miscalculated the distance.

Cale thought his lungs would burst, but he kept going. The gate, doubtless protected by a Tyrusian force field, was closer now. He could see the girl's face more clearly, and as their gazes met she smiled, tremulously.

Yosh! he thought, *she's beautiful!* He tried to summon a reassuring smile for her, but all his energy seemed to be concentrated on simply reaching her.

Pain exploded in his shoulder. He could smell his flesh burning from the blast even as he cried aloud and fell forward. He hit the earth hard, too racked with agony to even try to break his fall. He heard the girl gasp, cry, "No!"

He pressed his lips together until they hurt. Fighting against the blackness that threatened, he clutched his shoulder with his good hand and crawled forward. He could reach it. He was almost there.

"Hurry," urged the girl, pacing frantically on her side of the field. "You can make it! I'd turn this stupid thing off, but I don't know how—"

He pulled himself up to the force field, gasping. Slowly, Cale lifted the hand with the Exotar. He closed his eyes to aid his concentration. At first, it didn't respond; the pain was too much of a distraction. Angrily, Cale reached deeper, tried to banish the red-hot thoughts of pain that threatened to overwhelm him.

The sweet sound of the Exotar hummed softly. He reached, touched the field with it. Beneath his shaking fingers, the area that he touched began to become visible. Slowly, he raised his hand, stumbling to his feet. He bit back a cry. *Yosh*, but it hurt. . . !

He forced himself to keep going. Thank goodness— thank Rafe—he had the Exotar. And to think he had almost strode off without it, like a reckless fool! Rafe, though, had been smarter. . . . He desperately hoped his friend was all right. It would take more than a pack of Manglers to bring down Rafe, Cale thought to himself with a ghost of a smile.

At last, he was able to cut his way through. The girl on the other side of the fence now leaped into action, reaching forward for him.

"You did it! Come on, I've got to get you out of here!"

She pulled him to her, flung his arm about her shoulder. "Lean on me. That's it." He did, heavily, feeling the slim strength of her body. No soft, pliable Earthling, she. There was strength in her, and courage as well. He blinked hard to stay awake, and stumbled where she led.

He wasn't sure why he trusted her. He just did.

The fuel storage tank was about twelve feet high. Rafe scrambled up the ladder and jumped onto the top. Below him, the Manglers, thwarted, milled angrily. Their howls shattered the air. Catching his breath, Rafe glanced over at the gate where he'd sent Cale.

There was a vehicle of some sort a few yards from the gate, and as he watched, it took off into the night. Cale was nowhere to be seen. Earthlings, it would seem, were gentler to the Cale of Tyrus than his own kin.

The Manglers gibbered and howled below. He peered down at them and grinned ferally.

"Come on, then!" he taunted. "Come get me! I haven't got all night!"

The lead Mangler, a hideous thing much bigger than its fellows, stared up balefully at Rafe. Then, chittering, it lifted a claw and pointed upward to where the commander was perched. Slowly, scrabbling for each toehold, the Manglers began to climb.

Rafe stepped back, until he was in the center of the tank's roof. "That's it, you mongrels. Come on, live up to your names!" he cried. They responded by snarling fiercely and increasing their efforts. Finally, they had clambered atop the tank. They formed a semicircle, spittle dripping from their jaws in anticipation, ready to close in on Rafe and rip him to shreds.

"Thanks for coming," said Rafe mockingly. He went from stillness to movement in a heartbeat, bolting for the far edge. He leaped upward, turned a double somersault, and landed perfectly on the earth, weapon in hand. He fired at point-blank range. Not at the Manglers—at the fuel tank.

With a huge boom the tank exploded. Fire licked upward like a Mangler itself, greedily devouring the shrieking creatures as they writhed in agony. Rafe flung up his arm to shield his face from the scorching heat and flying fragments, then turned and ran into the night.

He felt certain that Cale was safe. But where in this world *was* he?

Rita's foot hurt from pushing the pedal down as hard as she could. A thousand questions tumbled through her mind, but she resolutely pushed them aside. She had to put some distance between them and whoever it was trying to hurt whoever it was in the seat beside her.

He groaned softly and eased up, clutching his injured shoulder. Rita was no doctor, but she knew a bad injury when she saw one. She hoped he wouldn't faint from loss of blood or something. Wordlessly, she handed him her canteen. He stared at it, then up at her.

What kind of city boy was he? Didn't he even see movies where those cowboys drank from canteens? She spared a glance from the road and looked at him briefly.

"Unscrew the cap. There's water in there."

"Ah," he said, and obeyed. He drank thirstily, and some water trickled down his face. Carefully, like a child, he screwed the cap back on and made certain it was secure. She felt his eyes on her.

"Are you an Earthling?" he asked.

Rita snorted, laughing. *"Earthling?* Yeah, I guess you could put it that way."

And suddenly her gut twisted at the significance of the words. Despite the risk, she turned to stare at him. Her mouth was dry as the desert around them as she squeaked breathlessly, "Then what the hell does that make *you*?"

He didn't answer. "Watch out!" he cried.

Startled, Rita jerked her gaze back from the young man beside her to the road ahead. From an arroyo beneath the bend in the road, she saw a helicopter rising. She heard the angry *chop-chop* of its blades just before the bullets started flying.

The windshield shattered. Rita screamed, and instinctively flung up her arms to shield her face. She heard the man beside her crying something, then she was seized in a strong grip. She went flying.

It seemed like forever before they hit, the stranger taking the impact of the fall and cushioning her with his body. She opened her eyes, only to close them again almost immediately.

The Jeep had veered over the guardrail, and in its tumble to the earth had been propelled up and into the helicopter that had been firing at them. The two machines collided and the resulting explosion nearly seared Rita's eyes. Heat rolled over them in waves.

Konrad lowered his binoculars. A shame about losing such an excellent chopper pilot, but it couldn't be helped. And the end goal had been accomplished.

"The Cale is dead," said Konrad soberly. He turned, a half smile on his lips, and bowed slightly as he faced the Dragit.

"Long live the Cale."

The Dragit grinned.

* * *

Rita's base camp wasn't that far away by Jeep, but on foot, with an admittedly gorgeous but heavy alien slumped over on her, it seemed like the trek took forever. When she finally stumbled into the cave's welcoming blackness, she felt as if she'd just finished the Boston Marathon.

Rita was meticulous about the layout of her camp, and was never more grateful for it than now, when she was able to put the man—alien—whatever—gently down on the cool earth and find the emergency matches within seconds. Everything she'd had in the Jeep, of course, was gone. Quickly, working by touch, she found and lit a lantern.

The light warmed the cave, and she felt a little better. She located another full canteen. With her Swiss Army knife, she cut away the strange maroon-and-black material that covered him to get a better look at the wound. God, she hoped it wasn't too b—

Rita blinked.

She'd seen him get hit, and while she didn't know enough to put a name to the weapon, she figured out that getting shot by it was pretty bad business. And yet there was not the blackened hole she'd expected to see, nor blood—only pale flesh, with just the barest hint of a pink, raised scar.

She poured some water on her bandanna and bent

to bathe his face. For an instant, she paused, searching those features as if they could reveal something to her.

Now that she knew what he was, she could see it. The temples were recessed slightly, and extended further up the hairline than in—in humans. The eyes, closed now, were slightly slanted. Beautiful, yes. Strong, yes. He'd displayed courage and, when they were about to become barbecue à la helicopter, a startling presence of mind.

But who was he? Why was he here? Why were those people trying to kill him?

She swallowed hard, and brought the cool bandanna over his face, gently stroking away sweat and dirt. He moved beneath her ministrations, shuddered—and opened his eyes.

They were an alarmingly unsettling shade of purple-blue. Confused by the sudden rush of emotions, Rita spoke bluntly. "Your shoulder is almost healed. Can you explain that?"

He blinked. God, his eyes were beautiful—strange, but beautiful. His high forehead creased in a frown and his expression grew contemplative. Suddenly his eyes flew wide and he bolted upright, crying aloud the single word, "Rafe!"

A name. He stumbled to his feet and raced to the cave entrance, only to slow and slump in defeat as he realized how far away they were from the base.

Tossing down the bandanna, Rita rose to step beside him. For a moment she was quiet, respecting his sorrow. Then she asked softly, "Who is Rafe?"

He smiled a little. "Hard to say. My teacher, my protector, the thorn in my side . . . Friend, I guess, is the best word. I'm—I'm alone here now."

She followed his gaze to the cold stars winking above them. "I know how that feels," she said softly, thinking briefly, painfully, of Eric.

He turned to her. She felt his eyes roving her features, felt the blood rise in her cheeks in response. She was glad of the soft lighting that wouldn't reveal the degree of her embarrassment and shyness.

"I owe you my life," he said sincerely. "What can I do to thank you?"

Rita thought of all the questions, and picked the most pressing one. Her lips curved into a smile as she replied, "Well, you could start by telling me your name."

He put his hand to his heart and bowed a little. "I'm Cale."

"I'm Rita," she replied, and extended her hand. He stared at it, then at her face, an eyebrow raised in question. She saw again his reaction to the canteen and said, "You put your hand in mine."

He did so. Her breath caught for an instant. Cale's hand was warm and strong, yet the grip was tentative.

He doesn't want to hurt me, she thought suddenly, and the comprehension brought a new flood of feeling in its wake. She curled her fingers around his and shook the hand. He caught on at once.

"It's a little custom we have here on Earth," she joked, to lighten the mood.

His face lit up. "Ah!" he exclaimed, pleasure flooding him. "Already, I'm learning!"

Her hand suddenly went cold in his. She licked her lips. "You—you really *are* from out there, aren't you?"

Cale smiled and looked a little sheepish and a little proud at the same time.

"Yes," he relied. "I am." He tried her name, almost tasting the syllables on his tongue. "Ri-ta."

She couldn't breathe. Excitement, fear, and—most of all—wonder rushed over her in waves. Cale saw her face change and lifted the hand that was not holding hers to her elbow, steadying her as her knees went weak.

"Oh," she managed. "Oh, Cale. I've got several thousand questions I'd like to ask you!"

The airmen all stood at attention, saluting their new ruler. Konrad thought the Dragit had changed, ever so slightly, since the death of Cale had been confirmed. He stood just a little straighter, carried himself with more dignity. Though he had not yet been officially coronated, it was as though he already felt the weight—the pleasant and highly desirable weight—of the crown.

Konrad gave the Dragit an Earth salute. Smiling a little, the Dragit winked and returned it with a nod. "You've done well, Colonel Konrad," said the Dragit.

"Thank you."

"You will be joined by many in the years ahead. You will all have much to prepare for."

"I eagerly await the day of your return!"

Konrad watched, holding the salute, as the Dragit ascended the light ladder into the shuttle. The mock *Enterprise* ascended and then sped to join the mother ship awaiting it.

Conquest. It would be sweet.

Over the last few hours, Rita had learned a great deal about this mysterious Cale, not the least of which was that he seemed to have a bottomless pit for a stomach.

He had devoured with good appetite and great enjoyment everything she'd prepared for him, from the macaroni and cheese to potatoes baked in the fire to hot dogs on a stick. It had been amusing and rewarding to watch the play of expressions cross his face as he experienced each different taste.

But now, finally, the food had been eaten, dishes cleaned, and they sat munching on candy bars, talking of other worlds and scientific developments that left Rita stunned.

"Now, wait a minute," she said, interrupting Cale as he tried to explain how the Tyrusian ships crossed the vast distances of space. "That can't be! Einstein says you can't *go* faster than light!"

"Who is Einstein?" asked Cale innocently, licking melted chocolate off long fingers.

Rita waved a hand. "Skip that. Somehow, you got here. What were you planning to do?"

Cale finished the candy bar, chewed, swallowed. "Make friends?"

Rita burst out laughing, looking first at him, then at the wrapper of the candy bar he'd devoured with such enjoyment.

"What's funny?"

"I'm really glad you don't look like E.T.," she chuckled. His look of utter bewilderment made her change the subject. "So—seriously—are you a scientist back home. On Tyrus?"

He hesitated for a moment, his wonderful eyes flickering away and then back.

"I'm . . . a student," he said at last.

"Well, one of the things you must have studied really hard is our language. You speak awfully good English."

"So do you," he replied sincerely, not seeming to see the humor in his comment.

Rita had opened her mouth to say something teasing when a dreadful howl shattered the night. Horrified, she whirled toward the entrance of the cave and her throat closed up with terror.

One of the dreadful things that had chased Cale earlier had found its way to the cave. *The food—I bet it smelled the food!* shrieked Rita silently, guiltily.

"Mangler," breathed Cale.

"Great name," Rita managed. Mentally, she went through the contents of the cave. No weapons—at least, nothing to stand against this thing.

Fire. Maybe it would flee from the fire.

She didn't have the chance to find out. Cale had risen with astonishing speed, grabbed the strange glove with which he'd cut his way through the invisible gate earlier, and met the monster halfway. Its shriek of rage shivered along Rita's spine. Now she realized that the thing was severely wounded. It was badly burned, and part of its face was nothing but black tissue. Would its wounds make it weaker, or only more dangerous?

She pressed up against the coolness of the cave wall and got to her knees, groping for a rock. Her hand closed on one and she got to her feet, seeking an opening.

Cale seemed to know how to fight the things. His handsome face was contorted with strain and Rita stifled a cry as suddenly the creature lurched and both Cale and the monster rolled through the fire. Embers flew wildly. The thing lunged at him, and Rita cringed inwardly as saliva dripped from the creature's sharp teeth onto Cale's face.

Cale. . . !

This was her chance. She surged forward and with a grunt of effort brought the rock down as hard as she could on the creature's head. It ought to have crunched the thing's skull, but to Rita's horror it seemed to have little effect. The thing snarled and batted her away with one great paw. Rita fell hard, the breath knocked out of her.

Though it hadn't hurt the monster, her courage had given Cale an opportunity. Growling like one of the monsters himself, Cale thrust upward with his gloved hand. The force of the movement and follow through sent the beast reeling backward, off-balance. With astonishing grace, Cale sprang to his feet and braced himself for the next charge.

And it came. It was as if the struggle had done nothing but energize the beast. But this time, Cale was ready for him. The thing gathered itself and sprang. Cale uttered a wordless cry and thrust forward with his gloved hand, seizing his foe by the throat.

Rita couldn't tear her eyes from his face. He was pale, sweating, his eyes narrowed in awesome concentration. The thing on his arm made a strange sound, and then to Rita's shock, Cale began to *lift the creature off the ground.*

It thrashed wildly now, its twisted but functional limbs flailing, sensing death was near, but to no avail. Then there came an unmistakable cracking sound, and its monstrous form went limp. Cale flung the beast away with a look of disgust. It slammed up against the cave wall, then tumbled to the earth like so much limp cloth.

For a long moment, he stared at it, gasping for breath. Then he dragged a hand across his forehead, gazed at the spattering of blood and sweat on it.

"That's some glove," Rita gasped.

"Rita," he said softly, turning to her. She stared at him, wide-eyed, trembling with reaction, and she struggled to smile. He broke into movement, hurrying to her and wrapping his arms about her.

Now, she could let go. Now, she let herself slump against his chest, and felt the hot tears spill down her face. Cale's hand came up to stroke her hair, and he murmured soft, soothing words in a language she did not know. Then, in English: "It's all right. It's over. You're safe."

She drew back slightly, gazing up at him. His face was all concern now.

"You—it—it could have killed you! I was so afraid for you!"

Something passed over his face, something bright and wonderful and amazed. Though he was from another world, she could read his expression clearly: he had assumed she was afraid for herself. It had never entered his mind that she would fear for him.

Gently, he reached up and brushed a tear from her face. Her heart had begun to slow, but now it sped up again. Their eyes locked, then he lowered his head and brought his lips tenderly to hers.

She melted into him, knowing only the warm strength of the circle of his arms, the infinite gentleness of the kiss. She had never before felt so complete as she did now, here, in the arms of this being from a far-distant planet.

The strains of "Magic Man" drifted into her thoughts. This was magic. *This* was her magic man, not Eric, but Cale—

He pulled back, and she let him, though she didn't want to. His color had risen and his eyes sparkled. Then they crinkled at the corners with an impish mischief as he said, a bit breathlessly, "Just a little custom we have on Tyrus."

She smiled with him. "I think I could learn to like Tyrusian customs," she murmured.

"Cale! You're alive!"

Guiltily, as if she'd been caught doing something wrong, Rita moved away from Cale even as he let out a loud whoop of joy and ran to the man standing in the entrance to the cave.

"Rafe!" he cried delightedly. The older man opened his arms to receive him and they embraced tightly, thumping one another on the back.

Rafe. Cale—what had he said?—teacher, protector, the thorn in his side . . . his friend. Rafe was all right. Cale wasn't alone anymore.

"My liege," said Rafe warmly as they broke the embrace and regarded one another happily.

My liege?

"We must go," continued Rafe, pleasure fading before urgency. "If I could track you, then they could. If they—"

"Excuse me," said Rita with false sweetness. She turned to Cale, hands on her hips. "*My liege?*"

Cale shrugged helplessly. "I . . . was getting to that."

"Oh, really?"

"Thank you," interrupted Rafe in an attempt to defuse the situation. "Thank you for what you've done for our Cale. I'll wait for you outside, Cale."

For a moment, Rita simmered with anger. Then, looking at Cale's chagrined face, she felt it ebb. He was in danger. He probably didn't want her exposed to the same threat, and thought to shelter her by keeping his true identity a secret. She smiled, and he understood.

Relief spread over his face, then it was shadowed by the sorrow of their parting.

He reached to touch her face, stroked it gently. "You said you understood being alone," he said.

Rita nodded. An ache was growing in the pit of her stomach. She was about to be alone again.

"Yes," she managed.

"I will feel very alone on Earth now . . . without you."

Tears stung her eyes. She didn't want him to leave. Something had happened between them, something sweet and unexpected and, above all, *steady*—like the rocks she loved. Steady and utterly dependable. Unshakable.

Magic man . . .

The words came to her lips and she was as startled as he was. "Then take me with you."

He raised his eyebrows in surprise, searched her face. Then a slow smile curved his lips. It was like the sun coming out from behind the clouds, thought Rita giddily. He seized her hand, squeezed it tightly.

"Come on!"

And as they ran out into the cool desert night to join the waiting Rafe, Rita glanced up at the stars and blessed them for the gift they had given her.

CHAPTER
FOUR

• • •

They say all secrets are eventually revealed. That you can't hide something forever, no matter how hard you try. That, eventually, destiny catches up with you.
   Things have a way of getting found out. . . .

Utah Badlands
The Present

Major Phil Stark gazed down at the swirl of browns and yellows of the Utah desert. Heat waves caused them to shimmer, putting Stark in mind of a waterless oasis. The black shadow of the helicopter seemed like ink sliding over the warmer colors of the earth.

Stark was silent, his sharp brown eyes scanning for the object they'd come to investigate. Beside him, piloting the helicopter with the same expert grace he'd seen her use on other, less tranquil occasions, sat Army Ranger Sergeant Angela Romar. She was a striking-looking woman, with her dark olive complexion and inky hair. The strong bones of her face and dark coloration gave away her Mediterranean—and Gypsy—heritage.

There had recently been quite a few scandals in the military involving sexual harassment. Stark suspected no one had ever tried something like that on Romar. She was certainly attractive enough, but Stark knew that she'd put anyone who attempted an unwanted pass in the hospital pronto.

Not for the first time, he wondered why the DoD had sent him out to this remote locale. Something about a scientific discovery. But that was for the book-worms, wasn't it, not for Military Intelligence.

Something as dark as the chopper shadow caught his eye. The yawning mouth of a cave. This was the place.

Wordlessly he pointed, but Romar had already spotted the cave. She set the helicopter down smoothly, the blades churning up clouds of dust. Stark tried not to cough, but he couldn't help it. He jumped out, followed quickly by Romar. Through the clouds of brown Utah dust, he saw one of the white-coated lab technicians waving to him.

Stark strode up to the man, drawing himself up to his full, rather imposing height.

"This better be good," he rumbled.

The whitecoat was unfazed. "Judge for yourself," he said, gesturing at a pile of white things nestled in the darkness of the cave. Stark removed his sunglasses and passed a hand over his dusty face, aware that the clinging sand lightened his naturally chocolate-colored skin by several shades.

He could see now that the things were bones. He knelt, peering closer. His eyes narrowed. Strange angles, unbelievable teeth, claws . . .

"What the hell is it?" he asked. Romar moved up behind him, gazing over his shoulder.

The whitecoat shook his head, gazing raptly at the bones. "Damned if I know, sir. I've never seen anything like it." He paused, and added somberly, "I'm not sure anyone else on this planet has, either."

Stark shot the whitecoat an unreadable glance. "Looks like it might be some sort of prehistoric species." He heard the soft sound of Romar moving away to inspect another part of the cave.

The whitecoat shook his head again, with more certainty this time.

"No way. I'm betting it's not more than twenty years old, tops."

"Hey, you guys," called Romar. "Come back here and check this out."

She had wandered toward the back of the cave. His eyes now accustomed to the dimness, Stark could see that there were remnants of camping equipment, abandoned here God knew how long ago. Romar pointed toward two tin coffee cups.

"Looks like we're not the first to find this thing," she said. She and Stark exchanged glances.

Stark fished a pencil out of his pocket and lifted one of the cups with it. Romar was a step ahead of him; she already had the sealable plastic evidence bag at the ready. He dropped the cup inside.

"We'll have the FBI check this for prints," Stark told the whitecoat. "If anyone else knows about that—thing—I want to know about *them*."

I'd always been a loner . . . I never seemed to quite fit in.

Mom said that all teenagers feel that way.
Adolescent paranoia, she called it.

But she always seemed worried when I'd bring the subject up. . . .

Glenport, Massachusetts

The day was bright, and David Carter had to slit his eyes against the glare of the sun. As he made his way toward the gym, his movements were quick and lithe. He never seemed to be consciously aware of his deep grace, nor of the longing glances cast in his direction by the pretty cheerleaders rehearsing energetically in the sunshine.

That wasn't where David belonged, and he sensed it. Not for him the football field, with its noisy huddle of testosterone-driven jocks, nor the track, racing around like a hamster on a wheel. He strode past the open field and track, headed for a private workout and a little solitude. He needed to clear his mind.

As he pushed through a press of youths all about his own age, laughing and exchanging crude jokes, David felt a pang of isolation. Why couldn't he laugh with friends like that? Go driving on hot summer nights, with a pretty cheerleader by his side? There were reasons aplenty, but the one that most mattered to David was, in his heart of hearts, he didn't want to.

He went to his locker and changed out of his jeans and T-shirt into a tank top, shorts, and gym shoes. On a day like today, most of the other students at Glenport High School would be outside, if they lingered here at school at all.

David had the gym all to himself. While light still trickled into this long room, it was softer, darker than the bright, unforgiving glare of a sunny afternoon outside.

For a moment, David watched the dust motes swirl in a beam of light from a window. The shaft of sunlight illuminated the gymnastic equipment that sat silently, as if waiting for him. He took a deep breath of the familiar and not altogether unpleasant fragrance of the place, wiped his powdered hands together one final time, and began.

He raced toward the parallel bars and leaped onto them with ease, as if embracing an old friend. Effortlessly he swung himself up, flipped, and grasped the bars again. His powdered hands were sure and strong. Up and over, up and over, leaping to catch the rings above and flip using them as well. On to the horse now, coming down into easy splits, whipping his lean and powerful body upward to walk on his hands before moving back once again to the comforting stability of the parallel bars.

Over, around, losing himself in the heady ritual of movement, of at last letting his slim, strong body do what it wanted to do without fear of repercussion. Much was in turmoil in his life; he suspected it was this way with all kids his age. His physical grace let him escape.

Sweat popped out on his brow, trickled under his arms. Faster, faster, tighter flip, that's it, now another handstand, then *flip*, hands up in the air, feet on the floor, heart pounding. Freedom.

There came the sound of slow applause from a single pair of hands.

"Seven-point-three," droned a voice, "seven-point-five, seven-point-six . . . Whoops, a two-point-four from the Russian judge that could seriously hurt David Carter's chances for the gold. . . ."

Startled, David whipped around. His pupil enlarged instinctively, contracted as he saw it was only his friend Jim Bailey.

Walking toward David, Jim winced. "Jeez, man, *please* don't do that eye thing. You know I hate that."

"Sorry," replied David. "You startled me. I didn't think."

"You done here?"

David glanced back at the gymnastic equipment. He wanted to do some more. The routine had only taken the merest edge off his tension, but Jim was waiting. "Yeah," he told his best friend, "I'm done."

They fell into easy step with one another, heading back down to the lockers.

"You just keep getting better and better on those things," said Jim, jerking his head back toward the gymnastic equipment. He patted his own, somewhat softer belly. "All I get when I try that parallel bar is indigestion."

"Thanks," replied David. He shrugged. "I like it."

"You really should go out for the team."

"I've told you, my mom won't let me." David could hear the bitterness seeping into his words as he spoke. "She's so paranoid about anything happening to me. It's like I'm made of glass or something. You know she won't even let me take Driver's Ed." This last was the hardest.

Jim reached into his pocket, pulled out a set of keys, and twirled them around his finger.

"Got just the cure for that . . ."

David grinned.

He showered and changed quickly, then they were racing toward the parking lot and Jim's bike. Jim was blessed among students in that he had a souped-up Harley clone, and suddenly the bright, sunny day seemed to include even David in its friendly embrace. For appearances, Jim drove the motorcycle out of town, but once the apartment buildings and houses gave way to trees and meadows, they switched places.

David eagerly hit the pedal, gripped the handlebars, and took off. Jim, clinging to David for dear life, admirably held his tongue. They'd done this before. Inevitably, David would start off like a house on fire, then calm down and simply enjoy the power at his command. This time, though, David didn't let up.

Finally, Jim said, "I said you could drive, not fly."

David ignored him. His eyes were fastened on the road, watching the tires devour it as they went. The white picket fences they passed seemed to streak by. The odometer kept on climbing.

Jim, looking a little anxious now, tried again. "How's about bringing it down to Mach One, okay? Personal favor."

No sooner had the words left his lips then they heard the unmistakable wail of a police siren. Jim glanced behind them, slumped against Dave and groaned. "Oh, man . . . the sheriff!"

David merely grinned wickedly, and gripped the handlebars even harder. Jim came out of his cocoon of self-pity to stare in disbelief.

"What're you *doing?* Are you nuts?"

"Let him earn it," David replied, the grin widening.

"David . . . !"

David shot him a look over his shoulder, his pupil dilating, then returned his attention to the road.

Jim leaned his head against David's back in surrender. "And here I was hoping to get into an Ivy League school. Do you think Princeton takes ex-cons?"

Now the sheriff's light was flashing. The red glow played over their faces—David's laughing, Jim 's pale and distressed.

The sheriff's car gained despite David's best efforts, and finally pulled in front of them. David slammed on the brakes. They screeched in protest and the cycle swerved hard before coming to a stop.

"You know, helmets aren't just the law—they're a good idea," gasped Jim.

There was the sound of a door opening and then closing. Footsteps approached the car. David, all traces of mirth gone from his face, gripped the handlebars and stared straight ahead.

A shadow fell over them. Behind David, Jim stared up and gave a feeble, sickly smile. David still didn't look up.

"What're you doing driving a motorcycle?" snapped the sheriff. "Driving without a license is a very serious offense. You could get in a hell of a lot of trouble for this."

Now David looked up at the man who had allegedly been such a good friend of his father's. He took in the short, graying hair, the lines of worry, the intense, strange, slanted eyes so like his own. And the odd, romantic name skittered through his mind: *Rafe.*

"Sorry, Sheriff," he said, his voice low and angry. He wasn't sorry, and Rafe knew it.

"I expected better from you than this kind of dumb teenage stunt, boy," Rafe growled.

David shot him a defiant look but said nothing. The silence lay between them.

Finally, the sheriff said, "You should both be in school." *Never mind that the last bell rang a half hour ago,* thought David, hot with anger. *Rafe couldn't be bothered to check things like that—easier to assume I'm guilty of cutting classes along with driving without a license.*

"Get going." Rafe glanced over at Jim, who quailed visibly. Rafe stabbed a finger at him. "*You* drive."

Then he was gone, striding back to his car and glancing back to make sure the boys traded places. They did. Still flushed with anger, David sat down on the seat behind Jim.

"What is it with you and the sheriff?" asked Jim,

revving up the cycle. "It was me, I'd be in solitary confinement!"

David shrugged, feigning nonchalance. "He was a friend of my father's. That's all I know."

No gymnastics team. No motorcycles or Driver's Ed. "He's a friend of your father's, David."

My life is one big goddamn question mark.

Rita fingered the silver chain around her neck as she spoke, her voice weary. "David's just a boy, Rafe. He's going to do things like that, no matter what you and I want." *What wouldn't I give to have a parent's ordinary worries. Dates, grades, what college will he get into, will he get a job. . . .*

Rafe paced in her living room. His body was tense as a cat ready to spring, she thought. He turned to her, his eyes blazing.

"He must be more than that! He must be Cale!"

The same argument, round—what? Hundred and forty? Around and around they had gone over the years, from the time David had started taking swimming lessons, to Rita's decision to enroll him in a public school. Always, this dire edict: *He must be Cale!*

Rita hadn't wanted to be a mother of kings. She just wanted to marry the man she loved and raise his child to be happy and healthy. For a time, it seemed as though she might get her wish. . . .

She leaned forward and picked up the pretty crystalline orb from where it sat on a pewter stand on the coffee table. Gently, she held it in one hand, ran the index finger of the other over its smoothness.

"You talk like his father were dead," she said softly.

That halted Rafe's pacing. At once, he replied, "I have no information to confirm that."

Rita placed the orb down and looked him full in the eye. "But you fear the worst, don't you?"

Rafe shook his graying head. "No." He paused, then replied, his voice full of emotion: "In my heart, he's alive."

They were linked, he and she; linked by their love for a man who had left this world a long time ago. Linked by hope, and fear, and by love for a son who wore that man's face.

Without another word, Rafe turned and left.

Rita watched him go, hearing the door close behind him. She closed her eyes and sighed. She was fond of Rafe, and his devotion to David was beyond question. But still, every time he came to talk with her, she felt worse, not better.

Like an addict reaching for a drug, Rita leaned forward and again picked up the crystalline orb. She could see her reflection in it, distorted, unhappy.

She closed her eyes and thought of the first time she had seen it . . . the last time she had seen Cale. . . .

. . . They had just bought the house. It was new, then, and the simple pleasure of sitting out on the porch swing on a summer evening, just the three of them, had lost none of its sweetness. Cale cradled the baby in his arms, the perfect, devoted father that she had known he would be from the moment she first told him she was pregnant.

He was clad now in human clothes, not a jumpsuit, and he had cut his hair in a style that mostly hid the deep recesses of his temples. He looked completely human. The swing creaked, a comforting, homey sound. David gurgled wordlessly, his little mouth trying out noises. Absently, Rita fondled the beautiful amulet Cale had given her, her fingers tracing the intricate design.

Cale's eyes, as ever, were on the stars. He never seemed to harbor a desire to return to Tyrus, but she knew that part of him would always belong there. She smiled, a little sadly.

"Can you see it from here?" she asked.

He nodded, lifting a hand to point. "I think that's it. The star that Tyrus circles."

They were silent a moment, rocking. David cooed and chewed on his fist. Then, dreading the answer, Rita asked the question that had been burning in her mind since she first met him.

"Do you miss your world, Cale?" She had to know.

He looked over at her, love shining in his eyes, and her breath caught, as it always did when he gazed at her like that. Then he glanced down at their son, touched one soft cheek gently. "Less and less every day."

Her throat closed up, and she blinked back quick tears. She leaned in, nestling her head against the warm strength of his shoulder. A comfortable silence fell between them, punctuated by the creaking of the swing and the sound of crickets. In the distance, fireflies blinked, adding a soft touch of magic to the moment.

Then another sound, of twigs cracking beneath approaching feet. Rafe emerged from the shadows.

"I'm sorry to interrupt, Your Majesty, but—"

Cale's face, a moment ago soft and relaxed, hardened slightly. He sat up a little straighter in the porch swing.

"The rebellion?" he asked, not really needing an answer.

Rafe nodded solemnly. "It has come."

Rita shivered in the warm night air. One hand went to clasp the amulet, as if gripping it could keep Cale here, here with her and the baby.

"Oh, my God," she whispered.

The preparations for his departure were a blur. Dimly, she remembered Rafe and Cale deep in conference in the kitchen while, moving like an automaton, she made coffee for the long night ahead. David slept in his father's arms, unaware of the tumult that had suddenly erupted in his young life. They drove to the arranged meeting place in numb silence, and it was only when they stood on the precipice overlooking the crashing gray Atlantic that Rita began to feel the first prickings of the pain that would be her constant companion for the next sixteen years.

Rafe stood at attention, little David clutched awkwardly in his arms. Cale was fingering a beautiful orb of crystal, not yet looking at Rita.

"You can't go back," she repeated for the hundredth time. "They'll kill you!"

"We've gone through this before," he chided gently. "You know I must. I'm their ruler. If the invasion of Earth is to be stopped, I must lead those who would stop it."

Rita had promised herself she wouldn't cry. Tears slipped down her face, proving her a liar.

"Come back to me," she whispered.

"I swear it," he said. Then she was in his arms. He was warm, strong, but not gentle, not this time as he had been with their first sweet kiss in the cave so long ago. He held her as if he could pull her into him, take her with him forever, and his lips were almost bruising as he pressed them to hers. She tangled her fingers in his black hair, felt wetness on her face, and knew that she was not the only one weeping at this bitter parting.

At last, he drew back. He pressed the orb into her hands, folding her strong fingers over it.

"Keep this. Use it only when you have to. You will know when the time comes." Nothing more. No words of love, or loss, and for that she was grateful. Had he said them, she wasn't sure if she could have let him go.

Now the Cale of Tyrus turned toward the heir, gathering the baby from an uncomfortable-looking Rafe.

"Good-bye, my son," he said to the infant. David smiled, tried to grab his father's face with his pudgy hand. "I wish so much that I could be here to watch you grow strong. Someday, you will understand why I had to go. I leave you my love until we meet again."

He paused, gazed intently into the baby's eyes. "Remember me!"

As Rita watched, Cale's iris widened and the pupil enlarged in what she had learned was a ritual greeting—or farewell. Her heart hurt as she watched David, still an infant, return the gesture as naturally and instinctively as he drew breath. Cale's child indeed.

Cale handed David back to Rita. He made as if to touch her one last time, then clenched his fist and turned away, facing out to the sea.

Slowly, a triangular ship rose up from its hiding place below the cliff. A ramp of light was extended. Rita had seen this before, had watched Cale first step down to Earth from one. She could barely make out two figures awaiting their Cale on board the ship. Their armor didn't match, and while she didn't know very much about Tyrusian weaponry, she suspected theirs was pretty beat up as well.

Rafe extended a hand, indicating that his Cale should precede him. Cale stepped onto the first rung, then turned to face Rafe. Rita was close enough to hear what transpired.

"You're not coming with me, Rafe," said Cale gently.

Rafe's eyes widened in astonishment, and a flicker of pain crossed his face. "Your Majesty? Have I offended—"

74

"No, no, old friend, far from it. I want you to stay here with my wife and child. Keep them safe for me until I return."

"I'm a soldier, not a nursemaid!"

"Rafe, listen to me. You are the only one I can trust for this. Serve them, as you served me; protect them, as you protected me. The child may be Tyrus's future; Rita is my life." He put a hand on Rafe's shoulder. *"And Rafe—teach him as you taught me."*

Rafe's shoulders sagged slightly. He bowed and stepped back. "As my ruler commands."

And then Cale was gone, lifted away in a strange, alien ship from her and David for who knew how long, possibly forever. She watched it go, not daring to blink, not daring to miss a second of watching his ship, until tears stung her eyes and . . .

"Mom?" Cale peered down at her—no, not Cale, David. She blinked, realizing her face was wet, and took a deep breath.

"I'm all right," she lied. She put the orb down. David watched her, his eyes serious.

"Mom . . . you've got to let him go. Dad died a long time ago. I hate seeing you like this."

She looked at him, his strong youth's body, the hair the same blue-black shade as Cale's, the purple-blue eyes as intense.

"There's so much of your father in you," she

breathed. It was wonderful, yet painful at the same time.

He sank down in the sofa beside her. "Why won't you tell me what happened to him?"

"I wish I could," said Rita truthfully. "But it's too dangerous for you to know. One day."

David frowned in annoyance. "I'm sixteen, Mom. I'm old enough to handle it. I mean—you've never even shown me pictures of him!"

He shimmered in her vision as the tears came again. "Look in the mirror," she replied softly.

David flung up his hands in disgust and frustration and stalked off to his room, slamming the door. Rita lowered her head into her hands and let the tears come unhindered.

David flung himself onto his bed and punched the pillows. He was sick of this. "It's too dangerous for you," his mom always said. Well, some kids were on their own when they were sixteen, and he knew that life on the street was pretty damn dangerous, too.

He rolled over, his face hot with anger, and grabbed the small hard plastic ball he liked to toss around when he was particularly upset. He flung it at the floor. It bounced up, hit the door, and came back in his direction. Without even thinking about it, he caught it easily in one hand and repeated the process.

Ka-thump pok. *Ka-thump* pok.

David thought about Jim's family. Screamingly ordinary. Jim, his kid sister Laura Anne, his mom, their dog, Scooter.

Ka-thump pok. *Ka-thump* pok.

Jim didn't know how lucky he was. Or maybe he did. David got invited over often enough for dinner to feel at least a peripheral part of that happy clan. No touch football or anything, of course, not for precious, made-out-of-crystal David . . .

Ka-thump POK. A particularly violent toss this time.

He was forced to admit, his mom tried—every summer they went to their little fishing shack out on Maple Island. And Mom was surprisingly good at a lot of nonmom things, like fishing and cleaning the fish and even baiting the hook. But David had dreams, sometimes, dreams of strong arms and a deep voice, dreams of his father.

Ka-thump pok. *Ka-thump* pok.

Suddenly David's face screwed up and he hurled the little ball out the window as hard as he could. Faintly, he heard it strike a tree, bounce off, and roll to a stop somewhere in the grass.

"Why'd you have to die, Dad? *Why?*"

CHAPTER
FIVE

• • •

Like any kid, I guess, I wanted something more than just being a regular teenager. I wanted to be special. Unique. I wanted to do something, make a difference, matter, somehow.

Until the day I got my wish, and the world I knew shattered like broken glass.

"The results are back, Mr. Stark."

Stark thought that the whitecoat seemed much more comfortable here in the lab, in his own natural environment, than he had in the field where they'd first discovered the mysterious skeleton. He glanced quickly at Romar, her black hair covered by a black beret, and caught a quick flash of excitement in her dark eyes.

"The DNA doesn't match anything in the animal kingdom," continued the whitecoat, consulting a clipboard. "The bones aren't carbon-based. They're some kind of silicon analogue, twice as dense. Tendon attachments are longer, too—our friend here is ten times stronger than a gorilla."

All nice, interesting information, but when the scientist paused to push his glasses back up the bridge of his nose, Stark asked bluntly, "What exactly are you saying?"

The whitecoat pursed his lips. "Bottom line: this critter ain't from around here."

Beside Stark, Romar inhaled swiftly. Her eyes widened as she stared at the bones—at the oversized skull, the legs that looked as if they'd been put on backward, the teeth longer than her hand.

"Then . . . where?" she asked.

The whitecoat shrugged. "I really don't like to speculate, but . . . put it this way. This could be a hell of a lot bigger than bugs on Mars."

Romar gazed triumphantly at Stark and poked a finger in his chest. "I *told* you," she gloated.

Stark frowned and gave her a warning glance. "You read too many tabloids, Sergeant."

Her beautiful face creased in a frown. Her body ramrod-straight, she strode to the telephone on the wall, seized the receiver, and thrust it toward Stark.

"I still think you'd better make the call," she said, an icy note of warning in her voice. "*Sir.*"

Stark hesitated. His dark eyes searched hers, saw no softening there. He looked again at the bones on the table, took in the massive skull with its small eye sockets; the teeth, the claws, the limbs that obviously worked, though by all rights they shouldn't.

Not carbon-based, the whitecoat had said. Something silicon, he'd said.

Ten times as strong as a gorilla.

Phil Stark made his decision. Wordlessly, he took the phone from her, his strong brown fingers closing over the white plastic. Romar did not let any expression show on her features as she kept her eyes on him.

Smart woman. He was not in the mood for any more *I told you so's* at the moment.

"Get me the White House."

Field trips generally interested David only inasmuch as they got him out of school. The Boston Museum, though, wasn't too bad as field trips went. It would have been more interesting had he not been here dozens of times before with his mother.

He glanced up disinterestedly at the *T. Rex* skeleton that stood poised, mouth open in a soundless roar above them. Absently, he looked at the gigantic teeth, thought the obligatory *He could swallow me in one bite*, then dismissed the creature. He'd seen *Jurassic Park*; now *there* were some scary dinosaurs.

Tyrannosaurus Rex was the meeting place. The class had broken up into groups after arriving at the Boston Natural History Museum, so as not to overly terrorize the pleasant but somewhat easily intimidated blue-haired ladies who led the tours. David shifted his weight, glanced at his watch, and sighed. At least another fifteen minutes before the last tour group would arrive. But, hey, better killing time here than in Social Studies.

He wandered back to Jim, who had apparently found something of interest. Jim gazed happily at a diorama. David glanced at the title: SPANISH CONQUEST OF NEW WORLD. The display featured several cowering Incas in traditional dress. Conquistadors in their shiny armor went to "greet" them before massacring them.

"I love these things," Jim sighed.

"Didn't think you liked history," said David.

"Oh, I don't," replied Jim heartily. "Ask me how I feel about topless native women." He waggled his eyebrows, and David had to chuckle.

"Barbaric, isn't it?" came a soft, female voice behind David.

Startled, he turned around. His heart sped up.

She was gorgeous.

David guessed she wasn't much older than he was. Tall, slim but perfectly proportioned, she gazed steadily at him from behind dark glasses. Red lips curved in a seductive smile. Long blond hair, so pale it was almost white, tumbled down the back of her chic short jacket. A tight black skirt barely covered long, shapely legs.

Jim could keep his Inca mannequins.

Suddenly recalling her statement, he stammered, "Uh, I guess so." He wondered if she meant the Spaniards or the naked mannequins.

Jim was gazing with open appreciation at David's new comrade. He leaned over and whispered in David's ear, "Not bad, Davie, me lad," he said.

"Jim!" hissed David, feeling the heat rise to his cheeks. Embarrassed, he backed away a little from both his friend and this mysterious, exotic young woman. She continued to smile and follow him.

"There's some cool stuff that way," she said, nodding her head in the direction of another wing. "Want to see?"

David's mouth was dry. Nothing like this had ever happened to him before. Girls generally ignored him, and none of the bright, peppy girls who attended his high school could hold a candle to the sultry allure of this platinum-haired beauty.

"Nah," he lied. "I better stay with the group."

Her smile widened. She took another step toward him, almost pressing against him. He felt the soft brush of her body against his, lightly. "Wouldn't you rather hang with me?"

"I, uh . . ."

The girl reached up a slender hand and removed her sunglasses. "Look at me," she whispered.

David gasped. Her eyes were exotic, slanted, and even as he watched, unable to tear his gaze away, the iris enlarged and the pupil dilated in the same strange gesture he'd made himself so often.

Automatically his own eye dilated in response. She chuckled, deep in her throat. "I knew you were . . . special. Come on . . ."

She turned and walked, hips swaying, toward a deserted side wing. David stared after her. More pressing than the desire to follow a beautiful young woman was the need to follow someone who seemed to know more about him than he himself did.

She rounded a corner. David hesitated, then made his decision.

At first, she was nowhere to be seen. David glanced around, then saw the long fall of pale blond hair. Nervously, he cleared his throat and said, "Excuse me . . ."

The figure turned around. It wore a grin, and the features, though very similar to the girl's, definitely belonged to a young man who had to be her twin brother.

"Gotcha!" snarled the youth.

"Who are you?" demanded David, embarrassment turning to anger. "What do you want?"

Now the girl stepped out of the shadows. The boy turned to her. "He *is* one of us. I don't know how, but he is. Come on. Let's go," he said. He grabbed David's arm, the fingers digging into the flesh.

"Like hell," retorted David. He tried to twist out of the youth's grip, but somehow the boy managed to catch hold of his other arm despite David's struggles. The grip was surprisingly strong. Genuinely alarmed now, David reared back, rammed his elbows into his adversary's chest, and twisted wildly. Grunting in pain and surprise, the boy loosened his grip, and David was free and pelting down the hallway as fast as he could go.

David heard them giving chase, their boots clattering in the stone corridor. Adrenaline surged through him, lending him wings. He ran as he had never run before, nameless dread driving him. David tore around a corner and vaulted over a display case without even pausing to think about it.

It was just like practicing on the gymnastic equipment, and his body rose to the challenge. He skidded and rounded another corner, finding himself in the Hall of Prehistoric Mammals now. David gathered himself and leaped. His hands gripped the tusk of a stuffed Siberian mammoth and he launched himself as if he were leaping off the parallel bars. Tucking and tumbling, he handed solidly on a fake rock ledge. Staring at him was a nuclear family of equally fake Neanderthals. He ran into the "cave" and hid behind Grandma Neanderthal, burrowing in among the "furs" for additional camouflage.

For a moment, there was no sound save David's heavy breathing and the sound of his racing heart. He gulped and forced himself to listen.

Nothing. Then: "Up there!" The youth. David closed his eyes and groaned inwardly. How had this strange boy known? He gathered himself, ready to spring on his attacker when he entered the "cave."

The noise made him cover his ears. Over on his left, the cave suddenly blew away. Good God, what had happened? He stared at the pile of chicken wire and papier-mâché, gaping in shock. Only when he caught a blur of movement out of the corner of his eye did he realize he was exposed. Recovering himself, he leaped off the ledge and took off running again.

This time he didn't hear the heart-stopping sound of them running behind him. For a wild, elated second, David thought he'd managed to shake the pursuit. The triumph that swelled inside him was short-lived. Something slammed into his back, sending pain shuddering up the length of his spine and knocking him to the floor. He hit hard, and gasped like a fish out of water.

Then he began to slide—backward, as if someone had a good grip on his leg and was hauling with all his might. Except no one was there.

"Whoa . . ." gasped David. He tried to slow his progression, but his fingernails could grasp nothing on the smooth stone floor. He began to move faster. Twisting, David rolled over onto one side, glancing frantically back at the two strange young people who had suddenly, for no reason David could fathom, become his nemesis. They stood motionless, their hands clasped, their faces still. Concentrating.

On dragging David.

David shot out a hand and grabbed ahold of the leg of a display case as he hurtled past. The action almost yanked his arm out of its socket, but he forced himself to hang on. He bared his teeth in a feral smile as he realized he wasn't being pulled toward the twins anymore.

Then he felt the invisible grip on his legs increase. David again began to move toward them, though more slowly now as they had to contend with the extra weight of the huge display case.

Who are they? What are they doing? How are they doing this?

But there was no time to ponder such esoteric questions. He had to stop whatever it was they were doing. Desperate measures were in order. David grasped the leg of the case with one hand and reached up, straining, with the other. With a wordless cry, he tipped the case over.

It shattered with an ear-splitting crash. Shards of glass pattered harmlessly over David's body, then lifted up, like leaves on a wind, to move with a dreadful purpose toward David's tormentors. Arrowheads and spearheads, liberated from the case, followed suit.

The boy cried out, flinging up his arm to shield his face. David watched wildly as a large sliver of glass embedded itself in that arm. He didn't want to see what the arrowheads and ax heads would do. He scrambled to his feet, nearly slipping on the pieces of glass, and took off.

Simon squealed in pain and fury. As quickly as it had begun, the rain of glass and weaponry ceased. The deadly shards fell with a bright tinkling sound in midflight. Simon clenched his teeth and worked free the shard of glass that had penetrated his arm. With a grunt, he flung it down and crunched it to splinters with his boot. Something warm dripped into his eye, stinging it, and he realized he had a cut above his eye as well.

The quarry had fled, laughing, no doubt, at Simon's attempts to capture him. Simon made a tight fist in anger, and heard the satisfying sound of another glass display case shattering in response to his impotent rage.

Sonia, bleeding from a cut on her cheek, grabbed him. "That's enough! Simon, please!" she cried, shaking him.

Taut as a bowstring, Simon whipped around, glaring at his twin. He quivered with rage that had no outlet. She had That Look on her face, that expression of worry and fear—fear of Simon.

Deliberately, Simon let the anger go. He took a deep, steadying breath and reassured himself that they wouldn't fail a second time.

They'd find him. They'd find this rogue hybrid and take him to where he belonged, or Simon would not be held responsible for what he did.

Gasping for breath, David pelted out of the museum only to see the big yellow bus pulling away from the curb. The thought that he might be stranded here at the museum, completely at the mercy of the mysterious and frightening pale-headed twins, terrified him.

"Hey!" he yelled, taking off after it. He ran alongside the bus, pounding on the doors. "Hey! Open up!"

Thankfully, the bus halted and the doors opened. David clambered on, aware of the stares he was drawing, and ran a hand through his tangled, sweat-matted hair. In the back, Jim waved frantically. David lurched down the aisle toward his friend as the bus began to move. He collapsed on the seat and plastered himself to the window, both hands on the pane, looking to see if he was being followed.

He was. The two strange kids—the boy and that

stunning-looking girl—had just emerged from the museum. David made eye contact with the youth. He shrank back from the look of naked hatred on the other boy's face. The girl pulled a cell phone from her purse and began dialing. The bus rounded a corner, and David dropped back down into the seat.

"Good God, David, you look like you've run a marathon!" said Jim, concerned. "What happened?"

David shook his head. He had no answer—not for Jim, not for himself.

Stark stood rigidly at attention in front of the general's desk as Konrad pored over the dossier.

"At first I thought it was some kind of hoax," he was saying. "But the lab can't explain it."

Konrad glanced up at him, his oddly shaped eyes narrowing. "Have you told anyone else about this?"

"No sir," replied Stark, bridling a little at the question and all it implied. "I thought the President should be informed immediately."

"He will be," said Konrad. "I promise you. Now"—and he glanced back down at the pile of papers and photos—"your report indicated that there might have been other people in that cave prior to our discovery of it. How many do you estimate?"

"Two or three, we think. Unfortunately, we were only able to get one clear fingerprint."

"Ah." Konrad nodded. "Have you been able to identify it?"

"We should know by this afternoon."

"I see. Do you—" The phone jangled shrilly, cutting Konrad off. He reached and picked it up. "General Konrad here."

"Sir, we have a problem." It was Sonia. "We're at the Boston Museum. We've found a new hybrid. Unauthorized. A male, about sixteen."

Konrad kept his face neutral, though his heart suddenly started to pound. His gaze lingered on the photo of the Mangler's bones. A terrible suspicion was starting to form in his mind.

"Indeed. I want very much to meet him."

David paced like a tiger in a cage, every line in his body radiating tension. His mother watched him silently, her eyes huge but not filled with tears, not now. There was no time for such luxuries as fear and grief anymore.

"It was like something out of a science fiction movie, you know? I mean, they were dragging me back to them with their *minds!* Too weird—"

He broke off from his frantic narrative, plopping down on the sofa and burying his head in his hands. More than anything, Rita wanted to hold him, comfort him, as she had done so often when he scraped a knee or stubbed a toe. But David had been suddenly plunged into manhood today, and she had no real comfort to offer—only her own simple, human strength.

A terrible thought manifested on his frightened face. "You do believe me, Mom, don't you?"

"Of course, I do," said Rita firmly.

"Who were they?" muttered David. "How could they do that?"

"I can answer those questions." Rita and David glanced up to see Rafe standing in the open front door. Rita's hand went to her throat.

No . . . not yet . . . please, God, not yet. He's still just a boy. . . .

David frowned angrily. "What's *he* doing here?" he asked his mother, not bothering to disguise the dislike in his voice.

Rita licked her dry lips. "David," she began, groping for words, "I didn't want it to happen like this—I didn't—"

Rafe interrupted her, his voice brusque. "There are things you must know, David."

Emotions warred on David's face. Totally confused, he glanced back at his mother. Not wanting to, Rita nodded.

"Take him, Rafe."

* * *

Rafe had said nothing during the drive out of town. David didn't want him to, although he was burning with curiosity. He had a distinct feeling he wouldn't like what he would hear. He sat slumped down in the passenger's side of Rafe's patrol car, leaning as far away from the sheriff as he could.

Rafe drove for about twenty minutes, until they were well out of Glenport. Then he parked the car and got out, indicating that David should follow. Defiantly, David slammed the door closed with unnecessary force. Rafe ignored the childish outburst, heading up a gently sloping hill. David followed, striding through the tall grass to keep up with Rafe's long steps.

Finally, he spoke. "Has this got anything to do with my father?" he asked.

Rafe nodded. "A great deal."

He said nothing more, and David could take a hint. He shoved his hands in his jeans pockets and strode alongside Rafe. It had been late afternoon when they left; now, evening was approaching. Twilight muted the bright greens, turned the blue sky lavender. Below them, as the shadows lengthened, David saw lights coming on in Glenport. It looked almost unbearably homey to him, and he felt a sudden ache inside. He wondered, not for the first time, just what the hell they were doing.

At last, Rafe stopped. They were at the very crest of the hill. A few yards distant, the earth gave way to rocks, and David could faintly hear the sound of the ocean below the precipice. Rafe looked about, as if searching for something. Apparently, he found it. David followed the sheriff's gaze and saw an ancient, weathered pine tree.

"See that pinecone?" asked Rafe, pointing.

David squinted. In the soft light of the evening, he could just barely make out a single pinecone dangling forlornly from the topmost branch.

"Yeah."

"Bring it to me."

David glanced over at Rafe, confused. Rafe's visage revealed nothing. David rolled his eyes, shrugged, and started toward the tree. Rafe's hand fell on his shoulders.

"No. From here."

"What?" David stared at him. "How can I—what does a damn pinecone have to do with anything?"

"It's got everything to do with it," Rafe snapped, his eyes blazing.

"But—but I can't—"

Rafe stepped nearer, towering over the youth. David flinched, ever so slightly, at the intensity in the older man's face. Something very big was going down here, whatever it was.

"Reach out with your mind!" hissed Rafe. "You have the power. *Use it!*"

For a second, David was completely baffled. Then he had a sudden, adrenaline-producing mental image of himself being dragged along the stone floor of the museum, dragged without anyone laying a finger on him, and—he didn't want to follow where that thought took him. Instead, he turned, fixed his gaze on the pinecone, and concentrated.

Nothing.

Unaware that he did so, he lifted his hands to the sides of his head, pressing fingers into his temples, his temples that always seemed to him to be a little bit deeper and higher than everyone else's. . . .

The pinecone remained still.

Damn it! Sweat beaded on his upper lip. Absently he licked it off, tasted salt. *The pinecone . . . it's just hanging there . . . come to me, come to me, damn it. . . .*

With a slight groan, he fell to his knees. His head ached severely, but he saw Rafe looming over him and kept his thoughts clear.

"Focus, boy!" said Rafe, intense but not angry. And David tried to focus, *wanted* to focus on this stupid pinecone and—

It trembled. There was no wind.

Elation filled him, gave him a fresh burst of energy, but it wasn't enough. His head was splitting, and suddenly he arched in pain.

"I can't do it!" he cried, collapsing onto the soft grass.

"Your father could." Rafe was implacable. "He could do that and things a thousand times more difficult."

On all fours, David stared up at him, shaking with the mental effort. Sweat poured down his face and his breathing was labored. Rafe's words both hurt and comforted him. As he locked gazes with this man, his father's best friend, something in his face made Rafe's own harsh countenance soften slightly.

"Rest a little bit," offered Rafe, his voice oddly gentle. "Then we'll try it again."

David caught his breath, and when he felt his legs were no longer made of rubber, he stumbled to his feet. He brushed dirt and grass from his hands and knees. Taking courage from Rafe's suddenly gentled demeanor, he said, "Rafe—tell me about my father."

Rafe smiled, a little sadly. "You remind me very much of him, when he was your age. Such a little hellion he was. He always wanted to do things his way. Trying to teach him was like—"

A sudden blast of something very loud and very bright whizzed past them. It struck the pine tree dead on, and David watched in horror as the old tree was vaporized by the shot. Beside him, Rafe pulled out his gun, reaching to shove a dumbstruck David behind him.

"Don't move!"

The voice was hard; it was the voice of someone used to being obeyed. David, huddled behind Rafe's bulk, stared as four enormous men stepped out of the woods. In addition to their remarkable height—six feet five, if not taller—they were unusual in their garb: fedoras, sunglasses even at night, and trench coats.

Even in the dim light, David could see that their heads were oddly shaped. Unaware that he did so, he reached and fingered his own temples—recessed, yes, but not as caved in as the temples on these guys—

The leader held a funny-looking snubby weapon. But David remembered the old tree that had weathered countless summers only to be vaporized just now, and suddenly it didn't look funny at all. It looked dangerous as hell.

The others had weapons, too, but more recognizable revolvers and automatics. No less dangerous, but more familiar.

The leader said something that sounded like gibberish, but he felt Rafe's body tighten in angry response. Then he heard, so softly that for a second he thought he'd imagined it: "Run, David!"

David ran.

We want the boy.

That's what the big Tyrusian had snarled at Rafe,

speaking in their native tongue. They'd never get him, not if Rafe had anything to do with it. Thank goodness the boy had had enough sense to run when he was told. He might yet get away, if only Rafe could keep these thugs occupied long enough—

Rafe threw himself to the right, falling into a tuck and roll and leaping back onto his feet. Where he had just been was scorched earth. As he rose he fired, wishing desperately he had an arbus, too. It might make this four-against-one fight a bit more equal.

One of his bullets found its mark. Rafe was rewarded by a shriek as one of the Tyrusians clutched his chest, stumbled, and fell off the precipice. His shriek lingered long after he had vanished from Rafe's sight.

Heh. *Three* to one.

His exultation was short-lived, for the leader had witnessed David fleeing for the safety of the woods. Ignoring Rafe, he turned to his companions and pointed after David. Rafe swore under his breath and kept firing. His shots missed them, however, and his swearing increased as he watched them execute their second plan.

The two Tyrusians obeyed their leader by reaching underneath their trench coats for something. Then they ran toward the precipice and leaped off. Even as their feet left the rocks their "trench coats" stiffened and flared outward, forming crude wings. Crude, but enough to take them safely down to where David had fled. Lights flashed brightly, dancing in the darkness, searching.

They were tracking David down like a criminal.

And Rafe had little doubt that they'd find him.

CHAPTER
SIX

• • •

It had happened so suddenly. One minute everything
was fine, the next, I was running for my life.

I had a sudden deep sympathy for the rabbit when
the fox comes out of nowhere. . . .

David could see the lights shining down, searching
him out, but not the men who held them. The illumination itself was sufficient, however, to spur him on
to greater speed. His chest heaving with the effort, he
leaped over a fallen trunk, used a low-hanging branch
to catch himself, and pelted on through the dark, unknown terrain.

He glanced back and his eyes widened with fear.
They were gaining on him. He cried aloud as the forest
suddenly lit up from a blast from the strange weapon.
Fire crackled, the rank smell stinging his nose and
eyes and making him cough.

Just ahead, he saw a culvert, sunk deep in the side
of the hill. They'd tracked him over open fields, even

through a smattering of trees. He desperately hoped this would be enough to shelter him from their blinding searchlights. With a grunt of effort, he launched himself, flying through the air to land with a thump inside the culvert. Not a second later, bright light flooded the area. David pressed back, smelling the clean, slightly damp scents of earth and grass.

And then the light moved on. The search continued. He'd lost them.

For a moment, he simply sat, catching his breath and trying to make sense of what had just happened. He couldn't. All he wanted to do was go home, take a hot shower, and—

Home.

Mom.

New fear flared through him. If they had found him, they might find her, too. He didn't worry about Rafe. He seemed to know exactly who these mysterious men were and how to fight them. He'd be all right—at least, David sure hoped so. David stumbled out of his hiding place, ascertained that the searching lights were far in the distance, and then headed for home as fast as his feet would carry him.

As he raced down the deserted street, he saw nothing amiss. He gave a weak grin of relief. There was the car, sitting outside; the porch lights were on. Mom was waiting for him. He ran up the steps, taking them two at a time, and flung open the door.

"Mom," he gasped, "I—"

He froze as if he'd been slammed up against a wall. Standing in the living room, two of them gripping his mother by the arms, were four of the tall, trench-coated men who had chased him earlier. Before he could react, the other two men seized his arms in tight, merciless grips. David felt sick.

"What do you want?" he demanded, sounding harsh despite the knot twisting in his stomach.

Silence was his answer. They merely stared at him, their expressions unreadable, their strange eyes disguised by the sunglasses they wore even in the house. Finally, Rita spoke. Her voice was tired, her face pale and drawn.

"They want you," she told her son.

"*Why?*" he cried, shouting the word in his frustration and terror.

"Enough talk," growled one of the strangers. They hauled roughly on Rita's arm, pulling her away from her son. That was the last straw for David. He began to struggle fiercely now, writhing in their powerful grips like a fox caught in a steel jaw trap, with about as much success as that hapless animal would have.

Like a spark borne on the wind, David's struggles ignited something inside Rita. She, too, began to fight, trying desperately to reach her child. One of the men pulled a gun, but she ignored the possible danger.

The man leveled the gun at her head. David saw, shrieked in anger, and managed to get one arm loose. He reached toward his mother, fingers stretching, straining to somehow stop what must surely be inevitable—

"*No!*" The word was a harsh scream, a deep need, ripped from David's throat without his even being aware of it.

The gun began to tremble. The man who held it grunted in surprise.

David thought of the pinecone.

He strained even more, focusing his attention on the weapon. And suddenly the thing jerked free of the stranger's grasp as if pulled. It flew through the air and landed in David's outstretched hand. He was as startled as the man and stared stupidly at the weapon.

Rita had no such handicap. She twisted like a salmon, taking advantage of the distraction. In a heartbeat she was at David's side. Seizing the gun from her son's limp fingers, she whirled and trained it on the strange man.

"Let him go!"

They did.

"Now back away slowly—that's it. One move and I swear I'll empty this thing in you. David, listen to me. Do exactly as I say."

David stared at his mom. This was a side of her he'd

never seen—the warrior, grim-faced and determined. She stood ramrod-straight, the veins in her neck standing out with tension. Sweat sheened her brow, but her eyes were clear and promised death if it came to it. As he stared at her, fascinated and filled with not a little awe, she yanked the amulet she always wore from her neck. The chain snapped.

"Take this," she told him. Never taking her eyes from their adversaries, she tossed it to him. He caught it without thinking, his own eyes still trained on her. "Now go outside and start the car. Hurry!"

"No! I won't leave you!"

The men had overcome their momentary surprise. Moving slowly and purposefully, they began to spread out and close in on Rita and David. Still grasping the gun with the knowledge of someone who knew how to use it, Rita aimed it at first one, then another of them.

"Go, David! *Now!*"

Something in the tone of her voice made David obey. He turned and fled, grabbing the car keys from a table by the door. He flung himself into the car and inserted the keys into the ignition with a trembling hand. Shaking, he looked back toward the open door. He could see his mother, gun in hand, backing up as the men closed menacingly in about her.

"Mom!" he cried over the purr of the engine.

"Come on!" His voice rose high. He was absolutely frantic now.

At the sound of David's voice, Rita turned to gaze at her child. Her face softened with love, and her eyes roamed over his features as if committing them to memory. That, more than anything else he had seen today, made David's heart lurch with unnamed terror.

My boy. My beautiful boy. Dear God, your father would be so proud of you. . . .

She dragged her gaze away from David's shocked, pale face and regarded her enemies. They were moving closer now, and she knew that she wouldn't be able to drop all of them before they got her. It didn't matter. As long as David got safely away.

Her face grew hard with hate. "You'll never get him, you monsters," she growled.

They closed in.

Bright light suddenly lit up the room. Rita had to squint, but she didn't dare close her eyes. Out of the corner of her eye, she saw what was causing the strange illumination. It was the orb, sitting on the end table. Something flickered as if trapped inside.

Still covering the men, Rita moved quickly to the table and picked up the glowing orb of crystal with her free hand. Her eyes flickered to it, and she almost dropped it.

Cale!

It was definitely her husband's face gazing up at her. He was older, as she was, his face lined and his eyes—

Eye! Cale wore a strange, tear-shaped patch over one of his eyes, the tail curling toward his ear, and the thought of what must have happened to him made Rita's heart contract with pain. His single remaining eye widened, then glistened; his lips moved, but she heard no sound.

Joy grew quietly inside her, spreading a warmth and a certainty deep in her belly that almost choked her with happiness. She understood.

Her mind flew back to that moment fifteen years ago. In her thoughts, she heard again the beloved voice as she recalled his last words to her: *Keep this. Use it only when you have to. You will know when the time comes.*

The men made their move, rushing her. The time had come, and as Cale had promised, Rita knew exactly what she needed to do.

She lifted the orb over her head. It was a better weapon than the gun, which Rita now let fall to the floor. She grinned like a wolf. The light emanating from the orb grew brighter, almost painfully so.

Cale!

And then there was nothing but light.

* * *

David opened the car door. Despite his mother's words, he was not about to let her get killed by those—those—whatever they were. It was at that moment that the light flooded out of the door and windows, almost blinding him.

He threw up his hands to shield his eyes, and through his fingers he saw what couldn't possibly be happening. The light, it was dazzling his eyes, surely—The noise came, and he cried aloud.

The house was collapsing in on itself. David screamed a single word, laced with horror and fear and loss: "*Mom!*"

The imploding house was greedy. It didn't want to go alone. The force began to inexorably haul the car toward the house, as powerful a pull as gravity. David snapped out of his near-catatonia and rammed the car into reverse. He floored the pedal, vainly attempting to pull away. The engine whined in protest. For a moment, the car edged backward, ever so slightly. Then it froze for an instant.

The force was too strong. Slowly, the car was dragged toward the house. David opened the door, trying to escape, but at that instant the car wedged between two trees. The door slammed shut, missing David's fingers by a fraction of an inch. David gasped for breath. He could feel the car shimmying around him, a quintessential example of irresistible force meeting immovable object. The car inched forward as the trees pressed in, keeping it in place.

He had to get out of there. Frantically, David scrambled over the seats to the back of the car and kicked at the rear windshield. A crack appeared. He kicked again, and again. At last, it gave way, showering him with pebble-sized bits of safety glass. Grunting with effort, he climbed out, bracing himself to resist the pull that would certainly be exerted on his fragile human body.

Silence. Whatever it had been, it was over.

David slid down the back of the car and landed on his feet, turning to stare back at his house. Or, rather, what remained of his house. All that met his gaze was churned-up earth. Everything else had disappeared.

Numbly, David took a step forward. A hand closed on his shoulder.

David shrieked and whirled, fists clenched, ready to fight. But it was only Rafe, his face covered with sweat and dirt. For a long moment, they stared at each other. Then David found his voice.

"She's . . . she's gone," he whispered.

"David." Rafe's voice was filled with compassion.

David sagged, all the energy leaving him in a dizzying rush. He stumbled and Rafe caught him. Suddenly angry, David seized the amulet his mother had given him before—

—before she died—

—before the house imploded and shoved it in Rafe's face.

"Don't you understand?" He was crying now, and he didn't care, didn't even wipe at the tears that streamed down his face. "She's *dead!*"

Rafe didn't say anything at first. He stared at the amulet, then took David's other hand and, with uncharacteristic gentleness, folded the amulet in the boy's hands.

"Perhaps," he said.

David started. "What?" Dazed, he looked back at the remains of the house, started to point at it, to protest.

Rafe seized the boy by his shoulders and shook him. "There isn't time for me to explain all this to you. They know who you are now—and they won't stop until you're dead. You've just got to do what I say."

David shook his head. There was so much he didn't understand. But he trusted Rafe; he had to. There was no one else. Gently but firmly, Rafe slipped an arm about David's shoulders, forcefully turning him away from the ruins of everything he'd ever known.

"Come on, boy!"

And David went.

I'd always been a loner; no real friends, but no enemies, either. Now I was on the run—with no home, and no place to hide. In a matter of hours, I have become trapped in a nightmare. I've lost everything I love. Strange people are chasing me. And nothing makes sense anymore.

David didn't know how much time had passed with him sitting slumped against the car door, his cheek pressed against the window. Rafe was silent, and that was fine with David. He didn't know what to say, what to feel—not even what questions to ask.

The glass of the window was cool on his heated face. After that first burst of panicked sobbing, David had been curiously calm. He suspected it was some kind of shock, that at some point when he least expected it, the pain and grief would hit him like a ton of bricks and he'd be absolutely helpless to stop the kind of crying he'd do then. But that was later. Now, dry-eyed, he merely stared wordlessly out the window at the moon-silvered landscape.

Now and then the recollection of all the strange and terrifying things that had happened would make him feel a fresh burst of fear. He'd turn in his seat, checking for any signs of pursuit. His heart slammed against his chest at those moments, but fortunately he and Rafe seemed to have made a clean getaway. How long they'd be able to stay ahead of their enemies was anybody's guess.

Rafe jerked the wheel with an unexpectedness that startled his passenger, and took them down a dirt road. After a few moments, the car screeched to a halt. David was confused. Rafe had taken them almost to the edge of a cliff that overlooked the Atlantic Ocean. It was an incongruously beautiful scene, the moon spreading its light over the waves, serving as host to two desperate people.

"Get out." Rafe's words were brusque, but not harsh. Without even thinking, David obeyed that voice, closing the door behind him. Now that he was outside, he could see that the cliff overlooked a natural cove. A dirt path twined from where the sheriff's car was parked down to this small inlet, clearly visible in the moon's light.

"Give me a hand." Again the voice, clipped and cool, like an order from a military man. David mutely followed Rafe around to the back of the car. Rafe set his shoulder to the automobile, and David automatically followed suit.

He was puzzled, though. "It's going to go over the cliff," he warned.

"Push!" grunted Rafe. They did. As David predicted, the car rolled a few feet and then, with a speed that startled him, it hurtled over the cliff. David stepped back a step or two without thinking. He watched the car falling, falling, to land with a loud splash in the ocean. It began to sink almost at once.

"Come with me." David dragged his gaze from the sight of the sinking car to the man who had suddenly become his last link to his past. Rafe had always been something of an enigma to the young man. The only clue he'd ever gotten was, "He was a friend of your father's." Now, he had become a teacher and protector, instructing David in that very weird thing with the pinecone, seeming to know exactly what was going on with the strange trench-coated men.

He wasn't just a small-town sheriff. That was for damn sure.

"David!" The word was a bark. David was startled out of his reverie and hastened to follow the retreating figure of Rafe down the trail to the little cove below.

More surprises; more mysteries. Sheltered in the natural cove was a small fishing boat. David wanted to ask questions, but suddenly he was a little afraid of Rafe. The big man clearly understood everything that was going on and had apparently even made plans for it. Now was not the time for questions, and David instinctively knew it. He didn't even wait to be told before he slogged into the water and clambered aboard the boat. Rafe grunted in what David hoped was approval.

Rafe steered the small boat with certainty, even though to David the ocean yawned ahead of them, massive and endless in its inky expanse. Finally, he was able to see what Rafe was heading for—a small island, barely a dot to his eyes even now.

Things just kept getting weirder.

Simon wanted blood.

To hell with capturing the rogue hybrid. Sure, they'd capture him all right, and they'd turn him over, too, just like they were supposed to. But not before Simon had the satisfaction of breaking a few bones and blacking an eye or two. At the very least.

He lifted the camera and began to film, focusing in on the little boat that was named *Rita's Dream*. He could see them perfectly now, thanks to the camera's night vision. The little rogue looked scared. Simon lowered the camera with a smile, glancing over at his sister. His smile faded as he regarded her profile in the moonlight.

If Simon didn't know better, he might have thought his sister was going soft on him. On previous missions, she'd always been as wild, as out for fun, as he. But she seemed troubled by this whole situation, the sheer thought that there could possibly be others like them that they didn't know about. Twice he'd caught her about to say something, then fall silent. But she'd gone along with everything so far, so Simon guessed she was all right.

She better be, he thought to himself. He was fond of

his pretty sister, but he had no scruples about bringing her in line if he thought she might do anything to jeopardize their mission.

Or get in the way of his pleasure.

They had been on the trail of the rogue since shortly after he'd managed to escape them at the museum, but it had frustrated Simon that all they had been permitted to do was keep tabs on him. Still, knowing that soon he would be within their reach was a comfort.

So they had lurked in the shadows outside his house, watching the sheriff come racing to the rescue. They had watched as the three conveniently split up, the mother staying behind, alone, and the sheriff taking the rogue hybrid out to "tutor" him. It had been child's play to notify Konrad and his men to move in and capture mother and son.

But something had gone wrong, somehow. The boy had escaped with the sheriff, and the mother—gone. It had taken precious time to round up transportation, and the boy had almost eluded them.

But now the twins stood on the cliff edge, their motorcycles softly purring, staring out at the small dot that was the boat containing the sheriff and the hybrid.

So long, the two of them had waited, patiently, waited for what was their birthright. And now this upstart bastard had come to mess everything up. He shouldn't exist. If Simon had his way, he wouldn't exist for much longer.

Simon growled deep in his throat. His hands tightened on the handlebars of his motorcycle. For a hot, pleasant moment, he fantasized that his fingers were tightening around the throat of the rogue hybrid instead. The thought gave him a measure of comfort.

Sonia turned to look at him, then glanced quickly away.

He was scaring her.

Good.

CHAPTER
SEVEN
• • •

I wondered what had happened to Mom. I wondered who these people were who were so intent on getting me that they were willing to kill for it. But more than anything else, I wondered why Rafe wasn't wondering.

It hadn't taken long for David to realize where Rafe was taking him. He'd never approached the island from this direction, or after dark, but he'd certainly been to Maple Island often enough.

Funny, he'd been thinking about the fishing shack just last night, sullenly sitting alone in his bedroom while his mother wept in the family room. He felt a pang of guilt at the memory. Had he only known—but how could he possibly have guessed at the radical and violent change his life would undergo in the span of a few short hours?

He returned his attention to the shack. The place was isolated, and frankly, the fish didn't bite all that well. But it hadn't mattered. David's heart hurt afresh as he recalled all the times he and Mom had been here together, just the two of them, walking the beach, digging in the sand. . . .

He walked around inside the little shack, occasionally reaching to touch an object. Here was the woodburning stove; nights could get chilly, even in the summer. And the bunks—how he'd fought to get the top bunk when he was young! Mom was always afraid he'd fall out of it—

"David," said Rafe, gently breaking in on David's thoughts.

David turned on Rafe, hurt and confusion in his eyes. "Why have you brought me *here*?"

"Because this place is half of your heritage," Rafe replied. "There is another half. . . ."

As David watched, curiosity overcoming the pain of memory, Rafe removed a strange object from his pocket and placed it on his temple. He walked to the center of the room, squatted, and held his hand over the wooden floor. He closed his eyes, concentrating. David wondered what he was doing, but said nothing.

The floor disappeared. David stumbled backward in shock. Where the solid wooden floor had been, now there was only a strange ladder that looked as if it had been made of light. Below, other lights blinked, casting their illumination upward into the dark room.

"Come with me."

Rafe swung his legs into the aperture, stepping without hesitation on the topmost rung. Like an escalator, the ladder began to descend, carrying Rafe with it.

David's mouth was dry. He was starting to tremble. But he knew he had to trust Rafe. Slowly, a little apprehensive and a lot excited, he stepped gingerly onto the ladder of light and let it bear him downward.

He'd crawled, toddled, and walked across that floor for fifteen summers, utterly ignorant of what lay beneath it. Now, he gaped, openmouthed, at a host of strange and colorful instruments, architecture, and furnishings. The colors were beautiful—blues and soft purples, the shapes of the bizarre objects so inviting he wanted to touch them. His ears caught the soft hum of machinery in action.

Rafe reached up to give him a hand. David scorned the gesture and jumped lightly off the ladder.

"Your father and I would come here to communicate with your homeland," said Rafe. If David's snub had bothered him, he didn't show it.

"Homeland?" David blinked. "Where?"

Rafe smiled a little. "Not here."

David was growing annoyed. "Then where?"

"On another planet, around another sun."

David's eyes widened, then narrowed with doubt. "Get out of here!"

Rafe continued, implacable. "It's called Tyrus. And half of you, David, is out of that place."

The youth laughed, but without humor. He was angry. He felt like Rafe was having fun at his expense. Surely, this couldn't be true! *Another planet, my—*

"You're out of your mind!"

Rafe shook his head, took a step toward David. His face was only inches away. David shrank back a little, but held his ground.

"No, boy. The proof is within you." He paused, and as David watched, enthralled, Rafe's eye dilated.

"Remember me. . . ."

And suddenly the room seemed to darken. No, wait, he wasn't in a room at all, he was outside, it was night. His body was small, so impossibly small. The face that peered down at him was enormous, and for a crazed moment David thought he was looking into a mirror.

He watched, his consciousness contained inside this tiny body, and a hand that was clearly his reached upward to touch the giant face. David felt the rough stubble scratch a hand that was impossibly soft.

"Good-bye, my son," said the giant face in a booming voice. It looked ineffably sad. Dad! *"I wish so much that I could be here to watch you grow strong. Someday, you will understand why I had to go. I leave you my love until we meet again."*

He paused, gazed intently into David's eyes. "Remember me!"

David watched, fascinated, as his father's eye dilated. He gazed deep into the strange dappled field, and felt his own eye return the gesture without his even thinking about it.

David shook his head and abruptly returned to the present, almost startled to find himself again inside his bigger body with its longer limbs. He took a deep, shuddering breath.

That hadn't been a trick. It had been a memory.

He stared up at Rafe. "Father . . ."

The big man nodded.

By the following morning, the inexplicable incident in the small town of Glenport, Massachusetts, was *the* hot story of the day.

Dozens of newspeople crowded around the site where Rita Carter's house used to be. There was no house anymore, not even a trace of a house, only a strange, granular material like that found on the black sand beaches of Hawaii.

The CNN cameraman listened to someone speaking through his headphones, nodded, and gave Amy Ngyuen the signal. The beautiful Asian woman, who until now had been looking bored and a little angry, snapped into broadcast mode.

"Shortly after ten p.m. last night," began Ngyuen

in the ice-cream-smooth, cool voice that had gotten her two Emmy nominations, "this quiet neighborhood in Glenport, Massachusetts, was awakened by a sound no one has been able to adequately describe. They discovered that here," she turned gracefully, pointing at the house that no longer was, "right behind me, a house that had stood for thirty years vanished without a trace. There was no explosion or fire, and the authorities refuse to speculate on what happened."

Ngyuen paused, waiting for her signal to introduce the pretaped interviews of the local law growling, "No comment." Instead, she got a frantic signal from Manny, who kept gesticulating, *Keep going, keep going.* Something had gone wrong. Someone hadn't gotten the tape ready.

Out of the corner of her eye, Ngyuen caught sight of an elderly man arguing with a police officer. She ran with it. "I believe we have someone here who knows something."

Poised, in control, she beckoned to the man to join her. He ambled over quickly and peered at the camera.

"Sir, you are . . . ?"

He adjusted his glasses and stood up straighter. "Meeks, Jacob Meeks," he replied in a movie-perfect New England voice. "Live over there." He pronounced it *they-ah.*

"Can you tell us what happened here?"

"Had to be Martians." *Maaashuns.*

Just great, thought Ngyuen bitterly. *I want some hot gossip, I get The X-Files.* She kept her broadcast face intact. "You think so?"

Meeks bridled and glared at her, his pale eyes enormous behind his spectacles. "Said so, didn't I?"

"What makes you think aliens are involved?" She turned to the camera, letting just the barest hint of Skeptical Smile #14 curve her lips. Let the audience in on the joke.

"House there yesterday, gone today." He shrugged his thin shoulders. "What else could it be?"

Ngyuen decided to wrap this up. "What else, indeed?" she replied rhetorically, turning to face the camera. "Until the authorities are willing to tell us what really happened, we can only speculate. Aliens? Terrorists? Who can say? Live from Glenport, Massachusetts, I'm Amy Ngyuen."

"Got it," said the cameraman. Amy's smile vanished and she rolled her eyes.

"Good God," she groaned. She turned to Meeks and gave him a withering look. "Aliens? Why didn't you just say Bigfoot captured them?"

"A-well," replied Meeks placidly, "because Bigfoot ain't been seen 'round these parts for years."

"It looks like a circus down there," exclaimed Sergeant Romar as she expertly piloted the chopper. She stared at the black-gray lot, at the swarm of newsmen, and cast a glance over at Stark. "What the hell's going on?"

"Set us down, Sergeant." The use of her rank coupled with Stark's cool tone shut Romar up. She and Stark had worked together for some time now, and he usually called her by her first or last name. Something big, obviously, was going on.

She pulled the chopper around and searched for a place to land. They were greeted at once by a state police captain, who barely waited for them to get out before verbally assaulting them. He carried a shotgun and looked more than ready to use it, should he feel it necessary. Romar raised a raven-dark brow.

"Hold it right there," he sneered, sounding like an escapee from a movie of the week. "Let's see some ID."

Stark was totally unruffled. Slowly, so as not to upset the jittery officer, he removed his badge and flipped it open. The man perused it carefully.

"Major Phil Stark, Military Intelligence. This is my aide, Sergeant Angela Romar."

"Military Intelligence?" The man visibly relaxed. "Maybe you can tell us what's going on here."

Phil shook his head. "Sorry. My orders are to search for a woman named Rita Carter. Seen her?"

"We're all looking for Carter." The officer nodded

his head in the direction of the square sandy lot. "That used to be her house."

Romar hid her shock. "We understand that she has a son," she said, trying to keep her voice cool and calm.

"Yeah. He's missing, too. So's the local sheriff. Damnedest thing I ever saw."

All at once, Romar forgave the man for his jitters. She gazed into Stark's brown eyes, seeking answers. There were none there for her to read. Suddenly she felt pretty damn jittery herself.

She didn't accompany Stark as he put a hand on the police officer's shoulder and walked him a short distance away. Their heads were close together as they talked in low voices. Romar moved as if drawn to the site where the Carters' house had once stood. A bright yellow ribbon of police tape prevented her from getting too close at the moment, but her eyes roamed over the flat surface.

No answers here, either. Romar sighed and squared her shoulders. Squinting against the sun, she looked around. Amid the flurry of newspeople, cameras, and gawkers, her eyes lit on the one person who was not in motion.

Across the street, slumped dejectedly on the bumper of a convertible, was a young man about the same age as the missing boy. He looked utterly miserable. Now and then, he would raise his head and cast such a glance of fear and pain in the direction of the house it made Romar wince in sympathy.

She walked over to him. "Hi," she said.

He glanced up. A vague shadow of hostility crossed his round face as he took her in from beret to boots.

"What are you, a recruiting officer?" His voice was thick.

"No," replied Romar. "I'm Sergeant Angie Romar. What's your name?"

"Jim Bailey."

"I'm looking for David Carter."

On his guard at once. "What for?"

"I want to help him." She was utterly sincere, and somehow the boy sensed it. He relaxed his defensive posture just the slightest bit. "Is he a friend of yours, Jim?" she inquired gently, already knowing the answer.

Jim shrugged. His eyes were bright with unshed tears. He blinked hard. "He was."

"You think he's dead?"

He shot her an angry look, as if he thought she was toying with him. "Isn't he?"

Romar shrugged. She leaned back against the convertible bumper as Jim was doing. She didn't look him in the eye as she continued.

"I don't know. Maybe he wasn't in the house

Paige awoke early in the morning, his subconscious mind probably telling him that he had important work to do that day, and it must all dove-tail in, just exactly, or it wouldn't work.

To his mother's distress he wasted very little time on breakfast, although he usually loved to linger with her over it. But he told her that he had promised to take June to the sick child as her father had to use his car in another direction, and he must go to the bank on the way.

Mrs. Madison had learned well through the years that when her menfolks said something *must be,* with a certain set of lips and jaw, it would be of no further use to argue. So she made the most of the brief time allowed her, and thanked the Lord that it was June and not Reva that he was taking on his morning drive.

The morning was bright and fresh and the two young people hurried away eagerly, looking forward to bringing help and joy to that poor discouraged family.

June had on another blue dress, this time with little pink rosebuds on the blue cotton background, and a decorous little white panama sailor on her head. She was taking no more chances in casual garb.

June hurried into the house and came out to report:

"Nannie slept well all night and her temperature is almost down to normal this morning. The nurse is going to sleep now and says she will be ready to take over by dinner time, or later in the afternoon. I'll tell you at noon when you return. There comes Mr. Shambley! He looks like a different man already. He walks almost steadily. I wonder if the doctor gave him some medicine to take if he feels faint or dizzy in town."

"Yes, he gave it to him last night."

"Well, brother, how are you feeling this morning?"

"Fine, I thank you. Did you succeed in getting the loan, Mr. Madison?"

"Oh yes, of course," said Paige. "Here, let me help you into the car and then I'll hand it over. There, are you comfortable? Now this in this envelope is the interest, plus the next to the last installment on your principal. Put that in your pocket where you can get it out easily as soon as you get to the office where you pay it. And don't worry about the last installment. When it comes due I think I know where I can get it for you till you get on your feet! And now this other envelope has money you can put in your bank. For use right along till you get going on your job. You have a bank, have you? Because it isn't wise to carry much money around these days. There are too many crooks abroad. You have a bank?"

"I used to have," said the man with a shamefaced droop of his head, "but when we got in all this trouble I had to draw the money all out."

"Oh well, it will be easy enough to open another account. Is it far from where you pay your mortgage?"

"No, just a few doors down the street."

"Well, is there some place there where you can sit while you wait for me? You know this will be rather tiresome, all this business, and you've been a sick man."

"Why, there's a drug store near by. I could get a glass of water if I feel faint."

"That's it! The very thing. Perhaps you better make it a cup of coffee and a sandwich if you feel like it. And then suppose you stay there till I come. I'll get away early if I can. That's Marshall's Drug Store, isn't it? Well, they have sort of little booths there with seats and tables and you can order your coffee and sit as long as you like."

"I'll do that," said the sick man, "I thank you kindly. You seem to think of everything I need."

"And here's a fresh newspaper so you'll have something to read till I get back. I may be able to manage it by half-past eleven, perhaps sooner. But don't you try any stunts on me. Remember you're still a sick man, and you want to get really well so you can take that job we're going to find for you. Here we are now. That's the door you go in, isn't it? Get that mortgage fixed up all right the first off. Good-by till I come back for you," and with a smile Paige drove off to the garage where he usually left his car.

With shaken, trembling steps Mr. Shambley entered the office where of late he had so often gone with fear and trembling, and with shoulders back and head up, went over to the window where he usually looked after his mortgage.

He could see the look on the face of the man at the window, that iron jaw, and those cold eyes. Expecting, no doubt, that he was coming to plead further poverty, and ask for leniency.

But Mr. Shambley, with Paige's envelope in his hand, walked proudly up to the window and handed out the papers, like any man of self-respect, and then handed over the money, counting out the new bills that Paige had arranged, tens, twenties, and a couple of fifties.

"Oh," said the man behind the window, "so you got around to pay on time, at last, did you?"

The quick color rolled up in the sick man's sallow cheek.

"I always pay on time when I have the money," said Mr. Shambley, and his tone was almost haughty. "The last two payments I had been sick and lost my job."

"Oh," said the receiver, "well, we have to get ready for unexpected things like that, you know. Can't expect a company to loan you money without interest. We are not in business for benevolence," said the man behind the window disagreeably. "You came mighty near losing your property, do you know it? I had orders if you didn't pay before noon today to foreclose on you."

Mr. Shambley turned away quietly, feeling suddenly faint and dizzy, but knowing he had still other things to do before he could give way to this feeling.

Slowly and with his head up he made his way out of the Chalmers' office, and walked down the street to his former bank. This was an exciting moment. He was going to deposit some money in his old account, and while it wasn't really his money yet, but was merely borrowed, it gave him an added feeling of self-respect to do it.

There was a long line of people before each window when he entered the bank, and just to rest his trembling limbs and get his breath he went and sat down on a vacant bench. Then as soon as the line was nearing the end he got up and took out his old bank book and his envelope of money.

But it was heartening to find that here he was welcomed. He may have felt shame when he drew out his last cent, but there had been no reproach connected with that, and now he was entering a deposit again. So the old cashier greeted him with a cheery good morning, and as he noted the three hundred dollars that were being deposited and wrote them down in the book, he added, "Glad to see you're back again."

Much cheered with the pleasant words and almost trembling with the gladness of it, Mr. Shambley walked out of his bank with a smile on his face. His mortgage interest was paid and he had a small balance in the bank again. There was food in his home, milk and bread coming on the regular deliveries, his little girl was getting well, and he would soon be in shape to take another job. Why should he feel so shaken? Oh, he had one more duty. He was to go to the drug store and get some coffee. He had promised, and of course his new friend would be here after him soon. He must be in good shape to go home with him. He must show he could keep a promise.

Of course he would like to go somewhere and enquire about a job. Perhaps after he had that coffee and a sandwich— But no, he must keep his promise. Besides, he was looking rather pale and feeble and it might not be a good set-up to try to get a job. He must get in good physical shape before he tried for a job. Nevertheless, he could enquire around a little if he saw anybody who seemed likely to know about jobs.

His trembling limbs carried him safely to the drug store where he was to meet Madison, and he slipped quietly into a vacant booth and smiled pleasantly into the eyes of the boy who came to take his order.

"Give me a cup of coffee. Yes, cream and sugar, please. And have you got any sandwiches?"

"Oh, sure, ham or cheese or both? Peanut butter, too."

"Give me one of each, " said the man who had been going practically without food himself that his family might have the few crumbs that his poverty might provide.

"I've got to get well and strong as soon as I can," he told himself as he munched the sandwiches slowly, and took great heartening swallows of the hot coffee. It seemed to him that he had never eaten anything so good. Of course that soup and coffee last night was wonderful, but after all he couldn't rightly savor it then, because there had been that mortgage looming with only a stranger's promise of the money to pay it. But now the interest was paid, and the next to the last installment of the principal, and he was going to get well and get a job, and now he could really enjoy eating and drinking.

He glanced at the clock over the door. It was half past eleven. The young man wouldn't be there until twelve at least, would he? There would be time for another cup of coffee and a couple more sandwiches. That would fortify him for the ride home, and then if all went well he would take a good long nap, and then he would try to go out and see if there was any chance of a job somewhere. If he could only get to work right away and begin to return some of that borrowed money, then after a while he could begin to live again. For as things were now he was really no better off than he had been yesterday. But he could feel new strength going through him. He would be well very soon.

It was ten minutes to twelve when Paige walked into the drug store and singled out his man who was just swallowing the last drop of coffee, and actually there was a new look to him that showed even at a distance.

"Well, brother, how did it go?" he asked with a keen look

into the man's face. For to tell the truth Paige had been tormented all the morning lest he ought not to have trusted this stranger with so much money. Suppose he should go and get drunk or go off somewhere and have a good time, spend all that money wildly? Then he would have a right to blame himself with having been rash. He hadn't even told June how much he was lending the man. He must have been crazy, he told himself when he thought it over.

Then hard work had begun and there came up more than one case where furtive words were spoken that showed that Harris Chalmers was not inclined to be lenient with any of his customers, and more than one man was turned away without a receipt for his mortgage money, or without a deed for his property, because he had pleaded that he could not pay all he owed that day. More and more the matter of the business itself began to worry the young man. Of course it was not in any sense his responsibility, yet if he knew these things to be going on how could he possibly sell, or urge upon poor men to buy, and that he knew he was supposed to do?

So the morning had dragged anxiously for Paige, and he was greatly relieved to see his man safe and sound apparently enjoying some food, and not in the least drunk. Also he was delighted when his protégé looking up recognized him with a hitherto unproduced smile that really made him almost good-looking.

"Oh," said Shambley with almost a ring of triumph in his voice, "it went fine. Thanks to you!" he added shyly. "I tell you it does make a difference for a man to go anywhere with money in his pocket. At least," he added with almost a sigh, "till one remembers that it is only borrowed and will have to be paid back before long—and—I haven't any job!"

"There, there!" said Paige, like a mother to a sick child, "Don't begin that yet. That will all come in good time, and you'll be able to see it through. Come. Are you through here? Is this paid for? Because I think we better hurry. I'll have to get back to my office later, you know."

"Oh, yes, it's paid for, thanks be!" said the erstwhile man of poverty. "I paid for it before I began to eat. You see, I've learned my lesson."

Paige smiled and led the way out to the car.

When they were seated and had made their way out of the thick of traffic, Paige said, "Well, how did the rest go? Have any question about your mortgage?"

Shambley looked up with a sort of a sheepish grin and shook his head.

"No," he said slowly, "only I thought they looked surprised. The man tried to be a bit sarcastic at first, but when he saw my roll of bills come out he began to sing a different song."

"Yes?" said Paige with a grin. "Well, that's the way to get the best of them. And did you go to the bank?"

"I certainly did. And you would have thought I was their long lost brother, or the prodigal son, or something, the way they welcomed me."

"Well, that's nice. Now let's keep it that way. No, don't look worried. You'll soon have a job. And now tell me your life history, your working history I mean. What work have you done?"

"Well, a little of almost everything," said Shambley. "Of course when I came back from World War Number One I had to take whatever I could get for a while, same as you do today, but I worked around on a farm for a few months and then I got me a job in an office, doing bookkeeping."

"Oh, are you a bookkeeper?"

"Yes, and they said I was pretty good. I've got some recommends that might come in handy. And besides all that I'm kind of handy with tools. Been a machinist now and again."

"Well, that sounds good. We'll see what we can do for you as soon as the doctor says you're able to work. I imagine he'll say you better begin at something out of doors until you get your health thoroughly established. Would you be willing to look after some gardens at first? Then you wouldn't have to work a whole day always if it seemed too hard on you."

"Oh, sure! I could work at gardens. That wouldn't tire me."

"Well, we'll see the doctor first. And for a start I think my father could use you in his garden. He's been quite sick this Spring and we're trying to persuade him to go a little easy. He's getting to be an old man and can't stand so much any more."

So they talked happily as they went on their way, and Shambley was much cheered. But Paige was more and more troubled as he thought ahead and wondered what he was going to do about his wonderful job.

June came out smiling to meet them as they drove up to the house.

"Nannie is decidedly better. Her temperature is down to ninety-nine and she ate quite a nice lunch. The nurse has just come back and she's going to stay until tomorrow at least. She is wonderful. And that kid brother is worth his weight in gold. He can do almost anything and do it well, and he's willing as can be."

"That's great! Now, I'll just see my man gets into bed comfortably and then we'll start. He's had a good lunch, coffee and sandwiches, and won't need anything more till he wakes up."

"That's splendid. I'll go tell the nurse. I promised I'd be back late this afternoon and get dinner so she could get a nap before night. Dad will bring me out."

"Okay. And I'll be out here after you later. There'll likely be other things to do. I'll drive right out from the office as early as I can get away."

"And by the way," said June, "mother has an easy-to-eat hot lunch for us ready the minute we get there right now. I told her you had to get back to the office and wouldn't have any time to eat."

"Oh, that is kind, but I don't need a lunch. I've often gone without."

"Of course you have," laughed June, "but this is one time you don't have to. Soup and coffee and chicken sandwiches and pumpkin pie and cheese don't take long to eat."

"Oh, boy!" grinned Paige. "Sure I'll stay. Even if I get fired from my job for being late I'll stay."

"Well, you needn't get fired this time," laughed June. "Mother knows you have to go at once, so you needn't stand on ceremony. And she'll have something you can eat quickly."

It was a pleasant drive and Paige had a delicious quick lunch and soon was speeding back to the office, thinking what a quiet, pleasant home the new manse had become, and how understandable it was with a background like that, that June should be so different from so many other girls. Was it thinkable that Reva Chalmers might have been like that with a mother and father such as June had?

The thought flitted through his mind that perhaps riches and ambition out-dominated sweetness and quietness. But he put it away and turned his thoughts to the immediate afternoon, and what the office would have in store for his faculties. He had spent too much time on outside matters in the last twenty-four hours, and it behooved him to get right down to business and work fast. Tonight he would run out to Shambley's and see how things were doing, and get the doctor's slant on the patients, and then perhaps he would be able to bring June home again.

That thought was pleasant.

7

WHEN Paige drew up at the Shambley house late that afternoon and stopped his car not far from the window that opened into Nannie's room he thought he heard the little girl crying again, and he sat still to listen. Was the child worse? Perhaps he ought to go for the doctor or after something that was needed for her.

"I'm glad you've come, Miss June," came the sorrowful little girl's words between sobs. "I got afraid again."

"But my dear, what were you afraid of?" asked June's gentle voice.

"I was just afraid I might get dying again— Every—body—hasta die—sometime, don't they?"

"Why yes," said June, "but if you have the Lord Jesus in your heart it is nothing to be afraid of. It is only your body dies then, but your spirit goes straight to be with Jesus, and He loves you, you know. He won't let any harm come to you."

"But—I've been—awful bad—sometimes—and—and— He would know that mebbe, and He wouldn't like me, and would mebbe send me out of Heaven."

"Oh, no, He would never send anybody who belonged to Him out away from Him. He loves you, and He took all your sin on Himself, just as if He Himself had done it, and then He paid the death price when He died on the cross for you, so there is nothing against you any more. When you accepted Him as your Saviour that meant that you had the right to all His righteousness. So you don't have to live under your old sins, because Jesus Christ will live in you and cover you with His own righteousness."

"How do you know that, Miss June?" asked the timid little voice. "What makes you think He would do that for me?"

"Because the Bible says so, my dear. See, I have marked it with a red pencil in your own little Bible that I am leaving for you, dear, and you can read it for yourself as often as you get afraid. It says, 'Who His own self bore our sins, in His own body on the tree.' There are a lot more verses in there that tell you how He loved you and died for you. I have marked a few of them, and when you get better you can read them for yourself."

"Oh, thank you," said the small sad voice, "but don't you think He'll forget me when you're gone Home? *Just me?* He wouldn't want to bother with me."

"No, my dear. He has said, 'I will never leave thee, nor forsake thee.' He won't forget you, because He loves you, and died for you. And the Bible says He has a book of remembrance, where the names of all those that fear the Lord, and think upon His Name, are written, and your name is there. He cannot forget you. You are His own. He never forsakes His own. He says He will be merciful to their unrighteousness, and their sins and their iniquities He will remember no more, and in another place He says: 'I, even I, am He that blotteth out thy transgression for mine own sake, and will not remember thy sins.' Now, can't you rest your heart on those words and go to sleep? Your head is nice and cool. You haven't hardly a speck of fever, and when you wake up the nurse will have a nice little pleasant supper for you."

"I'll try," the young voice said trustingly, and then Paige could hear soft steps, the closing of a door, and June came quietly out to meet him. He saw by her eyes that she was glad he was there.

June reported that the father was still asleep, had been asleep ever since he came home at noon, and the doctor had been in to see him, and seemed pleased. She had the dinner nicely started, the table set, things in the oven getting their finishing touches. The nurse had promised to report on the telephone if she needed any help, and to see that Mr. Shambley roused to eat some supper. There would be no need for them to come back that night unless she sent for them.

Then Paige suddenly felt disappointment. He wanted this pleasant association to go on.

"I was very much interested in the way you quieted Nannie's fears," he said as they started home. "The car was just outside the window and I couldn't help hearing. It was wonderful the way you had all those verses on the tip of your tongue."

"Oh," said June with a compassionate look at the young man, "I've known all those verses since I was a child. I presume you do too, if you stopped to think about it."

"Well, I'm afraid I wouldn't have had even the most familiar ones right on tap they way you did, and known which to use. I learned verses of course when I was a child, but it is so long since I've paid any attention to them that I doubt if I could finish more than half a dozen if I were to start."

"You probably could," said June. "Verses like those are not so easily forgotten."

Paige was still for a full minute, then he said shamedly, "Well, you see I was fairly familiar with the main facts in the Bible. I was a pretty good church member, I thought. I was doing church work to a certain extent. I always went to church. But it didn't really impress itself upon me as something I ought to do, to read the Bible much. I felt that I had been well brought up by Christian parents, and that was all I needed. I guess not many of us fellows that went over really thought that we were going to be killed, or got any idea there was a likelihood we might. Not till we got over there and were about to start out on our own on some mission. Then I'll own I was really scared, and began to search around in my mind for something I had been taught that would still that awful beating of my heart, and that appalling vacancy in my stomach. It took the nearness of the enemy to start that, I guess, and I would have given the world and all for somebody to tell me what to do, what to think—even what to pray. For somehow I couldn't really pray out there, only little stilted formal sentences, like 'God help me.' And I was wondering while I heard you talking to Nannie, suppose I had met you for a few minutes out there before I went out to meet the enemy, suppose I had asked you for help. What would you have said?"

June looked at him keenly, studying his face, and saw he was in earnest. Then after a moment she answered:

"Why, I would have asked you if you had ever willingly been crucified with Christ. Not just joined the church, but given up your whole self into His keeping, not just accepted Christ as your Saviour, but really been willing to die to the things of the flesh, the things of this world. Did you ever come to that place where you could honestly say, 'I am crucified'?"

"Do you mean that if I never did that I wouldn't be saved?"

"No," said June. "There are many Christians who really believe but never get to the place of privilege where they have surrendered everything and trust it all to Christ. If you are crucified with Christ, then you have the right to claim His risen power in your life. That means that we are identified with Christ in His death and have a right to the power that He brought out of the tomb when He rose from the dead. Why should one who has that power be afraid of death? Death was the last foe that He conquered, and death cannot hurt those who have once been crucified with Christ. Do you see?"

"That is a strange new doctrine to me," said Paige solemnly. "I'll have to think that over. I can see it is higher ground than I have ever thought was attainable on this earth. I would like to talk this over with you again when I have thought about it more. I wish it might be this evening, but I have an appointment with my boss tonight. He has some new plans to unfold to me. I'm not anticipating it with pleasure. I don't feel anchored enough myself to meet new phases of life. I wish—"

"I'll be praying for you," smiled June, as they turned into her driveway, and he knew they must part.

"Thank you," said Paige. "I have a hunch I shall need it. I don't know what is coming next. But I'll be seeing you soon."

"Well, here's a bit of poem for you that may help:

> There is a faith unmixed with doubt,
>   A love all free from fear;
> A walk with Jesus, where is felt
>   His presence always near.
> There is a rest that God bestows,
>   Transcending pardon's peace,
> A lowly, sweet simplicity,
>   Where inward conflicts cease.
>
> There is a service God-inspired,
>   A zeal that tireless grows,
> Where self is crucified with Christ,
>   And joy unceasing flows.
> There is a being "right with God,"
>   That yields to His commands
> Unswerving, true fidelity.
>   A loyalty that stands.

"That's wonderful. Give me a copy of that, please."

"I will. It's something I found in a book."

"Well, I'll be seeing you."

And then they parted.

June went into the house and her mother met her just inside the door with an anxious look on her face.

"Your Aunt Letitia has fallen downstairs and broken her hip. Your uncle just telephoned. She wants to know if you can come and run the house for her for a few weeks till her daughter Ella gets out of service. She's a nurse, you know, overseas, and there may be some delay about her getting home, but Aunt Letitia feels that everything will be all right till her daughter gets home, if you are there. You know Uncle Barnard is pretty feeble, and she will fret a lot if she has to go off to a hospital and leave him, but she has a good nurse, and a doctor who is devoted to them both, so it won't be strenuous for you. Do you think you should go, child?"

June's face was blank for a moment. Somehow this wasn't the pleasant next event that she was hoping for. It looked like a long hard task, no matter how many nurses were on duty, but she managed a faint smile.

"Yes, of course, I *should*," she sighed. "But mother, you'll have to take over Nannie. She needs a lot of help just now, spiritually."

"Yes, of course, child. I'll look after them all. And Miss Randall will help too when I can't go. She's a splendid help, and you know she's home for the summer now, so you needn't worry about me. But I'm sorry about your summer. I wish there were some other way out, but perhaps it won't be long before Ella gets home. We'll be hoping for that. Oh, dear child! I can't bear to let you go again when you've just got home to us."

"Yes, I know," said June with a catch in her breath and tears in her eyes. "But I can't say no. They've always done so much for us."

"Of course," said her mother. "And now I've looked up

the trains, and your best one leaves at quarter to twelve, midnight. Dad telephoned down and got you a sleeper reservation, so I guess it's all fixed. I knew you would feel you must go. And now, dear child, come in and have some supper, and then we'll go up and get your suitcase packed."

Gravely June ate her supper, and went upstairs to get her packing done. This was going to be hard. Aunt Letitia was one who was very particular and hard to please, and never by any chance did things in the way that June had been brought up to do them. It would mean her way must be sweetly put aside, and she must produce as good results as she could, working by strange methods. No, she didn't want to go, but she knew it was right that she should, and therefore of course she would go.

It was not until she was comfortably settled in her berth and trying to calm herself to sleep that she discovered in the back of her mind the real reason why she did not want to go. She was having too good a time here at home, doing church work with that nice, pleasant, generous young man who lived across the street.

And therefore, likely that was the reason why the Lord was sending her away. That young man was under the employ of the father of another girl, a girl who had no intention of letting him stray away from her world, and she ought to have seen that at once and been aware that such a friendship was not an abiding one for her.

So, she prayed in her heart and told her Lord it was all right, whatever He wanted her to do, and she would try to put such thoughts away and do her best in this new plan He had apparently marked out for her.

Then she remembered the little poem Paige had asked for, and thought that out. She had promised it, and she could write it out on a slip of paper and send it off from the station in the morning, without any return address. Then there would be no danger of his thinking that she was trying to start a correspondence. How should she word the note?

Just the poem on a slip of paper, and a word to explain:

> Duty suddenly called me away, but here's the poem you wanted. Sorry I couldn't wait to have that talk. With all best wishes.
>
> > Sincerely,
> > June

Then she turned over firmly and really went to sleep. In the morning she would write it and mail it on the train.

8

THE business that Mr. Chalmers wanted to talk over with Paige Madison was a commission to three different clients whose mortgages were to be foreclosed. There were some technicalities involved which Mr. Chalmers felt Paige with his courteous ways was well fitted to handle, and he had taken time to explain the whole matter carefully, so that there was no seeming unfairness in the whole transaction. Mr. Chalmers had learned by this time in his closer association with this young man that Paige was not easily fooled about such matters, and that his early upbringing had been in the old-time, strictly honest manner. In fact it was for this very reason that he had been so eager to get hold of this young man because of his reputation and his frank face. Harris Chalmers had found through personal experience that Christian reputation and apparent innocence counted for a great deal in the business world, especially when the business itself was a little shady. The only trouble in this case was that the young man he was trying to train into the ways of his own business methods was almost too smart and too conscientious for the place he had cut out for him. So this initial trip on which he was sending him, as an experiment, required much coaching that there might be no hitches.

Nevertheless, when Paige started home a little after midnight he was conscious again of that feeling of uneasiness about the whole thing. He hated this matter of foreclosure. He didn't want to be a part of it. And of course he couldn't just go around himself lending money to all these people who had failed to pay their interest on time. He had already gone rather deep into his slender savings for the Shambleys, and while he had no regrets about that venture, and felt reasonably sure that what he had loaned would in time be returned in full, still he could not go on doing the like indefinitely for a lot of other people.

He had felt uncomfortable about the whole matter of this commission while Mr. Chalmers had been presenting it to him, and had once told him that he would much prefer to stay in the office and work, than to take the responsibility of such a trip as was being marked out for him. But his boss made it plain that this was an emergency case, as their man who usually went on such trips was away in attendance on a very sick relative, and might not be back for a couple of weeks, and these cases must be attended to at once.

Moreover, it had occurred to Paige while they were talking that this trip might make plain to him a number of matters that had worried him, and he was anxious to get his mind at rest about his job. So he had quite willingly consented to go with that idea in mind. But on his way home he thought it over again, just as before when he came home from the first interview. Was he getting finicky? Was he becoming a worrier? He must put a stop to this. He must get rid of this question that was so shadowy in his mind, this question about his job. Well, perhaps this was a good way to settle it.

As he passed the manse it occurred to him that this trip was going to upset his work with the Shambleys, for he would be away at least two days and he must start early in the morning. But likely he wouldn't be needed there so much just now, and June would look after things.

How he would have felt about the Shambleys if he had

known that June was already on the train for the West, and uncertain when she could return, was something else. But he did not know, of course.

He had a vague memory that the best train he could catch in order to get his work well underway with dispatch would be very early in the morning. Perhaps that five-ten in the morning, and that would be too early to bother June. He would just have to ask his mother to call up, and explain to her. Mother would keep an eye on the Shambleys too, so of course he would not be missed, though he was going to miss the trips up there with June. But likely he mustn't count on that too much. Only he would like to finish that talk they had last night. She had told of a power that was at his service if only he were willing to meet the conditions, and he hadn't been sure he was. Well, perhaps this trip would help him to decide whether he wanted to get that power at any cost, or rub along without it, the way he had done all his life. Certainly he had no time tonight to think about it now. He must pack and get a little rest, and it was getting on to one o'clock. He must turn his mind to practicalities.

So he parked his old car. And there was mother waiting up for him, of course! Well, for once it was a good thing. He could tell her about the Shambleys and get her to phone June.

His mother was naturally ready to help with the Shambleys, and with his packing, and anything else where she was needed, and so in a short time she got him off to bed for his brief sleep. In the early morning, while June, in the lounge car of her train, was writing her bit of a note to him, Paige, on his train, was just settling himself for more sleep to piece out his curtailed rest of the night before, and the two trains were hurrying the two young people many miles apart, leaving the Shambleys in the care of the two mothers and the nurse. Of course they could not be in better hands, but the whole set-up was unexpected, to say the least.

It was odd though that Paige should waken with a strange dream. He was not given to dreaming, and it surprised him.

In his dream he seemed to see the car he had seen at the cross-roads with Reva and her crowd in it, and then somehow there was June sitting in their midst, looking distressed. It seemed to him that he ought to go and try to get her out of that crowd. She didn't belong there. And then suddenly Reva turned and gave him a languishing look and smile. Not that it pleased him to have her smile at him, but he found an oppression in his mind that somehow he was bound to her and must like it whether he wanted to or not. He could not seem to think this out, but when day came and the dream came back to his mind he reasoned it out that his subconscious mind had carried the thought of his job, and that he must placate this daughter of his boss to keep that lucrative job. Well, he must put this notion out of his head. He had the job and was under obligation to do the best he could for it, as long as he kept it. Anyhow, this trip must be accomplished, whatever he thought of his boss. So he bestirred himself and got in shape for the day, wondering what it would bring forth, and how soon he could hope to finish and go back home.

Sometimes the last conversation he had with June came to him, and he puzzled over some of the things she had said, and wished he might have had that talk with her before he took this trip. Somehow he was most frightfully dissatisfied with himself. Even his impulsive gesture of rescuing the Shambleys from their financial difficulties had not allayed his sense of being wrong in some way. It was ridiculous, of course, and it must be he was getting to think too much about himself. Perhaps Reva had been right when she said so much about having good times, and recreation. Perhaps he had better get out and play some golf or tennis or something. Could he, for instance, inveigle Reva into playing either one, and thus discharge any obligation he might have toward the daughter of his boss? Well, that would be something to think about later. Just now he had a day's work before him and no time to trifle with idle thoughts.

So he snapped his suitcase shut, gathered his other effects

together, and made his way to the dining car for breakfast. There was just about time for that before he would reach Boston. But as he hurried through the train he gave a passing wonder if his mother had remembered to telephone June. But of course she would. She never forgot things like that.

June was waiting for her breakfast in the diner about that time. When her breakfast arrived she had her missive ready and asked the waiter if he could get it to the mail car for her. His eye caught the gleam of the bit of silver she laid beside the letter, and he took it quite willingly, and then June settled down to enjoy her breakfast. But somehow she could not get her thoughts away from the letter she had just mailed and she found herself praying in her heart that it might reach the young man's need.

Meanwhile at home the two mothers were telephoning. It was Paige's mother who was the first to call.

"I hope I haven't wakened you all too early," she said, "but I was commissioned to let your daughter know that my son has been sent away on a business trip, and will not be able to help out in the work with the Shambleys today. He wanted me to call early lest June would think he had failed her. He didn't get home last night until a little after one o'clock and had to leave on the five o'clock train this morning. He wasn't sure but he might be away several days."

"Well, that was rather rushing orders, wasn't it?" said the other mother. "But don't worry about June. She isn't here. She had a call to the West and left on the midnight train, so you see our children are both on the way elsewhere. But don't worry about the Shambleys, either, for I promised to take over."

"And so did I," laughed Paige's mother. "I guess we'll have to take over in company. I have two loaves of brown bread in the oven. I was planning to take them over this morning. I have Paige's car, of course. Will it be convenient for you to go with me?"

"Why yes, that will be lovely!" said June's mother. "My

husband has to call on someone in the country who is very sick so I can't take our car, but I'd love to go with you, and if we both go they won't miss the children so much. I have an apple pie I think might appeal to the young lad. And some cookies."

"Fine!" said Mrs. Madison. "I should think that ought to do for a start. And I'll take a few flowers. That can't hurt anybody, and often brings a lot of cheer. The little girl will like them if she's well enough to see them."

So the Shambleys were likely to be well cared for.

Meantime Paige Madison was on his way to his first commission. He went at once to the taxi headquarters.

He had decided to go straight to the homes and deal with the men of the house before they went to business if he could possibly get there before they left.

The first name on his list was Reamer, and the taxi whirled out through the city streets, and into the country, mean streets with rundown houses. It reminded Madison of the Shambley street, only *they* had plenty of trees and woods around them, and this street was stark and bare, with a hot sun already bearing down upon little paintless houses. It seemed strange to Madison that Harris Chalmers should bother with poor little places like this, and he watched the begrimed numbers on the doors anxiously. Was there some mistake in the address? He had checked each address over himself before he left the office.

The taxi drew up in front of a fairly decent story-and-a-half brick house. Three bricks off the top of the chimney were lying on a broken roof.

With a quick look around, sizing up the neighborhood, Madison said a few low words to the taxi driver. "Wait! I'll call to you if I find I have to be longer than I expect."

The stolid driver nodded his head, and Madison went to the front door.

He knocked several times before there was a sound of footsteps within the house, discouraged footsteps shod in downtrodden shoes whose heels clomped down each step of the stairs, and hesitated now and again as if the person who wore them were almost undecided about coming to the door at all. Madison knocked again in a very business-like, determined way, and then the reluctant door was slowly unlocked and opened a crack while a discouraged-looking woman with eyes that had been crying, looked out with fright in her face.

Paige Madison put on his kindliest tone and asked, "Is this where Patrick Reamer lives?"

The woman gave a reluctant nod.

"Well, is he in?"

"Yes, he's in but he's sound asleep and I wouldn't dast to waken him."

"Well, I'm sorry," said Paige smiling, "but I've some very important business with him, and I guess we *have* to waken him. Would you like me to go up and rouse him?"

"Oh *no*," said the woman with a frightened look in her eyes, "that would never do. He'd half kill me if I let anybody come up and wake him."

"Oh, I'm sorry," said Paige, "but I guess we'll have to do something about it. This is important. You wouldn't want the law to take hold of it, would you?"

"Oh—no, *no*!" said the poor woman, two slow tears beginning to course down her worn cheeks. "What's it all about, anyway? Couldn't you ask me about it?"

"Why, yes, maybe I could. Do you know about your house? Your husband owns it, doesn't he?"

"Yes," gasped the woman, "that is he do an' he don't. You see we got a mortgage on it."

"Yes, exactly. That's what I've come about. Did you know that the interest is overdue and must be paid or the mortgage will have to be foreclosed?"

"Yes, I know, but we can't pay it yet. My man was ta get paid last night. He was gonta have money enough to pay you half, he said, and mebbe a little more, but he never cum home all night last night. I expect he stopped at the tavern for a drink, and that finished him. He didn't cum home till five o'clock this morning an' he tumbled right inta bed with his boots on, an' that's whar he is now. An' I looked in his pants pockets and everywhere else, an' he hasn't got a red cent left. That's the way he gets when he goes to the tavern first before he cums home. But mebbe next month ef I go ta meet him at the fac'try I can get him home okay, an' I'll do a bit of washin' here an' there, and then we can pay."

Madison's face grew troubled. Was this what he was in for? Hounding poor people for money they didn't have?

He looked down into the worried, pleading eyes of the desperate woman and wondered what he ought to do.

"Well, now, I wonder what we can do," he said. "Suppose I come in and sit down a little while and let's talk it over."

He called to the taxi man to wait a little longer, and he went in and sat down.

"Now, you know, my good woman," he started.

Then she began to weep and plead with him to be kind and wait till she could get the money. She said they had put all they had in this house since they got married, and now they would lose it all if the mortgage was foreclosed. And just when she had thought he was going to get a better job and they would be able to pay up real quick.

Paige studied her shifty eyes and her poor, troubled face and wished there were something he could do. He was in no position to be burdened with a decision like this, but yet he knew that the last thing Mr. Chalmers had said to him the night before had been to warn him not to get "soft" and give in to any amount of pleading. But wasn't there some other way out of this situation?

"I wonder," he said, looking at the woman almost hopefully, after a quick survey of the bare little room, "I wonder if there isn't somebody you could borrow the money from? Haven't you any friends or relatives you could borrow from? Or your bank? Wouldn't they lend you enough to cover this? You know I'm only employed by the company. I have no authority to allow you to pay later. Your contract says the money *has* to be paid on the date."

"I know," she mourned, "but my neighbors told me they didn't think any man would be so hard-hearted as to mind a few days' delay. Can't you see your way clear to being a little kind to a poor woman who has worked hard to get a home for her old age?"

"I'm sorry. I wish it were in my power to do something about this. But say, haven't you got something you could sell, that you could get along without? That would solve your problem."

The woman shook her head despairingly.

"I had a half dozen silver spoons when I was married, and I tried to sell them, but they told me they was only plated, and they didn't bring much. Besides, they're gone. O' course there's my little Mary's pianna, but I'd hate ta part with that, she loved it so much, and she's dead now. It's the last thing I've got that belonged ta her."

"Would you know of anybody who would buy it if you were willing to sell it?"

"Yes, there's a man lives at the end of the block wanted it once, but I wouldn't sell it."

"Well, now I'll tell you what you might do. I'll be willing to come back again this afternoon and get your money if you can succeed in getting it somehow, and then we won't have to foreclose the mortgage."

"Oh," groaned the woman, "that's awful good of you. I'll go out an' try my best. What time'll you be back?"

"I think about one o'clock," said Paige, glancing at his watch. "But you mustn't keep me waiting, for I have a train to catch, and I couldn't wait. I'd simply have to put the papers in the lawyer's hands and let it go through, and they would put you right out perhaps. If I were you, I'd wake your husband up now. Put cold water on his face. That will bring him to, and tell him this is imperative. Do you want me to go up and try to wake him?"

The woman looked terribly frightened.

"Oh, no," she said half frantically. "He wouldn't be any good until he gets his sleep out. I know, for I've tried it before. I'll go out and try to sell the pianna."

Paige finally had to be satisfied with that, though when he returned to the taxi he had to own that he hadn't much hope the inadequate little scared woman would accomplish much.

So he went on to his next stopping place.

It was a long distance, quite to the other side of the city, and when he reached there he found his man was out working on the road, so it took some time to find him and get a chance to talk with him. But when he accomplished that he found a new situation there. First the frightened man claimed that he had already paid a month ahead and this next one was not due yet. Paige showed him the records in the book and made him read over the contract, but when he found that the man couldn't read very well, he read it over to him carefully, explaining it to him as he read, and even then the man was befuddled.

"Me no can pay now," he said sadly. "Bimeby I pay. Wife sick. Baby die. Big doctor bill. Undertaker. Six months, then mebbe pay little. Mebbe pay half."

Paige gave the man a troubled look.

"Is there nobody you can borrow from?"

"Me? Borry? Naw, nobody mind me."

"How much have you paid in for this house already?"

"Me pay four hundred a'ready!" said the man. "Me got five hundred more yet ta pay."

"But don't you understand? If you don't pay this interest on time they have to foreclose on the mortgage. You signed your name to this agreement in the first place. You must have known it would be foreclosed if you didn't pay."

"Well, me no can pay now," said the poor man with another shrug and a sigh.

Paige looked at the man in despair. He would not understand, or else he *could* not. In despair he looked around among his fellow-workmen who were just finishing their noonday meal and closing up their dinner pails. Only one man seemed at all interested in what was going on, or noted the distress in the other man's eyes. But this one deposited his dinner pail under a tree and came striding over.

"Wha's a mattah, Pete?"

Paige's client looked up with another shrug and a torrent of a tongue unknown to Madison. He watched the two men for an instant, and then was surprised to hear the other laboring man say:

"Das arright, Pete. I got some money. I lend. How much?"

Pete lifted an astonished face.

"How much?" the other man urged.

"*Too* mooch!" Pete said with a shake of his head. "Long time I no could pay."

"*How* mooch?"

"Dwenty-five intrst., dirty-one principal. Too mooch, too mooch," said Pete sadly.

Then the other man.

"Dat's okay, Pete. I go get," and the man walked over to the boss, said a few words, and swung away on his bicycle.

"I be ri' back, Pete; two tree meenits," he called back.

Paige waited. He could not well do anything else with that sorrowful, desperate man watching his generous fellow-workman pedal away. Pete watched his friend out of sight, and then with a sigh and a shake of his head, he picked up his shovel and went on working as if nothing were going on, and there were no great matter hanging in the offing.

But in less than five minutes the bicycle came rolling back. With a businesslike look on his rough face, the man parked his wheel against a tree and strode over to Pete, producing a roll of bills, which he carefully counted out to the amazed Pete.

Then Pete laid down his shovel and straightened up. Proudly he walked over to Paige Madison, saying, quite as if this had not been a public transaction:

"*Now* I pay. You give me re-seet?"

"Oh, yes," smiled Paige, and carefully wrote the receipt.

A little while later, with a lighter heart and the necessary money he walked up the highway to where he had seen a bus plying its way back and forth. He smiled to himself as he remembered the smile on the face of Pete as he thanked his fellow-workman, and somehow he couldn't help feeling that the generous workman would stand high in contrast with Harris Chalmers, and yet was that fair? Harris Chalmers did not know Pete, his fellow-workman did. Then for the first time it occurred to him to wonder if he would be commended by his boss for having helped this man to pay what he owed. For in his briefcase he carried three foreclosure papers which he had been expected to serve on three men. And he hadn't as yet served any. Then he put the thought sharply away from his mind as unworthy. That would definitely mean that Mr. Chalmers was crafty. In fact, after the two experiences of the morning he had a strong feeling that the business in which he was employed was not one he liked. Well, it wasn't his business, of course, and he wasn't responsible. But still he knew one thing. Never again would he consent to be sent out on a mission of this sort.

The next person he was to see was several miles away from Boston, and he had also promised to go back to the poor lady who was trying to sell her "pianna" in order to pay her interest. He would have to go back that way. It was almost the time he had set to be back, and there was no telling how long the transaction would take, even if she had succeeded in selling the piano. So he had better take the third commission tomorrow. Besides, there were several other people he must see, some messages from Mr. Chalmers to give to men in their Boston offices, and one or two personal things he wanted to do, now that he was in this neighborhood.

He stopped only for a brief lunch when he reached the city again, and then took a taxi to the brick house once more.

But the little house gave no response, though he knocked several times. At last he gave one final, long pounding on the door, and a tousled head was poked out of the window over him and an angry voice demanded to know what he wanted and what business he had to make such an infernal racket on the door of a private house.

Paige decided this was the husband who had spent the night drinking and the daytime in sleeping it off, and he looked up at the man.

"Are you Mr. Patrick Reamer?" he asked.

"Yeah, that's my name. What's it to you?" was the surly reply.

"Why, I've been sent from the Harris Chalmers Company to contact you about your house. Do you know that you are behind in your payments?"

"Sure, I know," snarled the man, "but I'm gonta pay in time."

"But you know you have to pay *on* time, not *in* time. You understood when you signed the contract that there was to be no delay in payments, and now you are several days behind even the thirty days the law allows, and you know, don't you, that it means there will have to be a foreclosure on the mortgage if you run behind?"

"Yeah, they told me that, but I couldn't pay if I didn't have the money, could I? But I gotta job, and I'll have the money in time."

"I'm sorry," said Paige, writhing at the thought of what he knew he must say. "I was sent here to tell you that your mortgage is being foreclosed and you must get out at once."

"Okay! I don't like the old house anyway," said the man. "But I want my money back. I already paid a couplla hundred dollars on this."

"I'm sorry," said Paige, "but your contract says that you must get out and be foreclosed if a payment is missed. I'll have to put this in the hands of the law, so it will be better for you if you move right out and don't make any further trouble."

"Aw, that's all bologny. I know a fella had the same kinda contract I hev, and he let his payments go a lot more'n I have, and they didn't put him out. I'll take my chances with the law."

"Did you know that your wife has gone somewhere to try to sell your piano so she can pay the money today before the time is up?"

"*Pianna?* Well that's a good one! We never had no pianna. We haven't got a thing in this house we could sell if we wanted to, and if we did, nobody would buy it, so you can go your way and tell that Mr. Chalmers if I get the money I'll pay as soon as I can. And he can whistle for it till he gets it. I'll take my chances with the law, and I don't get out unless I get back the money I already spent on this here shanty."

So, with no further words Paige Madison turned and went on his way, sorry for the man and yet indignant.

9

PAIGE Madison arrived in the suburban town where his third client lived about half-past one the next day. He had been given to understand that this was the most important case of all three, as it involved a larger sum of money and was several days overdue beyond the thirty days the law allowed. It was definitely to be foreclosed. The man who held the mortgage had replied to none of their notices, and it was now long enough overdue to allow for no protest. On his way out he had gone carefully over the notes Mr. Chalmers had given him, and practically had them by heart. He felt fairly calm over the thought of what was before him. The two cases of the day before had somewhat taken away his dread, though he reiterated to himself that he would never willingly accept a commission like this one again. It might be necessary on some occasions, perhaps, but he would never feel that it was right to take it for granted that everyone who didn't come to time on the minute was a crook and had to be dealt with se- verely. Perhaps there was a right and wrong to it, but he couldn't see it that way, not at least with as little ceremony and human feeling as these cases seemed to be receiving from Harris Chalmers. But he would be exceedingly glad when this last item was completed and he was free to return home.

He took a taxi at the station and gave the man's address.

"You know where Mr. T. J. Washburn lives?" he asked the taxi driver.

"Oh, yes sir," the driver assured him, and started off down the street slowly. Paige observed that it was a pretty town and they were turning toward a pleasant neighborhood. Perhaps this wasn't going to be even as easy as those two cases of yesterday. The people on the street seemed fairly well-to-do, and people who had been prosperous did not usually take kindly to losing what they had.

They turned another corner and drew up slowly in front of a commodious brick house, painted white. There seemed to be a number of other cars parked on the street, and the whole effect was very pleasant, which rather served to heighten Madison's reluctance for the immediate duty before him.

"Is this the house?" he asked the driver. "Are you sure?"

"Oh, yes sir, I've knowed Mr. Washburn a good many years."

Paige got out and paid his driver, still feeling uncertain. The driver went away, and Paige turned to go up the front walk, and then halted again. The front door was standing wide open, and there seemed to be flowers around the porch, a mass of them. Could it be they were having a party? If so, it was certainly an inopportune time for him to arrive with his unpleasant message. But—it couldn't be a party at this time of day. Why it was scarcely two o'clock yet!

A quiet, elderly woman and a little boy were coming into the gate behind him, and to make sure he turned and asked the woman: "Is this the Washburn house?"

"Oh, yes," she answered gravely. She was very plainly dressed, perhaps a servant in the family, or a plain old relative. But reassured, he went quickly forward and mounted the steps, glancing about for a doorbell. But before he found any, a young man in a frock coat came forward and greeted him pleasantly. Could this then be a wedding he was barging in on and was this a bridegroom or a best man? How terrible that joy and tragedy could so easily mingle in a world that seemed so bright with sunshine! He was embarrassed and hardly knew how to act, but he must do something.

"I beg your pardon," he said hesitatingly. "Have I come to the right place? I want to see Mr. Washburn."

"Yes?" said the young man. "Right in here," and he motioned toward a wide doorway a little beyond the front entrance.

So Paige stepped into a large room, and suddenly was confronted by the sight of a coffin in which lay an elderly man with white hair, and a beautiful arrangement of lovely flowers banked about him.

Startled, he stood still, and was about to leave. It was not a wedding but a funeral he had come to! But he could not back out because there were a number of other people coming in behind him. They filled the doorway, and his friendly escort back of them was signaling to him and pointing to the coffin. He could not stop and say that he had not known where he was coming. It would create a scene. He would have to go on and act as if he had come here with intention. Eventually there would be opportunity to go, or at least to talk with somebody and find out who was now responsible for the man's estate, if he had any.

So Paige quickly adjusted himself to the situation and went forward to stand and look at the dead face, and while he stood there he could not help but think how but for a few days' happenings he might have faced this man and brought sorrow and disappointment to him. Of course it was all right to foreclose mortgages if one couldn't pay them, but wasn't it right to arrange things so the borrower would have more time given him if he had been unfortunate? Well, this was no time to consider a question such as that, and again he told himself it wasn't his business anyway. But somehow, as he stood and looked down at that dead face, his own heart was searched as it had not been since he was a little boy. Even deeper than it had been when he was across the ocean, about to meet the enemy.

It seemed to him that the man who lay there was a good man. He had the marks of right living written in his face. And he was probably now in the presence of God. He looked like one of God's children. And God Himself was there beside that coffin, he felt, looking at him as if he were challenging his presence there with one of His saints.

It was a strange, foolish feeling of course, a part of his embarrassing position perhaps, but he felt as if he had met God in a new way, and there was a tacit understanding now between himself and God that he would have to come back after this was over and have it out; have this matter between himself and God settled forever. A strange outcome indeed to have followed a mission like the one upon which he had been sent.

A good many people had come into the room now, and there were tears in evidence and softly murmered speech from one to another. Paige presently roused to the fact that he was in the way and that a great many other people were wanting to stand where he was, and wanting to look again upon their old friend for the last time. Paige looked around to see whether he could get out of the house now, or at least out of the room, or certainly out of the way; but a kindly old man, who very much resembled the man in the coffin, touched him on the shoulder and led him to a vacant chair. He sat down quickly to get out of the public eye. Of course it wouldn't look right for him to leave the house now before the service. It would make him all the more conspicuous.

A young man stepped up near the coffin at last and began to pray. Paige bowed his head with the rest, realizing now that the room was full. The wide hall was crowded with people sitting and standing, and the room beyond the hall, that was probably the dining room, was literally packed full. He had come to foreclose a mortgage on that home where death had taken the head. Intruding into their sacred sorrow! And when he closed his eyes and bowed his head, there stood God beside that coffin, as if He were waiting to take His beloved saint away with Him. He could see Him clearly, even with his eyes shut.

Paige had never experienced such a sense of being searched, accused. He had the same feeling he remembered from his school days when he was being called to account for some omission of duty. Yet he had not been actually conscious of wrongdoing. But now everything seemed wrong. His very presence in this strange house seemed more than an intrusion. It seemed the outward mark of something that he was beginning to see in his own life. Possibly not his job, but more his own attitude toward life as a whole.

All this was pressed upon him as he sat there with bowed head. He seemed to hear his own sins brought out before the God who stood so close.

The prayer over, there followed a wonderful collection of verses from Scripture, making so clear the way of salvation and life that the wayfaring man, though a fool, could not err therein. For the first time in his life Paige saw what he had been taking casually and not giving real heed to, though he had known the facts well from his infancy.

And God was still there. He was standing so near that, though his own eyes were looking down, he could feel His presence pervading the room, and looking into his own soul.

Then the speaker began to mention a few things in the life of the wonderful, gentle old man who was departed; to tell of little incidents in which he had witnessed to some soul about Jesus, and to say how "Our brother Washburn was one who had unquestionably experienced what Paul meant by being crucified with Christ. He had continually lived in that resurrection power that Christ brought out of the tomb when He rose from the dead, that power which is made available to such of His own as are willing to be crucified to the things of the flesh and the things of the world."

Paige's mind went back at once to that last talk he had had

with June. There were others then who believed this and preached it. Perhaps for aught he knew his own father and mother had thought that they had taught him so to believe.

Sharply it came to him now that he was here in the capacity of an agent to bring sorrow and loss and distress to this saint of God, this man who had lived in a lofty place with Christ by the power of His resurrection.

And now he, Paige, had the definite feeling that he had been sent up here by God to this funeral to meet the Lord and find all this out, understand it as he never could have understood it in any way except in this startling presence of the Lord. It was as if the Lord were waiting to take away His saint with Him to glory.

Paige lifted a haggard face at last and looked at that placid face again lying in the coffin, so still, so calm, so satisfied, and knew that here was proof that a life lived in the resurrection power brought joy and not sacrifice, eternal riches and not spiritual poverty.

Then came the young minister's voice again, strongly, with a ring of triumph in it:

"'I am the resurrection and the life. He that believeth in me, though he were dead, yet shall he live.'"

And it came to Paige as he listened that the deep meaning of that was to assure him that if he was willing to surrender all in that death with Christ, he would be losing nothing worth while, for there was a greater life that he would gain even here on earth. Why had he never understood that before? Why had he been so reluctant, even when June tried to make it plain to him? What was it he was trying to cling to? His lucrative job? He almost shivered at the thought that it was possible he had been willing to risk a life in close company with God, empowered with the strength of Christ for a job such as he was now out upon.

There was no question in his mind now about the job. It was not his idea of a place for a crucified Christian. But the question of just what he should do about it, just what came next, and how far he was already involved in it, could not be decided now. He had first to settle things with God, the God who was standing by him now, and looking into his heart.

There was a soft general stirring as a voice invited all who would to come forward and take a farewell look at the face of their friend, and Paige arose and moved back out of the way. Then he realized that this was the time for him to get out of the house and try to plan what he should do next about his errand. Should he abandon it, or call up the home office and ask for instructions, or what? But before there was a way for him to slip out, the white-haired man, who looked so much like the dead man, laid a kindly hand on his shoulder and said in a low tone:

"You will ride in the car with me to the cemetary."

"Oh, but—!" protested Paige. "I have no right there."

"Yes," said the other, "you were my brother's friend. I want you with me."

"No, you don't understand—" protested Paige, but the man had gone into the crowd with the parting words:

"Yes, I want it that way. You stay around with me."

Paige, bewildered, scarcely knowing what to do, retreated into a corner over near the hall door. Now was a time to slip away, of course, as soon as the crowd in the hall thinned, yet he scarcely liked to be so discourteous after the man had been so gracious. He had probably mistaken him for someone else, but still if there were opportunity he ought to explain who he was, and of course this would likely be the only opportunity he would have to find out where he could contact Mr. Washburn's executor, or whoever he should see about this matter of the mortgage. He hated to intrude matters of business now, at a time like this, yet he ought to get back home as quickly as possible, whatever he was going to do eventually. He must somehow manage to explain to this man before they intruded him into the funeral train. It was impossible that he should carry out this farce any longer, for while he knew in his heart that unspeakable good had come to himself through that service, still he had had no right whatever there, and there seemed no apology worthy to excuse his stupidity.

And now the people were moving away, the coffin was covered, and Paige moved out onto the porch, with a quick look around. He could slip away and come back toward evening to explain.

But the kindly hand lay on his shoulder again, imperatively.

"Come now," the man said, "they are waiting for us."

And suddenly a number of people swept him along. And though he did his best again to get the attention of his pleasant-minded host, there was no opportunity.

There were two other people already in the car, and though Paige hesitated at the door, beginning, "I must explain—" the older man only smiled, and said, "Yes, just a minute. I must speak to someone over there," and the undertaker urged him to take the seat across in the corner.

So Paige, much against his will, went to the cemetary, and it was not until the two people in the back seat were dropped at their home after the service that Paige had an opportunity to explain.

The other Mr. Washburn, for Paige had now discovered that that was his name, turned to him at last.

"Now," he said, "I'm sure you will understand how I had no time before this to talk. I was sure you would see how involved I was."

"Yes," Paige said, "but you gave me no opportunity to explain to you that I am not Mr. Washburn's friend, or even acquaintance. I never saw him before until I saw him lying in that coffin. I came to see him on business. I had no idea that he had passed away until someone ushered me into the room where he lay. I am merely a business man, sent up to look after some business with Mr. Washburn, and I had no intention whatever of barging in on a private matter like a funeral. I tried to get out, but everybody misunderstood, and I could not manage it without creating confusion."

The old man had been watching him earnestly as he talked.

"Oh, I'm sorry," he said. "I thought you were Joe's friend from Chicago. I am sure no one intended to involve you in a matter which couldn't possibly interest you."

"Of course I understand that," said Paige. "It was wholly my own blundering. But you are mistaken that I had no interest in what went on. I was much touched and *helped* by the service. I feel that I should thank someone for having let me in on it. But of course that is wholly apart from the business I came up to transact, and perhaps now it will not be out of place for me to ask where I can find Mr. Washburn's representative? I really ought to get the midnight train back to New York if that is possible, though if I can better get my business transacted tomorrow I could of course arrange to stay overnight. This is scarcely the time to talk business with a member of the family. Is there any business representative of the family whom I could see?"

"Just what was the nature of the business you had with my brother?" asked Mr. Washburn, watching the young man gravely.

"It is a mortgage foreclosure," said Paige firmly, finding that of all the missions of the occasion this one seemed to him to be the hardest to execute.

"Foreclosure?" said the other man. "But I understood that that was already attended to. At least I talked it over with my brother and he told me that it was his intention to pay in full the principal on that and have it entirely out of the way."

"Yes? But he *didn't*. And the interest is some *time* overdue. I don't know whether you understood that a failure to pay the interest on time necessitates a foreclosure. In this case it is quite over the legal thirty days."

"That seems strange," said Mr. Washburn. "My brother talked about that with me a few nights before he was taken sick. Are you sure that wasn't attended to?"

"I'm positive. I have all the papers with me. Several notices were sent on this matter and no attention was paid to them."

"Do you know the dates?"

"Yes, here they are. The first was sent on the usual date, of course; the second a week later, and others after that. Here they are."

The older man studied the dates for a moment before he said:

"Oh, well, then you see the first reached here about the time my brother was taken ill. It is possible he did not even see it, as no one dared to trouble him with his mail. That is a pity. It makes you a lot of unnecessary trouble, too. But suppose you come back to the house with me now. I can look through my brother's papers. His checkbook might tell something. We will see if the notices are there. He always attended to such business matters himself, but of course he often consulted with me."

At the house again the two men went to the neat little study where the dead man had his desk, now piled high with unopened letters.

The brother sat down, glanced hastily through the pile of mail accumulated and selected the envelopes bearing the Harris Chalmers' return address.

"Yes, here they are," he said as he laid them on the desk, studying the dates on the postmarks. He knit his brows over them a moment, then unlocked a drawer and drew out his brother's checkbook, turning over the leaves rapidly, and suddenly exclaiming:

"Yes, here the check is! The date of the first notice and the check all made out and signed. That must have been the last thing he did. We found him fallen forward on his desk, the pen in his hand, the night he was taken sick. And he was desperately ill from then on until now! None of us thought to look into his private affairs to see if there was anything that needed immediate attention. Joseph was always so methodical it seemed as if nothing was likely to go wrong."

Paige looked at the man bewildered, wondering what should be his procedure now? Would these people want the mortgage foreclosed? Then the other man spoke.

"This check would not be good now, of course, on account of Joe's death, and the natural process of the law would bring it under the jurisdiction of the managers of the estate. But since that would take some time, and you are in haste to return, and since it was our fault in a way that this was not paid before, would you be willing to accept my check at once for this whole matter, and give me a receipt? Of course allowing for the interest of the delay? I can give you a certified check."

"Oh!" almost gasped Paige. "Would you be willing to do that? I suppose that would be much simpler for us. But it is imposing upon you."

"Not at all," said the old man with a sigh. "Joe and I were very close brothers, and I think he would like me to do this for him. I would not want my sister-in-law to be disturbed by knowing of this, nor to have any idea that her home might have foreclosure proceedings on it. We are trying to have life go on as normally for her sake as possible. She has been through a great deal during the weeks of my brother's illness, and I'll be glad to finish this matter up definitely at once if you are willing to arrange that, and there need be no further question about it in the settlement of affairs."

Paige Madison breathed a sigh of relief when he received the certified check for the full amount covering the entire remaining mortgage. This was not what he was supposed to have come after, but surely his boss would be more than pleased at the outcome of his mission. So, in a little while he was free to hurry away to his train.

But he grasped the hand of Charles Washburn warmly and thanked him again for all he had done, and more than all for making his presence at that service possible. Then he looked back at the simple substantial white house where he had spent such a strange and unexpected afternoon, and thought he would like to come back there sometime and remember.

It was not according to his custom in riding on railroad trains, but Paige Madison spent a large part of that night in prayer, and it seemed to him that the Lord Jesus Christ had come with him, and was very close, ready to help him understand.

This would be something that he would not tell about in his report to Mr. Chalmers. Something all between himself and God. He might not even tell his mother. There was only one person he felt would ever understand, and that was June Culbertson. She would understand. Strange, and he had known her so short a time! But she had spoken of these same truths that had so stirred him at the funeral service.

10

JUNE'S brief letter was waiting for him the next morning when he got home to breakfast. It lay by his place. He tore it open and was filled with a strange disappointment when he read that she was away. He hadn't known that he was looking forward to seeing her and talking with her. And suddenly he knew that he had been going to tell her about that afternoon at the funeral. And now she was gone! Perhaps he would never see her again. She did not say how long she was likely to stay.

He turned to the poem and read it through. Almost he could hear her voice saying the words.

Then his mother came in with fresh coffee, and he folded the letter and enclosure and put them in his pocket. Somehow he did not feel ready to part with them yet. He wanted to read them over again. Meantime he was going to meet his boss, and perhaps they would be a sort of talisman to guard him from making any mistakes. For he felt a misgiving about how his boss would think he had handled this important business.

He swallowed his coffee, gave his mother another brief kiss, and darted out to his car, his hand on the folded letter in his pocket, taking comfort from it. He was cheered by the thought that June had remembered to send the poem. And somehow he felt, even just from the single reading, that it would chime right in with his experiences with his new Lord.

Back in his office he found a pile of mail that had to be attended to at once, and he and his secretary were deep into dictation when there came a call from Mr. Chalmers.

"Madison come yet? Send him in at once!" and the receiver slammed into place. Somehow the very click of the instrument sent a shiver through Paige's shoulders. How silly, he told himself, as he swung out of his chair and went toward the boss's office.

"Well, Madison, I see you have returned. I hope you had a successful trip."

"Why, I think so, Mr. Chalmers. I would have been in here with a report before, but I thought you would be busy the first thing in the morning with your mail, so I waited to get a few important letters out of the way."

"Well, I came down a little early this morning. I was anxious to hear your report. Did you have any trouble? Served all three foreclosures?"

"No," said Madison, "I only served one. The others both paid up."

"Paid up!" gasped Chalmers, springing up from his chair. "But I thought I gave definite orders that all three *must be foreclosed!* What business did you have to go against my orders?"

"I beg your pardon, Mr. Chalmers. I do not recall your having told me not to receive the money if it was given to me. I supposed of course payment was the most desirable." Paige's tone had a new dignity, and Mr. Chalmers cooled down and looked at him, realizing that by his blustering he was actually giving away one of the secrets of his business which he had not intended to make known to him at this stage of the game. His intention had been to go cautiously with this young man who was inclined to be so overconscientious, leading him gradually to see the necessity of the more subtle and clever ways of managing business affairs in order to be greatly successful.

Like a balloon that had suddenly been pricked with a pin he deflated from his blustering.

"Well, yes, of course," he said with a tone almost mollified. "That is, if they paid enough. But I had no reason to anticipate any such thing as that. Two of those people have been nothing but a nuisance, always having to be nagged. Well, go ahead, young man, and give us your story. I interrupted you."

Paige gravely told his story, beginning with the people in the brick house where the man drank all the money up and the woman went out to sell a piano she didn't possess to pay her interest. And he knew how to tell a story, so that in spite of his slightly haughty manner in telling it, he held the interest of his boss, who nodded approval as he finished with the foreclosure.

The boss was frowning when he began on the poor laborer in the road who couldn't pay, with the pathetic plea of sickness and death, and then the fellow-laborer who went home and got the money to lend to him. Paige told this story so well that the boss actually had tears in his eyes when he had finished, and remarked feelingly, "Now, whaddaya know about that? Not many fellow-laborers would be that generous," and he took out an expensive handkerchief from his breast pocket and blew his nose hard.

Paige had been rather dreading the story of the dead man, because by this time he had realized that the Chalmers temper would be more roused by the man who had ignored their several notices than by any of the others, but now in view of his seeming interest in the poor laborer he took heart of hope, drew a deep breath, and prepared for the worst if necessary.

"Well!" snapped the boss, ashamed now of his emotion. "Go ahead! What about the Washburn case? What possible excuse did he have for ignoring all our notices?"

"He was dead," said Paige solemnly.

"Dead?" shouted Chalmers. "Well that's a new one to pull!

How do you know he was dead? Who said so?"

"Nobody said so. I went to his funeral."

"You went to his *funeral*! Are you kidding, Madison?"

"No. I'm not kidding," said Paige gravely. "It was quite unintentional on my part. I went to the door of the address you gave me and asked to see Mr. Washburn. They motioned me to the door of the next room, and there lay Mr. Washburn in his coffin. I realized suddenly that I was at a funeral. Many people were coming in behind me, and there were some already seated. I backed away and tried to get out of the room, but some kindly person motioned me to a chair, and without making a scene there seemed no way to get out at present.

"You can perhaps imagine how I felt, for those first few minutes. After that the service was so impressive that I completely forgot why I had come."

"Did they know you were coming? Had you sent word and made an appointment? You're sure it wasn't staged for your benefit?"

Paige gave his boss a startled, indignant look, then answered solemnly: "No, I had not telephoned. I took the train out there and a taxi to the house. I noticed there were a few other cars parked on the street, and some flowers on the porch, but thought nothing of it, until suddenly I was in the room and there was the coffin right before me."

"Why, how extraordinary!" exclaimed the boss. "And afterwards I suppose you got out."

"No, they gave me a chair, and the room was full. I didn't want to make a scene. And afterwards I was glad. It was a very wonderful service, and it seemed to me as if God were standing there. I was glad to have had the experience."

Chalmers was deeply embarrassed and looked at his young employee in a kind of wonder, seeing that he had really been deeply affected.

"Well, I'm glad it wasn't too unpleasant. But afterward, were you able to find out why we hadn't heard from Mr.

Washburn, and what we should do to complete this business?"

"Yes, afterwards I talked with Mr. Washburn's brother Charles, and he took me to our Mr. Washburn's study, found all our notices still unopened among the mail that had accumulated during his illness, and then we looked in his check book and found a check made out for us at the date of our first notice, covering the entire loan, interest and all. It seems the brothers had talked it over and decided it was best to pay it all now."

"But that check wouldn't be good now until the estate was settled, of course."

"No, and so Mr. Charles Washburn, anxious not to have the widow troubled with the matter, offered to pay the whole check, with interest of course, to get it settled without further trouble for us. It seemed to me that would be what you would think was best, so I accepted it, and gave him a receipt. It is a certified check."

Paige laid the check down on Chalmers' desk, together with the roll of money the working man had given him.

The boss took up the check, counted the money, cleared his throat and said, "Well, I guess you have done fairly well with your first commission, Madison. I shall know where to find the right man to send again when I have a difficult commission."

Paige had arisen and was going toward the door, but now he turned back and shook his head.

"No," he said. "Never again. It is too soul-trying a job for me. I'm not cut out for that."

"Oh, you'd soon get over that squeamishness."

"No!" said Paige firmly. "But—I'm glad you're pleased. And now if you have nothing further I'll go back to my desk. There is a big stack of mail over there that needs immediate attention."

"Of course, Madison. I understand. But perhaps you'll arrange to take lunch with me. There may be some other questions I'd like to talk over with you."

Paige assented gravely, and went back to his office, wondering what might be coming next, and thinking that he ought to decide once for all what he was going to do. This uneasy uncertainty was utterly unfitting him for any kind of work. Well this was all probably ridiculous. Mr. Chalmers was very nice after he finally understood things. He had probably misjudged him, and had let his own first unpleasant impressions color every thought connected with his job, and he must stop it. He would just go ahead and do what was required of him, and likely some things that he was being put through now were just training, so that he might be in touch with every branch of the service. Besides, this was no way to face a new life, finding fault with everything that came his way.

This evening there was a big question he had to consider for the future, how his life was to be different since he had met the Lord, but just now there was his desk full of work, and that must have his undivided attention.

From time to time he remembered the luncheon he was to share with his boss, and wondered again what was coming next. He found himself with a great crying out in his heart for help toward the God who had seemed so near to him since yesterday. When had he ever, since he was a child, felt like crying out for help to God? Even during the war he had felt more or less that his mother's prayers would cover all the help he would need. And how was it that now since he had watched that still presence of God standing beside him he had learned that there was something he needed that even his mother's prayers could not provide? It must be his own cry for help, a real cry from a recognized need.

But he had no time now to consider that. His heart had sent out his cry, and it would be answered when the need came.

With these resolves made, a great deal of work was accomplished that morning in Madison's office, and he went with a lighter heart to meet his boss at the appointed place for luncheon.

It proved to be the University Club, where a few choice spirits in the business world were assembled, and after a pleasant flattering introduction they sat down to a luxurious lunch.

Paige would so much rather have been by himself to think out things, and go over yesterday's experiences, but it seemed that he was in a world just now, whether rightly or wrongly he was not sure, where he had to do what someone else wanted rather than order his life as he would choose. And once he thought longingly of that bit of a poem now residing in his vest pocket. He would so much have liked to be able to recall it. But that had to wait its time too.

So it was no private talk of criticism or new orderings that this luncheon had been planned for, he presently discovered, but a social mingling to introduce him to other well-known business men.

Why? How could that sort of thing make him to be of more value to his boss?

When the little company around the lunch table broke up and the various ones said good-by and hurried away to their respective offices, Chalmers lingered a few minutes, talking about the club, telling how advantageous it was to any man to belong to it, mentioning various reasons why every young man should belong to a club, and finally ending up by suggesting that he would be glad to propose Paige's name if he was agreeable.

The question was so unexpected that Paige scarcely knew what to say. Was this something he ought to think about and perhaps ask his new Guide? And yet, as long as he was staying with his job and his boss seemed to want this, perhaps he ought to accede to it. Meantime the boss awaited an answer.

"Why, that sounds very pleasant, and is most kind of you. But—it is something I haven't ever thought about before. May I think it over for a day or two?"

Chalmers gave him a quick stare. He had expected his man to be flattered and pleased and accept with alacrity, and here he wanted to think it over. Or was this a bit of lofty pose? He couldn't quite make up his mind.

The boss was a bit mortified perhaps, much as his daughter had been, that the younger man didn't immediately bow down to him, but he answered quite indifferently.

"Oh, all right. I just mentioned it because I thought it would be good for a young business man to have some such contacts. It's a very conservative place, and quite respectable."

"Oh, of course. I know its reputation. I was only wondering if I would have the time to come to places like this."

"Nonsense!" said the other man, "of course you'll have time. And I might often want to ask you to bring some one of our customers here for lunch. There couldn't be a better place to take them, good food, and a fine class of people always come here. It makes a good impression to take a customer to a place like this."

"Yes, I see," said Paige, "and of course if it's a matter of taking your customers somewhere I'll be very glad if you'll help to make it possible."

Mr. Chalmers' face brightened. For in truth he had had two reasons for urging this. One was connected with his business as he suggested, the other was at the instigation of his daughter Reva, who had implored him to do something about that new man of his to make him better company. "He's a perfect stick, dad! I don't see how he can be any help in the business world if he can't get on with young people," she had said. And to that end he had taken Paige to the University Club.

"Very well, Madison, I'll put your name in at once."

Some other business men came in then and one a very distinguished man with an international reputation, and Paige found himself being introduced to him, and having a few words of very pleasant conversation.

When they finally went together back to the office Mr. Chalmers said eagerly, "You see, Madison, that's the kind of a place it is, where you meet great men from all over the world, and make contacts that do you no end of good when you get down to business."

Yes, Paige could see, and felt that he had certainly done the right thing to consent to have an entre into a place like that.

On the way home he found himself wondering how the Shambleys were getting on, and decided that he would drive out there and find out before night. If Shambley was better it was about time to do something about getting him a job. Perhaps he had better stop at the house and call up the doctor before going out there. He didn't want to rush things too much and have the man break down right at the start.

Then he reviewed the morning hours and recalled to his mind the look on his boss's face when he got the news of payment instead of foreclosure, and felt again that Chalmers had been disappointed at the outcome. Queer that Chalmers should feel that way. Of course he must be mistaken. There wouldn't be any reason why he should *want* to foreclose. Not unless he owned the house himself! H'm! Perhaps that was it!

He was thinking about this when he noticed one of the men from the office waiting on the corner for a bus, and knowing he went his way for some little distance he stopped and invited him to ride.

The invitation was accepted with alacrity, and they soon fell to talking.

"Well," said Grainger, "you've been off up Boston way. Pleasant time of year to take a trip like that. How'dya make out? Foreclose everything?"

Paige smiled.

"No, not all of them. A couple of them paid up."

"You don't say! Not that Washburn case, I hope. Because that's practically sold to another party at a stupendous price. Houses are scarce these days, you know, and the day you left, Chalmers called me in and had me write to a party who works with him a good deal, and got the deal all fixed up. Chalmers was going to make a pretty penny on that deal."

Paige looked at him astonished.

"That's a bit strange," he said speculatively, "he didn't tell me."

"No, he wouldn't likely. He keeps his own council, that man. But stop, here's my corner! Thanks for the lift," and Grainger was gone. But Paige had something more to think about, and now he was sure he understood the black look that met him when he first told of his dealings in the Washburn case.

Well, here was another angle to be considered. What would God have him do? Before he went to that funeral he would not have thought of asking himself that question.

How he wished that June was at home and that he might talk it all over with her. Was this new life going to involve more perplexities than he was willing to undertake?

Then he got out the little poem she had sent and read it over, perhaps really taking it in for the first time:

> *There is a faith unmixed with doubt,*
> * A love all free from fear;*
> *A walk with Jesus, where is felt*
> * His presence always near.*
> *There is a rest that God bestows,*
> * Transcending pardon's peace,*
> *A lowly, sweet simplicity,*
> * Where inward conflicts cease.*

Would he ever get to that place, ever have a faith like that, on which he could rest, and inward conflicts would cease?

Paige drove home and learned that his mother was still at the church at some committee meeting which was lasting overlong. So he called the doctor and found that the Shambley invalids were improving rapidly. The little girl was able to sit up, and the father had been out walking every day for the last two days. The doctor saw no reason why he should not take an easy job, preferably an outdoor job.

Then Mother Madison came bustling apologetically in, announcing that dinner would be ready in fifteen minutes. Paige went upstairs to freshen up for the evening. He would find out from his mother more about the Shambleys before he went out to see them.

He snatched a minute or two before he went downstairs to read that little letter from June again, and went down in answer to the dinner bell with a pleasant look on his face which his anxious mother observed and rejoiced over.

"And how about the Shambleys, Mother?" he asked. "Have you seen them lately?"

"Yes, I was up there this morning. They seem to be getting on all right, only Nannie is broken-hearted that her beloved teacher has gone away."

"Of course," said Paige in a tone of sympathy. "By the way, mother, do you have any idea when she is coming back?"

"Why no, her mother seemed to think it might be some time, as she has to stay there till her cousin is discharged from the Army. She's a Wac or a Wave or something."

"I see. Well, I wonder if you can find out her address for me? She wrote me a note saying she was called away but she failed to give me any address to reply, and I want to thank her for a poem she sent that I had asked for."

"Why of course I can get it for you," said the mother comfortably. She did her best to keep the satisfaction out of her voice. It certainly was nice that Paige wanted to write to a girl like June.

After dinner Paige took a quick drive up to the Shambleys and found to his joy that Mr. Shambley was working at his own garden, and he looked up with a smile to greet his benefactor.

"Well, sir, I got me a job. Whaddaya know about that?" he said. "I start to work a-Monday, down at the filling station, and it's good pay too. I think I can begin ta pay ye back pretty soon."

"Don't worry about that," grinned Paige. "I'm glad you've got a job. Are you sure you ought to begin so soon?"

"Yes, the doctor said it was all right," and his face fairly shone with new joy and vigor.

Paige talked cheerily with his protégé for a few minutes, took a brief glimpse of the little girl sitting up in her invalid chair by the window, talked a few minutes with the sad little mother, her face now wreathed with smiles, whistled for the boy and asked a few questions about the duties he had left for him to do when he went away, slipped him a silver dollar for any errands he might have to go on, and then hurried home. What he wanted to do now was to write to June. Going to Shambleys had made him doubly anxious to talk to her.

But as he turned in at the drive he saw the Chalmers' car drawing up in front of the house. He hurried to park his own car and lock the garage door. He wanted to get upstairs before anybody saw him, so that he wouldn't be interrupted. He made a dash for the back door, stole softly into the kitchen and slid up the back stairs cautiously. But even as he passed silently across the top of the front stairs he heard a voice and a laugh that filled him with disgust. That false laugh! And what had she come here for? Was it a message from her father? In which case he would have to see her of course. Or was it some of her own fool nonsense? In which case he would lie low and not see her.

And then he remembered his resolve on his journey homeward, to be a little more friendly with his employer's daughter. Perhaps he owed that to him, since Chalmers had gone out of his way to be nice to him that day.

However, he would at least wait until he was called.

So he stole into his own room and lay down on the bed silently in the dark, while the false laugh and chatter went gaily on belowstairs. He found himself wondering what his mother thought of Reva Chalmers.

II

JUNE arrived at Aunt Letitia's in the middle of the afternoon and was eagerly welcomed. She found her aunt very comfortable with a fine nurse, two maids in the kitchen, and her uncle hovering here and there trying his best to carry out the orders of his wife.

She went up to her room and while she was removing her hat and coat she looked around on the immaculate room, and told herself indignantly that there hadn't been any reason at all for sending for her. She understood all too well that she was supposed to be a kind of an overboss to see that the other servants did their work properly. She had all too definite memories of the last time she had spent a week in this house and how she was cross-examined every hour or two to find out if she had nagged every servant about the corners being dusted and a thousand other little things that were not really so important when the lady of the house was laid aside.

But June told herself this was not profitable thinking in which to indulge. She was a Christian girl and she had come to do a kindness to a fussy old woman who was unnecessarily particular, but as long as she felt she must do it it must be done in a Christian way, and not with grudging.

So she hurried down to visit with her aunt, and to go over with her the things she wanted done.

Pencil and pad were ready on the little table by her aunt's bed, and she went quickly to work.

"Now the first things in the morning are important to start the day well. I always insist on having the front porch and the front walk swept down the first thing before anybody goes by to criticise. Thomas usually does that, but now for sometime he had been off in the armed forces, so of course Betsey has had to take over, and it will be one of your first duties to see that it is not forgotten. And you mustn't neglect to speak sharply whenever one of the servants forgets or omits a duty. You will find that is always the best policy. Never be lenient. It doesn't pay."

June dutifully wrote down these orders, but her gentle lips drew tight in an uncontrollable effort not to look angry.

"Jane will do the cooking, including making the coffee which I find has to be watched, for she always insists on letting it perk too long and the coffee is utterly ruined. You will have to watch that, for no amount of telling does any good, and your uncle is apt to take Jane's part. He hates to have the coffee sent back to be made over.

"Betsey will wait at table and help Jane with the dishes, and she knows about when the napkins should be changed, but doesn't always do it, and so you will have to be vigilant about watching that. And in that little pile of papers on the table beside you, you will find the list showing when certain duties are due. Washing on Monday of course, ironing on Tuesday, cleaning silver and brass on Wednesday, sweeping on Thursday, baking on Friday. Washing smeary windows whenever they need it, and you will have to go around and investigate where it is needed, for I never saw a servant yet that wouldn't slip by a duty when she could. And of course you must watch the dust in the corners and under bureaus and beds, or they will look as if the very pigs lived here."

June wrote on, down the long list of trivial household duties, things her own mother had taught her when she was a child. Yet mother never had made a burden of them. June wondered again as she had wondered before how an intelligent woman could make so much of such trifles, and worry so, lest each fraction of an operation was not performed in its exact ordered time, even during her own illness.

But this was no way to begin her life here. This wasn't something she was doing just for Aunt Letitia. This was something that had to be done "as unto the Lord," and that called for a gentle quiet yielding to the rule desired. She must not despise her aunt for being particular, even if her own mother's house was just as neat and dainty as a flower, and that without half the effort, and no servants at all at present. Well, never mind. She was here, and while she stayed she would do her best, though her heart longed to be back home, doing her work in the church and Sunday school, looking after the poor and sick of the church, trying to help them all to a knowledge of the Lord Jesus.

So with a Christian smile on her face she went on down the long list. Now and again she attempted to get her aunt to curtail her directions, pleading that she must be getting too tired, but the inexorable woman went right on, saying that it was good for her, that she could sleep better if it was all understood, just what she wanted done.

At last the ordeal was over and June carried away her sheaf of notes and tried to smile, saying she hoped she would be able to be helpful in every way.

Then the aunt uttered a weary sigh and said she was quite sure all would be well "now that Junie was here." "Of course," she added, "*I* am always here, and you can come to me if you have any trouble with the servants, or forget anything I have told you."

At last June was free to wander about the house and yard and try to relax and get used to the idea that she was snatched away from the midst of a life she loved, in her home, doing Christian work in pleasant company, and dumped down in this strange town, among people she didn't know, and some she did know and didn't like. If her cousin were only at home it wouldn't be so hard. But if she were, there would of course be no reason for her to be here. Well, she would get adjusted pretty soon she supposed.

She wandered into the kitchen and got acquainted with Jane, and Betsey, and after a brief talk with them the orders she had received from Aunt Letitia didn't seem nearly so formidable. She was sure she would have no trouble in getting along with these servants.

Jane was frying chicken, and it looked and smelled delicious. She found she was very hungry after her long train ride.

Then suddenly Aunt Letitia's little silver bell sounded imperatively, and admonished by Jane with a quick grin and a frightened look in her eyes, June hurried in to see what was the matter.

"Was there something you wanted, Auntie?" she asked gently.

"Yes. It's that awful smell of frying. Something is burning, I'm sure. Is it chicken she is frying?"

"Yes, it is, and it looks perfectly delicious. Are you getting hungry, Aunt Letitia?"

"*Hungry?* My patience no!" snapped the old aunt. "Not with *that* smell in the air. What on earth is she frying it in? Surely not that new vegetable shortening? It never smells like that."

"Why no, she told me it was lard. She said she couldn't get any more vegetable fat and had to take lard."

"The very idea. Why I *never* have a drop of *lard* in my house. I haven't had for years. You'll have to go to the phone and call up and see if they won't send up some vegetable shortening immediately. Jane knows I can't eat things fried in lard. It gives me awful indigestion. Just call up Fresnoes. They'll have the kind I always get. It's the top number on the second row of grocers at the right of the phone."

But when June called the number they verified what Jane had said. There was no shortening to be had in town except lard, and very little of that.

"Well then try Hardings. But this is ridiculous! I never knew Fresnoes to run out of staples. It's most careless of them."

So June tried Hardings with the same result, except that they didn't even have lard.

Down through the whole list of stores June went, but there was no vegetable shortening to be had, and the poor sick lady was in despair.

Then the nurse appeared on the scene.

"You are getting too tired," she said to the patient. "The doctor would certainly object to this. I think you had better close your eyes and rest awhile before you eat your dinner."

"Eat!" snorted the old lady. "I don't feel as if I could ever eat another mouthful as long as I live with that awful smell going through the house. And I can't possibly eat chicken fried in *lard.*"

"Why can't we *broil* a bit of chicken for you, Aunt Letitia?" suggested June. "I saw they were quite young chickens. They'll be tender. I'll slip out and tell Jane."

"I never liked broiled chicken," said the crochety aunt, "and anyway it would be tough as an owl I'm sure."

"You just wait," said June with a smile. She hurried into the kitchen again and had a conference with Jane.

June was diplomatic and soon had Jane on her side, and they managed together a bit of tender broiled chicken fit for a queen. They prepared a pleasant-looking tray, which June ventured to carry in and present to her aunt.

"Well, it *looks* well enough," vouchsafed the grouchy old lady, "but I don't see how I can eat a bite with the odor of that awful lard in my lungs. However I'll try a bite if you think it isn't too tough."

So as last June coaxed the old lady to eat a good supper of delicious broiled chicken and hot biscuits with honey. She finished it all, though she didn't get as far as saying it was good.

"Well, June, you're a bright girl," she admitted grudgingly. "I knew if you came I'd be all right. But just see that we don't get out of vegetable shortening again."

"Well, I don't see how I'm to manage that, Aunt Letitia, if there isn't any in any of the stores," said June with a smile.

"Oh, I'm sure you'll find some *somewhere*. If they don't have it here you can run into the city market and get it, I'm sure."

When June finally got her own dinner she was almost too tired and disheartened to eat it, but she did her best to be cheerful and bring a smile to her uncle's troubled countenance.

When they came to say good-night he actually smiled and said: "You're a good girl, Junie. They didn't succeed in spoiling you in college at all. I'm glad you've come."

And with that bit of praise June went to a well-earned rest. But when the light was out and she lay on her pillow she shed a few tears, partly of loneliness, partly of despair at the look of the immediate future, and partly because she was homesick.

And back in the home town Paige wasn't having a very much better time, for he had listened till he was sure that the voice downstairs belonged to Reva Chalmers.

For a minute or two more he hoped against hope that the family didn't know that he had come in, and therefore they would not call him. Then he heard that vivid clarion voice proclaim, from what sounded very much like the hall at the foot of the front stairs. "Why, yes, I'm sure he must be here. I saw him drive into your driveway just before I parked my car. He's probably gone upstairs. Can't you call him? Won't you tell him I have a very important message from my father? If it's too much of a climb for you I'll run up and tell him myself," offered the girl.

"No," said Paige's long-suffering mother. "I'll see if he's there," and he heard her tramping slowly up the stairs.

Paige sprang up from the bed and came out grinning.

"Okay, mom," he whispered as he passed her. And then he discovered his caller standing at the foot of the stairs looking up.

"Yes," he said, trying to smile, but really frowning down at his pursuer, "did you have a message for me?"

"I certainly *did,*" she said running up three steps to meet him. "Dad sent this card of membership, University Club, you know. He said you wanted it right away and asked me to bring it to you tonight."

"Oh, really? That was kind of you," said Paige trying to be courteous. "But let's go downstairs. You don't want to stand there on the step. But it wasn't at all necessary for you to bring it tonight. I shall probably have no opportunity to use it at present, unless your father sends some customers to be fed. I could have just as well got it from him at the office. There was no hurry."

"Oh yes, there was," said Reva, slowly descending ahead of him, and looking up into his face. "You're going to have immediate opportunity to use it, because I'm asking you to take me to lunch there tomorrow. I have something very special to talk over with you."

Paige looked at her hopelessly. Was this girl going to pursue him everywhere, and how far must he go in acceding to her requests? He gave her a troubled look, and ran his hand over his forehead wearily.

"Why—I—am not sure—I can manage that tomorrow," he said, trying to stall for time.

"Oh, you needn't begin to make excuses," said the girl eagerly, "because you're *going* to take me. You see I asked dad if there was any reason why you couldn't, and he said no, not that he knew of, and that it would be a very nice way to christen your membership card. So, we're going, and I'll come for you at your office at exactly twelve o'clock. That's a date. And now, will you kindly come out and see what's the matter with my car? I can't get it started."

"Why certainly," said Paige. "That is if it's nothing serious.

I'm not exactly a mechanic. However there's a garage not far away and I'm sure they can fix you up if I can't."

"Oh, a garage," said the girl with a pout. "I don't want a greasy old mechanic fussing with my car. I'm sure you can fix it. Dad says you're very clever at everything."

Paige made no answer. He merely opened the front door for her and helped her down the steps. Reva, however, chattered all the way out to the car.

"What seems to be the matter?" asked Madison as they arrived at the car.

"Why, I'm sure I don't know. It was going all right on the way over, though I thought it was making a funny noise. I don't know anything about machinery. But when I stopped and was about to get out I saw I was pretty far away from the walk, and I put the key back in and fussed and fussed with it till I lost patience. I saw I couldn't get it started by myself, so I just left the key in it and came on in. I do hope you'll be able to fix it. I just hate to deal with strange men from a filling station."

Without answering, Paige swung into the driver's seat and snapped on the lights.

"Poor shabby old car," sighed Reva, in the tone that expects prompt denial. "Of course I've abused it horribly. I do hope it's not entirely out of commission, for if it is I know dad won't get me another for ages. He said that when he got this one."

Paige was working with the key, trying to turn it, rattling it gently. Then he pulled it out and examined it carefully, looked at the other keys on the same ring, chose another and slid it in, turned the ignition and the car responded promptly, with expensive tones of eagerness, as if it too recognized the trick that had been played.

"Why, you've *done* it!" exclaimed the girl. "I simply knew you could. What was the matter with it?"

"You were trying to use the wrong key," said the young man with a courteous grin in the dark.

"Was I? Oh, can you imagine it? Dad says I ought to have a nurse, and I believe he's right."

"It could be," said Paige under his breath, as he swung out of the car and stepped back for her to take the driver's seat.

"Well, I certainly thank you a lot," said Reva with satisfaction. "And now you'll get in and take a little ride with me won't you, just to show you've forgiven me for bothering you?"

"Sorry," said Paige, stepping back up the curb of the sidewalk. "I have some important letters to write that must get into the morning mail. I don't think you'll have any further trouble with your car. And thanks for bringing me the message from your father. Good-night!"

Making a wry face in the darkness, Reva stepped on the gas and swung off with a flourish, soon out of sight down the road, her tail lights twinkling wickedly at Paige. He gave an understanding little laugh like an answer to the wink of the lights, and hurried into the house,.

He grinned at his mother as he went through the hall.

"Some caller!" he said with a wink at his mother.

"Oh, Paige! And you have to take her to lunch! Did you *have* to do that?"

"Well, I didn't see how I could get out of it, Mother. Her father has just had me voted into the University Club, and sent me down the card. It's only fair that I take his daughter to lunch there once."

"Once?" said his mother with a sigh. "Oh, Paige, she's not your kind of a girl."

"Of course not, mom; I don't have to be told that. Don't you worry. But don't I have to be polite, especially since her father gives me a job?"

"Why, of course, I suppose you do, Paige, but I do wish she were a different kind of a girl. Perhaps you can help her to be."

"Not much chance of that, moms. I'm sure you can see that."

"Well, not very hopeful material to work on," sighed the mother. "Still, people do change."

"Mebbe," said the young man, and then he stooped and kissed his mother. "Good-night. I want to write a letter. Did you get that address for me, moms?"

"Oh, yes, here it is," said his mother brightening, and producing a neatly folded paper.

So Paige went up to his room to write his letter to June.

12

IT was with a sense of deep peace and contentment that Paige read over the cherished letter which he had worn in his pocket ever since its receipt. And if his mother had been able to see the smile in his eyes as they lingered on those hastily penned words, she would not have sighed so deeply, nor lain awake anxiously praying quite so long.

Paige got up soon and went to his desk. There was a sweet thoughtfulness on his face, and one might almost have fancied that he was sitting opposite to June looking into her eyes as he wrote rapidly.

Dear June:

I have been having a wonderful experience and all the way home I had been planning to *tell* you about it. And then when I reached home I found only a bit of a note with the news that you were away indefinitely.

I confess I was somewhat stunned. I was sort of counting on the talk we had promised each other. But then all this mix-up occurred that sent us wildly off in different directions.

Probably it didn't matter so much to you, but to me

it was very upsetting, for I really was in need of advice and help along the lines in which we had been talking, and I was in haste to get home and have that talk.

Well, it seems that God knew my need, and sent me a strange kind of help, of which your little poem (for which I sincerely thank you) was a part. But I am getting ahead of my story.

I would so much rather *tell* you this by word of mouth instead of writing it, but I feel the need of telling someone, and I feel that you will understand, as we had talked of these things.

You see I was sent out to foreclose some mortgages and I hated the very thought of it.

He paused to think just how he would tell the story. Then his pen went rapidly on.

He wrote a few words about the first two houses where he visited, described briefly the kindly act of the fellow-laborer on the road, lending the money to one who did not seem to be even his friend, and then went on to describe how he came to walk into the Washburn funeral unaware.

I stood there startled, and looked down into that casket, shocked, and wondering how I could get out without making a scene.

There in that simple casket I saw an elderly man with white hair, and one of the most kindly saint-like faces I have ever seen. And I had come there to foreclose a mortgage on his home, and probably bring sorrow and humiliation on his household.

I felt ashamed and deeply troubled. Somebody offered me a vacant chair and I dropped into it greatly shaken. When I looked up again I saw that God was standing there beside the casket as if He were waiting to take that old saint Home.

Someone was praying and I shut my eyes but God

was still standing there. I could see Him, even with my eyes shut. It was the strangest thing that ever happened to me. It seemed that God was searching my soul, telling me all the wrong I had ever done. I never had my life turned inside out that way before, not even when I was about to face death in battle.

Maybe you will think I am crazy, but that same God came home with me on the train. And He has been beside me ever since in everything I do.

I thought that you might like to know that I have at last surrendered to Him, fully, I think, as you said. I think I can now honestly say, "I am crucified with Christ" the way you told me. And ever since, I've had that peace and rest that your poem talks about. It's a joy such as I never felt before.

And why am I telling you this?

Because you have been the one who introduced me to this subject, and pointed the way, and I felt sure you would understand. I knew you would be glad that I have met your Lord, and have surrendered.

I have been to see the Shambleys. They seem to be getting well fast, and the father has a job. The doctor has okayed it, and he starts Monday in a filling station.

It is getting late for I have been interrupted since I came home, but I'll be so glad to know what you think about this, if you have time to write me. Was this experience I had something real, or a figment of an overworked imagination?

But even if you think it isn't real, I *know it is,* because I have felt Him near me all day long. And I think you led me to the place where I could understand when I saw Him at that funeral service.

Thank you for writing me, and I hope you're coming home soon. Please write again soon.

Paige

Paige went to sleep soon after that, feeling as if he had just had a talk with June. His spirit was soothed and content. And it was not until the next morning as he was getting ready for the day that he remembered his luncheon date with Reva Chalmers. It hung over him like a pall, obstructing the sunshine that his new spiritual experience had shed on his soul.

About the middle of the morning it suddenly came to him that his great peace that had been with him since he went to Boston had fled. Was it not true then that this peace had come to stay? What had he done to drive it away?

What was that they had said, that Christ brought a power out of the tomb when He rose from the dead, and His own surrendered ones had a right to claim it? Ah! He would claim it.

For an instant he bowed his head on his lifted hand, closed his eyes, and prayed.

"Oh Lord, this thing is depressing me so! Please undertake for me. Be with me while it goes on, that I may do the thing that is pleasing to Thee."

Paige was ready for her when she came, and they went out together, the observed of the whole outer office. But there was something grave and dignified about the young man that almost overawed the daring girl, who was so accustomed to doing whatever came into her head, without consideration of anybody else.

Paige had a taxi waiting to take them to the University Club, though it wasn't far away, and they were soon seated in the pleasantest corner of the big stately room. It was a corner where two windows met, overlooking the city park on one side and the busy shopping district on the other. Paige had noticed it when Mr. Chalmers took him to the club, and decided that that was the most attractive as well as the most secluded spot in the whole place. Therefore he was pleased that they found the table unoccupied.

Paige had not been a society man to any extent, but his

home training, and his experiences on the other side of the
sea, had given him an easy manner, free from self-conscious-
ness, and Reva was surprised at the smooth way in which he
managed the simple affair. There wasn't an awkward minute
that the girl had to cover with some flip remark. In fact her
father would have been surprised if he could have watched the
little scene and seen how almost embarrassed the girl herself
appeared to be at times. For this young man whom she had
selected to bait for her own amusement turned out to be anything but the gauche youth she had fancied him to be. Of
course she had known little of him before her father brought
him into the scene, but his very quiet gravity, and his lack of
response to her gay modern lures, had made her think that he
would be easy prey. But now against her wishes she was being made to feel that he was very, very much older and wiser
than she, that he was a young man of wide experience, not
afraid of anybody or anything, and that he was going out of
his way now to be nice to her for her father's sake and not for
any wiles of her own.

Before she had quite got her bearings and decided what her
line was to be, he opened conversation with a string of bright
jokes, so high above the ones she might have chosen that
some of them she had to think hard to understand, though she
managed to give a surprised laugh a little delayed, for each
one. He was bright, he really was, though in a more distinc-
tive way than the young men she knew. It almost seemed as if
she were discovering that he was some wise professor who
was stooping to amuse her, or humor her, and she actually felt
almost inferior as the talk went on. It was a long time since
anyone had ever made Reva Chalmers feel in the least inferior.

Quite casually he asked her what was her college, and she
rattled off a list of fashionable finishing schools where she had
been endured for brief terms till she passed on to others. But
she saw to her amazement that he was not at all impressed.
Quite easily he began to ask her questions about where she

had been and what she had done, until little by little he had reversed the role she had intended him to play. He was exerting himself to be nice to her, to be really interesting, and as she watched him and saw the pleasant lights in his handsome eyes she began to admire him, and to think he was really worth angling for.

The ease with which he managed the ordering without any of the quips and sallies that accompanied that act in her crowd, just as if it were an everyday matter and not one of great moment, gave her again a respect for his judgment. And the way he took control of the conversation and sent it along any lines he chose was another thing. She was accustomed to take matters of that sort into her own hands, and now every time when she tried it she was checkmated, by some interesting incident of war, or travel, or even college life that completely frustrated her.

To the girl it was a new experience, like a new game she was trying to play in which Paige was always one ahead.

To Paige it was like a commission to be fought out, in which he must win, but afterwards he realized that he could not have won without the help of that new power into possession of which he had so recently come. He was really fighting this luncheon out as if it were a battle in which he must win, even to death. It was as important as that. It wasn't something he liked, and enjoyed, but there was a delight in feeling that he had done this in the right power.

He had the feeling that he was working in cooperation with his new Guide. Though of course he hadn't been talking religion nor trying to teach this girl anything, just interesting her in a new line of topics that had not come her way before.

There would come a time in Paige's life when he would realize that every Christian was here on the earth to do one thing, to witness for Christ, and he would be looking for such an opportunity, knowing that he must await orders before he attempted a word. Paige had not yet reached the point in his new life where he could understand that, but he was witnessing just as truly, perhaps all the more, because unconsciously.

So he led along with stories of battles, stories of braveries, stories of perils and storms at sea, brief stories of sadness, and found his audience had ceased to grin and sneer, and was listening wide-eyed.

Then suddenly their hour was over. It was time for him to go back to the office, and he led a subdued and very admiring girl out to the office building again, and bade her good-by.

She roused at the parting, and grew vivacious again.

"And how about taking me to the dance Saturday night? It's going to be a gorgeous affair, and I just know you'd make a wonderful dancer."

"No dancing, thank you, and no time for affairs of that sort. I have a lot of other things to do."

"But don't you ever have fun? Surely you must have *some* recreation. You can't live without that."

"Well, there are different kinds of pleasure of course. But a grown person can't give so much time to it."

"But what do you do when you want to have fun?" she asked with a puzzled frown.

"Well, I like exercise of course. Things like tennis and golf, horseback riding, but those take time too, and one has to be careful about taking time out from real things. Do you play tennis or golf?"

"Oh, yes," she answered with a shrug, "but I guess I'm too lazy for much exercise. I'd love riding I guess, only dad doesn't want me to ride. I'm sure I don't see why."

"Well, I'll take you on for a set of tennis sometime if you like."

"Okay! When?" she seized the idea with alacrity.

"Tomorrow if you like, in the afternoon. The office is closed on Saturday afternoon, and I can take a couple of hours. Say two o'clock. Where would you like to play?"

"Oh, the country club, I suppose," she said thoughtfully. "But two hours isn't much. We might finish up by coming to our house for dinner, and then going to a night club afterwards."

"Sorry," said Paige, "I wouldn't have time for a program like that. Saturday happens to be a rather busy day. I've just promised to take a class of boys in the Sunday School, and I have to get ready for that. I've been away from such things so long that I'm rather rusty on Bible teaching."

"Bible teaching!" ejaculated Reva aghast. "Why do you bother with dull things like that? Why don't you tell your boys some of those stories you've been telling me? They would adore that."

Paige grinned.

"I may use some of those stories perhaps. There's many a lesson in them of how to be saved and how to live a Christian life."

"Well, I think you are hopeless! I don't see how you make the grade living like that. But all right, I'll play tennis Saturday afternoon, and I'll meet you at the country club at two."

And so they parted.

Then with a great load off his mind he went back to his desk and did a good afternoon's work, satisfied that the Lord had taken over and helped him through the ordeal of the luncheon. As he thought it over it hadn't been so bad. And he had an idea that that girl was teachable and might even develop into something bearable, even pleasant, if she had the right environment and less money, but *he* did not want to be her *teacher*. She got on his nerves.

The day passed quickly, and closing time saw his work pretty well caught up. He would be ready to begin a clean slate the next morning. He got away early, for he had no notion of being held up by Reva again. There were things at home he must attend to, and he was anxious to see if there was any mail at the house for him. Of course it was too soon for June to have received his letter, but she might just have written another letter on her own account. Although, being

June, and not Reva, she would never have done so except under dire necessity. She would never be one to put herself forward.

On his way home he stopped at a florist's and bought his mother a plant of beautiful roses in bloom that he knew she wanted. Then he went home, presented his offering, gathered up his mother and June's mother and took them up for a quick visit to the Shambleys, and came back to the nice chicken potpie dinner to which both the Culbertsons had been invited.

That was a pleasant interval. He sat nearly all the evening afterwards, downstairs in the living room talking with both the fathers and mothers, and enjoying himself hugely. He liked June's mother and father, and he could see how she had grown to be the kind of girl she was, with home influences like those. He enjoyed listening to his father and Mr. Culbertson discuss some point of doctrine in their church.

And now as he listened and saw the great love of the Lord shining in both their faces, almost a glory light, he suddenly realized that God Himself was sitting in their midst, as if He enjoyed being with them. Was it possible that God could enjoy human beings? Was that why He had made them, to be His companions? He had a passing memory of that dead face in the coffin. That man had been one of those, he felt sure. He would have enjoyed sitting here with these men, talking as they were talking, loving their Lord. And Paige was humbly glad that he was one with them.

They went early and Paige lingered a little longer with his mother and father. When he went up to his room he looked up that verse about being crucified with Christ, and read the whole chapter, realizing how very little he knew of the Bible after all. He must fix a time every day for reading it. He must learn more about it than just the simple facts that he had been taught as a child. For now he began to realize that there was much more to the Bible than just those facts that everybody knew, and no one heeded. And June knew them.

13

JUNE was very happy when she received Paige's letter. She had thought he would be polite enough to thank her perhaps, though her first brief note did not require it, but she had not anticipated that he would write a long letter, and evidently expect her to write again. He who had a lot of friends of course, and especially that pretty wealthy girl who evidently liked him a lot.

And such a letter as he had written! Oh, she had been praying for him of course, that he might find the light on the problems he had talked about with her. But somehow her faith had not been strong enough to expect *such* an answer. He had really seen the Lord in his very soul or he would never have written her all that.

His letter greatly comforted her, for she had been through a hard day of fault-finding by Aunt Letitia; and grumbling on the part of the servants, and she was well nigh on the point of giving up and going home. She was watching every mail and hoping that there would be a word from her cousin that she would soon arrive. So Paige's letter came like a breeze from another world, a sort of a heavenly world where real things were still going on, and God was still caring for His own.

Aunt Letitia had had a bad time that day, and cried out with pain, scolded her nurse, and finally sent for June to come and read to her.

June was hoping she would want some Bible reading, but no, the crochety old person wanted a mystery story and June must needs walk to the village to get some new ones, with a full list of the many she had already read, so there would not be duplicates.

Back at the house the aunt was moaning. Her pain was worse. She insisted on having the doctor at once, and he was out in the country on a critical case and could not come. And now Aunt Letitia refused to look at the books June had selected, refused to hear any reading now, and set up more complaints. She sent June to the attic to search out a soft old blanket which she said was lighter than those they had put over her, but which after long searching could not be found. Then Jane remembered that her mistress had given that blanket to the missionary society to send abroad to the people who were starving and freezing, but Aunt Letitia could not remember that, declared it was not so, and sent June to look for it again. So June was tired when after the long futile search she came back to her room to rest. She read Paige's letter over again, and rejoiced in it. Tonight, if there was any time at all left to herself, she would answer it.

And Paige, the same night, was thinking of her, wishing he could get up right then and write another letter to her telling of the delightful evening he had enjoyed getting acquainted with her parents.

But of course it was too soon for him to write her again. He would have to wait and see if she would answer his other letter. Maybe she would think it had been fanciful. Though he knew in his heart she wouldn't think that. She was too much like that sweet mother of hers to get any such idea from his letter.

When Paige got up to a new day the next morning it came upon him heavily that he had promised to play tennis with

Reva Chalmers. Well, he must put it out of mind until the time came, and not let himself grow miserable over it. He had work to do, and he would take the tennis in his stride and not make so much of it. He had always enjoyed tennis and if Reva was a tolerably good player it ought not to bore him too much. Forget it, he told himself.

So he was in fairly good humor when he met Reva at the country club, racket in hand, arrayed in immaculate garments and trying to smile as if he were looking forward to the event with pleasure.

Reva proved to be a fairly good player, and gave him a stiff opposition, as long as she lasted, but when they reached the end of a set she professed to be weary and wanted to sit down and rest. What she really wanted was a chance for a good flirtation, and Paige had no mind for resting, so he sat down for five minutes and then said:

"Come. We are wasting our strength. We were just getting warmed up for a good fight. Let's get back to work again. You play a good game. You'll soon get your second wind and won't feel tired."

So they went back to playing and Reva found very little opportunity to talk.

When they had finished their two hours Paige escorted her down to the club, declined the offer of drinks, or other refreshments, and hurried away.

"You know I told you I had other things to do," he said with a farewell smile.

"Oh, just *Bible*! That's silly on a lovely day like this. Let the old Bible go and have a good time with me," she pleaded.

"Sorry, I couldn't," he said. "But I thank you for the game and maybe sometime if I get time we'll try it again. You can bring some of your other friends along to take over when I have to stop."

Reva sat gloomily on the club veranda and took a drink. Then she slammed into her car and whizzed off in search of a more peppy game. She wasn't sure but this guy was just a waste of time. There were plenty of other fellows who were ready to join in with any whim she happened to have, and didn't have to go off and study a Bible! Well, he was intriguing, of course, and stunningly handsome, and he certainly could smash the tennis balls across the net, and beat her every time. Anyway she could always use him for a filler-in, any time her regular dates failed. But really he would be worth cultivating if she could ever get a chance to cultivate him. Perhaps she and dad could do something clever for a vacation and rope him in to go along. So Reva went home to think up something devilish and plan how she could get her father to help her work it out. If dad told Paige that he needed him for some work this summer, he would have to go along wherever they chose to go, wouldn't he? Well, she would see what she could do about it, for she certainly didn't intend to let a little old religious notion or two spoil her fun, and she certainly meant to win over this reluctant swain.

Meantime Paige went home and after a refreshing shower went into a deep study of the Bible, specializing on the Sunday School lesson for the morrow, and then went to his knees in further preparation. This was his first opportunity for what was usually called real witnessing, and he wanted to make it count for the young souls who were to be put under his care for a time.

As he rose from his knees he looked out the window toward the Culbertson house and gave a wistful sigh. How he would enjoy a talk with June now! He would like so to talk over that Bible lesson and see what she thought on different points. She had a wonderful way with young people. Witness that Shambley kid. She could wind him right around her finger. She would know whether his plans were wise. Well, that was silly thinking. She wasn't here, and he had no right whatever to be making her the center of his thoughts, just because they had spent a couple of days in company working for the Shambleys. June probably had some intimate friends off there where she had gone, perhaps some very special friend, and she would soon forget that he, Paige Madison, existed. Well, that was that. If she ever wrote again he would know how to think of her. But at present he knew in his heart that she was the finest girl he had ever met so far. The most beautiful too. Reva wasn't to be compared to her, and it had not taken that afternoon of tennis to show him that. Of course he had never played tennis with June, but what difference did that make? If she did not play tennis already he would teach her to like it, that is if he ever got the chance, or if she didn't like it he didn't really care. He would certainly rather talk with June than with a brainless girl like Reva.

Then suddenly he called himself to order. What was he doing? Thinking about a girl he scarcely knew as if he were going to have opportunity to spend his life having a good time with her, when in reality he wasn't sure of ever seeing her again. He must get his mind off girls of all kinds and get this Sunday School lesson ready to hold the attention of those new boys, boys that he didn't know at all, and who very likely might not have any use for him.

So back he went to his study, and finally to his knees.

"Something else, dear Lord, that You need to take over. Just my wandering thoughts and hopes. Help me to lay them all at Thy disposal."

A little later in the evening Paige got into his car and took a turn up to the Shambleys just to have a few minutes' talk with Mr. Shambley and make sure he would take a thorough rest on Sunday, because Monday he was starting to work. There wasn't any need of it of course, but Paige was restless and wanted to get his mind away from himself and his various problems. So he talked with Mr. Shambley, and gained his confidence still more than before. During the talk more information concerning Harris Chalmers and Company came to the surface, and the impression of them that he had had from the first grew more unsettling than before. Of course Mr. Shambley was not a good judge of character, and was in a position to be prejudiced against the firm that had made life so hard for him of late, but after all it could not be denied that the firm he now worked for was *hard*. They might not be dishonest, they might not overstep the law, but they certainly were *hard*. Did a business firm have to be hard, unfeeling, unkind, in order to be successful? It suddenly came to him that he wished he could be in some kind of business for himself, and try it out.

There had to be business in the world, of course, and it had to have success or it could not be carried on, but did it have to be *hard*?

And did a Christian have any right to be hard? He had to be wise and use judgment of course, but when a man got into a tight corner did he have to be treated with almost cruelty? If he only had some money he certainly would like to go into business and try out some of his theories that were being developed.

He drove slowly, took quite a detour while he thought out these matters, and when he finally reached home his mother called to him from upstairs. For once she had not sat up for him. At least she had started to bed.

"Paige, Miss Chalmers called up twice, and said it was very important."

"Yes, I was afraid of that," grinned Paige. "I'm sure it was not important. Don't worry."

"And Paige, there's a letter for you, special delivery airmail. It came just a few minutes ago."

"A letter! Where is it?"

"Right there on the hall table. Do you find it, dear?"

"Yes, I have it, thank you, Mother, and —good-night!"

Paige came leaping up the stairs with the letter in his hand, and a shining in his face. His precious letter. It had come, and she had sent it special delivery! That showed, didn't it, that she knew how much he needed a word from her?

It was sometime afterward that that thought came to him again and he wondered at himself for having dared to think it. Yet it had given him a very welcome assurance. This was a matter of his Christian experience and he had asked her a serious question about whether it could possibly be real, or whether he was letting his imagination run wild. And he needed to know what she thought before he went to teach that new Sunday School class. So he need not condemn himself for thinking too much about June. She was a Christian friend, and there was nothing foolish about his feeling for her. They were merely new friends who had discovered they thought in the same way about spiritual things.

Then he turned on the light and sat down to read his letter.

And about that time Reva Chalmers was accosting her father who had just come into the house.

"Dad, I played tennis with your handsome assistant manager today, and do you know, I think he's sweet, and it really would be quite easy to humanize him. I got a start on him this afternoon, and I think he already likes me a lot. If you'll give me the job of educating him I believe I could make him quite easy for you to manage. You know all he needs is to get rid of some of his sentimentality and he'd be a fine businessman, ready for the hardest proposition you could hand him."

Oh, Reva was clever, and she knew exactly what her father wanted of Paige Madison, and just how he had failed in her father's scheme of business matters. She knew also how to get around her father so that he would eventually listen to her and see that her suggestion was not only wise but altogether interesting from more than one point of view.

"Oh? You don't say! And how could you bring all that about?" asked her father. His tone was sarcastic, amused. So he often humored his daughter's suggestions for the time being, and on occasion he found them to be worth trying.

"Well, come on and sit down in your big chair, daddy, and I'll tell you all about it. This is a real plan, daddy, and I'm sure it will work if you'll just back me up in it. And I have a nice cold drink in here for you. Come on, daddy."

So she cajoled her father into his big easy chair, put a cool little kiss on his forehead, and a cold frosty glass into his hand,

and then she settled down on a low hassock in front of him.

"Now, let's hear what your proposition is!" said the father, with an amiable smile.

So Reva began her story.

"Why, you see, dad, I've been getting quite a line on Paige Madison since you let me take that membership card for the University Club to him. He took me to lunch the next day, and he really was not half bad! He can talk, daddy, that guy can talk, when he wants to! And I believe all he needs is to get a different point of view. You see he hasn't been brought up the way we were. He doesn't know the ways of good society and he needs to be taught. I think I could teach him if I had half a chance to be with him enough. And that's where you come in, dad. You've got to give me a chance."

Her father grinned.

"I should think that was up to you, Reva. You seem to be able to get enough other young fellows around you without my assistance. I never heard you call for my help in that direction."

"Yes, but dad, he's very special, you know, and he thinks he's so awfully wise and grown up. And when you have to make a man practically over before you can do anything with him, you certainly do need help. Besides, dad, he's all hemmed around with ideas."

"Ideas? What kind of ideas?"

"Well, old fogy kind of ideas. He can't do this and he can't do that, and he won't do the other thing, and he seems to think it's practically wicked to have a good time. So if I'm going to make him over I've got to get him out of that idea. Don't you see how much more valuable he'll be to your business if I do? He's simply got to get so he can—what's that thing you say?—be all things to all men you know. He's got to get to be a good society man, rejoice with them that do rejoice. That's one Bible verse I learned that day you made me go to Sunday School when I didn't want to. But now, why he couldn't do that at all. He's glum as an owl most of the time when I see him."

"Why, I thought he was rather a pleasant young man. He has a nice smile."

"Oh, yes, when he uses it, but most of the time he doesn't. And I'm beginning to find out why he's that way. Dad, do you know what he's doing tonight, and what he's planning to do tomorrow, why he can't accept any of the invitations I've given him? Dad, he's going to teach a Sunday School class of boys tomorrow; and tonight he's studying his *Sunday School lesson!* Can you imagine that? For a full-grown man, and one that's been to war too?"

"Well, that's a commendable thing to do, isn't it?" asked the grinning father. "I was asked to take a class in Sunday School once myself. Of course I didn't do it. But it shows what good people think of the young man when they ask him to do that. It won't hurt his reputation a bit."

"Oh, *that!* What's reputation? But you couldn't expect a young man to mingle in good society if all he does for recreation is study the Bible. Why, my teachers in school, practically all the teachers in all the schools I ever attended, said that the Bible was an antiquated book, and practically *nobody* believed in it any more. And just fancy any businessman getting his education out of the Bible nowadays!"

"Well, they do claim there's some very wise sayings in the Bible," said Mr. Chalmers amusedly. "I suppose he could do worse. But I don't understand just what all this has to do with me. What did you want me to do about it? I can't call Paige Madison into my office Monday morning and tell him I don't want him to read the Bible any more, can I?"

"Oh, you silly! Of course not. But you can get him away from here on a vacation, and arrange it so I can come with you, and get a chance to work on him. Now dad, don't you begin to say no. You haven't given this enough thought yet. You are all tired out, aren't you? And didn't I hear you say you needed to get away and rest somewhere? And you said too that you couldn't get away from your business. But why couldn't you take your business with you? Take Paige along and let him write letters for you. He types, I know, for I saw him doing it the other day. That of course would be the only way you could lure him away with you, by telling him you weren't well and the doctor wanted you to have a change of air, and you would need him to go along with you. Then a few days later I would come down, wherever you want to go. I'd vote for the seashore. You know I adore swimming, and I'd work on him between whiles when he wasn't taking dictation for you. How about it, dad. Don't you think that's a good idea?"

The father smiled with a humoring look in his eyes.

"Could be," he said. "I'll think it over, and meantime you run along and get together your ideas and see whether you think it would really work."

As it turned out, Reva kept at her father persistently, and at Paige also, trying to get another tennis game, or a dinner date, and at last Mr. Chalmers yielded his opposition.

"All right, work away at him, and I'll see what I can do, but I doubt whether he'll go. He isn't hired for a stenographer or secretary and he may balk at the idea."

"But he's working for you, isn't he? Doesn't he have to do what you say, or you could fire him, couldn't you? Isn't he important to you?"

"He will be I hope after a while when I get him trained."

"Well then, couldn't you make this work out?"

"I suppose I could," laughed the father. "Well, run along puss, and we'll see what can be done. I suppose there is something in your idea, and at least it will give you a decent somebody to run around with—I won't have to sit up nights worrying about where you are, and whether you are staying out too late. It probably won't last very long with you, for I have a hunch you can't wind that young man around your little finger, even if you do get him off at the shore by himself where you can work on him."

"You'll be surprised, daddy, what I can do when I get a chance," said Reva coyly.

So Harris Chalmers went to his office and began to study maps, and make reservations at a favorite seaside resort, and ostentatiously sent for his doctor to come to the office so that the whole working staff would know he had been there. And afterwards he sent for Paige Madison.

14

WHEN Paige got the message that he was to come to the office at eleven o'clock that morning he frowned. Now what was going to happen? Another foreclosing trip? Because he simply wouldn't do it. If that was the kind of thing they were going to do with him every little while, nothing doing! There certainly were other jobs in the city and there was no reason why he couldn't find one if he made a business of looking for it.

So he put his desk in order, gave last directions to his secretary about the letters he had been dictating, and went to meet Mr. Chalmers.

He found the boss in a most amiable mood, so he was not probably going to find fault about anything.

Paige sat down in the chair the boss indicated, and prepared for orders. After a pleasant morning greeting Mr. Chalmers began, with a smiling face, as if he were about to confide in a close friend.

"Well, Madison," he said in a confidential tone, "I've just had a visit from my doctor." He paused to let that sink in.

"Doctor?" said Paige with a concerned polite lifting of the

eyebrows. What next, he wondered. Was the business about to fold up and was he being dismissed? "Why, sir, are you sick?"

"Well, not exactly sick," said the boss apologetically. "This is more a matter of prevention. There were certain symptoms that I knew ought to be checked up, and I found it was a wise thing. You know if you take a thing in time you can prevent almost any ill that human flesh is heir to."

"Yes, I suppose so," Paige answered, still puzzling over why he had been called into this intimate conversation. "But I wouldn't have supposed you had anything the matter with you. You always look so well."

"Well, yes, I still look that way, but it doesn't take long when anything goes wrong. However, the doctor thinks he can put me in shape soon if I'll do exactly as he says."

"Oh!" thought Paige. "This was probably a dismissal then, or else a plea for him to take over some disagreeable duty while his head was gone somewhere, to a hospital or sanitarium, or something."

But the pleasant cajoling voice went on.

"He wants me to spend some weeks at the shore, and to go at once; that is, within a few days."

"Oh?" said Paige trying to sound sympathetic. "But that sounds like a pleasant cure."

"Well, yes, it does sound that way, but you see, Madison, it means going away from my business, just now in a critical time. And just when Bill Arsdel has gone on that trip which is likely to take three months if he makes all the contacts I advised."

"Yes, I see," said Paige politely. Somehow he was going to be made to fit into this puzzle he supposed, but he failed to see how. He was only a *new assistant manager*.

"No, I don't suppose you do just see," smiled the boss, "but of course I couldn't go away without taking some of my business along. And as the doctor absolutely refused to have me write letters, and do the actual manual labor of carrying on what business I must do, I've got to take someone with me who is capable of doing these things for me. I was wondering about you, Madison? Would you like to go along with me? I remember you told me you could run a typewriter so there wouldn't be anything of that sort you couldn't do, and it would be a nice vacation for you. You wouldn't find the work too strenuous. Plenty of time for swimming and reading. I might even take you on for a few holes of golf, if the doctor is willing. And anyhow, when I don't feel up to it you can always pick up a good player on the links. Well, how about it? Does it appeal to you? Would you enjoy going?"

"Where are you going?" asked Paige thoughtfully.

"Well, I'm not sure yet. I'd thought of some fashionable resort where my wife would enjoy coming to see me now and then."

"Oh, isn't Mrs. Chalmers going with you?"

"No. Not at present. The doctor seems to think I would be better off without anyone who would get nervous over me."

"I see," said Paige, and was still again. At last he asked, "Then you would be alone over the Sundays, would you?"

"Why certainly not. Not if I had you along."

"Well, I'm sorry Mr. Chalmers, but I wouldn't be able to go with you then. I have duties on Sunday that would keep me practically all day."

"Duties?" shouted Chalmers. "What duties could you possibly have that would hinder you going with your employer for a little while?"

"Sorry, Mr. Chalmers, but I have. I would have to be at home on Sundays, and I can't possibly arrange anything else at present. Wouldn't you have someone who could come down and stay with you Sundays? Saturdays and Sundays. I would like to leave at noon on Saturday. That is, if you are going to be near enough to home for me to get here by Saturday evening."

They talked for a long time, but got nowhere. Chalmers tried to sneer and bully him out of his decision, but Paige still insisted that he was not willing to give up his Sundays. He would be glad to go with Mr. Chalmers during the week, but he must get home for Sundays. There were a number of obligations that he must fulfill at home, and no, he didn't feel that he was at liberty to get out of any of those obligations.

At last Chalmers sat disgusted. He had gone out of his way to be nice to this bull-headed boy and could get nowhere with him.

"I suppose it's some *girl*!" he said with an unpleasant sneer, at last.

Paige looked at him almost sadly and shook his head.

"No, it's not a girl," he answered. "If it were I might be able to do something about it. But it isn't. It's something I promised God I'd do!"

"Something you promised *God* you'd do? *Thunder!*" fairly shouted Chalmers. "That's about the most ridiculous alibi I ever heard. If you have access to God so you can make promises to Him, I'd like to know why you can't just go and tell Him, or send word to Him, or however you do a thing like that, that you'll have to be excused from that promise for a while. Say you'll do it in the fall when you get home from your vacation. Tell Him you're really *needed* to take care of a poor sick man. That ought to appeal to Him. This making bargains with God and then thinking you have to stick to them doesn't seem to me to be a rational thing. How did you know what duty was going to come up that would hinder you?"

"It has," said Paige firmly, "I can't be away this summer on Sundays. If you want me on that condition I'll be with you every day on weekdays, but I can't undertake the job on any other condition."

His employer narrowed his eyes and watched him keenly for a full minute and then he said sharply:

"Not if I pay you well for it?"

Paige looked at him with those steady eyes of his, and a smile of those firm lips, and said:

"Money would have nothing whatever to do with the question."

Chalmers put on an amused quizzical look.

"Do you honestly think God is such a hard master as all that, Madison, that He wouldn't be willing for you to have a little vacation during the summer months?"

"No," said Paige with a smile, "I don't think He is a hard Master. I don't think He is nearly so hard a master as you are, for instance—" he said it with a pleasant smile. "But I know that these things He wants me to do are pleasing to Him, and it means a great deal to me to keep my promises to Him."

"And what about me?" asked Chalmers, putting on a pitiful pleading look. "Me, a poor sick man, your employer, to whom you owe a certain amount of help and comfort. What about me?"

Paige looked up with another grin.

"Mr. Chalmers, what would you want me for on Sundays? You don't have your employees work on Sunday here at home in the office. You know there's nothing in the world I could do on Sundays that would be of any help to you. And God knows it too. So I'm afraid you'll have to get someone else to go with you unless you're willing to take me on those terms."

There was silence in the office for some minutes while the two men sat and surveyed each other, and at last the employer said with a sigh:

"Well, Madison, I've been hiring men to help me for a good many years, and some of them have been extraordinarily good fellows, but I'll own you are the first one who ever attempted to dictate terms *to me*. They generally were glad to get *my* terms, and they never lost out by it either. But I guess this time you win. I'll say this however. Maybe as the days go by down by the sea you'll change your mind and want to stay, Sundays and all. If you do, will you let me know?"

"Oh, certainly. But I know I won't change my mind."

When Paige went home and told his mother about the proposition his employer had made she looked troubled, but her eyes shone as he went on to tell of their conversation and how her boy had stuck by his principles and had not been afraid to talk about God as if he knew Him. And when she was praying for him that night she went on to thank God for the way He was leading Paige. But she added a wistful petition or two that he might not get interested in that rich girl, and that her Lord would please to send June home soon.

That night when Reva got her father in a corner of his library by himself and asked the outcome of his interview that day she was greatly disappointed at the outcome.

"Dad, I don't think you do as well with that stubborn guy as I do. I don't believe you kept at him long enough."

"Yes, I kept at him all right," said her father. "Oh, I kept at him till I fairly hung my head with shame. I never did coax anyone to work for me before, and I declare I never will again, not even if *you* ask me again. I kept at him till he put me up and compared me with God, and then I was licked. What a guy he is! I've never met his like before."

"Well, you see, dad, that's why I want you to get him. There aren't any like him and I'd like to conquer him and make him do what we want him to do, and *like* it. And then when we get tired of him we can always drop him like a hot cake if he acts up any time. See, dad?"

"Yes, I see. But I don't think you do. That fellow has what you call strength of character, and whether you think he's right or not in his conclusions, you'll have to have at least as much strength of character as he has to win him, and I don't believe *you* have, kitten. You're plenty stubborn and set in your way, but that's not strength, that's usually founded in weakness, and selfishness, and this man hasn't a selfish hair in his whole make-up. I can't help but admire him a lot, even when he makes me mad as a hatter."

"Well, but dad, I may not have strength of character as you call it, but I've got something else. They call it glamour now-adays, and you wait till I try my glamour on him. He's not had a chance to come in contact with that much. Wait till we go out to a few dances and I sport all my lovely evening frocks. Wait till we go swimming together, and he maybe has to rescue me a couppla times."

"Look out, baby! Don't you go taking any chances. He isn't worth risking your life for, you know."

"Oh, nonsense, dad, I can probably swim better than he can. He's been too much taken up with studying the Bible to waste much time swimming. And there are lots of other things we can do. Go out yachting, and deep sea fishing. I hate old fish, but it's a chance to lie around and look glamour-ous."

"I see," laughed her father, and pinched her pink cheek.

"Well, is he going to go with you?"

"Yes, on his own conditions, but it's up to you to change those conditions if you can. I wasn't able to find out what on earth is tying him to home so closely. He said it wasn't a girl, and I don't really believe that he lies, not unless he's an entire fake and putting on a religious act to make me trust him."

"Oh, no, he's not a fake. But I can tell you what it is he has promised God he'll do," said Reva.

"You *can*? What is it?"

"Teach a Sunday School class, and he's as much in earnest about it as if his life depended on it. He goes home Saturday night to study his Sunday School lesson so he can interest a lot of common boys and make them keep on coming to Sunday School. I bullied him until he told me. But I'll soon beat that out of him when I get a chance to see him every day."

"And you still want him to come, even if he isn't willing to stay over Sundays?"

"Oh, sure I do. I thing this is going to be fun. I'll come down to see you about Wednesday or Thursday. You're go-ing down Monday morning, you said? Well, I'll come down

Thursday morning then and we'll have the time of our life all day Thursday and Friday, all day and evening, and by Saturday noon he'll be wishing he didn't have to go back to that old Sunday School class. I don't suppose I'll actually accomplish much that first week, but the next week I'll still be there and I'll turn on the glamour, for all it's worth. O boy! And it's going to be my special mission to make him forget his old Bible, and really have a good time. By the second Saturday he'll be ready to telephone his mother or somebody to take over that class for him. You don't know how well I can work when I get the chance, dad!"

"Okay, kitten, hop to it and do all you can. I'll be betting on you, but I tell you truly I'm not so sure you can do anything with that stubborn lad, and I hate to see you disappointed."

"Oh, I never get disappointed," laughed the girl, with her head high. "You're a good old daddy to fix this all up for me."

"Well, I did the best I could, but at that I'm not sure but the lad will stand me up. He didn't seem keen on going."

"You didn't tell him I was going to be there, did you? You know this is a good excuse for me to arrive to stay with you while he is away Sundays. Only Sunday was the time I was counting on to get in my best work."

"Yes, I thought so," said her father. "Well, perhaps you'll be able to make him stay. We'll see how it works out."

So Harris Chalmers began hasty preparations for his migration to the shore, having carefully selected a resort not too far from home, so that his uncertain companion could go home Sundays and teach a class of little hoodlums. Ridiculous! Though perhaps if somebody had taken that much trouble for him he would have turned out to be a good boy like Madison. Although that wouldn't have fitted in very well with his ideas of success in business, and if he hadn't been successful Adella would never have married him. Well, he had had a fairly good life, and if he could put this over for Reva he certainly would be glad. He didn't feel at all sure that Reva meant anything serious with Madison. Still, if she did, it would be good to know that she had a *good* man. And of course *he* could make him a successful man in business lines. He was counting on being able to do a lot with the boy during this summer vacation.

So Chalmers' preparations went forward, and Madison was told to be ready to start the following Monday. They would go down in the car. Mr. Chalmers was counting on Paige to do the driving. Then if they ever got in a jam and Paige had to miss a train he could in a pinch drive home and get back Sunday night.

So Paige watched him solemnly, accepted in silence the decision, and went home to pack up the few belongings that he meant to take with him. Mainly some books that he wanted to study that would help him in his Sunday preparation. If he couldn't be at home until the late train Saturday night sometime, at least he would have ample helps for his study. Of course he was counting on giving Mr. Chalmers the main part of the day, taking dictation and typing the letters. He certainly would have been surprised and more than a trifle indignant if he could have known how very little Mr. Chalmers was counting on using him that way. To his mind this was wholly for Reva's sake, and she might do the planning after the first day or two. He was taking with him some unimportant letters that needed rather full answers, to have on hand when he got hard up to occupy Madison's time. Chalmers was an adept in any kind of deception, and he could easily use it for amusement.

One of the first things Paige did when he got home that night, after he had his boss's definite announcement, was to call up June on the telephone. At least he would not run any risks of missing or having to wait for a letter.

It thrilled him tremendously when he heard her voice over the phone. He didn't altogether understand it. He had been wishing with all his heart that she were back home, and he might have a good long talk with her, but now with his heart pounding like mad over just the sound of her voice hundreds of miles away over a telephone wire, he felt that this was something else. *This* was a reason for meditation, and of course he had no time to meditate just now.

Here was June on the wire and his own voice began almost to tremble as he answered.

"June! Is that you? *Grand!* This is luck that I could get you right away because I haven't very much time. But first, how are you? All right? That's good. And having a good time? What's that? Not so you'd notice it. Is that so! That's a pity. I wish I could send you a lot of good time by mail or radio or telegraph."

"Thanks very much. I'll take the will for the deed. But how are you?" said June.

"Oh, I'm all right, but not very happy over the way things have taken a turn. My boss says he isn't so well and the doctor tells him he must go to the shore for a while. He has picked on me to go along with him, and keep up with his mail that must be attended to. The man he usually uses that way has to stay at the office and hold the fort. He says I must go. He won't take no for an answer. I balked of course on Sundays being included, and finally he has given in and will allow me to come back for my Sunday School class. I told him I wouldn't go at all unless I could be home on Sunday. I'm telling you all this because I don't want to miss your letters, so act accordingly when you address anything to me, remember I'm at the shore from Monday a.m. to Saturday noons and you can get me by calling for the Larchmont, Crystal Lake. You remember Crystal Lake, don't you? I think you said you were there once. What? Yes, I guess it's an ideal place, but I would much prefer being at home this summer. Say, is there any chance of you getting home soon? I'm hungry for a real talk with you again. There are a lot of things that are not quite clear to me that I think you could help me about.

"Is that a bell I hear? Is it calling you? Am I keeping you too long?"

"No, Paige! No!" said June eagerly. "Yes, that's my aunt's

bell, but it won't matter. I'll explain it to her afterwards."

"Yes, I know, but I don't want to make trouble for you. Have you got that address? Read it to me. Yes, that's right. And you'll write to me tonight will you, June? Thank you. I shall be desperately lonely, because I don't want to go, and I'm not altogether sure it was the right way, yet no other way opened."

"Then it will be the right way, at least for the present, you know," June's voice came ringing the answer over the wire. "Don't forget! I'll—be praying!"

"And I too! And say, June, do you happen to have an extra picture of yourself? I'd love to have one if you could spare it. I'll be lonely, you know."

"All right, if you'll give me one of yourself. I get lonely myself sometimes."

There was softness in the tones that said more than the words could say. More than either dared to say because of possible listeners. But Paige turned from that telephone with relief in his heart to know that now there would be no reason for his missing any letter that June might have time to write him. And in his heart he gave thanks for a mother who had sense enough to stay out of sight and not make him self-conscious when he was telephoning.

He kissed his mother tenderly:

"I know you don't like this, Mother, and neither do I, but I couldn't see my way out of it, not yet, anyway. I hope you won't worry too much, moms dear. This is partly in the nature of an experiment."

"I won't worry, dear. I can trust you in God's hands. There's just one thing I've been wondering about a lot. It's that girl. Is she going along?"

Paige gave her a startled look.

"Oh no, moms, I don't think so. He distinctly said he was ordered to go off from everything and rest. I am being taken along for strictly business purposes. I have to take over anything in the way of business that has to be brought to his attention. That was where we had our first difference of opinion. I definitely refused to go unless I could come back for Sundays, and he pled in vain, telling how forlorn he would be alone. I suggested that perhaps his wife would come down occasionally for over Sunday, but he seemed to think the seashore didn't agree with her, and she wouldn't be down often. He didn't suggest that anybody else would come. I don't think your fears are well founded, mother dear."

She smiled questioningly.

"Well, my dear, you know I don't trust that girl. When she gets a spell that she wants you to fill in for some man who has stood her up she won't hesitate to run after you. Remember she has done it several times already."

"Yes, I know, but somehow I think this would be too tame a matter for her, attendant on a sick father. I don't believe I'll be bothered with her. If I am mistaken I'm sure to find a way out."

Then Paige went up to get another hour of study in preparation for his Bible class on the morrow before going to his rest.

15

THEY were to start away early Monday morning, while the freshness of the day was still in the air, and they were going in the Chalmers car of course. That fact alone seemed a pleasant thought, for Paige was not above enjoying a chance to drive such a car!

The mother kissed him good-by as if he were on his way to a second world war again, and his father stood behind, in the morning shadows out of sight, proud of a son who had attained a place with such a well-known firm of business men, yet fearful of what the outcome of such a connection with the alien world might be going to mean to him.

Old Phoebe the cook watched from the sheltering kitchen curtain, swelling with pride that the boy she used to care for as a mere baby was going out in such style.

Mrs. Harmon, next door, struggling to get her husband's breakfast in time for his train and in the absence of her maid, watched him drive away, Yes, there was no doubt about it. That was Paige Madison driving Mr. Chalmers in his handsome new car she had heard so much about. She neglected the bacon she was cooking until it burned and sent a message all through the house. She hurried back to the bacon, but resolved that she would renew her efforts with Mrs. Madison and *make* her join the woman's club.

And Priscilla Brisco from her modest little back room on a side street saw them turn to the short cut that went to the highway and bustled away to the side window to make sure who it was. This would be something worth telling! She even ran to the back hall window to verify just which way they were going, and just how many were in the car. No girl? No, no girl. Definitely no girl!

And there were others who would have been glad to look and wonder if only they had been on the line of travel, even so early in the morning. But the mighty car with its expensive set-up rolled quickly out of sight and even the suburban newspaper missed getting a sight.

As they drove along in the pleasant morning, and Paige realized that his parents had been where they could watch the departure, he reflected happily that mother had been wrong in her fears about that girl, and he was glad she was where she could see that she had been wrong, and that the obnoxious girl was *not* along.

How unhappy they all would have been could they have known that this whole expedition, including the magnate's severe threatening illness, was a figment of that dreaded girl's imagination, and entirely instigated by her. But they did not know it, and they settled down to be calmly, almost fearfully glad at their beloved son's earthly success.

Meantime June Culbertson was having a bad time out at her aunt's home. The old lady was undoubtedly getting better, but the more she improved the more impatient she grew at having to lie still so long and the "household going to ruin with the slipshod ways of those who were running it." June was practically in despair for she had never had to endure so much faultfinding in her life, and many times a day she was on the point of giving it up and going home. She was tired to death and not really doing anything herself of actual work, just going around from one part of the house to another passing on to others her aunt's faultfinding.

She was not writing all these things home for she knew they would distress her mother, but now and again something would creep in between the lines that the wise-eyed mother could read aright, and more by what June did *not* say than by what she *did* the mother knew things were not going happily with her beloved daughter. The parents talked it over whenever they were not too occupied with parish duties, and they really worried a lot about it, and wondered what they ought to do about it, or if they ought to do anything yet. Surely that cousin would come home pretty soon and relieve June.

It was the next day after Paige's telephone message that June decided to do something about a better photograph than any she had with her, and she told her aunt that she was going to do some shopping in the nearby town that day, if she didn't mind, and would she like any errands done for her?

But Aunt Letitia was in a very irritable mood, and was greatly aggravated by the idea that June would desert her duties and go shopping. What did she want to shop for? Surely if it was any clothes she needed there were enough things in the house she could borrow, if they didn't fit her right she could make them over. Anyway, this was no day to leave the house —sweeping day—it was her duty to supervise all that went on. She would have nervous prostration if she thought there was no supervision going on. And nothing that June could say could convince the good lady that her servants were amply able and willing to carry on without her. So, with a sigh, June surrendered and said she would not go.

Instead she went to the telephone and called up the photographers in the East where her last good likeness was taken, and ordered a picture sent at once to Paige. Then while she was at the telephone she called up a nearby city store and ordered a few slips and other garments sent to her C.O.D. She had come off in such a hurry that she hadn't brought many garments, and found herself greatly hampered. Certainly with all the requirements her aunt demanded constantly she did not have time to make over old clothes to fit her, especially since those that had been suggested were old ones of her cousin's and were much too long and wide without being entirely cut over.

When she answered her aunt's bell, which had been impatiently ringing while she was telephoning, she took her purse down with her, having asked the price on the long distance call she had made, but the old lady was too excited to listen to her at first.

"I should like to know *why* I can get no service when I ring my bell?" she demanded. "Isn't it bad enough for me to lie here all day long and have to endure agonies, knowing what must be going on, how my house is being neglected, without being able to get anybody to come when I call?"

"I'm sorry," said June meekly. "I was on the telephone and didn't hear until just now."

"Well, really! If you were gossiping on the telephone I should have supposed you might have excused yourself and gone on with your gossiping later."

June laughed.

"Gossiping!" she said pleasantly. "Just who would I gossip with? I don't know anybody in this town well enough to gossip with them. And I was on long distance besides, so it would have been rather expensive to cut it off and call back again." She was trying her best to put a humorous side to the situation, but nothing did any good.

"*Long distance!* Did you actually *dare* to call long distance without asking permission? Don't you know I never allow that? So this is what has been going on. This explains why my telephone bills have been so enormous since you have been here."

"I beg your pardon, Aunt Letitia. This is the first time I have ever called up on long distance since I came, and I asked the operator just now to give me the amount of this call that I just made, and I brought my pocketbook down to pay for it so it wouldn't be forgotten."

"Oh!" said the indignant lady. "Well, I don't like it! I tell you I don't *like* it! Who did you presume to call? Your home? I should think you could say all you needed to say to your people in a *letter,* and there wouldn't be any special rush about that. You seem to have been brought up in a very wasteful way, *telephoning* long distance! And who was your other call to? Some young man I suppose."

June's eyes were flashing indignantly, but she held her peace till Aunt Letitia's snorting was done.

"Who, I say, were you telephoning to?"

"No, Aunt Letitia, I did not telephone to my home, nor to any young man. I was simply sending to a business house for something I wanted. The other calls were to your city store. I was ordering some garments I needed. It didn't seem convenient for you to have me go shopping today, so I thought it would be quicker to get the things sent C.O.D. I'm sorry I annoyed you. But here is the money for the telephone bill. I called up to know how much it was. The whole bill was seven dollars and fifty cents. You can check that up with your bill when it comes, and here is a ten dollar bill to cover it. Now, is there anything else you wanted? You rang your bell, I believe."

"Why yes, I did, but you have distracted me so with your nonsense that I forget what it was that I wanted. Oh, yes, I remember. I want a dose of soda in hot water. Something I ate for breakfast didn't agree with me, and I wanted the soda *quickly* before I get started on one of my spells of indigestion."

June quietly went down to the kitchen and got some soda, bringing it back swiftly, and trying not to have an annoyed look on her face when she handed it to her aunt. This day seemed to be the one when nothing went right.

It was three days before the incident of the long distance telephoning was forgotten. Aunt Letitia brought it up on every possible occasion, with sarcastic remarks about people who had so much money they had to use the long distance telephone instead of writing a postal card.

By the end of that week June's nerves were all in a jangle and if it had not been for her habit of constantly calling for help from above, she would probably have broken down and cried. Some of this bottled-up agony undoubtedly crept into the tone of her letters home, for more and more her parents were worried.

But there was one source of comfort that came to June and that was her letter from Paige. There was another now, and Aunt Letitia grew curious to know why the postman came so often.

"Are you engaged?" she asked June abruptly one day.

"Engaged? Oh no," laughed June.

"Well, why do you get so many letters then?"

"Do I get a great many letters?" laughed June, feeling as if she wanted to cry, but wouldn't.

"You certainly do," said the accusing voice of the aunt. "You know I'm well acquainted with the postman's ring, and nobody else seems to get letters. Who do you write to? If you're not engaged to him you ought to be."

"Why, Aunt Letitia! I don't know what you mean. I'm not engaged, and most of my letters are either from my father and mother or from my Sunday School class of girls. There's one of them who has been very sick, almost died, and I was taking care of her for two or three days before I came away. She writes to me every few days, just little childish letters, misspelled and funny, but she's very faithful, writing at least twice a week. And mother writes me every day almost. Dad, too, writes often, and several of my friends in the church. You see I was doing a lot of church work when you sent for me, and I was president of the young people's work, and they keep writing to me to know what to do about this and that—."

"Oh," said Aunt Letitia, "how long did it take you to make up that story? I can't think a girl would come all this way out here and keep up her interest in a lot of common young people in a church. You needn't try to make me think those weren't men you were writing to. Maybe only one man, maybe several, though I hadn't thought that a daughter of your parents would be a common flirt."

"Aunt Letitia, *stop!* This is *awful!* I won't listen to another word like that!"

"Oh, you won't won't you? Well, my young lady, you'll listen to just what I choose to tell you."

"No, Aunt Letitia, I won't listen to another word. You've practially told me that I lied. I was telling you the truth and you know I was. You know I don't lie." And then suddenly June's self-control gave way, and she burst into terrible tears and rushed from the room, upstairs, and threw herself on her bed, shaking with sobs.

After a little her sobs calmed and she lay utterly still and tried to think. Just what was she weeping so bitterly for? What difference did it make that Aunt Letitia had been utterly insulting? She would get over it after a while. And she, June, had no right to say those sharp things, even if her aunt were insulting. Her Lord was caring for her. Nothing could really hurt her under her Lord's protection.

Finally she got up and washed away the signs of her weeping, made herself bright and pleasant, and then sat down to consider what she should do next. Of course, she could get all her letters together, tie them in little bundles, labeled, and take them down for her aunt to look them over, but she resented that idea. She was old enough to run her own life, and the letters were her own. She would not subject her precious letters to her aunt's critical eyes. No, not even her own dear mother's letters would she show, nor of course not Paige's few letters that were so dear to her. She could not stand the cold prying questions that would surely be asked. No, there was no reason why she should have to submit to that. But she would be quiet, dignified, speak gently if she had to go into the room. She would try to carry on in such a way that there could be no charge of resentment or hatefulness in her conduct. Just gentle kindliness.

But while she was thinking it over, and just as she rose from her knees after praying it over, there came a tap at the door.

It was her gentle uncle's voice that answered as he opened the door and came in.

"Junie," he said and his voice was almost deprecating as he took the chair she offered him, "your aunt is in a terrible way. She says you have been very rude to her, and she is almost in hysterics. I have had to send for the doctor, and the nurse says you'll have to do something about it or she'll do herself some harm. She's flinging herself about in the bed, and the nurse is afraid there will be some harm to the injured bone. Could you, *would* you come down and see if you can do anything about it? I know she must have been very trying to you. I know her, what she can do to the people she is fondest of, and I can't blame you if you answered her back, but Junie, you have always had such a sweet forgiving nature I thought perhaps you would forgive her this once and come down and see if you can help. We're all beside ourselves with her actions."

"Why yes, of course, Uncle. I was just coming down, though I wasn't sure she would want to see me."

"Well, I think she would, but it isn't likely she'll tell you so. I hate to acknowledge it, Junie, but your aunt is a very self-centered woman, and has a very stubborn nature. She is most outspoken, also, and never realizes how hard she makes it for other people. If you could find it in your heart to forgive this time—."

"Why of course, Uncle Barnard, I'll come," and she reached for his hand and gave it a quiet little squeeze. "I understand she is sick, and probably didn't realize that she had told me I lied. We'll forget it." For June still felt the Presence of the Lord with whom she had just been talking.

"That's my Junie!" said the old man with an almost pitiful tone. "I just knew you would come."

So June went down and entered the sick room as if nothing had happened, although her quiet face had no real smile on it, still there was no animosity in her eyes.

But more and more after that day June began to question whether this was the place that the Lord would have her to be. There really wasn't anything important for her to do. The two maids were doing the work and doing it well. She never had to check them up. They had been in the house for years and, better even than she did, they knew the habits of the mistress, and when they were not too mad at her for her crankiness they did their work well. The nurse was a quiet practical person who knew how to save herself as well as take good care of her cranky patient, and there just didn't seem to be any place where June fitted in except it might be as a buffer to bear the blame that might otherwise have fallen on some other hapless member of the household.

But at last one morning there came a letter from the cousin, and her heart leaped as she carried it to Aunt Letitia. Now at last there was going to be a message that her cousin was coming home and she would be free to leave!

But her heart fell when the word drifted back to her by way of angry complaints from the invalid. Cousin Ella was not coming back. She had re-enlisted and was going back to work in the Navy because she thought it was her duty, and because she loved it.

So now June had to do some serious thinking and finally sat down and wrote a despairing little letter to her father, asking his advice about what she ought to do. She dreaded to broach the subject of her staying as she knew her aunt considered that was what of course was her duty, especially just now when there was such a loud complaint about Cousin Ella and her decision not to return.

Of course June couldn't blame her, not if her mother blamed her as much when she did her best as she blamed June, but somehow she felt it was Ella's mother, and burden, and not hers indefinitely. And yet she wanted to do the right thing.

When June's father got that letter he sat down and wrote one back to her, very brief and very gentle.

> June dear,
>
> Your mother is very much tired out, and I think she needs you. She isn't exactly sick, but I'm afraid she is heading for illness. So, dear, if you can possibly be spared I think you should come home as soon as possible. After all, you owe something to your own dear mother, and she has been doing both your work and hers since your absence, not only in the house, but also in the church, and I think we should begin to look after her at once before she becomes a chronic invalid.
>
> Mother doesn't know I have written you, for she would of course protest that she is all right, as she always does, but I shall feel easier in my mind if you find it possible to come at once. "We're just a wearyin' fer you."
>
> Your loving father

He sent this letter special delivery, air mail, and it was not long in reaching June. Her heart leaped as she caught sight of the envelope in the postman's hand and she rushed upstairs to read it before anybody found out what it was, for if Aunt Letitia discovered that such a letter had arrived from June's home she would have raised such a hue and cry that all the joy of the letter, whatever it was, would be extracted before she had even read it.

So June read her letter carefully, several times, read it on her knees, praying for her mother, but reading clearly between the lines that her father did not mean her to be worried about her mother. Only to bring her sense of duty to her own to bear upon the problem that had been worrying her. Then she went down on her knees with thanksgiving, and with petition that she might be enabled to make this break with her relative in the right way.

With a sweet serious face she went downstairs at last and went to her aunt first. That would be the hardest announcement to make, for she knew there would be an outcry.

"Aunt Letitia," she began sweetly, "I've had a letter from my father. He says my mother is not at all well, and he thinks I should come home at once and look after her."

The old face on the pillow hardened.

"What's the matter with her?" she snapped. "Is it just a passing indigestion, or something like that? Because if it is I don't see any sense in your breaking up here, now that you are so well established in our home. Your mother would understand how much more, in my condition, I would need you than she does. If it is just some passing illness that she'll be over in a few days, it's such a long expensive journey it wouldn't be worth your while to go all that way and come right back here."

June gasped at the idea, and took a deep breath before she would trust herself to answer.

"Of course they must have all understood that when you came here this position you are holding was to be considered more or less permanent," went on the merciless aunt.

"Oh no," said June quickly, "they did not understand any such thing, and neither did I. I could never consent to that, and I know they would not. But Aunt Letitia, when I came, if I had realized how very little you need me, I would not have thought of coming. You do not really need me here. Your servants are well trained. I scarcely ever have any admonition to give them. They know far more than I do about your ways, and they never need me to tell them. And your nurse is devoted. You really don't need me at all."

"I consider those very hard unfeeling words for one who has been practically a daughter in our house. But I'll give you the benefit of the doubt and take it for granted that they are spoken as a bid for praise for what you consider you have done here, and it's not my way to praise people. The reward for well doing is the fact of duty well done. I am sure you are bright enough to understand that, and therefore I am giving you no praise. If you come to your senses and realize that your duty is here, and your place is here, especially while I am bed-ridden, I shall be relieved of course, but I am not going to get down on my knees and beg you to stay. I do not believe in that way of doing."

"Even if you did, Aunt Letitia, I could not possibly stay. My precious mother needs me, and my father needs me, and my place is in my home and not here. If you were suffering and had no one to bring you food and attend you I might feel that I ought to help you in some way, but not under any con-sideration would I feel that I could stay here now. I am sure Uncle Barnard would understand that."

"What is that, my dear?" questioned the old man gently, coming in just then.

"Oh, Uncle Barnard! I have just had a letter from my fa-ther. He says my mother has been overworking and is not at all well, and he feels that I should come home and be with her as soon as I can get there."

"Why, of course, dear child. That is right and good that you should do that. We are deeply grateful that you have been with us so long, and though we shall miss you greatly, we know it is right that you should go."

"Yes," said Aunt Letitia sourly. "You might have known that he would say that. He never was known to think as I did about anything in his life. Barnard, this settles it. You've sim-ply got to exercise your authority as a father and *insist* that the government shall cancel that second enlistment, and let Ella come home. I demand that you send a cable this morning, *now,* and order Ella to come home at once! I feel that I am going to be very sick over all this excitement, and you had better let her know, so there'll be no trifling."

The old man lifted mild worried eyes.

"But, Letitia, we couldn't do that. Ella is quite fully of age and I have no right as a parent over her comings and goings. I can *ask* her to come, but the decision would rest entirely with her, after the government. They have the first say of course."

"It's ridiculous!" snorted Aunt Letitia. "The *government!* Why should they have rights beyond those of a parent? And we are both sick and feeble. You can tell them that, Barnard. They would be inhuman not to listen to that!"

Poor Uncle Barnard! What a time he was going to have, standing mildly protesting, trying to make his unreasonable wife see reason.

In the midst of it all June slipped out. She was no longer the subject of discussion, and she was sure her uncle understood the situation and the rightness of her position. So she hurried upstairs to pack.

16

PAIGE'S first few days at the shore were fairly interesting and restful, although he did not consider himself in any need of rest.

Chalmers professed to be under orders to take a great deal of sleep and rest, and didn't let himself be wakened until late. After a luxurious breakfast in bed, he spent a half hour with the morning papers and then sent for Paige. There followed an hour or two of dictation, interspersed by oratory intended to gradually set forth his business policies which he still hoped to have break on his new assistant's consciousness so gradually that he would not be shocked into realizing that it was contrary to all his own earlier conceived ideas of righteousness.

Chalmers' idea of ethics was that if you went at matters of that sort deliberately enough the sharp contrast between good and bad would soon be eliminated and there would no longer be left the sensitive conscience with which the normal average male of worthy parents was born. This was, to the Chalmers' way of thinking, the path of success for a right-minded man who had been hampered at the start by strait-laced puritanical ideas. This was the way to be a financial power in the world with a good handsome veneering of Christianity on the outside, to give confidence to clients.

Paige's day began with a dip in the sea while the beach was still fairly empty of people, and he could have the whole ocean to himself. Then came a time with his Bible, and on his knees, and he felt fit for the day, both physically, mentally and spiritually! It was good to him that Chalmers was not bothering him early in the day, and he could get the right start.

After a hearty breakfast, and a few minutes listening to his radio for the news of the day, if there was any time left before Chalmers called him for dictation, he wrote letters, or began on his Sunday School lesson for the next Sunday.

Chalmers was most affable, and he almost began to like him when they talked together, except when that shady side of his character began to come to the front, and then his defense finally was silence. The two men soon began to understand each other, and to plan each to offset the other, as if their present life were a sort of game, in which some questions were batted back and forth to see which would win, and though Paige didn't say much, never tried to argue with his boss on business matters, and seldom on any other subject. Chalmers soon began to see that he would have to be up and coming if he would keep ahead of the alert young mind he had taken over to train. It soon began to be interesting to the older man to plan answers to the simple steady convictions of the younger man.

But Chalmers grew weary of this continual lying around. He was not by nature a lazy man. He was used to leading an active life, going from one interesting thing to another, and this role of invalid he was playing was not to his liking. He even took to playing chess because he discovered that his young business assistant had in earlier days started somewhat in that game. The actual work they did with dictation was limited, especially until word came from the city regarding letters that had come in which needed the boss's suggestions.

Paige was quick at taking dictation, and expert in typing, having used it a great deal during his college years, both to expedite his own class work, and also to help increase his income. More and more as Chalmers observed these things he commended himself for having picked out this young man for future promotion in his own business. More and more he was satisfied that at least for the present his crazy young daughter had chosen to set her fancy on this bright young man, and mentally commended her idea of getting him to come down to the shore and promote their acquaintance.

But even the limit of three days of invalidism was growing irksome to Chalmers, before Reva would arrive, and he took occasion to call up his so-called "specialist" a couple of times for permission to walk or ride and so vary the monotony.

So at last he professed to have gained such permission, and the program was slightly varied. The first day Paige took him a short drive, and Chalmers felt so well after it that he insisted on going down to the dining room to dinner that night instead of having it served in his room.

Then came Thursday, and Chalmers had a sudden spurt of dictation, getting things out of the way so there would be time for Reva to carry out her plans, leaving Madison without any actual duties for Friday.

But he reckoned without his host, for he found that his assistant had provided himself work by writing out some lists that he said he knew would be needed later, typing several copies for the different men in the office, and generally organizing a number of things to send back to the filing clerk. Chalmers was surprised at the ability shown in these things, and commended Paige for what he had done. Although he said it wasn't necessary now while he was on vacation, and he wondered if he wasn't going to have difficulty in tearing the boy away from his regular morning working hours.

Thursday evening Reva arrived, most "unexpectedly" of course, and her father seemed rejoiced to see her. He felt that now she was here she would take Madison off his watch for a while and he himself could run down to the bar and find some of his old cronies perhaps.

Paige looked his surprise at Reva when he came on her amid a small mountain of suitcases. He thought at first she must be on her way to some famous resort for the summer and had stopped off here to see her father, and doubtless to beg a big check for her summer use, but his heart sank as he realized that she would be underfoot all the next day probably. Then in almost her first sentence she made it plain that she had come to stay over Sunday with dad. Well, that meant he would have to be nice to her until it was time for him to leave. Her father would resent it if he wasn't.

He considered asking if he might go a little earlier, but that would not be in keeping with the letter of his contract. He was supposed to stay here until Saturday noon, and he couldn't just beat it because the daughter had arrived. Maybe it might mean a little more leisure for him to study his Sunday lesson, but he thought not. Somehow he began to think this was intentional. Reva was the clever girl. His mother had been right about her. Well there was only another day before Saturday, and he would be gone, and maybe she would be gone before he returned on Monday.

Friday morning Paige carried out his usual program, a brief swim, and then his devotions. He came down to breakfast as arranged and met Reva already at the table reading the society column of the morning papers.

"Hi!" she called gaily. "Aren't we going to have fun today?"

"Are we?" asked Paige in surprise. "Did your father make new plans last night after I went to my room?"

"Father nothing. What did he have to do with it?"

"Oh, then you didn't know that I'm down here working for him?"

"A lot you are. Not today! I'm boss here now!"

"Oh, are you? But I didn't agree to work for you." Paige grinned pleasantly.

"Well, you're going to. Today! See! I fixed that all up with dad last night after you went sleepy-bye. See? Would you like to go for a swim first or shall we take a yacht and go sailing, and then go swimming after lunch?"

"Why, you see I've had my swim," said Paige good naturedly. "I always take my swim around sunrise. There's more ocean then and less naked people. You know I like people better when they are dressed."

Reva stared at him unbelievably.

"Oh, why, the very idea!" she said. "You don't mean that!"

"Yes, I do," asserted Paige gravely.

"But isn't the water awfully cold then? And lonesome?"

"I like it that way," said Paige pleasantly. "Cold and lonesome."

"Well, I certainly don't," affirmed the girl annoyedly. "You certainly cut yourself out of a lot of fun in life doing the way you do."

"Well, I don't seem to miss much," said Paige. "But say, you spoke of going sailing. We might get a sailboat and go out. Your father might enjoy that."

"Oh," said Reva with diminished fervor. "Well I don't know whether the doctor would let him, or he would want to, but I'd love to go. Can you sail a boat? Because I could help. I've gone sailing a lot. But why can't we go this morning?"

"Sorry," said Paige, "but I have work to do this morning. Some typing that must be finished for the office. They need it."

"Heck!" said Reva with an ugly look. "Dad will see to that if I tell him to. But anyhow I'd rather go swimming this morning and sailing this afternoon."

"Very well, suppose you go swimming this morning while I am working and then everything will fit in nicely."

Reva pouted.

"Dad might make a fuss if I go alone. He always thinks I'm going to get drowned."

Paige knew this wasn't true, but he only smiled and said:

"Oh, you wouldn't be alone. There are plenty of life guards."

"Oh, life guards! There's no thrill to a life guard!"

They strolled out into the lobby of the hotel, and went to see if there was any mail. Paige's heart thrilled as he saw a package with his name on it. It wasn't possible for June to have sent a picture so soon, was it? And then he caught the name of the photographer on the envelope and quickly hid the large flatness under some magazines, for Reva was just behind him, all eyes out for the mail. And Reva had no reserves; at least she was determined that nobody else should have any.

He gave a hasty glance at the rest of the mail, saw there were several letters for his chief bearing the home office mark. There would be letters for him to answer.

With his package carefully protected under his arm and his hands filled with letters, one of which he was sure was from June, he bowed courteously to Reva.

"Excuse me," he said. "There are some things here that I must attend to at once and get the answers off in the morning mail," and he made a dash for an elevator just about to close its doors, and disappeared out of the girl's eager sight.

Once in his room he locked his door and opened the picture. There she was! It was perfect! He feasted his eyes upon it, and finally stood it up on his bureau and walked away studying it from a distance. It was like having her in the room, and he wondered at the tumult in his heart, over just a picture.

But a picture of *June!* He hadn't realized before how much this meant to him.

Then he opened her letter. It was brief, written just after his telephone message. It didn't exactly say that her own heart was in a tumult over hearing his voice again, but it conveyed the impression that they had the same feeling about their brief conversation.

Then suddenly the handful of letters he had brought up

with him slid out of his fingers and slithered to the floor. He stooped to pick them up and saw that three were forwarded from the office, and bore the return address of firms that had been considering a contract with Harris Chalmers and Company for some time. These letters ought to go to Mr. Chalmers at once.

He went to his phone and called up Mr. Chalmers' room. A sleepy voice answered.

"Mr. Chalmers, there are three forwarded letters in this morning's mail, two from New York, and one from that Mr. Harrigan. I thought perhaps you ought to see them at once."

"What? You say Harrigan? And New York. Bring them right to my room. And yes, probably they will need immediate answers."

"All right sir. I'll be with you at once," said Paige, feeling greatly relieved. This would probably relase him from further attendance on Reva for that morning at least.

He paused only to put June's picture safely away out of sight until he could get a suitable frame for it, and then hurried to his boss.

It was a busy morning, and thanks to an old pal of Reva's recently on furlough from the service, they were not disturbed, for Reva was enjoyably busy elsewhere, swimming with someone who did not object to modern bathing suits.

At lunch time, with the three letters answered, signed by Mr. Chalmers, and mailed down the chute in the hall, both Paige and his boss were tired and hungry and happy. And then Mr. Chalmers bethought him of his daughter who had been the instigator of this sojourn by the sea, and felt compunction. What had Reva been doing, and was she very angry? Perhaps she had even been so angry at his lack of attention to her this morning that she might have packed up and gone home. There had been times when she was capable of gestures like that.

"Have you seen my daughter this morning?" he asked Paige.

The young man looked up pleasantly.

"Oh yes," he said with reassurance in his voice. "She wanted me to go somewhere but I told her that I had work to do until noon. She spoke of swimming, and I think she probably found plenty of company. I saw her stop and speak to a group of young people as we came out of the dining room."

"Well, that's probably where she is then," said the father with relief in his voice. "She's a great swimmer and loves it." Paige noted that there was not a particle of the nervousness about her swimming that Reva had implied. He was coming to see that this girl said whatever was to her advantage to say, regardless of the truth, and sometimes even regardless of being found out. A great many people lied habitually, but few of them cared to be found out in a lie. This did not seem to be the case with Reva.

"Well, Paige, you might do a little scouting around and see if she has come out yet. She will think it strange that I didn't look her up. You might call her room and see if she's there. If not, the desk might know if she has come in yet."

So Paige spent a few minutes in locating the young woman, and found her at last under a becoming umbrella down on the sand discoursing with a much-tanned youth of former acquaintance whom she introduced with an air of triumph, showing him that she had not gone lonely when he wouldn't go swimming with her.

Paige gave her her father's message. He wanted to see her and they would go down to lunch together. So Reva had an elaborate farewell scene with the youth who was leaving on the afternoon train, and went back to the hotel with Paige.

Paige went silently through the lunch hour thinking of the letter he had read so briefly, and the lovely picture he had hidden away out of sight. He would so much rather have gone without lunch and read the letter again and looked some more at the picture.

It developed that Mr. Chalmers delighted in sailing and was sure he was equal to a couple of hours spent that way that afternoon, quite sure his doctor would approve. In fact he had asked him about that very thing, and had been told it would be splendid for him, but not to get too tired.

So they went sailing. And Paige showed that he knew a lot about sailboats and was at home on the ocean. At first Reva tried to show off by insisting on handling the tiller, but her father was nervous at her erratic moves and quickly put a stop to that.

However they had a pleasant sail and came in tired and ready to rest awhile. So Paige had opportunity for his letter and picture and Reva spent her time calling up some nearby seashore resorts to see if some of her intimates were there yet, and then made a rather stunning hasty toilet for the evening. She meant to do great things tonight. She had found that a dashing friend was located about ten miles away and she meant to get Paige to take her to see her. There would be a dance going on there of course and she would begin to get Paige to take an interest in gaiety. That was the first step. But of course she said not a word about a party. She just wanted to see her dear friend so much. There was nothing for Paige to do but acquiesce. Of course he would drive her. But when they arrived at the great hotel where Reva's friend was staying he found himself involved in a dance. His indignation rose when he saw that Reva had planned this to put him in an embarrassing position, to see if she could not force him into things that she knew he did not care for.

He gave a quick glance about the beautiful room with its throng of merrymakers, and his pleasant lips stiffened a trifle. Then Reva's friends approached and there were introductions, and a gay welcome for this good-looking young man, from all the girls. Almost he was swept against his will right into the center of things. He stood there quietly listening to their chatter, trying to reply with courtesy to questions that were being asked him, and yet with a kind of withdrawing of himself, as if he were not a part of their gathering and had only come for a moment.

He had cast another quick look around to find a way out that would make the next few hours possible, when suddenly an officer in full dress uniform dawned on his vision with hand outstretched eagerly:

"Paige Madison! my boy! to think of finding you here! I have hoped to hear from you. How long have you been out of uniform?"

His old captain was now a colonel! And more than that, Paige knew him to be his dear friend. Many times during his overseas experiences Paige had gone to him, and received kindnesses and great help. He would not have presumed to walk up to him and claim that old friendship in the presence of such a throng. But the fact that the colonel had come to him merely turned the heads of all beholders and left him free to stand a moment and talk. And it was quite natural when this great man put a hand on Paige's shoulder and said:

"I'm so glad to see you, Paige. How about stepping out here on the porch and sitting down for a little talk? I'm rather tired and I'd like to check up on what you've been doing since I saw you, and what you know of any of the other fellows in your company."

The giddy girls that were a part of Reva's crowd made ugly little faces at this, for they would have liked to be included in this close intimate group around a great man, but other younger men were surrounding them, so they all melted away with the hovering partners, and Reva herself seemed quite satisfied. Paige would come back in a few minutes, covered with glory from his friendship with an officer like that one, and she would shine with reflected glory. Oh, she was glad she had brought him, and she kept an eye out toward the door for his return.

But Paige did not come back. Not for a long, long time. The two had found comfortable chairs as far from the noisy clamor of the ballroom as possible, and were having a happy time reminiscing.

It was an hour later when the colonel bade them goodnight

and went up to his room. Then Paige looked at his watch and wondered if it wasn't almost time for him to do something about the young woman he was supposed to be escorting. Thank the Lord for sending that old friend of his to help him get away for a time into a restful atmosphere! How cool and quiet it was out here, with scarcely anybody around and nothing that demanded his attention for the time being. God had done that for him. He had asked Him to take over before he left his room that night, and this was the way he had done it! Well, and now what procedure should he use to find that crazy girl and get her to come home? For her father presumably would be worried about her if they came home too late. Which only goes to show that Paige didn't yet really know his boss, or he never would have thought that.

He began to walk slowly the length of the piazza, stopping now and again to look in a window and try to identify Reva, and once he saw her in the arms of a young sailor, looking raptly up into his face as if she had no idea of stopping her play, all night long.

He went back and sought his chair, but two other young people had taken possession of the place where he and his colonel had sat, so he walked on.

At last he grew restless. He must do something about this, mustn't he? Did he have to go back to that obnoxious, crowded place and extract her?

And then, wonder of wonders, she came walking out on the arm of the same sailor with whom she had been dancing, still looking up adoringly into his face, as if he were the only sailor on earth for her. He spied her at some distance and started up to meet them.

"I was just coming to find you," he said. "Don't you think it is time we should be starting back? Your father will be troubled, I am afraid, and you know a sick man should have his rest."

"Oh, dad won't be troubled," she laughed gaily, "I'll risk that. But I do suppose we should start now. May I introduce you to Larry Keene? He used to play with me in my back yard when we were kids, and climbed over the back fence together. Larry, this is Paige Madison. He believes he works for my dad in the office, but I steal him away sometimes to take care of me."

Reva turned it off very neatly and they said good-night and were soon away, but the girl was silent for a long time, and it was evident that she was very angry. At last she broke forth with:

"I think that was the meanest thing I ever saw anybody do. Take a girl to a dance and then go off and leave her. I thought you had been brought up with good manners."

"Yes? And what about taking a man to a dance that he didn't know existed, when you knew I didn't dance and wouldn't have gone if I had known that was included in your program? I think you will find my bad manners couldn't compare with yours, for you knew what you were going to and I didn't. Now, suppose we forget it and get some pleasanter topic to talk about, unless you want me to feel that I have to say no to everything you ask me to do lest you will play some trick like this?"

"Oh, well, that's ridiculous! You ought to get over this notion that you can't dance, or *won't;* I don't know which it is. You know you ought to do it for dad's sake if for no other reason. By and by he'll have some swell people he'll want you to take out somewhere and put something big across with them, and you won't be able to fill the bill because you can't dance with their daughter and win the whole family over. Don't you see how silly you are?"

"No," said Paige. "I do not. It's a question I have thought over carefully, and decided against, and no amount of argument will change my mind. And if my job with your father depends on anything like that I had better begin to look for another one right away."

"Oh, you silly! I didn't mean that of course. Dad would be horrified if he knew I said that to you. But didn't you think that hotel was perfectly spiffy? And where in the world did you happen to come across that stunning looking officer? He acted as if he knew you very well."

"Yes," said Paige, "he was my first captain when I went into the service."

"He *was!* You don't *mean* it. No *kidding?*"

"No kidding," said Paige. "He was a very swell person. Everybody in the company loved him, and went to him with all their troubles. He made himself a personal friend of all his boys."

"Why yes," said Reva with amazement in her voice, "that's the way he acted to you tonight. You know I thought he was perfectly spiffy. I do wish you had taken me out there with you and I could have talked to him. I should have adored that."

"Well, I'm sorry, but you see I had no idea he was going to stay out there so long, and I didn't suppose you would care to leave a gay scene and go and sit quietly in the dark."

"Well, but it would have been so wonderful to hear him tell about great battles and things. It would have thrilled me so!"

"But he didn't talk about battles. He was talking about the different fellows and what had come to them since we were together. And he told me how some I knew had died so bravely, doing great things."

"Oh, I wouldn't have liked to hear about dying. I just hate the thought of death. It doesn't seem fair that anybody has to die."

"And yet it *is* fair," said Paige thoughtfully.

"What do you mean, fair?"

"Why, God made people to be His companions, and put them in a beautiful garden with only one rule they had to keep, and He told them beforehand that if they broke that law they would bring death into the world, and everybody that came after them would have to die. And yet they broke it! He made another way for them to be saved because he had to keep His word and punish them with death."

"Well, I say that wasn't fair. We didn't *all* eat that apple in the garden and *we* don't deserve punishment."

"Oh, but you would have eaten it, wouldn't you, if you'd had the chance? Are you sure you wouldn't have done it?"

"Well, I don't like apples so very well, but I think likely if I was told I couldn't do anything I would go and do it. I always did."

"Exactly. Then why do you say it wasn't fair."

"Oh, Heavens! Let's talk about something pleasant. Don't you ever think about anything but preaching?"

"Oh, yes," said Paige. "I think about beautiful things. Look at that ocean out there with the moon just rising on it putting a path of silver across it."

"Yes, it's sort of pretty, but why rave about something you can see almost any pleasant evening? I saw the most gorgeous dress tonight. It was on a bride and it was sort of cloth of silver with little flashes of diamonds over it. I mean to have one like that when I'm married."

"Now the moon is all the way up and walking like a boat on the water. See! Would you like to run down that silver path on the sea?" Paige asked.

"Oh *don't!* That would be *horrible!* I think the sea is terribly desolate at night, and to think of *me* all *alone* out there would be the most poisonous thing I ever heard of."

"Oh, but the path is *silver,* you know, and it would match your silver gown with the diamond sparkles on it," laughed Paige.

"Goodness, I believe you are a poet," said Reva and looked at him almost as if he were something to be avoided. "Well, anyhow you'll go swimming with me tomorrow morning, won't you? Just because you played a trick on me tonight."

"I couldn't possibly go swimming tomorrow. There were some very important letters in today's mail, and more are likely to be in, in the morning. I must get those answered and off before I leave."

"Before you *leave?*" she exclaimed unbelievably. "You

don't honestly mean that you are going away and leave dad, a poor sick man, all alone."

"Sorry," said Paige, "that was the agreement. I couldn't have come at all if it hadn't been for that. And he's not alone. You are here."

"Oh, piffle! I never heard such a silly man. You don't have good judgment, that's what's the matter with you."

But though she talked and pleaded the rest of the way back to their hotel she was not able to do anything about changing his mind. And yet strange to say, he began to seem to her still more intriguing. Of course there were plenty of other men down here for her to keep in practice on while he was gone, but she felt that even for a short few days it was worth while waiting for him.

So with great relief he was free at last to go back and take out June's picture and gaze at it a long time, just to make sure she was all that he remembered she was.

17

PAIGE had bought a blue and gold tooled leather frame for June's picture and it stood on his bureau now looking quite at home.

He turned his eyes toward it for good-morning when he awoke that Saturday morning at his usual time.

After his early morning dip in the ocean Paige came back to his room and dressed for the day, remembering happily that he was to leave for home at noon, and would have little time for preparations later. There were bound to be more letters to answer which he should carry back to the office.

It did not take him long to pack, and he sat down with his Bible for his early morning reading. He glanced at his watch. There were still fifteen minutes before he was supposed to meet Reva at the breakfast table, time for his chapter at least.

He was sitting there happily reading, his Bible open in his hand, conscious now and again of the picture that looked down upon him. He liked to feel that June was there reading with him.

He did not know that the door had opened. In fact he did not realize that he had not locked it when he came in from the sea bath in such a hurry, fearing to be late for the day. But he suddenly became conscious of someone standing there in the doorway, and he looked up, startled. There stood Reva, her eyes upon the picture, with actual hatred in them! He had a sudden feeling that the picture was desecrated by that look. But before he could move, her eyes still dark with hate, came to look him over, and then to concentrate with a still darker look of hate mingled with a queer kind of fear she saw the Bible, This was what had spoiled all her plans! This Bible, and that picture! That *girl,* whoever she was, was probably at the bottom of it all, and she longed to tear that picture into shreds, to grasp that Bible and twist it out of shape, stamp on it, only she was just a little bit afraid of the Bible.

Her angry look lasted only a second as she lifted frustrated eyes toward the young man whose room she had invaded.

But Paige was alert now, and sprang to his feet.

"Oh, is it time to go down?" he said. "Were you waiting for me?" Quietly. Just as though he had not seen the look of hate in her eyes, that scorn of the Bible.

Suddenly she turned her baleful eyes on him and with a quick motion reached out and snatched the Bible from his hand, flinging it angrily across the room.

But she found her own hand seized firmly in a grip that frightened her.

"That will be about all," he said in a cold voice. "Now, will you please to *get out* of my room?" and he firmly propelled her into the hall, closed the door and locked it behind her with a determined snap.

Reva, thus ejected, stood amazed alone on the outside of the door where she had so arrogantly intruded. She had never dreamed he would dare do that! Just for a *Bible!* If it had been the picture she had torn (and she had carried that intention too in the back of her mind) why that might have made him angry perhaps, depending on who the girl was and how much he liked her, but a *Bible!* He could get dozens of them in the stores. A mere Bible! He must be superstitious! What harm could it do to throw a Bible?

She waited for a full two minutes. Surely he would come out and apologize. He pretended to be so courteous.

She could hear him moving around in his room, quick, masterful steps. He had gone over by his bureau. He was putting something in his suitcase. He was putting that picture away where she couldn't lay hands on it. It was as if he must have read the hatred of it in her eyes. He was pulling out drawers in his dresser, folding garments rapidly, angry and getting out, it sounded like. What had she done? She hadn't meant to make him do that. Her intention had been merely to rouse him out of his silly ideas and make him see that wasn't the right way to live. She had never had anyone treat her this way. That masterful grip on her arm, that being forcibly ejected from his room! She had thought it might be intriguing to dare to enter. The world she lived in did not think evilly of such a thing. It was merely being a little daring and she had always practiced such little dares on her men friends. It was just something they did not expect, to have a girl barge into their room. Of course if her father should find out about it he would create a terrible rumpus, but surely this goop wouldn't dare tell dad. If he did she would simply say that *he* had *pulled* her in, and tried to kiss her. That would fix him, and dad too.

It was very quiet now in that room beyond the door, and she couldn't quite figure out what the occupant could be doing. What she would have thought could she have known he was kneeling beside his bed praying, enquiring what should come next, is a question.

But presently she heard a stir, a step, and the click of the telephone. She heard him call the office and ask for a porter to take his bags down. Bags, he said, not bag. He must be planning to take *all* his things home. If he was angry he was liable to make a lot of trouble for her with her father. Dad would be angry then if he found out what she had done. Then she heard the sound of the elevator coming up. That would be the porter after those bags and she did not want to be caught standing here in front of his door all alone. Stealthily she made her way with swift sneaky steps to the end of the corridor and vanished around an angle into the side hall, just as the elevator door slammed open, and she heard the reverberation of the porter's knock on Paige's door. Well, she would just go down to the table and order her breakfast, and when he came down he would see that she had not waited for him. He would see that she was very angry at what he had done to her, putting her out of his room that way. Just because she was teasing him a little, throwing his old Bible across the room.

But Paige did not come down to breakfast. He went instead to get the mail and then at once to Mr. Chalmers' room.

"Good morning! Am I too early for you?" he asked respectfully, in a tone a little more grave than usual. "I found there were some more of those office letters, and I thought perhaps it would be as well for me to get them answered and take them up to the city with me at noon."

"Well, you are an early bird," said the boss, yawning and giving him a sleepy look. "Let's see what letters you have. Not another from Harrigan yet? Yes, there is. Well we better get that answered while he's in the mood. Are you ready?"

Paige assented.

"Okay! Let's begin! Start on Harrigan."

Paige sat down and went to work. He turned the letters off rapidly, went to the typewriter and typed them, took them to be signed, and had the whole lot addressed, sealed and ready to go. Then he looked at his watch.

"I've just barely time to catch my train," he said. "Is there anything more you need before I leave?"

"Oh, no! You might just tell Reva to come up pretty soon, in case you happen to see her around. Otherwise if she doesn't come I can simply call the desk and have her paged. They'll find her. Don't worry. And oh, come back as soon as you can get free on Monday, or catch a ride. I'd tell you to take the car only Reva will probably want it, and the mischief would be to pay."

"Thank you sir," said Paige gravely. "I'll do my best about getting back."

"Well, you'd better, boy!" laughed the boss as Paige closed the door quickly and rushed down the hall after the elevator that was just about to stop a few feet away.

Reva was hovering down on the first floor where she could get a good glimpse of all elevators coming down. She meant to get hold of Paige and give him a large sharp piece of her mind before he left, and *perhaps* make him miss his train.

But Paige had been around this hotel long enough to know many pleasant abbreviated ways of getting away. Before he left his room he had told the desk to send his baggage to the station for his train and he was assured it would be there on time, so he had nothing to do but race after it. Getting off a floor above the first he hurried down a back way, taking the servants' stairs, and dashing out the kitchen hallway. So he arrived on an alley that presently came out at the station. Retrieving his luggage he kept in hiding behind a pile of freight until his train came in sight, and swung on the last car. Reva was even capable of chasing him to the station. But not even a swift survey of the station as the train swept away city-ward gave any glimpse of Reva. He was rid of her, at least for the weekend. And he hadn't had to have any altercation with Mr. Chalmers about it either. Of this he was glad, for there had been no time to decide what was the wisest and fairest way to approach the subject with Chalmers, if at all.

After he was well out of the town he went through the train to make sure Reva hadn't come along, for she was clever enough to have done so if she could find a way to play a trick on him. She had known what train he was to take, and wouldn't hesitate to be annoying if it suited her purpose. But there was no sign of her. He also went to the baggage car and identified his baggage. Then his mind was free to think, but somehow there was nothing he could think about that didn't rouse his indignation beyond control. The indignity that had been put upon his Bible. The hate that had been directed toward June's picture. They were matters not easily dismissed. Yet he must forget them. A Christian might not harbor such thoughts against anyone. And the girl was not so much to blame as her parents who had let her come up having her own way, carrying out any whim that came into her head.

So he closed his eyes and asked for strength to straighten out this matter the way God would approve. This was not a something that concerned his job exactly, though it well might do so if that girl chose to lie about what had happened. Yet he felt that it was going to be most awkward to remain in that job where he would constantly come into contact with that girl. He dreaded to go back, yet there seemed no way out until Mr. Chalmers got better, or some other solution came to make a change possible. If only Bill Arsdel would return, perhaps he could somehow persuade the boss to let him change places with him, or *something!* But that was not a matter in his hands to arrange. Well, he had a better Manager himself, who knew how to upset the arts of man and bring around things for the good of his children when He felt it was for their good. So he could rest and not worry.

Oh, if June were only at home how he would like to ask her to help him pray about this. Then he wondered if there would be a letter from June at home waiting for him, and so his thoughts were drawn away from unpleasant matters. When the train arrived at the home station he felt really rested, and could forget his unpleasant visitor of the morning. One thing he knew, he would never again trust that precious picture of June out in the open in any hotel that also housed that snooping Chalmers girl. He wished he had a tiny snapshot that he might carry with him in his pocket and look at sometimes.

Perhaps her mother had one he could coax from her. And so pleasant thoughts brought a smile for his homecoming that his mother should not be fearful for him.

He wondered, should he dare tell his mother about what had happened that morning? She wouldn't be surprised, for somehow she seemed to have a prescience of what was coming. That undoubtedly explained some of her worries. Yet he knew his mother trusted God, and would not allow herself to go on worrying unduly.

So thinking, he swung off the train, gathered his effects together, even his box of books which in his anger he had decided to take with him, called for a taxi, and went home. Somehow he had a feeling within him that maybe he wasn't going back to the shore at all, yet he couldn't see how it could honorably be arranged. But definitely he did not *want* to go back and would be so glad if he did not have to. More and more he was getting out of conceit of his job, and wished there were a way out of that.

His mother welcomed him with open arms, told him the news briefly. June was not happy out with her aunt, and her mother was greatly worried about her. Her cousin had re-enlisted and would not be coming home at all in the near future. June's mother was overworking, and they couldn't seem to get a maid anywhere. Her father was talking about sending for June. It seemed to him she had about finished her usefulness with an overbearing aunt, and might come home.

This news filled Paige's heart with joy. It seemed to him that if she came back things would be getting pretty nearly right again.

But he could not linger long at home. He must get in touch with the office. Someone would be there, and he must give them Chalmers' messages, and the letters must be mailed at once.

But when he called the office the voice that answered him was Bill Arsdel's and he answered him wistfully.

"How did *you* get in these parts, Bill? I thought you were West indefinitely."

"Well, you see the men I went after were all on vacation and there wasn't any point in my just hanging around living in expensive hotels, so I came home. I hear you've got a cinch of a job. I envy you, Paige. And here I have to come back and stick in that old office all summer. You lucky boy!"

"Well *say,* how would you like to change with me if the boss is willing? There are reasons why I *want* to be at home, and I wouldn't mind the office work, if before you go you'll just line up for me what you think ought to be done. I'll call up and ask Chalmers if he's willing. How about it? You could take your wife down with you and give her a rest, too."

"Oh, she's off in the mountains with her sister and I'm stuck here alone. I'd be delighted if I could take your place, even if it were only for a week or two."

"Okay. I'll call right up and let you know this evening what he says. There are reasons why I very much want to be here."

They talked about the letters and several office matters and Bill advised what to tell Chalmers.

So Paige called up his boss and found he'd gone off somewhere, but he got in touch with him.

"Is that you, Madison?" asked the boss, "I didn't expect to hear from you till Monday. Nothing wrong is there?"

"No, nothing wrong, but Bill Arsdel is back. His men were all on vacations. And something has come up that changes my plans. I would very much like to stay home, at least for a week or two, and I thought perhaps you'd like to substitute Bill for me. He's got a lot of things he wants to talk over with you, and I know he's better than I am for what I've been doing. How about it? Can you see it that way? I asked Bill if he'd be willing if you were, and he's all for it. He's horribly tired with so much travel, and wants some sea air. And as for me, I'm glad to take over in the office if you don't mind."

There was a silence on the wire for a long minute. For it just happened that Reva had turned up at lunch time and told a long story of her own. She said she was fed up with Paige, that he and she had had a fight, and she was done with him forever. She didn't want to see him ever again, and so far as she was concerned the deal she had proposed was off. She was going to her friends up in the mountains, and he might fire Paige as soon as he liked.

Chalmers hadn't much of an idea how long this state of mind might last with his daughter, or whether she wouldn't presently be demanding that Paige be brought back and reinstated, but he was all in a dither about how he was going to manage with these two young people. If Paige came back Monday, as per agreement, and Reva was not gone yet it was going to be most embarrassing to Him. He hated such things and he well knew what uncomfortable situations Reva could arrange, so this suggestion of Paige's seemed to him a godsend. He could tell Reva he had sent Paige away and he wanted her to stay with him here for a while, where they could do things together. He would promise to show her a good time. Perhaps even a pony to ride was possible.

All these things flashed through the boss's mind while Paige waited, fearfully, for he found that he had quite been counting on it. Well, it wouldn't last forever, of course, and that unspeakable girl would surely soon get tired of trying to work on him. Then he heard the boss's most important voice.

"Well, of course, Madison, you know I dislike changes of any sort, and I thought we were getting along fairly well together, but since you say that something has come up that makes it imperative for you to be at home, and since Arsdel has unexpectedly returned and of course I'll be needing to talk over things with him, I suppose I can manage it to excuse you. I should like however to have you hold yourself in readiness to return if I should send for you. It might be possible that I would have to send Arsdel elsewhere, yet I am not sure yet that I would have to. However, you'll hold yourself in readiness to return. Can you do that?"

"Why, I suppose I *can*, Mr. Chalmers, though it would suit my needs much more conveniently if I were to *stay* here this summer. Have you any idea how much longer the doctor is going to keep you there?"

"I'm not sure," replied the older man importantly. "I've invited him down for a few days to look me over and it may be that he will dismiss me, I really feel so much better."

"That's good, Mr. Chalmers," said Paige, "and I thank you for your willingness to let me stay here. Don't hesitate to call me if there is anything I can do for you at the office. And now would you like to speak to Mr. Arsdel? He is right here."

"Why yes, you might put him on the wire. Good-by and I hope you have a good summer, Madison."

"Thank you, Mr. Chalmers. Good-by" and Paige handed the receiver over to Arsdel and turned away, drawing a quiet sigh of relief. At least he was free from Reva Chalmers for the time being. He hoped he wouldn't have to take up his residence in some far land to escape her in the future. Then he went upstairs and began to study his lesson in a real way. He wanted to make his classwork tomorrow something really worth while.

18

REVA was planning to put Paige through a series of mental punishments before she took him back into her favor, and to that end she would spend a gay weekend, fortifying herself for the few days while she was disciplining him for further attendance upon her.

She had not been to her father's room yet, and he had not sent for her, since Paige had left him after the dictation hour. As he usually took his lunch in his room she let him severely alone. She wanted to be sure what Paige had told him about their flare-up, and to give him time, in case he had made a full tale, to recover from any annoyance that might have succeeded Paige's revelations.

So at dinner time she came to her father's room and knocked, in all the glory of an elaborate green evening frock that stood out around her in filmy folds, *many* of them, and swept the floor effectively, giving the idea that it had slipped down from her shoulders as low as it dared. Green roses in her hair, above her wide red lips, hair swept high in most astonishing lines to meet the green roses.

Her father stared at her speculatively. She had that look on her face that told him through wide experience that she had recently perpetrated some wicked little act that needed to be hidden by great attractiveness. His own perspicacity told him this might have something to do with Paige's quitting the shore. He was a keen man, and that was one reason why he was so successful.

"Well, come on dad. Aren't you going down to dinner? I've got a date for tonight and I want to be ready when the man comes for me."

"Yes?" asked her father hopefully, wondering if she had any idea what Paige had just done. "Well then, kitten, before we go down to dinner suppose you tell me what you've done to Paige."

"I? Done to Paige? Why, what in the world do you mean? I haven't done anything to Paige. He's gone home to his Sunday school class for the weekend, hasn't he?"

"Yes, he's gone home, but there's something else again. He isn't coming back!"

If Paige could have seen her face then he would have been surprised. She actually turned white under her rouge.

"Dad!" she faltered, looking almost frightened, "he's not coming back! Dad, you're kidding!"

"No, I'm not kidding!" snapped her father, for he was disappointed himself to have his experiment turn out this way. "What did you do to him, kid?"

"Oh, we just had some words."

"What over?"

"Oh, that old Bible of his. He got sore at me."

"What did you have to bring that up for, kitten? You knew how he felt about that. It doesn't seem that that was a very wise subject to attack—not yet. I thought you were going to take it easy?"

"Oh, stuff and nonsense!" said Reva. "I was just fed up with that religion of his. You can't count on anything because he has his stubborn mind made up that there are things he won't do, and things he will, and he can't adjust himself to other people. He just won't change any of what he calls 'principles.'

I don't see they are any different from other people's principles. And I thought the time had come to make a stand. So I made it!"

"Well," said her father indifferently, "perhaps it had. Certainly if you don't care any more about it than that, it had."

"What do you mean, dad? He'll be back."

"No. He won't be back," said her father gravely. "I guess your game is finished."

"Oh, bologny, dad. He'll come crawling back and apologizing to you. By Sunday night at the latest. He won't break his promise to you."

"He called up and asked my permission," said the father. "He's sending a substitute. He ought to be here this evening. Might be here in time for seven o'clock dinner."

"Dad!"

"That's right. He's fixed it so that he won't have to come back at all."

"But you didn't have to let him go, dad. Didn't you say you had a contract with him? He works for you. You could have told him he *had* to come back."

"But I didn't!" said the father. "I didn't see that you were getting anything out of this, and I certainly didn't want a young man working intimately with me who desperately wanted to be somewhere else, so I finally gave my consent, especially as I wanted to talk with the other man."

"Who is the other man, dad? Anybody I know?"

"Bill Arsdel. I guess you know him."

"Oh, that poor fish? Why, he's married, dad. He would be no good to me. And besides he's getting gray hair."

"There! I hear footsteps coming from the elevator. He may be arriving."

"Heavens, dad! Let me get out. I don't want to be tied for the evening. I'll eat my dinner with Arthur somewhere. Good-night," and Reva made a quick exit, and went to her room to meditate.

So! He had really been angry! Well, perhaps that was a

good thing. Maybe when he came back—or even if he didn't come—when she got back, eventually, he would be more subdued. He must know that his job would depend somewhat on the way he treated her father's daughter.

And in the meantime there were plenty of other young men to help her wait. Waiting with plenty of swains was dead easy. And another thing that might help, she could have some neat paragraphs put in the society columns of the different papers. Hints that she was about to be engaged, or was already engaged. Hints of who were her different admirers. But then of course, did Paige ever read society pages? Well, it might not be natural to him, but still if he was beginning to be in love, or at least *interested* in her, perhaps he would be led to go to the most likely places to seek for information about her. And anyway, if he didn't read the paragraphs perhaps his mother did, and would tell him. Surely none of that family could fail to see what an advantage it would be to Paige to be in the good graces of the daughter of the house where he worked so acceptably.

As she thought these things, there would come back to her memory the thought of the sweet girl whose picture had stood on his bureau, framed in gold-tooled blue leather. A very expensive frame that she had seen in the shop window on the boardwalk, until it disappeared. And the first time she had glimpsed that picture on the bureau as she passed the room when the maid was making the bed, there had been *no* frame on that picture, she was sure. There hadn't been any opportunity of course to be sure then, because the maid was closing the door just as she passed. That was why she had made that bold dash into the room that morning, to see if the picture was really that girl he had had with him eating dinner at The Sterling that night. And when she snatched that silly Bible she had meant, next, to ask him who the girl was. But she would do it yet. She would find out about that girl, and she would *cut her out*. Just the way she had snatched his Bible and flung it across the room, so she would snatch that girl away from him. There would be a way, and when she got home she meant to work it out. Even if she didn't want him any more herself by that time, she would crush that girl. Even if it broke his silly heart, she would do it. Even if it made his own words about her come true, that she only cared for herself and for no one else. Well, perhaps she did. Why not? You never got anywhere in this world if you didn't look out for yourself, and if Paige didn't come back to her of his own accord by fall she would crush him, too. There were ways. She would take her revenge for his indifference.

Reva sat a long time considering ways in which she might crush that unknown girl, and through her get sweet revenge on Paige. That girl was the sweet religious type, probably, the kind that is horrified at all kinds of amusements, scandalized at a girl who would do anything unconventional, like what she had done today. Very well, then she would get a story around about that girl, hints that *she* was not so good as she pretended to be. She could get such things into the papers, and she could tell Priscilla Brisco. Priscilla got around to most of the houses in their town, dressmaking, and she loved to be interesting and tell news. Just a few words here and a few words there. It wouldn't be difficult to spread a story. And if she could find out who that girl was, who her parents were, perhaps she could extend her punishment to them too.

Of course she would have to find out a lot about the girl and her family, and a lot of other things, before she could really crush that girl, and Paige. But she would do it! And then when Paige came crawling back to her and begging her to take him over, she would laugh with a sneer in the end of the laugh, and run away. He was running away from her now, because he loved that old antiquated Bible better than he liked a girl with a pretty face and a lot of money. That was Paige, and she would certainly have her revenge on him. And anyway she would find that girl and smash her! It was going to be interesting. It would take time perhaps, and she hated taking time for anything, but after all, things that took time were the best of course.

Meanwhile, back at home in his pleasant familiar room, with his own books all about him, and his father's old commentaries, and Bible dictionary and concordance to consult when he got into some difficulties that he had to solve, Paige was hard at work. He never even thought of the girl who had dared to snatch his precious Bible and fling it away. He was only thankful that he was not required to attend her any more.

Across the road June's mother, knowing nothing of her husband's letter to their daughter, had written June a letter telling her of all the happenings in the church and at home, and one sentence read: "Your Paige Madison is still faithful to his Sunday school class. He comes home from the shore before evening on Saturday and is with his class on time on Sunday, and from their rapt expressions during lesson time I can see they already adore him. I was watching them last Sunday while Mrs. Beech taught my class for me, and was amazed to see those bad boys who used to carry on so not only during opening and closing exercises, but all during their class time, sitting quiet during the whole session, finding the hymns for their teacher, finding the places in their Bibles, and seeming to be answering questions eagerly. I tell you when a young man can do that with a class of boys he is worth his weight in gold."

That letter reached June the day she started home and gave her pleasure on the way.

June was sorry to leave her uncle for she could see that he had depended on her greatly. He had been most kind and gentle with her. Gentle, too, with his grouchy old wife, whom he treated as tenderly as if he were her young lover, and June could not help but think how her aunt must have bullied him all these years. Yet they were both Christians and doubtless had no idea what a jangle their lives had become!

Before she left for her train that night June had taken time to write a short earnest little letter to her cousin Ella, telling her that her father had written calling her home, as her own mother needed her, and imploring Ella to ask to be released and come home to her own parents. She especially stressed the need of Uncle Barnard, who was very feeble and greatly worried by all conflicting voices. She suggested that Ella would be able to manage all these things and keep both father and mother from harassment; as the servants, if left to themselves, seemed both willing and capable. She closed by a few words of loving greeting and sent up a prayer that somehow this appeal might reach her cousin. Then she addressed it, and gave it to her uncle to mail. He accepted it with a smile of understanding, and promised not to mention it to anyone.

Then June went in to say good-by to the hard aunt who was still aggrieved that June was going off and "leaving her to suffer," as she put it.

"You'll be sorry, June, I'm sure you will. I had great plans for what I meant to do for you in the future." Then she vouchsafed a hard little cold peck of a good-by kiss, and that was all. It left June with a feeling that she had been cast out in spite of her most earnest efforts. But when Uncle Barnard put her in the taxi that was to take her to the train he pressed a goodly check into her hand and said it was his thank offering for the sweet way she had kept her temper through all the trying weeks, and there were tears in June's eyes as she drove away, waving a good-by to the household. The two maids and the nurse were standing in the doorway shedding a few tears themselves at her departure. A trying duty well done had brought a loving reward. Jane and Betsey had each of their own accord told her how beautiful she had been and how she had set an example to them of bearing blame pleasantly, even where there should have been no blame. They had promised faithfully to try and follow her example. And the nurse had praised her and told her she was "a true Christian."

Seated at last in her train, all the parting, pleasant and sad, thought over and put away for future memories, she read over her last letters that had come in just before she left.

She began with her mother's letter, and was thrilled at her news about Paige and his Sunday school class. How wonderful that he was developing this way, with nobody earthly to help him, and plunged as he was into unpleasant circumstances. She kept reading that part of the letter over and over again, until she finally began to realize what she was doing. She simply must not let her mind dwell so much on one young man. He was only a friend, and they had known one another so short a time. Of course he had asked for her picture, but that meant nothing in these happy-go-lucky days. Not that Paige was a happy-go-lucky young man. But pictures were not counted so much today, and he was her friend at least. Besides he was down there at the shore all the week, and there was no telling but that rich handsome daughter of his boss would turn up sometime. Well, that was none of her business. He was her friend, and she was glad he was interested in his Sunday school class. Then she read the letters from her own class and was pleased to see how some of those girls had grown spiritually. Of course her mother had been teaching them during her absence, and mother was a wonderful teacher. They would have had the right truths and would have grown.

She read her father's tender letter. How wonderful it was going to be to be home with her own dear parents again. Oh, why had she ever thought she had to leave them for Aunt Letitia? Still, there was that sorrowful looking nurse, who seemed to have been impressed. Perhaps she had been sent there to witness to her and the two maids. And gentle Uncle Barnard had been so happy to have her. If there ever was a saint of God he was one, although *he* didn't think so in the least himself. Oh, but she was glad it was over! And then she read her mother's letter over again, and took a deep breath when she came to the part about Paige. It was so very good to know that he had found the Lord and gone straight to work for Him.

But now she must definitely stop thinking about him. She had her work to do, and he doubtless had his. They would meet from time to time and be good friends, but she mustn't be silly, and imagine that this meant more than it did.

She must plan for her girls in Sunday school. Perhaps they would be interested to come to the house once a week and have a little Bible class. They needed to learn more than could be taught in the brief Sunday school hour.

How good it was going to be to get home! That was her last thought before she dropped asleep.

19

IN the home city where the Madisons lived there was another firm of financiers for whom Paige Madison used to work as a boy, before he went overseas, even sometimes on vacations while he was in college. They were not so loudly advertised as Harris Chalmers. Their offices were not so luxuriously furnished as the Chalmers outfit, nor so ostentatious in their ways. They were more quiet and conservative, yet sterling true in their dealings and standards. It was with them that Paige had often found himself comparing his present successful job, and finding the contrast not good. They were the Brown Brothers, Christian men whom wise people knew and trusted, firm substantial men who stood high as conscientious Christian men. Nobody questioned their integrity. Everybody respected them, even the ones who called them old-fashioned.

The senior Brown brother died while Paige was overseas, and Paige had not seen the other brother since he returned from service. He had always understood that the son of the other brother was to come into the firm when the war was over, and hence he had not himself applied to them for a job when he came back. He did not know that it was through his connection with the Browns that Mr. Chalmers had heard of Paige.

It was Tuesday evening of that first week after Paige was at home that Mr. Samuel Brown called to see him.

Paige was surprised and very much pleased to see him. He had always been fond of both brothers, and felt honored to be remembered.

It was good to feel the hearty handshake, and see the kindly eyes searching his face the way they used to do.

"Well, Paige, I guess you know my brother died in the spring, and my boy went off to war and got killed, and now I'm alone."

"Yes sir, I knew about your brother. My father wrote me while I was overseas, but I didn't know about your boy. I just got home myself, you know, and I haven't had much time to get around and find my old friends. Oh, but I'm sorry, sir. I guess you'd know how I'd feel about them both. They were always so nice to me."

"Yes, I know," said the older man struggling for self-control. "Yes, it's hard to have them go, and hard to be left alone, and now I don't know just what I'm going to do. I hate to see the business go. I thought my boy would take over one day, but I guess he's got a better job up in heaven now."

"I'm sure," said Paige with a ring in his voice. "But you're not going to sell out, are you? You look well. Can't you carry on?"

"That's what I came to see you about, Paige. Thinking over everybody I knew you were the only one I'd like to have with me. I know you're with Chalmers now. Is that a permanent job or just a temporary thing? Are you entirely happy there?"

Paige's heart leaped, and he lifted honest eyes.

"No, I'm not happy nor satisifed," he said "Not the way I hoped to be. Not the way I was with you people."

"Would you like to come back if we could arrange the terms? I suppose you're getting big money where you are?"

"I certainly would like to come back, Mr. Brown," said Paige, a great eagerness in his eyes. "It wouldn't matter so much about the amount of money if I could be with you. You know I just don't seem to fit where I am. But I'm not so sure whether I could be released at once, and you want someone right away, don't you?"

"As soon as possible of course, but if there were hope of getting you I'd get a temporary helper and wait. What's your contract? How much notice do you have to give if you resign? You see it's this way. My boy's gone. There are no relatives that I want to pass my business on to. Of course my brother's widow will have a share, but she has no children to inherit a partnership. I'm looking for you to sort of take the place of my son."

"But I've almost no money to invest in it," said Page sorrowfully.

The older man waved his hand:

"That's all right, boy, I'll see to that part for a while till you have some. You put *yourself* in, and I'll put the *money* in, for the present. Got your contract here? Go get it and we'll see how we can fix it. I don't want to steal you away from Chalmers, of course, if things are going all right with you there, but I'd like you to know there's a place for you with me, if you want it, and we'll fix the terms up, though I don't want you to lose anything you value by making the change."

Paige went upstairs and got his contract and together they discussed the matter.

"Well, I guess you'll have to give at least thirty days' notice if you resign," was the conclusion. "How soon can you manage this? Of course you want to be perfectly honorable about it. I'll manage somehow till you come. Before I do anything I'll wait to hear from you after you've had an interview with Chalmers. He may change your mind, you know. Besides I've been told you are interested in his daughter. They tell me you're engaged to her. Is that right?"

"It certainly is *not* right," said Paige, his eyes flashing.

"Where did you hear a thing like that?"

"Oh, I've heard it here and there. They said you'd gone down to the shore with the family, and were pretty chummy with them all, taking the girl to dances and all that."

"Well, I don't know where you got it, but it's *not true*. Mr. Chalmers was supposed to be sick and wanted me to go with him to the shore to answer the mail and attend to business for a while. I didn't want to go, and wouldn't promise at first, but finally it seemed I had to promise part time, he made such a song and dance about it. And then after we'd been there a few days that girl came barging down and changed the whole thing. I found myself roped into taking her places, dances and all sorts of things, and I *hated* it. I just don't fit with a girl like that, Mr. Brown. And don't get an idea I'd ever be engaged to her. She is not my style."

They talked rather late and Paige was greatly elated at the outcome. Now if he could only get Mr. Chalmers to agree to release him! He puzzled all the next day on just how he should make the approach for it, and finally asked the Lord to show him what to do or say. Soon after that prayer there came a letter from Chalmers, written by Bill Arsdel, telling Paige that he would like him to take over that western trip he had told him about. There were seven mortgages to be fore-closed, and he wanted them *"foreclosed"* this time, *all* of them. *"See?"*

Paige wasn't long in answering that letter, and sending it by special delivery, air mail.

Dear Mr. Chalmers:

Your letter concerning the western trip is received. I'm sorry. I can not do that sort of work, and I'm find-ing out more and more that I am not cut out to fit in with your policies.

I feel that under the circumstances you will agree with me, and I am therefore handing in my resignation, to take effect at once if you are willing. I know that the contract asks for thirty days' notice on leaving, and if you want me to adhere to that I'll be glad to finish the thirty days in the office work for which I was originally hired, but I would be deeply grateful if you could find it convenient to allow my service with you to terminate at once. I am sorry of course that I have not been all that you wanted me to be, and I shall be interested to know how you are. Hoping your health will soon be fully restored, and thanking you for your kindness.

With all best wishes,
Paige Madison

Paige sent the letter on its way posthaste. And then he went back to his desk and worked as he had never worked before, doing each smallest duty meticulously. He wanted to be ready to go if and when allowed, and to leave everything in such shape that his absence might be regretted, rather than rejoiced in.

Late that afternoon a telegram arrived from Chalmers.

Your resignation accepted with regret to take effect immediately. Sorry you couldn't see things my way.

Signed,
Harris Chalmers

So that was that. Mr. Chalmers was angry, of course, and might regret it later and come back and try to get him to change his mind, but Paige, though he was sad at the abrupt way Chalmers had replied, rejoiced that he was free. He gathered up his belongings from his desk, said good-by to his secretary, and one or two others who were still in the office doing late work, and went home.

He went at once to the telephone and called up Mr. Brown, telling him the outcome of his letter, and received a glad welcome.

"Come down next Monday morning and we'll start with a clear slate and make our plans," said Mr. Brown.

"And you aren't sorry yet that you asked me?" questioned Paige.

"Not even a little bit," came the hearty reply that warmed Paige's heart.

Then Paige went to his mother with the news, his eyes shining, till she said he looked as he used to when he was a little boy and someone had given him a football.

"Oh, my son!" she said, "you don't know how glad I am about this! I've been so very troubled about your staying in that firm of worldly men, I felt almost from the start that it was not the place for you."

And then suddenly a cloud came over the brightness of her face.

"But—that *girl,* Paige? Will she hang on to you?"

Paige laughed.

"I think not, mom. Wait till I tell you how we parted," and he sat down and told his mother the whole story, not at length, only the main facts, but she watched him and drew a deep breath of relief.

"Oh, my dear!" she said, "we'll have to pray for that girl! How she needs the Lord."

"Yes," said Paige, "but she doesn't *want* Him, mom!"

"No, they don't, not when they want their own way, and don't realize they are sinners. But I'll pray. Also I'll thank my God that you don't have to be around her any more."

Paige grinned at her then.

"Why, moms! You didn't have to worry about *that* girl. I never would have taken up with her, no matter if there wasn't another girl in the whole wide world. I just couldn't abide her!"

But his mother only smiled in a wise way. Well she knew from her long life of experience, how easily the wrong girl could wind even a good man around her silly little finger, and never let him guess what she was doing until it was too late.

With his heart full of joy Paige went upstairs to write to June about all the wonders that the Lord had wrought for him.

And that was the night that June was taking the train for home and would be gone when that letter arrived, but of course Paige didn't know that.

June had sent a telegram to her father what train she was taking, but he had not told her mother about it yet. He was going to wait and let it be a surprise in the morning. So nobody had run across the street to tell the Madisons, or even telephoned, and Paige was writing his letter, carefully, not to tell too much. Not too certain just how much to tell yet. It was all so new he couldn't get used to it, and so he wrote and tore some of his letter to little bits and wrote it over again. He sat up quite late to finish it, and had it ready to mail in the morning. He knew he didn't have to get up early, for Chalmers had freed him from the office, and he could just enjoy his home and be lazy for a little while.

And so when he finally did get into his bed he was tired with all the excitement of the day, and fell right to sleep, but later dreamed of June. Where do dreams come from? Are they real, like radio voices floating around waiting to be picked up, or are they just formed out of the inner consciousness? That was something that Paige thought about long afterward, but he hadn't time then. He was too busy sleeping, and dreaming.

20

JUNE'S dreams were sweet and pleasant. She had been through so much that was unpleasant back at her aunt's and now that she was on her way home she seemed to have dropped it all and was just luxuriating in rest.

The train droned on mile after mile, steadily, dependably, getting ready for morning and its destination. Morning was already on its way. The sky was growing lighter at the edges, and the villages and cities were getting closer together. Here and there they passed a station in the darkness with yellow sleepy lights blaring out, and tired officials and trainmen standing around in the murky light waiting for the train to pass, and one more day to dawn.

Then the train rolled on, taking up its monotonous tune again, faster, a little faster! They were half a minute behind time. Where was that New York train? It ought to be in sight now behind that far mountain.

On and on, and on. Till suddenly the sharp blast of a whistle just outside the tunnel ahead, and a quick crash that shook the whole train to its very foundation. There was the sound of splintering glass, groaning machinery, torn wooden structures, and then the shuddering of the other train as it poised itself on the edge of the embankment, and quivering in every fiber of its being, rolled down to the river! Some of the cars turned over in the water and came to a tortuous stop.

June suddenly sat up and then as suddenly was jarred down again by the impact of the two engines disputing with each other which should occupy the slender track that seemed all so uncertain.

It was deadly still for an instant as if the trains were deciding what to do, till the New York train decided to turn over and roll. Then began screams and outcries, yelling of frightened children, groaning of the injured, the moaning of the dying. And fire sprang up and raged ahead.

June lay still stunned, scarcely knowing what to think. There had been an accident of course, but she wasn't hurt. She was thankful for that. She was in one of the last cars and had not been so close to the wreck as some.

Gradually her senses came back to her, and she could look around. She tried to open her window shade but one end seemed jammed shut. She pulled the fabric aside and saw the glow of the starting fire. She caught her breath. Fire! One should get out as quickly as possible!

She felt around for her shoes, which were usually the extent of her undressing in a sleeper. She found her light switch but it did not work. Her little flashlight was in her suitcase under the berth and she hadn't time to search for it. Better get out, no matter what she lost. Her purse was in her handbag, and with it held close in one hand, her arm slipped under the strap, she swung her trembling limbs out into the aisle which she found was on a distinct slant and crept forward to where the door had been.

There were other people ahead of her now, some women sobbing as they hurried, one screaming. A man telling her to shut up.

They reached the door, and the man wrenched it open with a great effort. They crowded out, all eager to be the first, June halting to let a woman with a little frightened baby get ahead, and at last she was outside, with the cool night air blowing in her face. Oh, it was good and reviving to feel it.

It was a motley sight outside. They could see the wrecked cars, twisted as if they had been made of tin like children's toys, the submerged cars down below in the river, with a few frantic people struggling to get out of windows, not far from where the fire was raging. It was weird and terrible. People in all sorts of dress and undress, milling around and crying out, trying to understand what had happened and why? Trying to do something to help, and doing the wrong thing!

Suddenly June saw a little neglected child crying at the edge of the embankment, her mother unconscious lying beside her. June hurried to them and knelt to see what help she could give, and so began her labors.

A little later someone sent a radio message that presently the broadcasting center took up, and started to tell the world what had happened.

The minister coming in from an all night visit to a dying parishioner, turned on the radio to see if his watch was right, and heard the cry:

"Terrible railroad accident! Head on collision between New York train and midnight express from the West. List of casualties not known yet. One train submerged in the river, the other on fire—" He shut it off quickly and dashed out the door. He didn't want his wife to hear this yet, though of course she did not know that June was on that train.

The minister hurried across the road to the Madison house. They would help. Was Paige there yet? He knocked at the door, rang the bell, and called. Paige in his bathrobe came sliding down the stairs.

"What's the matter?" he said when he saw the wild look on the minister's face.

"There's a terrible accident, over in Ohio I guess it is. And June was on one of the trains! Can you go with me to get her? I don't know if she has been injured or is even living."

"June?" Oh, his heart cried out to God for help. "Yes, of

course I'll go. I'll be with you in a minute. My car has gas. We'll go in that. I'll send mother over to your wife. Does she know?"

"No, she doesn't even know June is coming. I got the telegram late last night and didn't want to excite her."

"Well, mother will be with her. Do you know the exact location of where we're going? I'll get dad to phone the station and find out about the accident."

It was extraordinary how quickly they got started. How quietly all those two households of frightened people kept their heads and did the things that ought to be done. And then the two men were off, leaving the others at home to pray, and to watch the radio messages that from time to time kept coming in.

The two grave-faced men said little to each other, save now and again to ask a question about the route, but each knew that the other was praying and trusting, and Paige learned a lesson of trust that day from the frantic father who thought he had been the cause of his child's being on that train. Once he voiced that thought, in his desperation, and Paige looked up and shook his head.

"No, you weren't the cause," he said, "nothing can happen like that without God's knowledge and consent. You said that yourself last Sunday in your sermon. If God orders this, all will be well, because He can protect His own."

A look of sudden light came into the distracted father's face and he actually smiled.

"You're right, dear fellow," he said. "We'll just trust in that. Thank you for reminding me."

When they stopped at a filling station Mr. Culbertson did some telephoning, found out that the rescue was still going on. Most of the casualties were in the New York train, though there were several from the western train. Still they could take heart of hope, and press on. They were halfway there now.

Mile after mile of trustfulness, hour after hour of looking to God, and during that time the two men's hearts were knit in a deep strong love for one another, because they were out together to work for the one they both loved. Nothing was said about that, but each recognized the truth of it.

The last few miles were the hardest, for both men were very weary, the father almost to the breaking point, and they rode on, their faces gray and worn.

And then they came within sight of the wreck!

There was no room for their car to drive down there. It was the railroad track and the river, with only a narrow road a little above.

Paige drove as far as he could go, parked his car and then they got out and began to walk down, finding it very hard to get anywhere because there were so many others searching for dear ones, just as they were.

They marveled as they went on that anybody was saved alive out of that wreckage.

There were great crews of wreckers, trying to clear the tracks for the other trains to pass. There was another crew laying a temporary track. And how were they going to find June? They traveled from one end of the wreckage to the other. They asked questions of people who didn't know how to answer them. They found a couple of conductors and a few brakemen who couldn't tell them about the girl they were looking for, and at last they decided to separate, one going to one end of the wreckage, the other to the other, and meet again in a few minutes to decide what to do next.

A moment's questioning of a passing conductor informed them that no passengers had left for other locations yet, except as some were gone to hospitals, a few to the nearest morgue. But at last they found the man who had taken all the names of those who could tell them. Oh, it was anxious work of course. If they failed to find her here they must go to the distant hospitals and search. They *must* find her. If they only were near a telephone and could discover if possible whether someone had taken her home, yet they would not dare telephone and let her mother know that they had not found her yet.

So the thoughts went beating through the brains and hearts of the two, and now and again it would come to them that this wasn't trusting the Lord. They had handed their burden over to Him, and then taken it away with them and were carrying it themselves.

There was no time to kneel down and get quiet with the Lord, and no place to kneel. It was all confusion and clamor about them, souls in a panic crying out, yet so many of them not knowing to whom to cry.

Paige's heart ached for the father. Poor man. He was almost dead on his feet. He had been up all night with that desperately sick man, had helped him die, and then come home to this. He could scarcely keep going, yet he tumbled on. She was his little girl who was missing. What must it mean to him not to be able to find her?

So Paige quickened his own steps and stumbled on. Down closer to a bend in the river, and just beyond the clamor of the crowd he caught a glimpse of a light dress, some mother likely, sitting or lying beside a child. It wasn't in the least likely it was June, but he had resolved to pass no group, or single person, without looking into their faces, and making sure. That was the only way, after all. The person or persons he saw were a little off the general road where everybody was stirring around, and almost he thought it wasn't worth while to take the time to go, and then as he neared the trees, that half hid the group, he could see that two were lying on the ground together.

Heartsick he took another step till he could plainly see the two lying beneath a tree, fast asleep. A tiny little child, with a quivering sob shaking her small shoulders, now and then, trembling her pretty lips, and a young girl with a lovely protecting arm across the child, drawing her into a sheltering embrace. The attitude and the gentleness were so like a thing that June would do, that he stepped closer to look for her face that was turned away; and, too, there was something familiar about a blue wool coat that was spread over her shoulders. So he bent over and look intently at the girl's face half hidden beside the little child.

Then suddenly he was down on his knees beside her, his own hand on the sweet little ministering hand, rejoicing that her hand was not cold but warm. She was *alive,* at least!

"June!" he whispered softly. "Oh my darling June! Have I *really* found you?"

June stirred and opened her eyes, looked at him with bewilderment, and then a queer little tired smile dawned in her eyes.

"Paige!" she murmured softly. "Are you *real*—or—only—just a dream?"

Paige's heart leaped.

"I'm *real,* darling," he said joyously; and tenderly he stooped and put a reverent kiss on her forehead.

Afterwards he wondered how he had dared, but at the time it seemed the right and beautiful thing to do. Her face bloomed into radiant joy, but still there was that little pucker of bewilderment on her forehead and in her dear eyes.

"But—*how* did you—come to *be—here?*" she asked, as if still thinking it might be but a dream.

Paige smiled down tenderly at her. "Your father and I came to find you," he said.

"But—how did you *know?*"

"Your father heard the accident announced on the radio. He came over for me, and we've been searching some time for you. By the way, I must go and find him, and tell him the good news. Will you let me carry you?"

"Oh, I can walk!" said June. "But I don't know that I should leave this poor frightened baby. Her mother has been taken to the hospital and somehow they missed taking her. There were so many desperate cases. I promised her I would look after her till the ambulance comes back."

Paige smiled to himself to think that when he had seen her first she was being called to serve a little needy one, and here it was again. He had found her in service for a needy one.

He wondered what he ought to do. He couldn't bear to leave her now he had found her. There was so much confusion around she might get lost. Still he must meet her father.

Then all at once a tall person in Red Cross uniform came toward them and looked down at the two on the ground.

"Is this the child whose mother was taken to Mercy Hospital? The little one called Mary Lou Fenner? Her mother is frantic lest she'll be lost."

"Yes, she told me her name was Mary Lou," said June.

"Don't stir, please," said the Red Cross. "I'll lift her away from you. Perhaps she won't wake up."

The nurse stooped and lifted the little girl with accustomed ease, cradling her gently in her arms, as the child stirred; hushed her, and turning, strode over to the ambulance with her. As she left, Paige, with a great sigh of relief, stopped and lifted June in his arms, a precious burden, and carried her across the poor people huddled on the ground awaiting help.

"Oh," said June in a protesting little voice, "you mustn't try to carry me. I can walk."

"Yes, I know, but you are tired. I can see that, and—besides I *like* to carry you!"

"But I'm too heavy to be carried over this rough ground."

"No, no you're not heavy. You are—*precious!* Excuse me, but you don't know how we feel about you after hunting for you so long. And besides this is the quickest way to get back to your father and relieve his anxiety. Just lie still and relax till we get there. It isn't far."

So June relaxed smiling and lay thinking how strong and restful his arms were, and how glad she was to be taken care of.

The minister was already at the place appointed, waiting,

for it was some minutes past the time they had arranged for meeting. His face was ashen with anxiety, and he certainly needed to be reminded again that there was a state called "trusting" for such as he.

Then he saw them, June in Paige's arms, and his fears leaped up again. Was June dead, that Madison had picked her up and was carrying her; or was she hurt, disabled? Nevertheless he drew a breath of relief that the long search was over, even if there was more trouble to come.

But almost at once he saw that June was smiling, turning toward where he stood and waving her pretty hand. That gave relief, and then suddenly she was beside him and Paige was setting her down.

"Are you all right?" asked the anxious father.

"Oh yes," said June, "all right, but you look tired to death you dear, *dear* daddy."

"I thought when I saw you being carried," explained the father, "that you were hurt."

"No," explained Paige, "I just thought this was the quickest way to get here, and I was afraid too that she might be tempted to stop at every troubled person she saw and constitute herself a rescue squad. That's what she's been doing, I gather, ever since the accident. So I carried her. Besides, I found her asleep under a tree, and I figured she was pretty tired."

"Well, of course," smiled June. "but I'm quite all right, daddy, truly I am."

"Thank the dear Lord for that!" said the father with his face a-shine.

Paige's voice quietly echoed the word.

"And now," said he, "I think what we ought to do is to get to our car as quickly as possible and get started somewhere for something to eat. There obviously wouldn't be anything around here. Have you any baggage or anything? Were you able to bring anything out with you, June?"

June shook her head.

"I had two suitcases with me and my hat was hanging in the berth, but when I went back to the car I couldn't get in, so I just let them go. I can get home without them and all I want is to get home anyway."

"Well, I'll ask one of the officers about it. It may be possible to have your things sent on if they are not available before we get started. I'll get you folks over to the car, and then I'll ask the baggage master. Would you like me to carry you up the embankment, June? I'd be pleased to do it, if I may."

June laughed and shook her head.

"I'm perfectly able to walk. I think we'll both have to help dad. He looks about all in."

"Yes," said Paige. "You know he was up all night with a dying man before we left, and this has been a trying day for him. And there's another thing we must remember. We should telephone the two mothers. They will have been anxious all day."

So as swiftly as possible they made their way to the car. Then Paige went back to see about June's belongings and then they were soon on their way to a place where they could get a meal and telephone home.

They put Mr. Culbertson in the back seat to go to sleep for a while, and June insisted on sitting in front, saying she wanted to catch up on her acquaintance with Paige.

And so they started off joyously.

Mr. Culbertson was soon sound asleep, but the two young people in the front seat were suddenly terribly conscious of that kiss that had been given when Paige first found June, and the words of endearment that had slipped out in the stress of finding her. Paige wondered if she had heard them, had realized that he had kissed her, and June with a glad quiver in her happy heart, remembered them both, and was wondering if Paige had *cared,* or those had just been pleasant expressions of anxiety relieved.

But they were both too happy over having found each other again, and knowing that they were going to their beloved home to stay and not be separated, to let any sad thoughts spoil their joy.

They were soon quietly chatting. Telling of the accident, and of the trip in search of June. Telling of why Paige happened to be at home to come with June's father in search of her. And that opened the way for Paige to tell of his shore experiences and how he came to resign his job.

June looked a little grave when she heard he had resigned.

"But isn't that going to disappoint you terribly?" she asked. "Weren't you a bit hasty doing that?"

"No," said Paige decidedly, "I put it in the Lord's hands, and that was what He indicated." Then he told her of his old friend Brown, and the good proposition for the future he had made, and her face grew glad.

"Isn't God wonderful, the way He answers when you trust *entirely?*" she said. "That was the way He took care of me when I didn't think I could possibly stand Aunt Letitia and her faultfinding ways any longer and then came that letter of dad's asking me to come right home, that mother needed me."

Paige began to laugh, and June looked at him curiously.

"I'm laughing," Paige explained, "because your father was worrying a great part of the way over that *he* had *written* that letter. He said if anything happened to you it would be *his fault,* because he had told you to come right home."

"Oh, that's lovely," smiled June. "Just another instance of how all things work together for good to them that love God. God let that letter come, knowing that He would take care of me when the accident came. And He did."

"Thank the Lord," murmured Paige softly.

It was growing dusky now and the stars were pricking out one by one. By and by the moon would be coming up, but it could not bring to mind the last time he had watched it rise, making a path of silver on the sea. He had something better beside him now than a girl who despised him because he loved God's Word.

There was quite a silence between the two as they drove through a village, and then June asked casually:

"Did you ever get to know that daughter of Mr. Chalmers any better than you used to?"

Paige grinned.

"I certainly did," he said. Then with sudden resolve—"and I guess here's where I tell you all about it. Then we'll cross her off our list for all time, and make no more mention of her."

"Oh!" said June with a little gasp in her breath. Was there something coming that was going to hurt?

So Paige told her the whole story in detail, from the first arrogant barging in of the daughter of his boss, through the dancing incident, and on to the morning when she walked into his room, snatched his Bible and threw it across the room.

"Poor child!" said June sadly, "what a life to live!"

"Yes, isn't it?" said Paige.

And so he went on to tell more of the Brown's offer and how his business prospects had all been changed into something that he felt sure was going to be wonderful for him by and by; and how relieved he was to be out of the atmosphere of Harris Chalmers and Company.

It was quite dark now, and the moon was making a silver rim over the mountains as they drove.

"You must be very tired," said Paige. "Wouldn't you be willing to put your head on my shoulder and rest? Shut your eyes and go to sleep?"

June's cheeks grew hot with pleasure, but she laughed.

"I couldn't go to sleep when I'm having the time of my life now enjoying myself! There will be time enough to sleep later, I'm sure, and I like to hear you talk."

"Well, then," said Paige, after a pause in which he was weighing his chances, "at the risk of making you change your mind about hearing me talk, may I tell you something I've wanted you to know for a long time?"

"Oh, *do!*" said June eagerly.

"I *love* you, June dear. I've been loving you almost ever since I first saw you, and my heart has been longing for you ever since you went away. June, am I telling you too soon? Should I have waited until you know me better?"

June's head went down on his shoulder now, and she whispered softly, "No, Paige, no. It's not too soon. I've been loving you for a long time, only I was afraid you might come to love the ways of the world, and that attractive girl of the world with whom you were being thrown so much. So I didn't dare let my heart have its way about loving you. Because in case you finally fell in love with that other girl, I didn't want to have something to fight all the rest of my life."

Paige took one hand off the wheel and put his arm around his dear girl.

"You darling!" he said, stooping over he kissed her thoroughly.

"Look out!" said June, emerging from his lips, "don't run up a tree to the moon, not tonight. I'd like to get home in one piece and kiss mother once before we go on from here."

"Yes, certainly," said Piage, stopping his car suddenly. "We'll pause to get ready to drive carefully the rest of the way."

"What's the matter?" said an anxious voice from the back seat. "Has something more happened?"

"Yes, father," said Paige joyously, "I've just stolen your daughter away. I thought you ought to know before we get home. Do you mind?"

"*Mind!*" said the bewildered father. "I mind very much. I can't think of anything I would like better! Now, may I go on with my nap, or would you like me to drive awhile?"

"No," laughed Paige. "I think we'll manage without you very well. But you're sure you aren't going to feel badly about it when you get thoroughly awake and take it all in?"

"No, son. I'm very glad! And what's more, mother will be glad too."

"Well, I think I can safely say the same for my mother and father," said Paige. "At least I judge so from hints that have been dropped at our house from time to time. But now we must get on, or we won't get home till morning. Go on back to sleep, father, I'll drive carefully."

About the Author

Grace Livingston Hill is well-known as one of the most prolific writers of romantic fiction. Her personal life was fraught with joys and sorrows not unlike those experienced by many of her fictional heroines.

Born in Wellsville, New York, Grace nearly died during the first hours of life. But her loving parents and friends turned to God in prayer. She survived miraculously, thus her thankful father named her Grace.

Grace was always close to her father, a Presbyterian minister, and her mother, a published writer. It was from them that she learned the art of storytelling. When Grace was twelve, a close aunt surprised her with a hardbound, illustrated copy of one of Grace's stories. This was the beginning of Grace's journey into being a published author.

In 1892 Grace married Fred Hill, a young minister, and they soon had two lovely young daughters. Then came 1901, a difficult year for Grace—the year when, within months of each other, both her father and husband died. Suddenly Grace had to find a new place to live (her home was owned by the church where her husband had been pastor). It was a struggle for Grace to raise her young daughters alone, but through everything she kept writing. In 1902 she produced *The Angel of His Presence, The Story of a Whim,* and *An Unwilling Guest.* In 1903 her two books *According to the Pattern* and *Because of Stephen* were published.

It wasn't long before Grace was a well-known author, but she wanted to go beyond just entertaining her readers. She soon included the message of God's salvation through Jesus Christ in each of her books. For Grace, the most important thing she did was not write books but share the message of salvation, a message she felt God wanted her to share through the abilities he had given her.

In all, Grace Livingston Hill wrote more than one hundred books, all of which have sold thousands of copies and have touched the lives of readers around the world with their message of "enduring love" and the true way to lasting happiness: a relationship with God through his Son, Jesus Christ.

In an interview shortly before her death, Grace's devotion to her Lord still shone clear. She commented that whatever she had accomplished had been God's doing. She was only his servant, one who had tried to follow his teaching in all her thoughts and writing.

Don't miss these Grace Livingston Hill romance novels!